WOLFEHEART

A Medieval Romance

By Kathryn Le Veque

De Wolfe Pack Generations
Grandsons of de Wolfe

WWW.KATHRYNLEVEQUE.COM

ARE YOU SIGNED UP FOR KATHRYN'S BLOG?

You'll get the latest news and information on exclusive giveaways, exclusive excerpts, coming releases, sales, free books, cover reveals and more.

Kathryn's blog followers get it all first. No spam, no junk.

Get the latest info from the reigning Queen of English Medieval Romance!

Sign Up Here

kathrynleveque.com

KATHRYN LE VEQUE NOVELS

Medieval Romance:

De Wolfe Pack Series:
Warwolfe
The Wolfe
Nighthawk
ShadowWolfe
DarkWolfe
A Joyous de Wolfe Christmas
BlackWolfe
Serpent
A Wolfe Among Dragons
Scorpion
StormWolfe
Dark Destroyer
The Lion of the North
Walls of Babylon
The Best Is Yet To Be

De Wolfe Pack Generations:
WolfeHeart

The de Russe Legacy:
The Falls of Erith
Lord of War: Black Angel
The Iron Knight
Beast
The Dark One: Dark Knight
The White Lord of Wellesbourne
Dark Moon
Dark Steel
A de Russe Christmas Miracle
Dark Warrior

The de Lohr Dynasty:
While Angels Slept

Rise of the Defender
Steelheart
Shadowmoor
Silversword
Spectre of the Sword
Unending Love
Archangel
A Blessed de Lohr Christmas

Lords of East Anglia:
While Angels Slept
Godspeed

Great Lords of le Bec:
Great Protector

House of de Royans:
Lord of Winter
To the Lady Born
The Centurion

Lords of Eire:
Echoes of Ancient Dreams
Blacksword
The Darkland

Ancient Kings of Anglecynn:
The Whispering Night
Netherworld

Battle Lords of de Velt:
The Dark Lord
Devil's Dominion
Bay of Fear
The Dark Lord's First Christmas

Reign of the House of de Winter:
Lespada

Swords and Shields

De Reyne Domination:
Guardian of Darkness
With Dreams
The Fallen One

House of d'Vant:
Tender is the Knight (House of
d'Vant)
The Red Fury (House of d'Vant)

The Dragonblade Series:
Fragments of Grace
Dragonblade
Island of Glass
The Savage Curtain
The Fallen One

Great Marcher Lords of de Lara
Lord of the Shadows
Dragonblade

House of St. Hever
Fragments of Grace
Island of Glass
Queen of Lost Stars

Lords of Pembury:
The Savage Curtain

**Lords of Thunder: The de Shera
Brotherhood Trilogy**
The Thunder Lord
The Thunder Warrior
The Thunder Knight

The Great Knights of de Moray:
Shield of Kronos
The Gorgon

The House of De Nerra:
The Promise
The Falls of Erith
Vestiges of Valor

Realm of Angels

Highland Warriors of Munro:
The Red Lion
Deep Into Darkness

The House of de Garr:
Lord of Light
Realm of Angels

Saxon Lords of Hage:
The Crusader
Kingdom Come

High Warriors of Rohan:
High Warrior

The House of Ashbourne:
Upon a Midnight Dream

The House of D'Aurilliac:
Valiant Chaos

The House of De Dere:
Of Love and Legend

St. John and de Gare Clans:
The Warrior Poet

The House of de Bretagne:
The Questing

The House of Summerlin:
The Legend

The Kingdom of Hendocia:
Kingdom by the Sea

The Executioner Knights:
By the Unholy Hand
The Promise (also Noble Knights of
de Nerra)
The Mountain Dark
Starless
A Time of End

Contemporary Romance:

Kathlyn Trent/Marcus Burton Series:
Valley of the Shadow
The Eden Factor
Canyon of the Sphinx

The American Heroes Anthology Series:
The Lucius Robe
Fires of Autumn
Evenshade
Sea of Dreams
Purgatory

Other non-connected

Contemporary Romance:
Lady of Heaven
Darkling, I Listen
In the Dreaming Hour
River's End
The Fountain

Sons of Poseidon:
The Immortal Sea

Pirates of Britannia Series (with Eliza Knight):
Savage of the Sea by Eliza Knight
Leader of Titans by Kathryn Le Veque
The Sea Devil by Eliza Knight
Sea Wolfe by Kathryn Le Veque

Note: All Kathryn's novels are designed to be read as stand-alones, although many have cross-over characters or cross-over family groups. Novels that are grouped together have related characters or family groups. You will notice that some series have the same books; that is because they are cross-overs. A hero in one book may be the secondary character in another.

There is NO reading order except by chronology, but even in that case, you can still read the books as stand-alones. No novel is connected to another by a cliff hanger, and every book has an HEA.

Series are clearly marked. All series contain the same characters or family groups except the American Heroes Series, which is an anthology with unrelated characters.

For more information, find it in **A Reader's Guide to the Medieval World of Le Veque**.

Author's Note

And now, we're into a new generation of de Wolfe's. Brace yourselves.

Here comes the hard part.

I swore I'd never write a death scene of a major hero, and I won't, but we're in the year 1300 A.D. in this novel. William de Wolfe was born in 1201 A.D., so by this time, he has passed away. Most of the original de Wolfe Pack has passed away from sheer old age. I kept them alive as long as I could, I promise, but by the time this book takes place, William has been gone for four years. Paris passed away four months after William did. Jemma is gone, also, as is Adam de Longley, Deinwald Ellsrod, and Michael de Bocage and pretty much everyone of that generation. Who's left, you ask?

Jordan.

She's still kicking, though she is extremely old. She was ten years younger than William, so that puts her in her late-eighties in this novel.

Why am I telling you this? So you won't be surprised when you start reading and realize most of your old favorites are gone. We are into a new generation and, unfortunately, that means the old generation, at some point, must pass. But you will see how alive they still are through the eyes of Scott (the new head of the House of de Wolfe), Troy, Patrick, Blayth, and the others. And the grandchildren you meet all knew them and loved them.

Old knights never really die. They live on in their grand-sons.

And what grandsons they are.

Markus is quite a man. He's taller than his father, if you can believe that. I think Patrick, or Atty as he is called by the family, is my favorite brother. He was the very first brother who had his story told when I started writing Sons of de Wolfe. Therefore, it's natural that Markus would be the first grandson to have his story told. Already, Markus is my favorite grandson.

You'll see knights you recognize in this, like Hermes and Atreus de Norville, the "idiot" grandsons of Paris and William. Hector is their father, Evelyn their mother. Remember them from *BlackWolfe*, how they fought each other like morons? That was several years ago and now they're all grown up with children of their own, but they still act like young knights in a fight. You'll love the first chapter. There is also a new Kieran Hage, grandson of our beloved Kieran. He is a younger son of Alec Hage and Katheryn de Wolfe and very much like his grandfather. I hope to explore him more in the future.

Someone else you're going to see in this story, very briefly, is Kerk le Sander. Remember him from *Nighthawk*? He is a long-time friend of Patrick's who popped up when Patrick hastily married his wife. What some readers may not know is that Kerk is an Immortal – he's a son of the God, Poseidon (no kidding), and has his story told in *The Immortal Sea*, part of a romance duet I did with NYT Bestselling author Sharon Hamilton. But in this book, Kerk is just a knight, still at Chillingham Castle, and, of course, they have no idea who he really is.

Let's talk briefly about the history of Trastamara, which is a ruling house from Aragon in the 14th century. Before that, it was simply a noble family, which is mentioned in this book, but the House of Trastamara really didn't rise to power until about sixty years after this book is set. The Kingdom of Aragon, and the Kingdom of Sobrarbe (Aragon's precursor), make for interesting reading and was linked to the French dukedom of Aquitaine and, in later years, to the House of Hapsburg, among others.

And now, the usual pronunciation guide:

- Roget de Sauque: You'll see this name throughout the book, so his name is pronounced ro-SHAY (soft "g" sound) duh Sock. That's pretty much it – Sauque is pronounced "sock"
- Aleanor: Al-lenore
- Shand: Like "Shawn" with a "d" on the end – Shawnd
- Amabella, the heroine, is of Spanish descent. Her term of endearment is *querida*, which means "darling" in Spanish.

Now, I truly hope you enjoy Amabella and Markus' story because it's a good one full of really fun characters that I had a blast writing. You'll fall in love with Amabella's youngest children – they're a hoot!

Happy Reading!

THE PARENTS, CHILDREN, AND GRANDCHILDREN OF DE WOLFE

<u>William and Jordan Scott de Wolfe</u>

Total children: 10

Total grandchildren: 75 (including 4 deceased, 7 adopted, 3 step-grandchildren)

Scott (Troy's twin) – (Wife #1 Lady Athena de Norville, has issue. Wife #2, Lady Avrielle Huntley du Rennic, has issue)

With Athena

- William (married Lily de Lohr, has issue)
- Thomas
- Andrew (deceased)
- Beatrice (deceased)

With Avrielle

- Sophia (with Nathaniel du Rennic)
- Stephen (with Nathaniel du Rennic)
- Sorcha (with Nathaniel du Rennic)
- Jeremy
- Nathaniel
- Alexander
- Seraphina
- Jordan

Troy (Scott's twin) – (Wife #1 Lady Helene de Norville, has issue. Wife #2 Lady Rhoswyn Kerr, has issue)

With Helene	With Rhoswyn

With Helene

- Andreas
- Acacia (deceased)
- Arista (deceased)

With Rhoswyn

- Gareth
- Corey
- Reed
- Tavin
- Tristan
- Elsbeth
- Madeleine

Patrick – (Married to Lady Brighton de Favereux, has issue)

Markus

- Cassius
- Magnus
- Titus
- Thora
- Kristiana

James – (Wife #1 Lady Rose Hage, has issue. Wife #2, Asmara ap Cader, has issue)

With Rose

- Ronan
- Isabella

With Asmara (as Blayth)

- Maddoc
- Bowen
- Caius
- Garreth (known as Garr)

Katheryn (James' twin) – (Married to Sir Alec Hage, has

issue)

- Edward
- Axel
- Christoph
- Kieran
- Christian

Evelyn – (Married to Sir Hector de Norville, has issue)

- Atreus
- Hermes
- Lisbet
- Adele
- Aline
- Lesander (goes by Zander)

Baby de Wolfe – (Died same day. Christened Madeleine)

Edward – (Married to Lady Cassiopeia de Norville, has issue)

- Helene
- Phoebe
- Hestia
- Asteria
- Leonidas
- Dorian
- Dayne
- Stephan
- Pallas

Thomas – (Married Lady Maitland "Mae" de Ryes Bowlin, has issue)

- Artus (adopted)

- Nora (adopted)
- Phin (adopted)
- Marybelle (adopted)
- Renard & Roland (adopted)
- Dyana (adopted)
- Alexander
- Cabot
- Matthew
- Wade
- Tacey
- Morgan

Penelope – (Married to Bhrodi de Shera, Earl of Coventry, hereditary King of Anglesey)
- William
- Perri
- Bowen
- Dai
- Catrin
- Morgana
- Maddock
- Anthea
- Talan

Holdings and Titles of the House of de Wolfe and close allies as of 1300 A.D.

Scott de Wolfe – Earl of Warenton

Troy de Wolfe – Lord Braemoor

Patrick de Wolfe – Earl of Berwick (Heir: Markus de Wolfe, Lord Ravensdowne)

Blayth (James) de Wolfe – Baron Sydenham

Edward de Wolfe – Baron Kentmere

Thomas de Wolfe – Earl of Northumbria

Wark Castle (Wolfe's Eye):

Larger outpost for the Earl of Warenton. Literally sits on the border between England and Scotland.

- Thomas de Wolfe (son of Scott de Wolfe, known as *Tee* to the family <his mother's nickname>), commander

Berwick Castle (Wolfe's Teeth):

Massive border castle, strategically important, de Wolfe holding and now the seat of the Earl of Berwick, Patrick de Wolfe

- Markus de Wolfe, Viscount Ravensdowne, commander
- Cassius de Wolfe, commander
- Edward "Eddie" Hage, commander

Castle Questing (Wolfe's Heart):

Massive fortress, seat of the Earl of Warenton, Scott de Wolfe.

- Apollo de Norville, second

- Nathaniel Hage
- Hermes de Norville
- Tobias de Bocage

Rule Water Castle (Wolfe's Lair):

The largest outpost in the de Wolfe empire, known as The Lair. Seat of William "Will" de Wolfe, Viscount Kilham, heir apparent to the Earldom of Warenton.

- Magnus de Wolfe, second
- Perri de Shera, son of the Earl of Coventry and Penelope de Wolfe de Shera

Monteviot Tower (Wolfe's Shield):

Smaller outpost in Scotland, strategic. Holding of Troy de Wolfe.

- Andreas de Wolfe, commander

Kale Water Castle (Wolfe's Den):

Larger outpost on the England side of the border, strategic.

- Troy de Wolfe, Lord Braemoor, commander
- Troy also commands Sibbald's Hold, former home of Red Keith Kerr (his wife's father). A minor property commanded by son Garreth de Wolfe.

Kyloe Castle:

Seat of the Earl of Northumbria, Thomas de Wolfe

- Christoph Hage, second

Roxburgh Castle (Wolfe's Claw – unofficially)*

Large royal-held castle near Kelso, formerly manned by knights from Northwood, but awarded to the House of de Wolfe by royal decree for meritorious service to the crown. Volatile location, often attacked by Scots, and is manned by both royal and de Wolfe troops.

- Blayth (James) de Wolfe, Lord Sydenham, commander
- Axel Hage, second

*Note: Because of the extreme volatile location and nature of this garrison, Blayth (James) de Wolfe was given the title Lord Sydenham and the Sydenham Barony, a small but strategic barony between Wark Castle and the town of Kelso.

Northwood Castle:

Massive border castle, very important and strategic. Belonging to the Earls of Teviot. Not part of the de Wolfe empire, but strongly allied to de Wolfe by marriage and blood. The Earl of Teviot is John Adrian de Longley, Adam de Longley's eldest son. Adrian's mother is Cayetana Fernanda Teresita Silva y Fausto de Longley, Princess of Aragon.

- Hector de Norville, captain of the guard
- Atreus de Norville, second

Edenburn Tower (House of de Norville):

Smaller tower on the southern end of de Wolfe properties belonging to the House of de Norville. Owned and commanded by Alec Hage, Lord Bowmont.

Castle Canaan (Kendal):

The Earl of Warenton's southernmost holding, not directly related to the Scottish border but a source of additional troops if needed. Inherited the property when he married the widow of Castle Canaan.

- Stephan du Rennic, commander

Seven Gates Castle (Kendal):

- Seat of Edward de Wolfe's Barony – Kentmere in Kendal that adjoins brother Scott's lands at Castle Canaan
- Isleworth House, Surrey

DE WOLFE PACK GENERATIONS

The grandsons of William de Wolfe are referred to as "The de Wolfe Cubs". There are more than forty of them, both biological and adopted, and each young man is sworn to his powerful and rich legacy. When each grandson comes of age and is knighted, he tattoos the de Wolfe standard onto some part of his body. It is a rite of passage and it is that mark that links these young men together more than blood.

More than brotherhood.

It is the de Wolfe birthright.

The de Wolfe Pack standard is meant to be worn with honor, with pride, and with resilience, for there is no more recognizable standard in Medieval England. To shame the Pack is to have the tattoo removed, never to be regained.

This is their world.

Welcome to the Cub Generation.

De Wolfe Motto: *Fortis in arduis*

Strength in times of trouble

PROLOGUE

Year of Our Lord 1300
Mordrington Manor
Scottish Borders

HE'D COME FOR a meal and maybe a sexual favor.

But that's not what he was facing.

This was his damned property and all he could see where dirty, grizzled Scots in the courtyard, sitting around a giant fire they'd created right in the middle of it. They'd dug up the cobblestones in the courtyard that had been so carefully laid down last year to keep the mud and erosion at bay and they'd built a bloody big fire right in the middle of it.

Bastards.

He was going to get rid of them once and for all.

This was *his* property, after all. Mordrington Manor had been left to Roget de Sauque by his wife's father, a rich and producing manor with fat, brown sheep who multiplied in copious amounts in the springtime. He'd moved his mistress into it when she was pregnant with their first worthless bastard and since that time, she'd given birth to a second worthless bastard. Stupid sons because they took after her side of the family. The only reason Roget kept her around was because she was clever in bed and she did anything he wanted, something his wife wouldn't do.

Fenella Foulden Hume was the perfect whore.

But with her came her useless family of inbred Scots and he knew it was her brother's men he saw sitting around the bonfire in the courtyard. The longer he looked at them, the angrier he became.

Roget had entered through the front of the manor, with its giant oak and iron door, so fortified that a hundred men couldn't pull it down. That led to the great hall with the courtyard in the center of the manse's complex. It was surrounded by living quarters, kitchens, and a chapel, among other things. It was also protected by a wall walk on the second story, with battlements overlooking the hostile countryside.

He headed to this wall walk because he could get a full view of the Scots camping in his courtyard, eating his food and drinking his wine. He didn't know where Fenella was and, at the moment, he didn't care. He was enraged that she was housing her brother and his *reiver* brethren.

Aye, he knew exactly who they were.

What they were.

Taking the stairs to the gallery above the great hall, he emerged from a doorway on the gallery wall and out onto the wall walk. From this perch, he could see everything perfectly. The first thing he realized was that there must have been more of them than he suspected because the smell of human habitation was more powerful than the smoke that was filling the night sky. It smelled like a barnyard and given the beauty of the manse, that was a tragedy. Mordrington was a truly beautiful example of a country manse with gardens and a bucolic moat, but now it was filled with reivers.

Outlaws.

In truth, he'd always suspected that was the case, as far as a couple of years back when it seemed that Fenella's brother, Baldwin "Win" Foulden, had come for a visit with his friends and never left. Rumor had it that they were attacking small farms and villages in the area, and anything of value, from Berwick to Coldstream. Massive castles like Northwood and Questing came out to do battle with them, chasing them back into Scotland.

But Win's group of cutthroats was only a piece of a larger group who comprised a band of Scottish and English outlaws who liked to call themselves *Na Bràithrean*, or The Brothers. The Brothers had been responsible for a good deal of death and destruction along that stretch of the borders and as Roget looked around his property, he could see horses and sheep that he didn't remember buying. There were even black cattle in the fields to the south; he'd seen them coming in. Those didn't belong to him. The smelly courtyard was filled with barrels and possessions shoved into corners, possessions stolen from others.

His pretty, elegant manse had become a den of thieves.

It wasn't as if he hadn't noticed this before on his frequent trips to visit Fenella. He'd seen it but he'd ignored it for the most part because, usually, Win and his reivers kept their activities out of his sight. He didn't care about what he couldn't see, but over the past few months, they hadn't been so careful in hiding their ill-gotten gains. When he told Fenella that he wanted Win and his cohorts gone, she would simply smile, untie his breeches, and put her mouth on his manhood. The woman could suck the shine off steel. Then he'd forget about his anger until the next time.

But there wasn't going to be a next time.

As Roget stood on the wall walk overlooking the smoky courtyard, he could see three young women huddled in a corner, dressed in what looked like bed clothes. They were dirty, weeping, and frightened. Having heard about a raid against the small village of Hutton two days ago, Roget suspected who they were.

Spoils.

If the larger castles along the border heard about this, Mordrington would be destroyed. They couldn't stand against the Earls of Teviot, Warenton, Northumbria, and Berwick, the dominate warlords in the area, who would undoubtedly come to wipe them out.

The Earl of Teviot had just inherited the title from his father, a young earl named John Adrian de Longley, who had spent most of his years in Edward I's court. He was a fierce warlord and nothing to be trifled with. The Earl of Warenton was an older man who had inherited his title upon the passing of his father four years ago. Scott de Wolfe was the new earl, but he'd been in the north his entire life and was feared as much as his father, the great William de Wolfe, ever was.

The Earl of Northumbria was also a son of William de Wolfe, having married into the de Vauden family and inheriting the title from the heiress. He commanded one of the largest armies in the north. Then, there was the Earl of Berwick – the third son of William de Wolfe had been granted the title before his father's death. He was a man known as "Nighthawk" for distinguishing himself for many years along the border.

Patrick de Wolfe held Berwick and a few other properties along the coast and, along with several of his brothers, secured a massive portion of the north of England and a section of the borders of Scotland as well. They were enormously powerful and, fortunately, Roget was considered an ally and a vassal to Berwick, but that wouldn't last if the Brothers de Wolfe discovered he was harboring reivers.

He had to get them out before they ruined everything.

He could no longer ignore the obvious.

"You men," he boomed down to them. "Shut your lips and

listen to me! Shut them, I say! *Quiet*!"

The soft drone of conversation died down as men turned to him, pale and bearded faces through the blue haze of smoke. Roget frowned at the lot of them as a few stood up, looking up at him unhappily.

"If you do not know who I am, then you should," he bellowed. "I am Roget de Sauque and this is my property. I do not want you here. Take your ill-gotten gains and get out. If you do not do this in the next hour, I will rouse my army and bring them here to physically remove you. Am I making myself clear?"

The Scots simply looked at him. Then, they looked at each other, shrugging. Roget could see that there was no sense of urgency to move. Clearly, they didn't care what he said because he'd let it go on for so long that they didn't take him seriously. As he prepared to shout again, a woman suddenly appeared on the wall walk.

"My love?" she said timidly. "What is the matter? Why do ye shout?"

Roget turned to look at Fenella. She had been a beauty only a few years ago, but childbirth and age had crept upon her quickly, turning her body into soft mush and putting lines on her face. She used to be quite lush, with full lips and curly, auburn hair, but now she just looked… hard.

Hard, as if life had been unkind to her.

"Get your brother and his devils out of here," he said. "I have tolerated his presence far too long. They have turned this manse into a pig sty. Worse still, they are raiding and killing, bringing abducted women here to abuse. Did you know that?"

He was pointing to the frightened women down below. As they watched, a big Scots walked up to one of them, grabbed her by the arm, and dragged her off while she screamed for mercy. Roget turned to Fenella with dark, angry eyes.

"Murderous garbage," he growled. "I have overlooked it because every time I have brought it up to you, you have distracted me with your whore's tongue. That's all you are, Fenella. A whore. An ugly, disgusting whore. I want you out, too. Go with your brother and live in whatever filth he provides for you, for I am finished."

Fenella looked at him, hurt and distressed. "Ye dunna mean it," she said. "Ye're simply weary. Come inside and let me…"

She reached out to grasp him, but he rudely brushed her off. "I mean every word," he said. "Pack what you can carry and get out. And take those two worthless lads with you, too."

She gasped in shock. "But they are yer sons!"

Roget shrugged. "They may be, and they may not be," he said. "Do not think I don't know about the other men you've taken to your bed since you came to live here. I know; I have heard the rumors. You bestow your sexual favors on them for a price, so there is no guarantee either boy is my son. But because I am a man of honor, I have provided you and them with a place to live. But you have taken advantage of that. You have let your brother do as he pleases and use my property for his nefarious activities. He will leave and so will you. I will not tell you again. I will bring my army here and move you out by force."

Fenella was stiff with anger, with concern, but she knew better than to fight with him. It wasn't the first time he'd tried to kick her out and it wouldn't be the last because she fully intended to remain.

She knew how to change his mind.

Sauntering up to him, she reached out, putting a gentle hand on his crotch. "Ye're overwrought, my love," she said seductively. "Let me bring ye peace and calm. Let me…"

He shoved her away, roughly, and she ended up smacking her hand into the banister of the wall walk. It was wood, just like the walk itself, but it was hard and unforgiving, and she yelped in pain.

"You'll not use your whore's tricks on me," Roget growled. "I told you to get out."

Fenella used the next weapon in her arsenal. She began to weep loudly. "How could ye be so cruel?" she sobbed. "How could ye hurt me? I've done nothing wrong!"

Roget was so angry that his lips were turning white. Abruptly, he pushed past her, heading back into the gallery that lined the second floor of the hall. Fenella's tears stopped instantly as she ran to the door, watching him move towards the steps that led down into the great hall. It was clear to her that he was leaving, presumably to summon his army. Roget had been angry before but not like this. She'd always been able to calm him down, but today… today, he acted as if he meant every word.

Fenella's attention turned to the smelly, smoky courtyard.

"Win!" she cried. "He mustna leave!"

Win was standing by the fire, blending in with the other Scotsmen who were crowding the courtyard. He was big and brawny, not an unhandsome man, but wicked to the bone. He looked up, seeing his sister pointing towards the hall, and he grabbed a couple of his men as he rushed into the hall.

At that point, Roget was just coming off the stairs, right in front of him. With Win's men crowding into the doorway and into the hall, Roget was cut off from the exit. Win stood in front of him, looking at the man as he stood on the bottom stair.

"Ye're not looking at this the right way, laddie," he said to Roget. "If we're here, then no one will bother this place. We're like an army, protecting it. It makes it safe for my sister to live here."

Somewhere in the complex, Roget could hear a woman screaming and it distressed him. He may have been a man who kept a mistress, but he wasn't barbaric. He sighed heavily.

"Get out of my way," he said.

Win shook his head. "Not until ye see reason," he said. "We *will* protect Mordrington. That's a benefit to ye. Dunna ye see?"

Roget's gaze began to dart among the crowd of men in the hall. He'd come alone and it was clear that he was coming to regret that decision.

"You are not protecting Mordrington as long as you raid the countryside," he said. "You bring your booty back here and sooner or later, the bigger warlords of the area like de Wolfe and de Longley are going to figure it out. They'll come here and they'll destroy this place."

Win shook his head. "Why should they?" he said, grinning a gap-toothed smile. "Ye're an ally, Roget. They'll never look here."

Roget simply shook his head. "Let me pass," he said. "I told my men I would return tonight and if I do not, they'll come here looking for me, so it is best if you let me leave."

Win sighed, with regret. "If I let ye leave, ye'll return with yer army."

"I will not need to if you leave."

"We canna leave. We've nowhere to go."

He said it in a way that suggested hazard. Feeling threatened, Roget took a step back, up the stairs.

"This place does not belong to you," he said, trying to sound brave. "It does not belong to your whore sister, Fenella. It belongs to me and I am telling you to leave. Get out and there is no need to bring my army. Remain and I will have you burned out, if necessary."

Win scratched his chin, looking at his men. "Burned out, he says," he said to his men, who were nodding as if intrigued by the suggestion. "The man says he wants tae burn us out. What say ye?"

They started to laugh. The situation almost seemed humorous. But it was a deception; the laughter abruptly faded, and a roar went up among the men. They rushed Roget before he could run back up the stairs, grabbing him by the hair and arms. He was swarmed as they dragged him back out into the courtyard that had been ruined by their habitation. The massive fire was burning in the middle of it and as Roget screamed, they tossed him straight into the fire.

The group of men roared in approval.

On fire, Roget scrambled off the pyre and tried to run, but they pushed him back into it and he fell face-first. At that point, everything ignited, but he still tried to run, only not as forcefully this time. He slithered off the pyre, onto his knees, fully engulfed in flames as he tried to get to his feet. But someone hit him in the belly with a chair from the great hall, a chair that had been dragged out into the courtyard, and Roget fell back onto the pyre, squirming helplessly as the flames consumed him.

It was a heavy, oily smell that began to fill the air as his flesh burned. Win and his men stood back, watching until he stopped moving before carefully pulling him off the pyre. He was burning and smoking, but clearly dead, and they let him burn a little while longer before Win had his men doused him with buckets of water.

By then, Roget was a charred shell, but he was still somewhat recognizable. Fenella, lured by the shouting and screaming and smoke, stood just outside the doorway leading into the hall, seeing what had become of the man who had been her lover for twelve years.

Win caught sight of his sister.

"I'm sorry, lass," he said. "Ye know I had tae. Ye know what he was going tae do."

Fenella wasn't quite sure how she felt; that was clear from the expression on her face. She was shocked and sickened, but not particularly grieved. In fact, once she realized what had happened, she seemed to take a deep breath as if to reconcile herself to it.

There were no tears.

"He had wanted ye tae go before this, but I always put him off," she said, fixed on the smoking, wet body. "Ye did what ye had tae do, I suppose. But why not burn him tae ash? Why leave him like… that."

Win went to his sister, putting a brotherly arm around her shoulders. "Because if he disappears and his men knew he came here, they'll come looking for him here," he said. "We'll take the body back towards Trastamara and make it look like he came across bandits and they put him on their fire. These woods are full of outlaws' camps. He stumbled across one and they killed him for it."

Fenella watched the smoldering body, wondering what her life was going to be like now without Roget's money. That was the only thing on her mind – not his loss of companionship or the loss of the sex between them, but his money.

That was the only reason she'd ever stayed with him.

It had been that way since the beginning. Roget had been handsome and mildly amusing, but he was mostly rich. There was some money at the manse, but Fenella depended on a stipend from Roget every month. However, she was, if nothing else, resourceful. There were sheep to sell at Mordrington. There were fine furnishings and the jewelry Roget had given her. She could sell everything for a load of coinage before Roget's widow came and threw her out.

There was time yet to strip the place clean.

"It will have tae do, I suppose," she said after a moment. "But this place doesna belong tae me. It belongs tae Trastamara. Did ye ever think about that? They'll come tae throw us out, eventually."

Win shrugged. "Then we'll find another place tae hide, but until then, we'll bleed Mordrington dry. Cheer up, lass. The man who kept ye as his whore is no more. Ye can find another man tae keep ye. Keep *us*."

He laughed, heading back to his men, who were starting to drink heavily as Roget's body smoked a few feet away. Killing a man was all in a day's work to them and they thought nothing of it.

A man's life had no meaning to them. All they were concerned with was their immediate situation. Transient as they were, they didn't think much beyond that. It was kill or be killed, live for the moment or die a fool's death. Life, love, and noble pursuits had no meaning to them.

That was the mentality of The Brothers.

The next day, Roget's body was found in an abandoned camp five miles away, charred over an old fire, but the wheels set into motion that day were not anything Win or Fenella or any of The Brothers could have anticipated.

The countdown to a greater upheaval on the borders than they could have ever imagined had begun.

CHAPTER ONE

Bamburgh Castle
Northumberland

G OD, HIS EARS were ringing.

He was on his feet, but everything around him was muffled and strained. He found himself staring up at the sky above Bamburgh Castle. It was a bright summer's day, but puffy gray clouds were blowing in from the sea, looming above. He wondered fleetingly if it was going to rain before nightfall.

He could hear his father yelling at him.

Markus! Move!

He wasn't sure he *could* move. Everything was rocking around him and his knees felt like jelly, but there was no way he was going to fall. He was the tallest man on that field other than his father, but he wasn't going anywhere. Someone had tried; using their helm like a hammer, they'd hit him in the head with it, hoping to topple the mighty Markus de Wolfe.

All they'd managed to do was ring his bell.

But it was only momentary. The blood was suddenly rushing back into his head and his wits soon followed.

He was back.

With a vengeance.

Whoosh!

A massive, armored arm swung out, catching the man next to him and sending him sailing back onto his arse. Fury unleashed, Markus blinked away the lingering stars in his vision and went after the men on the opposing team. Behind him, his father, brothers, and cousins followed.

Markus was always the first man into battle and the last one to leave it.

He was fearless in a way few men were.

But this wasn't a battle; not really. It was the much-anticipated mêlée that started off the games in celebration of the marriage of Lady Mabel Chestwick to the son of the garrison commander of Bamburgh, Sir Lars de Vesci.

Young Edmund de Vesci, a relation to the Lords of Alnwick Castle, was an arrogant knight but the life of any party, and the celebration of his marriage to the fair Mabel had been going on for three days at his insistence. People had been drunk for three days, eating and drinking and vomiting as if it were a great Roman orgy. Everyone who was anyone in the north of England had been invited and the marriage festivities were culminating in a tournament and games.

The House of de Wolfe had come out in force.

It wasn't often when there were such vibrant and well-attended games this far north, and it wasn't often the men participating had the chance to do something that didn't involve fighting Scots and deadly battles. For a chance like this, to drink and feast and beat down one's allies in good-natured victory, was something they'd all been greatly anticipating.

It had truly been something to behold.

In fact, it had been so greatly anticipated that the men at each de Wolfe property had drawn lots to see who would attend. They couldn't empty out the castles and towers of every powerful knight, so a select and unhappy few had to remain behind to maintain security.

From Berwick, Markus had been able to attend along with his father, Patrick, and his brothers, Cassius and Titus. From Castle Questing, Scott de Wolfe, the Earl of Warenton, had remained behind while his eldest son, William "Will" de Wolfe had been able to attend along with younger brother, Jeremy. Andreas de Wolfe, son of Troy, was present along with Axel and Christoph Hage. Lastly, Atreus and Hermes de Norville were in attendance, who were always a formidable team to beat. If they weren't trying to kill each other, they were raining hellfire on everyone else.

Fortunately for Markus, his fiery cousins were on his team. He could hear them behind him, beating on some hapless Alnwick knight until the man caved in and fell to the ground. They hooted and bellowed with victory, jumping on the man and stealing his daggers, before moving to set in on someone else until Markus called them off.

"Nay," he boomed. "We move in a team or we will not survive this. Close ranks and we will move to each group. If they divide us, we will fall."

Atreus and Hermes were excellent knights for all of their wild ways. They understood. Markus set them, along with his two younger brothers, on a group of knights from Kyloe Castle, seat of his Uncle Thomas, and stood back as the younger knights went to work. It was like watching flies cover a pile of shite; the younger de Wolfe knights were hungry and ruthless. Markus and his cousin, Will, covered their backs along with Patrick, laughing as Atreus and Hermes kissed their fallen prey and then yelled like barbarians.

They were pure entertainment.

"God, that pair," Will muttered. "How is it we were stuck with them?"

Markus lifted an eyebrow. "We are *always* stuck with them.

They haven't seen each other in a couple of months and now that they are together, they are invincible."

Will knew that. As the eldest of the grandchildren of William de Wolfe, Markus and Will and their cousin, Andreas, always seemed to be in charge of the youngers in situations like this, and Atreus and Hermes were at the head of that pack. They were very close in age, and brothers, but they served in separate castles – Atreus at Northwood Castle and Hermes at Castle Questing. Therefore, opportunities like this were a chance for them to reaffirm brotherly bonds.

No matter how violent.

Will finally shook his head.

"Uncle Hector is a coward," he said. "As their father, he should be here to manage his wild sons. I'm afraid they are going to kill someone someday and we shall be to blame."

Markus snorted in agreement. When he wasn't watching Atreus and Hermes, he was watching the giant field around them. It was so huge that there had to be two hundred men on it, all competing for the top prize. There was much yelling and beating going on.

"Hector had to stay at Northwood Castle." Patrick spoke up. "He has a conference with Clan Gordon and he could not break away."

"I know," Will said. "I simply find it ironic that Uncle Hector sends his unruly boys with us so they can run wild in a mass competition."

He said it with disapproval, but Markus grinned. "When I go into battle, I will always want that pair with me," he said. "They are wild, but their courage is limitless."

As Will reluctantly agreed, Patrick kicked back a roaming knight who came too close. As the man stumbled away, he glanced at Markus.

"Speaking of courage," he said. "Did you see Lars de Vesci's daughter? She was in the lists earlier when the teams were announced. Lovely girl with brown hair."

Markus instantly knew where this subject was going and he eyed his father. "What took you so long to bring her up?" he said wryly. "That's the entire reason you brought me here, isn't it? To get a good look at Emmalina de Vesci?"

Patrick pretended like he didn't know what his son was talking about as Will, having been married for several years, snickered annoyingly. Markus' resistance to marriage was well-known in the family.

"She is an eligible young woman from a fine family," Patrick said casually. "Your mother knows her mother. They are friends."

"And that naturally makes her an excellent prospect, eh?"

Patrick watched Markus fend off another roaming knight by lashing out a massive fist, sending the man to the ground.

"It simply makes her a prospect," Patrick said. "Markus, you know I hate to bring this up, but you are my eldest and heir. As the son of an earl, you have enjoyed the courtesy title of Viscount Ravensdowne and you have seen over thirty years. That makes you prime marriageable material. It is time for you to think about taking a wife and you know it. Just… look at Emmalina. She is a pretty girl."

Now, the well-known subject was being openly discussed and Will, with a sympathetic glance to his cousin, thought it was better to leave this conversation between father and son. As he headed over to the rumble to give the pair some space, Markus grew increasingly frustrated.

"Papa, I do not want to have this conversation with you right now," he said. "I appreciate what you are trying to do, but I simply do not want to discuss it at the moment."

"You either discuss it with me or you will discuss it with your grandfather," he said. "You know that Magnus has ten women from his village picked out for you to look at. Unless you pick a woman yourself, you are going to have to marry one of his. He's going to bring them in longships across the sea and, like it or not, you'll have to marry one of them. So… it is better if you select your bride and *not* your grandfather."

Patrick was speaking of his wife's father. Magnus Haakonsson was the King of the Northmen, a man known as the Law-Mender. He was a great man, benevolent and generous, but he was also a ruthless warlord and a spectacular ally for the House of de Wolfe. He was loving, kind, demanding, and invasive when it came to his grandchildren, much to Patrick's distress, and Patrick wasn't jesting when he said the man would bring ten women for Markus to choose from.

Markus knew it, too.

"I am not marrying a woman who does not even speak my language," Markus said flatly. "I do not care how much he bullies me. I will not do it."

Patrick's attention was on the next group of knights that Atreus and Hermes and the rest of the younger knights seemed to be focused on. "Then you had better pick one yourself," he said. "Emmalina de Vesci isn't looking so bad now, is she?"

Markus started laughing. He simply couldn't help it. His father was trying to bully him and help him all at the same time. But his attention, too, was on the younger knights as they entered into a fist fight with a group of knights from Chillingham Castle. It was one of the bigger group of knights, like the de Wolfe group, and no one wanted to be an easy target.

The blows were flying.

"Should we enter that?" Markus asked his father.

The subject was changing from marriage to the skirmish at hand, and Patrick came to stand next to him, observing the beating that the younger knights were giving each other. He finally shook his head.

"I've no desire to lose teeth," he said. "But go ahead. They'll scatter when they see you coming, anyway. They're already running from Cassius and Titus."

Markus was laughing again, watching his brothers as they grabbed men by the neck and threw them to the ground. They were so tall that they looked like beasts among children sometimes. Patrick de Wolfe had inherited astounding height from some long-dead ancestor and was easily a head taller than his brothers, and all of his sons except for Magnus had inherited that height.

It was a family of giants.

Markus was slightly taller than his father's seven inches over six feet, while Cassius and Titus were slightly shorter than their father. Magnus was a few inches shorter than all of them, but he was so powerfully built that it more than made up for the height difference. No one would tangle with Magnus. He was also the only brother who had been born with blond hair, a fine tribute to his Northman ancestors.

But Magnus had been unable to come to the festivities, so it was Markus and Cassius and Titus using their height advantage to terrify their opponents. At least, Cassius and Titus were. Markus hadn't made his move yet.

Patrick gave his son a shove on the shoulder.

"Get in there," he said. "Make short work of this. We already have eleven hostages that we shall ransom for a tidy sum, so go in there and procure nine more. Twenty hostages and we shall be rich."

Markus flashed his father a grin. The lure of money was always a great motivator. He charged in just as an older knight emerged from the Chillingham group and headed in Patrick's direction. The knight, whom Markus knew, passed him on the way and the knight chuckled when he saw Markus.

He knew the fight wouldn't last very long now.

"What have I ever done to you that you would send your beastly sons after me and my men?" the knight shouted at Patrick. "I thought you were my friend?"

Patrick smiled broadly at the approach of his old and dear friend, Sir Kerk le Sander. He'd known the man for years. Kerk was the captain of the army for Chillingham Castle. Powerful and muscular, with white-blond hair and eyes the color of the sea, Patrick only laughed when Kerk reached out to slap him affectionately on the shoulder.

"I *am* your friend," he told Kerk. "That is why I am not having my men beat yours into the ground. They are simply forcing them to sit the rest of the competition out. They are weary; your men must rest."

"How thoughtful of you."

"I knew you'd think so."

"How much is it going to cost me when you ransom my men back to me?"

"I have not decided yet."

As Patrick grinned and Kerk rolled his eyes, they watched as Markus flattened a Chillingham knight who tried to use a club on him. Clubs were allowed, as were shields and anything else that could take down a man as long as it didn't have a sharp edge. Some mass competitions allowed real weapons, but de Vesci had been adamant that he didn't want anyone crippled or killed.

That meant brute strength won out.

"Markus is a tribute to you, Atty," Kerk said quietly, using the nickname for Patrick that he'd had since childhood, one that close friends and family used. "Truly, he is something to be proud of."

Patrick was watching his sons with great pride, and in particular Markus. "He is," he said. "I do not know what I ever did in my life to warrant such a gift from God, but there he is. He is my pride and my joy."

Kerk grinned at the reverence in Patrick's tone. "I heard about his royal appointment," he said. "News travels quickly here in the north. When does he take his position with Edward?"

"Next month," Patrick said proudly. "In fact, Edward is coming north to collect him because he's heading into Scotland. And it is not just any position; it is Lord Protector to the King, the exact same position I was offered from Edward's father, Henry, those years ago. I was set to take the position when I met and married my wife and decided to remain in the north. But Markus... he is destined for far greater things than I ever was, Kerk. To have the prestige of Lord Protector of the King is exactly what he deserves. Edward knows greatness when he sees it."

Kerk nodded, imagining the future for the big, young knight. "Think of the adventures he will have," he said. "Traveling with Edward, although I imagine he'll spend a good deal of time in either Scotland or Wales, but he'll make a name for himself. I envy him, really. I wish I was young enough for that kind of adventure."

Patrick gave him a lopsided smile. "Don't we all?"

As they grinned at each other, another Chillingham knight went down and the remaining Chillingham knights banded together to go after Atreus and Hermes, who had felled at least three men between them.

It wasn't simply dropping the men; it was the *way* they'd dropped them. Standing on their backs and declaring themselves invincible. The arrogance was no longer tolerable, so with Atreus and Hermes now being set upon, Markus and Cassius went to help and a full-scale brawl resulted. Punches were thrown and men went down in the muddy grass of the field.

Wiping blood from his mouth, Markus helped his brothers

take down a big knight with a club and a shield who had been swinging both around and clipping men in their faces or necks. As Kerk surrendered to the inevitable and headed back into the fray to help his men surrender honorably, Patrick stood out of the fight, watching with pride and amusement as his sons and nephews managed to take down the rest of the Chillingham gang. He was preparing to move in and help them drag men away so they could ransom them later when he caught sight of something on the edge of the field.

Someone was trying to get his attention.

"Papa, Kieran is here," Markus was suddenly by his side, pointing to the north side of the field. "What in the hell is he doing here?"

They were referring to Kieran Hage, a young knight from Berwick who had been left behind to help man the fortress. Named after his grandfather who had died about thirteen years earlier, he looked exactly like his namesake – enormous shoulders, vast brute strength, with dark blond hair and brown eyes. He was the son of Alec and Katheryn de Wolfe Hage, making him Patrick's nephew.

And his presence here wasn't a good thing.

"I don't know," Patrick said after a moment. "But I am certainly going to find out."

As Patrick headed off, Markus followed. They pushed their way through the pockets of fighting, finally coming to the edge of the field where Kieran was standing.

Patrick didn't give the man a chance to speak.

"What's happened, Kieran?" he asked. "Is Berwick standing?"

"Aye, Uncle Atty," Kieran replied. "Berwick is fine."

That brought Patrick a good deal of relief, but he was still concerned. "Then why have you come?"

Kieran had to dodge out of the way when a competitor from

the mass competition came hurtling off the field, narrowly missing him.

"Can we step away from the field of battle?" Kieran asked. "I bear concerning news, enough that Eddie believed I should bring it to you personally."

He was referring to Edward Hage, his eldest brother, who was in command of Berwick at the moment. Patrick nodded, already moving away from the field as Markus followed. They pushed through the crowds encircling the field until they broke free into the open area between the field and the visitor's encampment. That was when Patrick came to a halt and faced Kieran again.

"We are away from the noise," he said. "Now, tell me what has happened. Why did Eddie send you?"

Kieran nodded. "Concerning news that he wanted you to know," he said. "Early this morning, we received word from Trastamara Castle. Roget de Sauque has been killed."

Patrick's eyebrows lifted in surprise. "What happened?"

Kieran's gaze moved back and forth between Patrick and Markus. "Apparently, he was going to visit one of his properties and was set upon by outlaws," he said. "You know that entire area north of the border where Trastamara sits is filled with outlaws and murderers. He was robbed and then burned alive."

Patrick's eyes widened "What of the men he brought with him? Was there a battle?"

"He was traveling alone, we were told."

"Christ," Markus hissed. "The forests in that area are full of such cutthroats. De Sauque should have known better than to travel alone. Who sent you this news?"

Kieran held up a hand. "That is the strange part," he said. "It did not come from de Sauque's soldiers. We received the news from a servant of Lady de Sauque. She says that Roget is dead and the army is under the command of his knight, Sir

Shand Bexwell. She has no control over anything. Lady de Sauque is fearful of what that will mean for her and her children. She asks that we send help to supersede Bexwell and help her regain control of Trastamara Castle for her son and heir, Atlas."

Patrick stared at him a moment before sighing heavily. "God's Bones," he muttered. "Atlas de Sauque is fostering at Castle Questing. Does he know of his father's death?"

"Eddie sent word to Uncle Scott about it. He should know by now."

It was indeed troubling information, all of it. An ally was dead and the army was under the control of the man's captain, not his son and heir, who was a squire at Castle Questing. Trastamara Castle protected an important bridge over the River Tweed, a strategic location and one that was important.

One the Scots would love to get their hands on.

No wonder Kieran had come all the way to Bamburgh.

"This is a situation that involves the House of de Wolfe quite unquestionably," Patrick said quietly. "In truth, I am not surprised to hear that Bexwell has taken control. It's Roget's fault, really… I always thought the de Sauque marriage was an odd arrangement. Roget married Lady Amabella and gained Trastamara from her father when he died, but the man took it over and treated his wife like a possession. He provided well for her and the children, but the woman had less rights than his soldiers. It makes perfect sense that Roget's captain would take command and disregard her."

Markus was nodding to his father's assessment. "And now, she wants our help to wrest control from Bexwell."

Patrick looked at him. "Bexwell is not in command," he said. "If he ignores that fact, then we shall have to remind him. It *is* Atlas' castle even though the lad has only seen seventeen years. He is his father's heir."

"And what if Bexwell will not relinquish it to the boy?"

"He'll have no choice," Patrick pointed out. "Roget swore Trastamara's allegiance to me about ten years ago when we helped him fend off a series of attacks from Clan Gordon. We even had de Wolfe troops stationed at Trastamara for a couple of years after that. You were newly knighted at the time, Markus. Do you recall this?"

"I do," Markus recalled. "I've had limited contact with Trastamara since, however. I've only met Roget once or twice in all the time I've served at Berwick, but I know he has been a loyal vassal. But now…"

He trailed off, implying the obvious, and Patrick simply wriggled his eyebrows. "Now, we may have a situation on our hands if Bexwell does not relinquish control peacefully," Patrick said. "Even if Lady de Sauque had not asked, I would still take men to Trastamara to bolster her ranks and secure the castle. When the Scots hear about Roget's death, they could very well try to move on the fortress because they will consider it vulnerable. Trastamara is important and strategic, so I do not want it to give the illusion that it is weakened. Markus, you and Kieran ride back to Berwick now and begin preparations. I will make apologies to de Vesci and have the men break down our camp. I think we can make it back before nightfall."

All three of them glanced up at the sky, noting that the puffy gray clouds were growing heavier. The smell of damp was in the air.

"It might rain," Markus said. "I will return with Kieran and begin the preparations, but why don't you spend the night here and return early tomorrow morning? Avoid the bad weather if you can."

Patrick glanced up again, scratching his cheek where the mail was chaffing him. "Possibly," he said. "Muster five hundred men and have them ready to move by noon tomorrow.

Even with all of those men, it will take us an hour at most to make it to Trastamara."

"Aye, Papa," Markus said. "Anything else?"

Patrick shook his head. "Not now," he said. "But I want Atlas to meet us at Trastamara, so send Hermes back to Castle Questing and have him escort Atlas to Trastamara. Now, off with you both. And, Markus – wave to Lady Emmalina as you leave the area."

Markus cast him a long look as the conversation veered back to a distasteful subject. "I will not."

"Do it or I will be forced to make apologies for my rude son."

Markus made an unhappy face at him. "Then make those apologies," he said, grabbing Kieran by the arm and dragging the man along. "If I am rude, it is your fault. You raised me that way."

Patrick sighed with exasperation as Markus and Kieran took off running for the de Wolfe encampment to collect Markus' belongings and, as it turned out, Lady Emmalina never even saw him. By the time Patrick made his way over to her father to make his apologies for departing early, Lady Emmalina was surrounded by at least three young beaux who had her full attention.

Patrick found himself frustrated that Markus wasn't one of them, but that frustration quickly faded. He had enough on his mind with a dead ally and a vulnerable fortress without the added burden of an heir who had no intention of finding a wife any time soon.

But not if Patrick had anything to say about it.

One problem at a time.

CHAPTER TWO

Trastamara Castle
Five miles northwest of Berwick

"AMA? DO YOU think we can send someone into town for the honey puffs?"

The timid question came from a pale, frail girl who had seen thirteen years. Seated in her mother's small solar, the tiny one that her father had allowed the ladies to use, she was positioned in front of the hearth because, even on warm days, she had a chill to her bones. Young Aleanor de Sauque had never been very strong.

But she liked her honey puffs.

The woman sitting across from her, on a cushioned chair with a footstool to prop up her feet, glanced up from the intricate sewing in her hand. She was creating a cover for a pillow that would adorn her youngest son's bed, a horse's head because he liked horses so much. She was also the young woman's mother and although *"ama"* was another name for "mother" in the Spanish language, it also happened to be a nickname of her given name – *Amabella*.

Amabella Hemada Abril de Sauque smiled at her daughter.

"Is that what you would like, *querida*?" she asked softly.

"The day is growing late, but mayhap tomorrow. Would you like it if we all went? That way, you could pick them out yourself."

Aleanor appeared intrigued by the suggestion, if not downright interested. But she was a fearful child; fearful of the world, of people in general, of nearly everything around her. At her age, she had never fostered because she had been too terrified to leave Trastamara Castle. Therefore, the question had her both frightened and curious.

"Will you go?" she asked.

"Of course," her mother said. "We will bring Alfie and Ambra. Your brother and sister would like to go into town, too. There is a man there with dogs he has trained to jump on each other that they like to watch. Do you remember that from the last time we went? You liked them a great deal, too."

Aleanor nodded, but the thought of venturing out was too intimidating, even with the lure of honey puff pastries, so she lowered her gaze and went back to her sewing. She was very good at sewing, perhaps even better than her mother, and she was making a surcoat for herself modeled after one she had seen the last time she'd gone into the town of Berwick. It wasn't too far away and it was the largest town this far north. There were many people in it, the town dominated by a massive castle that was perched over the River Tweed.

But Berwick frightened her and the only reason she had gone was because her father had forced her to. He'd bellowed at her when she started crying, so she was forced to huddle in a wagon with her mother so her father would not become overly angry.

But he was gone now.

Truth was... she wasn't sorry.

"Allie?" her mother said gently. "Answer me, *querida*. Would you like to go get the honey puffs yourself?"

Aleanor glanced at her mother. "Mayhap," she said. "Do you think we could learn to make them here? They do not look too difficult to make."

Her mother smiled. "Why would you want to try when we can simply buy them and they are already wonderful?"

It was her mother's way of encouraging Aleanor to go out into the world, but the young woman wasn't convinced. She set her sewing back in her lap.

"Because you can do anything, Ama," she said. "Dada said you have a great talent for the kitchen and you can prepare any dish he likes. Or liked. When he was here, I mean."

Her head dipped down again, back to the sewing, but the gesture or the words didn't go unnoticed by her mother.

Lady Amabella Hemada Abril de Sauque eyed her daughter. These were difficult days following the death of Roget, the father of Amabella's four children – Atlas, her strong and noble son who was fostering at an allied castle, Aleanor, who had such a timid view of the world, Alphonse, her young and bright and strong son, and then Ambra, her baby. Four children who had been treated by their father like cast-offs.

Four children who had never known the love or gentleness of a father.

Four children who weren't sorry that he was gone.

Truth be told, Amabella wasn't sorry, either, and she had been struggling with that guilt. When she should have felt sorrow, she felt relief. As the man's wife, she should have grieved his death, but she couldn't bring herself to do it. Whatever she might have felt for the man had died a long time ago when he'd married her simply to gain her castle and her father's wealth. Once he had it, he showed her very little consideration.

None, in fact.

No, she wasn't sorry he was gone in the least.

But his death didn't improve her situation much.

Roget had made it clear to her from the outset of their marriage that the army of Trastamara Castle belonged to him. Her family's hereditary home, the place where she was born, became Roget's when her father died a year into their marriage. It was then she saw Roget's true nature. She had absolutely no say in anything about it and because he treated her as if she had little worth, most of the men did, too, including his captain of the guard, Sir Shand Bexwell.

Shand wasn't an evil man, not really. He'd shown more respect to her than her husband had at times, but he treated her as if she was of little consequence, just like Roget had. He only followed Roget's lead. Even now, he had taken over Trastamara as if he'd inherited it from Roget. He was making all of the decisions now, something Amabella had been forbidden to do. The woman hadn't made an important decision since her marriage to Roget twenty years earlier.

She lived like a prisoner in the home she'd been born in.

That was why she'd had to send one of her maids on a dangerous journey, alone, to Berwick Castle. Shand hadn't notified the allies yet of Roget's death and Amabella was frankly afraid of what the man might do with her and her children now that he believed himself to be in command of Trastamara. So, Amabella wrote a missive to Patrick de Wolfe, Earl of Berwick and Roget's liege, notifying him of Roget's death and asking for help.

She could only hope the man would respond.

Time would tell.

Meanwhile, she had to pretend that life was normal for the sake of her children. Aleanor had no great love for her father and the two younger children had hardly even had any interaction with Roget, so they were indifferent. Alphonse, known as Alfie to the family, had seen seven years while his sister, Ambra, had just seen her fifth birthday. As bad off as the children had been when Roget had been alive, she could only pray that it didn't get worse in his death for one very good reason – Atlas, her eldest son at seventeen years, was now the Lord of Trastamara.

That was exactly why Shand hadn't notified the allies yet.

He didn't want to relinquish the fortress to an inexperienced young man.

Unable to continue with her sewing, Amabella stood up and made her way over to one of two big lancet windows that overlooked the vast bailey. It was well-organized, full of men who might as well have been her enemy for all of the regard they gave her. She was trapped here, caged like an animal, with the title of Lady of the Castle and none of the rights that went with it.

She could only pray that Berwick changed that.

"Ama!"

The door to the solar slammed back on its hinges as a shout roused her from her thoughts. Amabella turned to see her youngest son in the doorway. Like her oldest boy, Alphonse Abril de Sauque had the dark personal traits of her Moorish ancestors, the Abrils from Aragon on her father's side, and also from her mother, who had been born in Algiers. He had inherited black hair and pale skin with the dark green eyes that were the purest shade, like an emerald. Those eyes were lit up at the sight of his mother.

"Ama," he said rather petulantly. "I want to ride my pony and Shand will not let me. I must ride. My guard is waiting!"

Amabella smiled faintly at her demanding, vivacious son as she came away from the window. "What did Shand tell you?"

Alfie frowned. "He told me that he could not be res… res… responsible for me and told me to go inside to you," he said. "What does responsible mean?"

"It means that he cannot watch over you," she said. "Where is Savia?"

That only deepened Alfie's frown. "She is sleeping with Ambra," he said, speaking of the old nurse the children had since birth. "Ambra is a babe and I am not. I want to ride my pony with my guard. Please, Ama, tell Shand that he must let me."

Unlike the older children, who understood how Roget and Shand had treated Amabella, the younger children still weren't entirely aware. He naively thought his mother had some control.

Amabella wished with all her heart that she did.

Were it up to her, he could ride with his "guard", which was made up of eight children belonging to servants – the cook's three young sons, two daughters belonging to the stablemaster, and three more boys belonging to various other household servants. They were all under ten years of age and Alfie was their leader.

And what a leader he was.

Alfie positioned himself to be the King of Trastamara and his horse guard would ride sticks with pieces of cloth on one end, like reins, escorting their "king" around the compound. Sometimes, they even used leaves or pieces of wood as "standards", following him around as he rode his fat, brown pony that Roget had given him. It was one of the only kind things the man had ever done for Alfie as a father.

Unlike Roget, Alfie treated his horse guard well. He would bring them food from his own meals, or play games with them, even allowing them to win on occasion. He had the beginnings of great benevolence, something Amabella hoped he never lost. The little boy had heart. None of Roget's indifference and greed had tainted him.

It was one of the few things that gave Amabella joy.

"You have been out with your guard all morning, have you not?" she asked him. "Why don't you come inside with me and play quietly? Your guard can rest and then you can resume playing tomorrow. Mayhap Shand will allow you to ride your pony then."

Oh, but the suggestion made Alfie unhappy. Grossly unhappy. He stiffened up and fell forward onto a cushioned chair, groaning and hissing because he didn't want to play quietly. Kings were not supposed to play quietly. But he wasn't unhappy enough to argue with his mother, whom he loved with all his heart. He also obeyed her without question. Well, at least most of the time.

… some of the time.

"Come, *querida*," Amabella said, reaching out to pick up her big boy and cradle him. "Come and play quietly. Do you want to play with your sticks? You can build a fortress with them like you did the last time. It was a fine fortress, Alfie. Good enough for a king."

That had Alfie's attention. He kept a stack of sticks and pieces of wood in his mother's solar and he'd built many a castle with those sticks. He slithered out of her arms and went over to the corner where he kept his sticks, piled in a basket to keep them from scattering. He sat down beside the basket and grabbed a handful as Aleanor sat up in her chair and frowned.

"But what of my honey puffs?" she asked.

Amabella shook her head as she sat back down to her sewing. "It is too late in the day to set out for Berwick," she said. "Mayhap tomorrow. Let me think on it."

"*Please*, Ama."

"I said I would think on it. Now, return to your sewing. It is looking beautiful, *querida*."

Aleanor blamed her little brother's appearance for her mother's reluctance to go into Berwick on this day. It was only early afternoon and there was plenty of time for a journey there and back as far as she was concerned.

Alfie was always spoiling everything with his demands and pushy nature.

But Aleanor didn't argue. Instead, she settled back with her garment. It never did any good to argue when it came to Alfie. She had just taken the first stitch when there was a sharp knock on the solar door.

"I'll answer!" Alfie said.

Eagerly, he raced to the solar door and yanked it open only to reveal his greatest enemy in all the world. The man who had denied him his pony.

Shand Bexwell stood in the opening.

Alfie immediately frowned and moved away, rushing over to his mother and throwing himself in her lap even as Amabella tried to stand up. She was forced to push Alfie to his feet as she faced Shand.

"Sir Shand," she said politely. "To what do we owe the honor of your visit?"

Shand wasn't un-handsome; he was average in height, with long blond hair and piercing blue eyes. He wasn't particularly large, but he was deceptively strong. He had great skill with the sword and with a bow and arrow. Roget had put a great deal of faith in Shand.

The man forced a smile in response to Amabella's question.

"I was hoping to have a word with you, Lady de Sauque," he said. "Is this a convenient time?"

For lack of a better response, Amabella shrugged. "As good a time as any," she said. "How may I be of service?"

Shand glanced at the children in the room. "Privately, please," he said. "This does not concern your offspring."

There was something ominous in that statement, which put her on her guard. Amabella could only pray that it had nothing to do with the servant she'd sent to Berwick. She'd done it secretly, pretending to send servants to Berwick to purchase foodstuffs when what they really did was head straight to the massive castle that overlooked the city. She knew the servants wouldn't tell, for they had no great love for the army or for Shand, but it was possible he'd had the servants followed.

Paranoia was a common world Amabella lived in.

"Certainly," she said calmly, looking to Aleanor. "Please take Alfie with you and go to your chamber."

Aleanor was rising from her seat nervously. "But, Ama…"

Amabella put her hand to her daughter's cheek. "Please," she said. "I will come for you when I have finished with Sir Shand. Please go."

Aleanor was still nervous but she did as she was told. She grasped Alfie by the hand and pulled him from the room, but the boy wasn't particularly keen on going and did everything but throw himself on the ground in order to delay the inevitable. Finally, Aleanor was able to take him from the chamber as Shand closed the door behind them.

"Please open the door," Amabella said steadily. "It is not proper for you and me to be alone in a chamber behind a closed door."

"What I have to say is private," he said. "I do not wish for the entire keep to hear. I will stay here by the door if you feel uncomfortable."

Amabella studied him for a moment before finally nodding, but she moved away from her chair and back over to the lancet window so she was about as far away from him as she could get. Moreover, her sewing kit was on the table next to her, including big iron shears, which she could use like a dagger if she had to. Not that she didn't trust Shand, for she'd never felt threatened by him, but she didn't like that he had shut the door.

"Speak, then," she said. "I am listening."

Shand cleared his throat softly. "It has been four days since the death of Lord Roget, my lady," he said. "We have put his body in the vault, but you've made no mention of where you wish to bury him or when. May I know of your plans?"

Amabella felt a little relieved by the question but she wasn't sure why he needed a closed door for it.

"My family has been buried at St. John's near Berwick for four generations," she said. "It is where we attend mass every Sunday. Summon the priest from the parish and I shall make the arrangements with him. Roget can be buried with my father, a man he was glad to see die so that he could take his castle. Let him explain that to my father in the afterlife, buried next to the very man he plotted against."

There was bitterness there, but Amabella had never made any real effort in concealing the disdain she held for her husband. Shand simply nodded.

"I will send for the priest, then," he said. "But there is something else I wish to speak to you of, something Lord Roget and I discussed on several occasions."

"What is that?"

"In the event of his death, he wished for me to marry you."

Amabella felt as if she'd been hit in the chest. All of her calm resolve left her and she stared at the man in shock.

"He…" she stammered. "He wished for you to *marry* me?"

Shand nodded and, contrary to his assurances when he shut the door to the chamber, he took a couple of steps in her direction.

He didn't stay by the door.

"Lord Roget did not wish for you to be without a husband," he said. "He wished for Trastamara to continue as it always had, now with me as Lord of Trastamara."

Amabella couldn't believe what she was hearing. "But you would not be Lord of Trastamara," she said. "Atlas is his father's heir. By birthright, the castle is his."

Shand lifted his shoulders. "He is not yet of age," he said. "He is fostering at Castle Questing and it was his father's wish for him to continue to foster there. He will be knighted by de Wolfe and once he is of age, then we will discuss his birthright. But not now. Trastamara is an important castle and, more importantly, it maintains control of The Orchard crossing over the River Tweed. It is one of the most important bridges in this area. Therefore, all of this must be commanded by a seasoned knight."

"You?"

"Me."

Amabella stared at him for a moment before turning away. She wasn't sure Roget had ever said such a thing to Shand, but then again, Roget had never discussed his business with her. Shand had never come across as particularly ambitious, but he could very well see this as an opportunity.

She couldn't be sure.

"There is no need for me to ever marry again," she said. "Atlas is now the Lord of Trastamara. I am only his mother. I hold no value to anyone."

Shand was watching her closely. "Untrue, my lady," he said. "Atlas is underage. As your husband, I will have the right to act as his regent. It was Lord Roget's wish."

"He never spoke of such a thing to me."

"Do you doubt my word, my lady?"

She turned to look at him. "I did not say that," she said. "All I said was that my husband never spoke of such a thing to me."

"But he spoke of it to me," Shand said. "I would not say it if it was not so. Until Atlas is able to assume his duties, he will need a regent."

"And you must marry me to accomplish this?"

"As I said, it was Lord Roget's wish."

He wasn't being aggressive in his stance, merely factual. Or, so he seemed. But Amabella didn't want to consider it or even talk about it. After a moment, she shook her head.

"Forgive me, Sir Shand," she said, "but my husband has not even been buried yet. At least let me get the man in the ground before we discuss this."

Shand nodded, but it was with reluctance. As if he'd been expecting an instant answer.

"As you wish, my lady," he said. "I will send for the priest today so we can bury Lord Roget before the week is out."

Amabella merely nodded, turning away from him. She had nothing more to say and the fact that she wouldn't even look at him was Shand's invitation to leave. He did, quietly, and shut the door softly behind him. Amabella turned to make sure he had left.

Only then did she emit a sigh of relief.

And frustration.

Something told her that Shand would be right back at her the moment Roget was put into the ground, and the next time, she might not be able to brush him off so easily. He didn't need to be married to her to be acting regent of Atlas' inheritance, but perhaps marrying her would make his position stronger. It would also give him cause to deny Atlas and retain Trastamara for himself.

It might even put Atlas' life in danger. Alfie, too, as another of Roget's sons.

It was possible that Shand wanted Trastamara all for himself.

With those horrible thoughts rolling through her head, Amabella found herself looking from the window that faced south, praying that the Earl of Berwick was soon on his way to Trastamara. If she was convincing enough, Berwick might take her side in this and deny any claim Shand thought he had to her and to Trastamara. At the very least, he could protect Atlas from his father's overly ambitious knight.

Amabella prayed the situation wouldn't get any worse before it got better.

If it ever became better.

Time would tell.

CHAPTER THREE

"WHAT DO YOU know about Trastamara Castle, Damien?"

The question came from Kieran Hage, proposed to a knight who had been at Berwick for twenty-five years. Sir Damien d'Vant from Cornwall was as far away from the home of his birth as he could possibly get, but he'd come to the House of de Wolfe as a pledge and ended up staying. As he told the story, there was excitement in the north that never happened in Cornwall.

He rather liked the thrill of the edgy northern borders.

Damien glanced at Kieran, a smile playing on his lips. "How long have you been at Berwick, young Kieran?"

"I've was born at Berwick," Kieran said, reminding Damien of what he already knew. "It is my home."

Damien would not be schooled by an arrogant young knight. He held up a finger. "You were born at Berwick, but you left when you were seven years of age and sent south to Norwich Castle with your older brothers for several years. Then you served at Ramsbury Castle in Wiltshire before returning home last year. Just because you were born at Berwick does not mean you know it, or the area, as well as I do. Otherwise, you would not be asking me the question you just asked."

Properly put in his place, Kieran wasn't pleased that he'd just been publicly humiliated. He was riding at the head of a five-hundred-man army from Berwick Castle along with his Uncle Patrick and his cousins, Markus and Cassius. Titus had remained behind with his eldest brother, Edward, but another Berwick knight had accompanied them, an old knight who had served his Uncle Patrick for as long as Damien had. Sir Anson du Bonne heard Damien's answer and snorted.

A cocky young knight wasn't going to find any sympathy here.

"Very well," Kieran said, listening to the older knights snicker at his expense. "I concede to your extreme old age and knowledge. I have heard of Trastamara, but I do not know the history behind it. Would you enlighten me?"

He was respecting Damien and insulting him at the same time, which had Damien fighting off a genuine laugh. He looked at Anson.

"Please, tell me we were not like this one when we were his age," he said.

Anson started to laugh but Patrick, riding behind them, heard the comment. "Must you seriously ask that question?" he said. "Damien, you and Anson were the worst. My father used to laugh at you two because of it. Papa used to say that he found it amazing you could walk without effort considering your pride had the weight of an anchor. It was an awesome burden to bear."

That brought Damien's smile full-bore. "Ah, the great Wolfe of the Border," he said. "I miss the man, Atty. I miss his wisdom, his sheer presence. God, to bask in that man's aura was truly something to behold."

Patrick was riding without his helm, his graying dark hair exposed to the weak sunlight of a mild day. Damien's comment had him reflecting on his father, who had inarguably been the greatest knight of his generation. The name William de Wolfe meant something in England and in Scotland. It stood for strength and honor, and a type of magic that can only be found in men who had achieved something extraordinary in life. That was the aura Damien spoke of – the inherent quality of a legend.

The pain of William's passing was as fresh to Patrick as if it had only happened yesterday. It was like a weight, pressing on him, threatening to crush him, though over time, the weight had lessened. He and his father had been so close, in every way, and like most children, he viewed his father as immortal. Surely such a man could never die. But one winter's night, after a brief illness when William seemed to be on the mend, he went to sleep and never woke up. The old knight died warm and safe in his bed, with his wife beside him.

It still brought Patrick to tears to think about it.

"It was," he agreed, fighting off the familiar grief. "It still is. I can still feel it, every time I go to Castle Questing, only now it's coming from my mother. She was his heart and that heart is still beating."

Damien turned to look at him, smiling. "That she is," he said quietly. Then he gestured to Kieran. "Would you care to educate your nephew on Trastamara Castle? Beyond the oddness of Roget de Sauque, I mean."

Torn from sad thoughts of his father, Patrick looked at the host of knightly faces around him and realized the younger men might not know everything, as Kieran had said. Berwick had many allies, and the scope of their influence was dotted by many small castles and pele towers, each one with a particular story. But none so unique as Trastamara. They were riding to aid an ally and that was all they knew, so a little background would be helpful.

Just so they knew what they were getting into.

Patrick spurred his horse forward so everyone riding on point could hear him.

"Trastamara Castle, first and foremost, guards the only crossing over the River Tweed between Berwick and Northwood Castle," he said. "When you hear men speak of The Orchard crossing, that's the one. It is an old stone bridge that was built many years ago, using a sandbar as support and built where the river narrows. The Scots cannot burn the bridge, but they've tried to gain control of it. Several times. If that happens, the Scots will have an easy way to invade our part of England, so it is imperative that Trastamara maintains control of that bridge."

Everyone had heard of The Orchard crossing, but Patrick had clarified the importance of it.

"What about Roget de Sauque?" Kieran asked. "I've heard men say he married for his property."

Patrick nodded. "He did," he said. "But many men marry for their property, so that is nothing new. Trastamara was built by the House of Abril, a family from Aragon who fought for Henry the Third. Henry granted them the lands north of the River Tweed and they built Trastamara Castle, named for the Trastamara family of Aragon. They are part of the nobility of Aragon. Some say the family will produce kings someday."

"They're royalty, then?" Kieran wanted to know.

Patrick shrugged. "They are old Spanish nobility," he said. "The lord who served Henry received the grant of land and built his castle, and acquired other properties through marriage. There are at least three that I know of. Roget de Sauque acquired Trastamara when he married the heiress, Lady Amabella Hemada Abril."

"Her mother was born in Algiers," Damien interjected. When Patrick looked at him, he nodded. "That is what I was told by a soldier who served de Sauque. I've never seen the woman, but they say she has the look of the Berbers."

"I have seen her and she looks like an Englishwoman to me," Patrick said. "She's quite beautiful from what I remember, but it has been a few years. That may have changed."

"How old is she?" Kieran asked.

Patrick lifted an eyebrow. "Too old for you if you've got any ambitions to be the next Lord of Trastamara," he said, watching Kieran flush. "She has been married to Roget for twenty years, so that should give you an idea of her age. In any event, it does not matter. Trastamara has lost its liege, Lady de Sauque is fearful that her husband's army may try to wrest the place from the rightful heir, and we are going to ensure that none of that happens."

"Papa," Markus said from behind him. He'd remained mostly quiet through all of the chatter, listening. "If the army is threatening to take control of the castle, and they do not know Lady de Sauque sent us the missive of her husband's death, then how are we to approach this? We have five hundred men with us. Do we just march up to Trastamara's gatehouse and demand entry?"

Patrick scratched his head. "I am their liege," he said simply. "They will open their gates to me or suffer the consequences. Trastamara does not carry more than two hundred men. I have brought five hundred with me. They would be foolish to resist."

"But if they are trying to wrest power from Lady de Sauque?"

"It is power she does not have," Anson du Bonne spoke up. "If you have lived in Berwick as long as we have, you have heard the rumors. Roget de Sauque treated his wife no better than the cattle in his fields or the horses in his stable. All you have to do is ask her son, Atlas, to hear that. If you ever want to hear a lad spew hate about his father, then talk to Atlas de Sauque. There is no love there."

Patrick held up a hand to silence Anson from speaking ill of the dead or of the bitter young man who was now the Lord of Trastamara. "Atlas should already be on his way to Trastamara," he said. "Hermes went to fetch him and he knows to wait for us before entering. I do not want Atlas walking into a group of men who would take his inheritance from him by force."

It didn't seem like an ideal situation all the way around, but at least they all knew what was happening. There was the potential for trouble, but it was clear Patrick was hoping there wasn't any.

"Papa." Markus reined his massive, dappled warhorse next to his father. "Let me ride ahead and announce our approach. Let me give them time to politely open their gates before we show up with five hundred men to overwhelm them."

Patrick looked at his son. He'd inherited the gift of diplomacy from his great-grandfather, Edward de Wolfe, who had been a diplomat for Richard the Lionheart and subsequently his brother, John. But he had also inherited it from his grandfather, Magnus. The man wasn't called the Law-Mender without reason. Markus was clever and silver-tongued, and coupled with his size and skill made him a formidable man, indeed. Enough of a man that the king himself had noticed.

Markus was the perfect candidate for Lord Protector, a position that Patrick very much wanted for his brilliant son.

"I do not think that is a good idea," he said after a moment. "You would be a lone knight and it might put you in a precarious position, especially if they are intent on keeping control of Trastamara. Nay, lad, it would be best if we approach them as an army. They'll have to take us seriously."

Markus lifted his eyebrows. "It may also put the Lady of Trastamara in danger."

Patrick knew that. In fact, he'd had that very same thought.

"Not if we do not tell them how we know of Roget's death," he said. "News travels fast. We will tell them that we have arrived before the Scots caught wind of Roget's death to help protect Trastamara from any potential attacks until the new Lord of Trastamara can be established."

"The new lord is a lad who has seen seventeen years," Markus reminded him quietly. "I know Atlas; he's bright and he's powerful, and he learns quickly. But is he man enough to hold a strategic post like Trastamara?"

Patrick sighed heavily. It was yet another thought that had crossed his mind. "What would you suggest?"

Markus turned his gaze to the road. They would soon be seeing the great towers of Trastamara Castle. "That you leave a de Wolfe knight in charge," he said. "Cassius or Anson or Damien. I cannot remain, of course, as I am due to join Edward when he comes north very soon, but if Atlas is fighting off a coup, then we cannot let him fight it alone unless you plan to remain at Trastamara until the threat has passed."

"I do not intend to remain there longer than necessary."

"Then leave a de Wolfe knight there. You are going to have to unless you want to worry about The Orchard bridge when you go to sleep at night."

Patrick didn't want to. He looked at his son, nodding in agreement. It wasn't ten minutes later that the gray-stoned bastion of Trastamara Castle into view.

Now, the crisis would begin in earnest.

CHAPTER FOUR

"**M**Y LORD, THERE was no reason for you to come. As you can see, Trastamara is quite secure."

Shand was standing in front of Trastamara's gatehouse. Literally, right in front of the open gate. He wasn't preventing Berwick from entering, but he wasn't inviting them in, either. His question had been directed at Patrick, who wasn't pleased with the man's response.

Markus could see his father's expression. Patrick was more a man of action than diplomacy in his later years, a man who had earned the moniker *Nighthawk*. He was a hunter and although hunters were patient when sighting prey, once that prey was cornered, there was no mercy. Patrick wasn't afraid to show force these days when there had been a time, years ago, when he'd had great patience. The older he became, the more he didn't tolerate foolery.

Therefore, before he could order the full invasion of Trastamara Castle, Markus took over the negotiation.

"Bexwell, is it?" he said, clarifying the name. When Shand nodded, Markus stepped closer to him. "You and I have been in a couple of skirmishes together, but it has been some time. The last time was last year, I believe. You manned the castle while my men did battle over at The Orchard crossing. Do you know me?"

Shand peered at him. "I believe I do, my lord. You are one of the earl's sons."

"I am his heir, Viscount Ravensdowne. My name is Markus de Wolfe."

Shand nodded in realization. "Of course, my lord," he said. "Forgive me for not remembering."

Markus waved him off. He wasn't concerned if the man didn't remember his name because he hadn't remembered his, either.

"It is of little matter," he said. "But we have come for a purpose. As you know, Roget was a great ally of Berwick and when we heard of his death, we immediately came to your aid because if we have heard of it, others have heard of it, too. Meaning Scots. They would like nothing better than to take charge of The Orchard crossing and we are here to ensure that does not happen. When a man dies, his enemies try to take advantage of that. Would you not agree?"

Shand nodded hesitantly. "But I am telling you that we have seen no trouble," he insisted. "It has been four days since Lord Roget's death and we've seen no trouble at all."

Markus pretended to be patient. "There is always tomorrow," he said. "The Scots can come out of nowhere and go after the bridge, so you would do well to have your numbers reinforced during this difficult time. Now, I have five hundred men who need shelter for the night. I will not ask them to turn around and return to Berwick tonight, so please give us shelter. We will not drain your stores, I assure you. We have brought our own with us. But I would prefer to get them inside the walls of Trastamara before the sun sets. May we be invited in, please?"

It was clear that Shand didn't want them there, but given

that he was faced with the Earl of Berwick and the man's son, he couldn't very well refuse. With a reluctant nod, he turned around and motioned them to follow.

That was all the knights needed to throw up the cry to move out.

Everyone was moving.

Markus gave his father a rather triumphant look as he followed Shand through the gatehouse. Patrick wasn't far behind, fighting off a smirk because his son was quick to criticize the arrogant young knights in the family when he, in fact, could be counted among them.

But it wasn't as if he didn't have good reason to be arrogant.

Markus could move mountains.

The moment the knights were through the gatehouse and the army started to pour in, they began to take over. They shoved aside Trastamara men to make way for Berwick men, and Markus stayed close to Shand in case the man took a dislike to it.

In fact, Markus was with Shand for a reason, and that was to separate him from his men. Divide and conquer was the way to keep them from rebelling against the Berwick presence and they were doing it very well.

Everything was proceeding as planned.

As Markus and Shand stood over by the south tower, watching the incoming army get organized, it gave Markus a chance to get a good look at the interior of Trastamara Castle, a place he'd never even been inside of.

There was a reason for that.

Markus had served at Berwick for the past nine years, ever since he'd been knighted by his grandfather, William de Wolfe. Markus had fostered at Lioncross Abbey in his youth, the seat of the House of de Lohr, but upon receiving his spurs, it had been expected that he would return home to help share the command burden with his father at Berwick Castle.

Berwick was one of the largest castles in the north, sur-rounded by a large city, and it covered a vast amount of land to the south and southwest. There were many allies, and Markus knew all of the major ones in-depth, but Trastamara, for its relative closeness, had never been a particularly close relation-ship. They mostly stayed to themselves unless they needed help, and that was only if The Orchard crossing was sufficiently threatened.

Still, Roget de Sauque showed up to Berwick when Patrick called his vassals together and he had never refused a com-mand, but Trastamara seemed to prefer its own company.

It was a castle of loners.

Markus could see that it was true given the lack of warm welcome they'd received from Shand Bexwell, the very knight Lady de Sauque had been concerned with in her missive. As the army began to settle into Trastamara's vast bailey, Markus took a look around at the castle, which was an interesting one.

Trastamara had three massive towers at each corner of the curtain wall, while the fourth tower was actually the keep. It was built right into the northwest corner of the wall. In the center of the bailey was the great hall and the kitchens, while the western portion of the bailey was sectioned off into the stables and kitchen yard.

As Markus took it all in, he could see his father on the ap-proach. The man had just come from the stables as his men oversaw the settling of the army.

"Bexwell," Patrick said as he drew near. "I would speak with Lady de Sauque now. Will you announce me?"

Both Patrick and Markus could see Shand's expression tighten. "She is in the keep with her children," he said. "She is grieving, my lord."

It was fairly close to a denial but Patrick didn't back away.

"That is understandable," he said. "But I will see her. Announce me."

It was a command. He wasn't going to plead with a subordinate, no matter how much the man thought he was in charge of this castle, and Shand seemed to take a step back. It was clear that he knew he'd just received an order and, being an obedient knight, he was conflicted. It wouldn't do to deny his liege, in any fashion, but it was blatantly obvious that he simply didn't want them here.

He grasped at the last strands of control that were inevitably slipping from his grasp.

"My lord, I do not understand any of this," he said, trying not to sound as if he were complaining. "We are not in any need, yet you bring your army here as if we have begged you to aid us. We have not requested, nor do we need, your assistance, but it seems as if you wish to push us aside and take over. And now you demand to see Lady de Sauque when I have told you the woman is grieving the loss of her husband. Forgive me, my lord, but your presence is both confusing and unwanted."

There it was, plainly spoken, and Markus looked at his father. The response would have to come from him, but it was clear to both Markus and Patrick that Shand was throwing up blockades at nearly every turn. Lady de Sauque's fear that Shand intended to take over Trastamara appeared to be well-founded.

Patrick didn't mince words.

"Bexwell," he said. "I want you to listen to me carefully. Do I have your full attention?"

"You do, my lord."

"Good," Patrick said. "I need to explain something to you. As you know, I am the Earl of Berwick. My brother from Castle Questing is the Earl of Warenton, but better still, my youngest brother, Tommy, is the Earl of Northumbria. His standing army alone numbers in the thousands. I have not even mentioned my other brothers who also have castles and thousands of men between them. It would be safe to say that one word from me and I could have fifteen thousand English soldiers swarming over Trastamara and you and your paltry army would not survive. If I was truly here to take over, as you have asserted, then I would have brought more than five hundred men. Does that make sense to you?"

Shand's jaw was ticking faintly. "It does, my lord."

"Then suffice it to say that we are not here to take over," Patrick said, his tone decidedly colder. "But I am here to ensure The Orchard crossing is secure, and remains so, in light of Roget's death and I will speak with Lady de Sauque. Is this in any way unclear?"

"It is clear, my lord."

"Then announce me to your mistress or I will find her myself."

Shand swallowed hard. There was nothing more he could say, no more fight he could give. Without another word, he turned on his heel and headed across the bailey, towards the enormous corner-keep.

Patrick and Markus followed.

Shand took them up the steps leading to the first floor, stone steps instead of the usual wooden retractable stairs. It was strange considering how much trouble Trastamara had from the Scots over the years, but they evidently had a good deal of faith in the tall curtain wall.

Coming through the entry into the cool, dark innards of the keep, they were on a level with only two rooms – the room the entry opened up into and a larger second chamber. Shand turned to them.

"Wait here," he said. "I will summon Lady de Sauque."

But Patrick shook his head. "We will go with you," he said. "Lead the way."

"But, my lord…"

Patrick cut him off. "I said lead the way."

Thwarted, Shand took them to a small spiral staircase built into the corner of the keep and they moved to the second floor. This floor was divided into thirds with three chambers, and Shand went to a closed door, rapping on it. A soft voice answered.

"Who comes?"

Shand glanced at Patrick and Markus. "It is Shand, my lady."

Before the woman could answer, there was a burst from the other side of the door.

"Go away if you will not let me have my pony!"

It was a child shouting. Patrick looked at Markus, who was fighting off a smile at a clearly angry little boy. Shand, however, appeared incredibly embarrassed.

"My lady, the Earl of Berwick has arrived," he said. "He is asking to see you."

The door suddenly flew open. A woman of unearthly beauty was standing in the opening, clad in a simple but lovely garment the color of mustard. Her eyes widened as she caught sight of Patrick.

"My Lord Berwick," she said, astonished. "I… I saw your army come through the gates. I would have come to you, my lord, I swear it. You did not have to trouble yourself by coming to me."

"Lady de Sauque," Patrick greeted politely. "It was no trouble at all. I came to offer you my sympathies on the passing of your husband."

The woman nodded briefly. "Thank you, my lord," she said. "And thank you… thank you for coming. We are honored by your arrival."

She was looking at him with a tremendous amount of uncertainty in her eyes, stumbling over her words. Since she was the one who had sent the missive about Roget's death without Shand's knowledge, Patrick tread carefully. He could see that she was frightened and he didn't want to give her subversion away.

He wanted to get to the bottom of things.

That meant talking to Shand, too, in order to determine the man's mindset. Perhaps this was a big misunderstanding, but perhaps not. Looking at the fear in Lady de Sauque's eyes, he was coming to think there was no mistake at all. Now that he could see for himself that Lady de Sauque was unharmed and well, he could focus on what needed to be done.

He motioned to Markus.

"This is my son, Markus de Wolfe, Viscount Ravensdowne," he told her. "Would you allow him a moment of your time, my lady? He would be happy to extend the service of the House of de Wolfe to you while I speak with Bexwell."

Lady de Sauque appeared somewhat baffled as she looked at Markus. When their gazes met, Markus suddenly found himself much more interested in the situation than he had been. He knew what his father was doing; he wanted Markus to speak with the lady to discover why she had sent that missive while he cornered Bexwell for his side of the story.

Divide and interrogate.

But now, Markus found himself more than happy to speak with Lady de Sauque. On the ride to Trastamara, his father had said that he remembered Lady de Sauque to be a woman of great beauty, but that it was possible that situation had changed. As Markus looked at her, he could confirm that nothing about that situation had changed.

Lady de Sauque was… stunning.

"Alone?" Lady de Sauque said, breaking into his thoughts. "You would have him… us… speak alone?"

She looked between Patrick and Markus with great fear and confusion. Patrick quickly sought to ease her.

"My son may be the size of a mountain and twice as intimidating, but I assure you, he is most kind and gentle with women," Patrick said. "He will leave the door to the chamber open, rest assured, and I will be on the floor below. I can easily hear a scream if you should feel so inclined. But I assure you, my son is the finest of men. He is worthy of your trust."

Lady de Sauque still didn't seem too convinced, but she graciously nodded. As Patrick took a reluctant Shand back down the stairs, Lady de Sauque ushered Markus into her chamber. It was a comfortable solar, a little cluttered, with two other people in it. One was the little boy who had yelled at Shand while the other was a girl, barely a woman, who looked at Markus with a terrified expression. In fact, she turned her back on him and lowered her head over whatever she held in her hands as if to hide from him. But the young girl didn't have his attention for more than a cursory glance.

He only had eyes for Lady de Sauque.

She was older than he was, perhaps by as much as ten years, but she had such an ageless beauty about her that it was difficult to tell. Her skin was pale, like cream, and she had beautiful dark red hair. He'd never seen a shade like it. It glistened with copper flecks in the weak light of the chamber even though she had it pulled to the nape of her neck and pinned it modestly.

But it was her eyes that had his attention. They were wide, slightly tilted at the edges, and the color of an emerald. He'd never seen such a color before. Even at a distance, there was no mistaking that deep, clear green. Everything about the woman reeked of beauty and poise, but as he stood by the door, the little boy who had shouted at Shand was suddenly standing in front of him.

"Are you a knight?" he asked.

Markus tore his gaze away from Lady de Sauque long enough to look at the child, who had Lady de Sauque's green eyes. Guessing he was a de Sauque offspring, Markus nodded.

"I am," he said. "Who are you?"

The child stared at him a moment as if trying to determine what to tell him. Finally, he puffed his chest out. "Alfie."

"Greetings, Alfie. I am Sir Markus."

Alfie jabbed a thumb into his chest. "I am *King* Alfie," he said imperiously. "I am the King of Trastamara. I have my own horse guard. Do you want to see them?"

"Alfie," Lady de Sauque scolded softly. "Do not pester Sir Markus, please. Come over here and sit with me."

Alfie looked at his mother, undecided whether he should obey her. New knights at Trastamara were far and few between, and the one before him was a giant. He'd never seen such a big man and was naturally quite interested in him. That curiosity won over and his attention inevitably returned to Markus.

"You may be part of my horse guard," he said. "Can you fight good?"

A smile played on Markus' lips. "I can."

"Have you been in a real battle?"

"I have."

"Did you kill a man and cut his head off and cut his hands off and watch him bleed?"

Markus started to snort but Lady de Sauque was there, pulling her cheeky son away. "Enough, Alfie," she said, yanking the reluctant boy with her. "I apologize for his manners, my lord. It is not often he sees a knight he does not know. He is very curious."

Markus was grinning at the lady. "I can see that," he said. "I am more than happy to continue the conversation with him after I have spoken to you."

Lady de Sauque nodded, forced to sit back in her chair

when Alfie climbed on her lap. "If you wish to shut the door, I will not protest," she said quietly, settling her squirming son. "You have come a long way. I am sure you have many questions."

Without a word, Markus shut the door, but he remained standing by it. He didn't want to frighten her and with his sheer size, he was used to frightening women. But not her; he didn't want to frighten her.

His gaze lingered on the woman with the alabaster skin and red hair.

"We received your missive," he said after a moment. "I am sure you realized that when you saw our army."

Lady de Sauque nodded, sighing heavily with relief. "I thanked God when I saw you," she murmured. "I am tremendously grateful that your father responded as fast as he did."

Markus nodded, acknowledging her gratitude. "Tell me quickly and succinctly what has happened since your husband's death," he said. "I do not know how much time we will have privately, so we must speak quickly on it. Has Bexwell taken control of Trastamara?"

She nodded. "He has," she said. "But, in fairness, he was my husband's second-in-command. That is his duty. But he does not want to relinquish that responsibility."

"What makes you say so?"

"Because he was in this chamber not two hours ago, telling me that Roget wished for him to marry me upon Roget's death," she said, distress in her features. "That is something my husband never told me, my lord. I do not know if it is true."

Markus' eyebrows lifted. "So he wants to marry you because Roget told him to?" he said. "But why? Your eldest son is now the Lord of Trastamara. Surely Bexwell has nothing to gain by marrying you."

She glanced at Alfie, at Aleanor, and shook her head sadly.

"He says that he will become my son's regent should he marry me," she said. "He told me he can administer Trastamara for Atlas until he comes of age and can assume his duties. But I must say that I do not believe him. If he marries me, Atlas and Alfie stand in the way of him assuming full control of Trastamara. I am afraid he will try to harm my boys and I cannot… I *will* not…"

She faded off, close to tears. Markus watched her hug Alfie tightly, who was starting to doze off against his mother. The little boy probably hadn't heard a word they'd said because he seemed completely untroubled, the relaxed nature of untroubled youth.

But that wasn't Markus' nature.

He *was* troubled by what he was hearing.

"Interesting," he finally said. "It is interesting that he thinks you would actually believe such an excuse for marriage. Bexwell may be calculating, but he is not intelligent. If he thinks you are the way to gain Trastamara, he is quite wrong."

"I realize that, my lord."

"Has he been cruel to you since Roget's passing? Has he been harmful?"

She shook her head. "Not in the least," she said. "He has not troubled me at all except for today. He came under the pretext of wanting to know where and when I wished to bury my husband, but I fear his true motive was the marriage proposal."

"Lord de Sauque has not yet been buried?"

"Nay. He is in the vault, kept cold until we can manage a burial."

Markus digested what he was being told, envisioning it from Bexwell's perspective. All he could see was a man who finally saw his opportunity to move up in the world with his liege's death. As he'd told his father, he didn't know Shand at all so he couldn't know the man's true mind or motives, but given everything he'd heard, he could guess.

Ambition took many forms – especially those pretending to be well-meaning.

"You should be aware that we have sent for Atlas," he said, leaning thoughtfully against the door. "He should be arriving at Trastamara shortly and I suspect Bexwell might show his true colors when the new Lord of Trastamara makes an appearance. Either he will respect the young man's position or he will not. Either way, you have my father and me here to discourage any revolution against Atlas to take his lordship from him."

Lady de Sauque was looking at him fearfully. "Sweet Mary," she murmured. "My dear Atlas is coming. Does Shand know?"

"He will when Atlas rides through the gates."

But Lady de Sauque shook her head. "Be cautious," she said. "The army is loyal to Roget and, consequently, to Shand. If they want him for their liege, there may be trouble as soon as Atlas returns."

Markus nodded. "Possibly," he said. "But take heart; I have several high caliber knights in the bailey along with five hundred men. If your army makes a move against Atlas, they will be very sorry."

It was as good as Lady de Sauque could have hoped for. "As I said," she said softly. "I am grateful you are here, Lord Ravensdowne. You bring me more comfort than you can know."

Markus gave her a crooked smile. "You may call me Markus," he said. "My men tease me when they hear my title because they think it sounds pretentious."

She smiled in response and it was as if the storm clouds parted and the sun suddenly burst forth. She had a radiant smile, as bright as anything he had ever seen. It was something that turned her lovely face into something quite extraordinary.

"It is not pretentious," she said. "It is something to be proud of. You have worked hard for the respect you enjoy, so do not let jealous men take that away from you."

He laughed softly. "They do not take anything away from me," he assured her. "But you are correct; they *are* jealous. There is much to be jealous of."

There was a hint of a jest in that statement and she laughed softly. "I can see that," she said. "Your father must be very proud."

Markus was enchanted by her gentle laughter. "Of course he is," he said. "So is my mother. Have you ever met my mother?"

Lady de Sauque shook her head, her smile fading somewhat. "I have not," she said. Then added quickly, "Though I would like very much to make her acquaintance, given the opportunity. My husband and I did not socialize much. He preferred the company of… well, it does not matter. I am most certain your mother is a lovely woman. She has a son that honors her with his kindness."

Markus dipped his head to her in thanks. "She has taught me much," he said, his gaze moving to the snoring child on her lap. "As you have taught your children, no doubt. I know your son, Atlas, but I was unaware he had siblings."

Lady de Sauque nodded, putting a gentle hand on Alfie's black hair. "He has three," she said. "You have met King Alfie, but he also has two sisters – Aleanor and Ambra. Ambra is napping with her nurse, but that is Aleanor sewing in the corner."

She gestured to the young woman hunched over her sewing, now looking up at Markus with veiled terror. She was a pretty little thing, tiny and pale. He smiled pleasantly at her.

"It is a pleasure to make your acquaintance, my lady," he said.

Aleanor nodded stiffly, glancing at her mother, who smiled encouragingly. Aleanor's gaze moved back to Markus.

"T-thank you," she said nervously.

She went back to her sewing.

Markus wondered what had the young girl so terrified, but given the state of Trastamara, he supposed it could have been any number of things. Politely, he returned his attention to Lady de Sauque.

"If you will excuse me, I will join my father and Bexwell," he said. "Thank you for your time, my lady. Should you need anything, do not hesitate to send for me."

He started to turn for the door, but she stopped him.

"Wait, please."

By the time Markus turned back around, she was on her feet, with Alfie laying across the chair. She approached him cautiously and Markus tried not to look at the figure beneath the mustard-colored surcoat. She had big, lovely breasts and a small waist, but that was all he could really see in his periphery. He tried to keep his eyes on hers and not look at all of that lushness below.

"Shand does not know I sent you the missive," she said quietly. "I would appreciate it if you did not mention it."

Markus shook his head. "Have no fear," he said. "We suspected as much. Your secret is safe. But I must ask – was your husband really burned to death by outlaws?"

Something in her features seemed to harden. "So Shand tells me."

"You do not believe him?" Markus cocked his head. "Do you think Shand had something to do with this?"

She shrugged, averting her gaze. "I do not know," she said honestly. "The truth is that I do not know him very well. He has served my husband for ten years, but we barely know one another. Roget made sure of it."

Markus simply nodded, seeing that the subject distressed her and not wanting to delve into it too much. He had the information he'd come for.

The rest could wait.

"I will go to my father now," he said. "Not knowing what he and Bexwell are speaking of, mayhap it would be best if you bolt this door for now. There is no telling what an ambitious man will do when he realizes he has been discovered."

She looked at him, fear reflecting in her green eyes. "My youngest will soon awaken and she will want for something to eat," she said. "I must be permitted to go to her."

Markus held up a hand because he could see she was becoming a little panicky. "Lock it for now," he said. "I will return as soon as I know something. I will stay with you and your children until we know how Bexwell is going to react to all of this. You should not be without protection, my lady."

Lady de Sauque simply nodded. Markus dipped his head at her, silently begging his leave, and departed the chamber. As he headed to the stairwell, he could hear the door behind him shut and the bolt thrown. Satisfied that Lady de Sauque was safe for the moment, he headed down the stairs.

That was when he heard the shouting.

CHAPTER FIVE

"WHEN IS THE last time you were home?"

The question came from Hermes. He was shouting to his companion as they cantered down the road, the pale gray walls of Trastamara Castle in the distance, gleaming against the late morning sun. His companion was a young man of seventeen years, tall and lanky, with a crown of dark hair and eyes as black as night.

Atlas de Sauque was fixed on the place of his birth.

"At least two years," he said above the thunder of hooves. "You would think I would visit my mother and sisters and brother more often, but the truth is that I could never stand to see Roget because he always wanted to get me drunk and press me for gossip from Castle Questing. At least I do not have to worry about that any longer."

Hermes didn't reply. He had been listening to a young man torn between jubilation over the death of his father he addressed as Roget and the shock that he had suddenly inherited an important border castle. From what Hermes could see, there was guilt tempering that jubilation, making it a strange combination, indeed.

Atlas didn't seem to know what to feel, but he did know one

thing for certain – he wanted to make it home as fast as he possibly could.

There was a sense of urgency there.

So, they headed out when the sun had been in the sky for about an hour after daybreak. Scott de Wolfe, the Earl of Warenton, had seen them off, sending them with an escort of about ten men considering Atlas was now the Lord of Trastamara and worthy of such protection. But the knight that Atlas has been squiring for, one of Scott's older knights by the name of Tobias de Bocage, had been very sorry to lose him. He'd even pleaded for him to stay, promising that he would purchase his armor for him when he was fully knighted to ensure he was properly outfitted.

The offer had been made half in jest, half-seriously. Atlas had grown from a timid, rather immature lad into an efficient squire who was the envy of most other knights. He was bright, skilled, and could hold his own in a fight. Both Scott and Tobias believed he had the makings of a great knight if they could get his reckless streak under control. With his father's death, however, those plans were somewhat blurred.

Atlas now had a lordship to deal with.

From what Hermes had seen, however, he wasn't dealing with it very well. Hermes had known Atlas since he first came to Castle Questing, and Hermes' oldest son used to follow Atlas around like a puppy. There was something strong and magnetic about Atlas. But he had a clear hatred for his father that he wasn't afraid to voice, and Hermes wondered how that was going to be viewed by an army that had been loyal to Roget.

They would soon find out.

It took a few hours to ride from Castle Questing to Trastamara because there was no easy way to get there. Trastamara was close to Berwick, but the most direct route to the castle was up into Scotland and Scott had specifically forbidden them to go into Scotland and attract the attention of the Scots. Therefore, they made their way to Trastamara on the English side of the border, traveling roads that were in some disrepair, before coming to the stout stone bridge of The Orchard crossing.

From there, it was a short journey.

Hermes could feel the tension mount as they drew near. He was apprehensive, but he had his orders. He had been told not to enter with Atlas unless Berwick had arrived. But very quickly, he could see Patrick de Wolfe's bright blue Berwick tunic with the wolf's head emblazoned upon it on one of the men at the main gate.

Berwick had, indeed, arrived.

With that in mind, Hermes charged ahead and began shouting, demanding that the gate be opened for the Lord of Trastamara. The men at the gate were so shocked at the sight of Atlas de Sauque that they automatically complied and the great gates began to swing open. Hermes and Atlas didn't even wait for them to fully open before they were storming through.

The bailey was full of Berwick men.

Feeling quite relieved that he was in the company of allies, Hermes dismounted his sweating steed, handing it off to a stable servant as Atlas did the same. Only Atlas didn't even pause to look around the bailey to get a good look at the situation. He didn't look at his father's men, or the condition of the castle, or anything else. His focus was on the keep and he immediately headed in that direction.

Hermes had to run to keep up with him.

Atlas had long legs and he covered a good deal of ground in his determination to get to the keep. There was almost a panicked sense in his movements. Taking the steps two at a time, he entered the cool, dark structure, hearing voices in the larger solar that was next to the entry. He immediately pushed into the chamber, only to be met by the Earl of Berwick and his father's captain.

Shand Bexwell's eyes widened at the sight.

"Atlas?" he gasped. Then, he suddenly looked at Patrick accusingly, his features stiffening in rage, but he was wise enough to keep his mouth shut. His focus returned to Atlas. "Atlas… you have come. Your mother will be pleased."

Atlas was tired from the ride, but he'd also had time to build up a substantial rage. He knew very well that it was his mother who had sent word to Berwick about his father's death and that Shand Bexwell hadn't, as of yet, sent any word to Castle Questing to notify him that he was now Lord of Trastamara. It was his right to know.

But the captain of his father's army hadn't sent him a bloody thing.

"Aye, I have come," he growled. "No thanks to you. How long has Roget been dead?"

Shand blinked in surprise at the harsh question. "His body was discovered four days ago, but…"

Atlas cut him off. "And when did you think to send me word? I heard it from Berwick, not from you. Just when did you think to tell me, Bexwell?"

Atlas had grown a great deal since the last time Shand had seen him. The lad was tall and he had filled out, with broad shoulders and a booming voice. In truth, it was a tremendous shock to Shand, who only remembered the skinny young man with the dark hair and oily skin. Now, Atlas' voice was deep, his tone commanding, and somewhere in the time since he'd last made an appearance at Trastamara, the lad had grown up. Two years had made a huge difference. He was a man now.

A man who was burning with rage.

Shand kept calm.

"I was going to send you word as soon as your mother decided upon a time and place for burial," he said evenly. "As you can imagine, the situation has been… chaotic. I am sorry if you think I was withholding information."

"But you were," Atlas practically shouted at him. "You *were* withholding it. Had my mother not sent word to Berwick, I still would not know of Roget's passing and neither would anyone else. By what right do you withhold information about my rightful inheritance? Who gave you this power, Shand?'"

As Shand struggled for an answer, Patrick watched the situation carefully. It was clear that Shand was cornered. He could see it. The man didn't have an excuse good enough to give to a rightfully furious Atlas and Patrick was curious to see how things were going to transpire. He wouldn't be at all surprised if Atlas attacked the man in his rage, but if that happened, Patrick would be forced to step in. Nothing would be solved by a physical fight, but most definitely, Shand was in a precarious position.

But there was something more that Atlas had divulged in his rage – he had mentioned who had sent the information regarding Roget's death, something Patrick had hoped to keep from Shand. But now it was out, which put Lady de Sauque in a potentially precarious position, too. If Shand thought the woman had betrayed him, there could be trouble.

Not that there wasn't trouble enough already.

"I told you that the situation has been chaotic," Shand said after a moment, though his poise was slipping. "Your father left Trastamara four days ago, but we only discovered his body two days ago. Your mother should not have sent word of his passing to Berwick, not before we had all of the facts and a time and place for his burial."

Atlas jabbed a finger in his face. "You do not make the decisions here," he seethed. "My mother is the Lady of Trastamara. With Roget's death, you serve her, but I realize the example Roget set for you over the years including shunning my mother and treating her like a ghost. That ends today, Shand. Do you understand me? I am in command now and you are not. If I am not here to give the orders, then my mother shall. Is this in any way unclear?"

Shand was beginning to twitch, his composure chipping off piece by piece. "You have been away a long time, Atlas," he said through clenched teeth. "You do not know the trouble that goes on here. I have had to do what is necessary to…"

Atlas cut him off. "Save your excuses, for I do not want to hear them," he said. "All I know is that I should have heard this from you, yet you have deliberately withheld information from me, as your liege. It was not your right."

Something in Shand's self-control fractured. "Of course it is my right," he snapped. "I have served your father faithfully all the time you were away. I know more about Trastamara than you could ever hope to. While you were off serving de Wolfe, I was here with your father. Unlike you, I never left him."

"That is because you are his knight," Atlas said, slow and deliberate. "*Only* his knight. You are a hired hand and nothing more. But I am everything, for this place is my birthright. Do you know what I think? I think you deliberately withheld telling me in the hopes that you could somehow usurp my command here. I think you are trying to steal my birthright."

He boomed the last few words, echoing off of the stone walls, and Markus suddenly stuck his head into the chamber, his expression both concerned and curious. Atlas noticed Markus and it was enough to break his focus against Shand. He emitted a hiss of frustration and turned away, struggling to compose himself. He'd just accused a man of treacherous behavior, but that man had yet to answer. The entire situation was hanging in the balance between them.

It was dark and ugly.

Meanwhile, Patrick took the opportunity to focus on Markus.

"How is Lady de Sauque?" he asked quietly. "I hope she is finding peace."

Markus nodded, his gaze moving from his father to Shand. "She is well," he said. "I intend that she should stay that way. I told her that I would remain her protector for the duration of my stay here. She and her children are not to be alone, for any reason, until this is sorted out."

Patrick could hear something hazardous in Markus' tone, leading him to believe that Lady de Sauque must have told him something concerning about Shand. The way he was looking at the man only reinforced that belief.

That brought concern to Patrick.

"Of course she will be guarded every minute," he said.

Markus nodded, but his gaze was still on Shand as Atlas paced on the other side of the chamber, grumbling and hissing.

"Bexwell," Markus said as he stepped into the chamber and shut the door. "I am curious about a few things. Please indulge me while I voice my thoughts, but I am curious as to why Lord Roget was alone when he was attacked and murdered. The forests around here are full of reivers, so knowing that, why did he travel alone?"

Shand was feeling attacked and verbally abused. Since Atlas had entered the room, he'd been on the defensive. His gaze was on Atlas but he tore it away long enough to look at Markus.

"Because he preferred to travel alone when he went to Mordrington," he said. "He often traveled alone on these roads and without fear. It was not unusual."

Markus cocked his head curiously. "Mordrington? What's that?"

"It is a manse not far from here," Shand said. "It is part of the Trastamara properties. Lord Roget always preferred to go alone when he traveled there.”

“Why?”

“Because he keeps his whore there,” Atlas said from his position on the other side of the chamber. He was looking at Shand as he spoke. “Is that where he was going? You did not think I knew about her, did you? I know. My mother told me. I heard about that the last time I visited here. Roget has had that whore for years, who has borne two bastards, and he provided her with a lovely place to live in Mordrington. A beautiful manse that belongs to my mother, in fact. My grandfather specifically left it to her, but Roget took it from her and housed his whore there. Such disgusting irony.”

He seemed wounded as he finished speaking, as if his father’s actions had greatly harmed him somehow. But his hurt was clearly for his mother; everyone could see that. Shand sighed faintly.

“You cannot blame me for that,” he said. “Your father did as he pleased.”

That was true and Atlas acknowledged that with a nod of his head. “I know,” he said. “But that is going to stop, too, now that Trastamara belongs to me. I will throw that bitch from Mordrington and into the sewage where she belongs. Her and her two beastly bastards.”

Shand wasn’t sure what to say to that. He eyed Patrick and Markus before lifting his shoulders in a resigned gesture. “I make no moral judgments against Lord Roget,” he said. “He was indeed traveling to see Lady Fenella when he was killed.”

Patrick and Markus exchanged rather disbelieving glances at that distasteful revelation before Markus finally scratched his chin. “Then that is why he risked the dangers of traveling alone,” he muttered. “To see his mistress.”

“Aye. And he did not like anyone to go with him, not even for protection.”

Markus thought on that. Lady de Sauque hadn't mentioned the part about the mistress and he didn't blame her. Surely it was a painful and shameful subject. But seeing what he had of Lady de Sauque, Markus couldn't imagine why Lord Roget even had a mistress. With a woman of Lady de Sauque's beauty, surely a man couldn't want for anything more.

It was all quite puzzling. Markus finally gestured to the door.

"You may leave now, Bexwell," he said. "But Hermes de Norville will go with you. You are no longer permitted in this keep or anywhere near Lady de Sauque. Hermes and a few other de Wolfe knights will be your shadow from now on. My lord, do you wish to add anything?"

He was addressing his father now, as the superior officer in the room, but Patrick simply shook his head. "Nay," he said. "Bexwell, we may have more questions. You are to obey Hermes in all things and do not stray from these walls."

Caged and bound, Shand could do nothing more than nod. He silently quit the chamber with Hermes right behind him. Once they departed and the door shut, Patrick turned to Markus.

"What did Lady de Sauque say about him?" he asked.

Markus glanced at Atlas, who was very interested in what Markus had to say. "She seems to be a virtual prisoner here, but from what I gather, that is nothing new," he said. "But it also seems very possible that Shand has designs on Trastamara. Lady de Sauque told me that he proposed marriage to her today so that he could be regent until Atlas comes of age. She believes the man means to marry her, kill her sons, and assume Trastamara himself."

It was damning and shocking information. Upon hearing of Shand's purported plans, Atlas' face turned red.

"*Marry* my mother?" he hissed. "Not if I have breath left in my body. And he intends to take my birthright, does he? I will kill him first!"

Patrick held up a hand. "Easy, lad," he said quietly. "Atlas, the first thing you must learn about becoming lord and master is patience. Patience and reason must rule; otherwise, everything turns to chaos. You must be a fair lord above all. Do you understand me?"

Atlas was still red in the face, but he nodded, struggling to contain his volatile, youthful emotions. "Aye, my lord," he said. "I will be a good lord. Better than Roget ever was. But I will not permit Shand to marry my mother, not ever."

"And he shall not," Patrick said evenly. "May I offer you my counsel?"

Atlas looked at him, realizing at that moment that he was no longer a squire. He was the lord of the Trastamara estates and that was an important and vital role. Patrick de Wolfe was his liege and he very much respected the man. He wanted to be respected in return, which was what Patrick was exhibiting. Realizing all of this, he suddenly grinned, embarrassed.

"Aye, my lord," he said. "I am sorry if I shouted at you. It's simply… well, my mother. Roget treated her so horribly. I will not let any man treat her that way ever again."

Patrick smiled, putting a hand on the young man's shoulder. "You did not shout at me," he said. "And I understand your passion. You are a good son to be so protective of your mother. But you must see the situation for what it is – Shand was with your father for many years, as he said. The army trusts him. The army does not know you yet, but if I could guess, I would say they want to trust you, too, as Roget's son. That being said, you cannot kill Shand as much as you want to. We have no direct proof that he wants to murder you for your inheritance, although I would believe that simply from his behavior since your father's death. It has been most suspicious."

Atlas was looking at him seriously. "Then what do I do?"

"Send him away," Markus muttered. When they both turned to look at him, he shrugged his big shoulders. "If it were me, I would send him away. Give him money, thank him for his service, and send him on his way. A man with Bexwell's ambition can always find a position elsewhere. But not here. The army must see that you are a fair lord, but that you will not tolerate interference in your rule, which is what Shand did. He interfered. Send him away and tell the army why you did it, and pledge to them that you will be a good lord but that punishment for an offense will be swift."

Atlas was listening intently. When Markus finished, he looked at Patrick. "Is that what you would do?"

Patrick nodded. "I would," he said. "Show your men from the beginning what they can expect from you. Be fair and open with them. Meanwhile, I am going to station a few hundred de Wolfe men here along with one of my knights, at least until everything settles down and your army is comfortable with your command. You must admit that you are a wee bit young to have control of an army, Atlas. It might do well for them to see an older, more seasoned knight as your advisor, at least for now."

Atlas didn't really have to think on that because it was wise advice. Truth be told, he would feel better having an experienced man at his side.

"I am happy to accept, my lord," he said. "I am not too proud to admit that I may need help and guidance. At least, for a little while."

Patrick patted his shoulder and dropped his hand. "Good," he said. "Now that it is settled, I would suggest you go to your mother. She is on the floor above us and I am sure she is most anxious to see you. Meanwhile, I will make arrangements to leave a knight here and after you speak with your mother, you must send Shand on his way. There is no sense in delaying that because he is already threatened by you. You do not want him turning the army against you, or worse."

Atlas nodded firmly. "Aye, my lord," he said. "Let me greet my mother and then I shall see to Shand. Will… will you stand with me when I do?"

"You know I will."

Atlas sighed with relief, a timid smile on his lips. "Thank you," he said. Looking to Markus, he nodded. "And you, too. Thank you for your assistance and for whatever you have done for my mother. It means a great deal."

With that, he left the chamber, heading up the stairs to see his mother. Markus and Patrick stood there for a moment, looking at each other, before Patrick finally shook his head.

"I suspect we may have averted a disaster here," he said quietly. "Did Lady de Sauque tell you anything else that you did not want to repeat in front of her son?"

Markus shook his head. "Not really," he said. "But it is obvious that she is terrified of Bexwell."

Patrick grunted. "Not after today," he said. "We will send the man on his way and let that be the end of it."

"It may not be that easy, Papa."

"I know. But hopefully Bexwell will go quietly. If he does not…"

"If he does not, we have five hundred soldiers that would be happy to muzzle him." Markus paused. "We were speaking earlier about Atlas being man enough to hold Trastamara. What do you think of him now?"

Patrick lifted his eyebrows thoughtfully as he headed towards the door. "I think Atlas de Sauque will be an excellent lord someday," he said. "Mayhap someday soon. Already, I feel better knowing he will be in command."

Markus turned to follow his father out of the chamber. "Who do you intend to leave here with him?"

"Probably Anson," he said. "He is old and wise. He'll help Atlas along where it matters."

Markus simply nodded, following his father as they headed out of the keep. All the while, however, thoughts of Lady de Sauque kept poking at him, not enough to cause him to really think hard on her, but enough to be annoying. That red-haired beauty with the lush body had truly been something to behold.

He almost found himself wishing he would be the knight to remain behind.

Almost.

CHAPTER SIX

A MBRA WAS AWAKE.

Eggggggggggs!

Having seen five years in the spring, Ambra Cayatana de Sauque was vocal, demanding, and adorable, much like brother, Alfie. The two of them were two years apart in age, but together, they were quite a handful. A delightful handful, but a handful nonetheless.

Ama, I want yellow eggs!

Those were the first words Amabella heard when she opened the door to her red-haired, green-eyed daughter. Her nurse, Savia, was a round Scottish woman with freckled skin and hair the color of dried grass. The old woman came running up behind Ambra, huffing and puffing because the little one had gotten away from her.

Amabella bent over and scooped her daughter up, kissing her soft cheek.

"Yellow eggs, is it?" she said. "I will have to see if the cook still has some."

That wasn't good enough for Ambra. She put her little hands on her mother's face, forcing the woman to look at her.

"She has them," she said seriously. "I know she has them.

She makes them just for me. The yellow eggs with the raisins in the middle."

Amabella smiled at her daughter who was not only a glutton, but a gourmet glutton. Unlike her older sister, who preferred simple and sweet things like honey puffs, Ambra loved finer foods that most children wouldn't touch, hence her request for yellow eggs. They were saffron-dyed, hard boiled eggs with a stuffing of yolk, raisins, cheese, and mint. The flavors were strong, but Ambra loved them.

Amabella could see that she was destined to head to the kitchen for said eggs.

"Very well," she said, kissing the girl one last time and setting her to her feet. "I will go get you the yellow eggs with the yellow things in the middle."

"M'lady?" the old nurse was still standing by the door, glancing towards the staircase that led below. "Who is down in the lord's solar? It sounds like men."

Amabella's smile faded. "It is," she said. "Come in and close the door, Savia. While you were sleeping, the Earl of Berwick arrived. They are taking charge of Trastamara until Atlas can arrive."

The old woman's eyes widened. "And Shand?"

"I have been told he will no longer be a concern to us," Amabella said softly, seeing the look of shock on Savia's face. "I do not know if they are sending him away or what they are doing, but he will no longer be an issue. Oh, Savia… I can hardly believe it. First, Roget and now Shand. Is it possible this hell we live in is finally over?"

The old nurse's face turned red and her eyes watered. She stepped inside the room, wiping at her eyes as she closed the door softly.

"Is it truly possibly, m'lady?" she whispered. "Tae finally know peace. Tae finally know… I pray 'tis true."

Amabella nodded, overcome with the very idea of it just as Savia was. They'd lived so long in a cage, in a world where they didn't matter, that to think that oppression was finally lifted was almost more than either of them could bear. For Amabella, it had been considerably worse, but Savia had suffered on the fringes just the same.

"The Earl of Berwick is speaking to Shand, even now," Amabella said. "Berwick's son was just here and we spoke briefly. He knows I sent the missive to Berwick and he knows that Shand did not know about it. He promised to protect me."

"From Shand?" Savia wiped at her eyes. "The man is a viper. He would have tae be a great knight, indeed, to protect ye from such a man."

Amabella thought back to the extremely tall and extremely large knight that had so recently been in the chamber. She'd never seen such a big man, with cropped dark hair, a shadow of a beard, and blue eyes that smoldered beneath dark brows. To say the knight was handsome was an understatement; he was far more than that. He was probably ten or twelve years younger than she was, a fine young man in his prime.

In fact, it did her heart good to have such a handsome, noble man pledge to protect her. It satisfied something deep, something kept beaten and buried by years of Roget's disregard for her.

Was it possible she was worth protecting?

"Ama!" Ambra piped up again, cutting into her daydreams. "Yellow eggs!"

Sighing heavily, Amabella knew when she was beaten. Her youngest would not quiet down until she had her yellow eggs and even though Amabella had promised Sir Markus that she would remain in her chamber and lock the door, he was also aware that she'd already asked permission to get her child something to eat. That was the routine when Ambra awoke from her nap. Amabella knew she could slip out to the kitchens and return before he even realized she had gone.

"Ama?" Aleanor spoke up. "I am hungry, too. Will you bring me something?"

Since her husband saw fit to strip her of servants except for a few kitchen servants and the nurse, it was common that Amabella fetched her children food or did any number of things servants usually did. Living a life of leisure as the Lady of the Manor was something unknown to her, but the truth is she didn't mind when it came to her children.

"Of course," she said. "I will bring something for all of you, but you must remain here until I return, please. There are many soldiers out in the bailey and I do not want anyone falling into trouble."

She meant Alfie, who was over by the hearth building a mighty castle with his sticks in an oddly quiet moment for him. But he wasn't paying any attention to her, so she turned for the door. The moment she opened it, however, a big figure was coming off of the stairs in front of her. It took her a moment to realize that it was Atlas.

Amabella's mouth popped open in shock.

"Atlas!" she gasped. Then, she was running at him, throwing her arms around him. "Oh, Atlas! You are finally here!"

She hit him so hard that Atlas was in danger of falling back down the stairs. He had to grab the wall for support before righting himself and hugging his mother warmly.

"Ama," he murmured, giving her a squeeze. "Aye, I've come. Did you think I would not?"

Amabella was close to tears as she hugged her first born. The moment was both joyful and surreal. As if she didn't truly believe he would ever come until this very moment, the young man who would inherit an awesome and turbulent mantle.

She stood back, looking at him in awe.

"Look at you," she said. "You have grown up since I last saw you. You are so tall!"

Atlas grinned. "I am certain I am taller than Roget."

He had never been able to call his father anything but his given name. Even now, he spoke of the man as if he were a stranger, someone distant. Amabella put a hand up, gently touching his cheek.

"I know you are."

Atlas was puffed up proudly as he caught sight of his siblings pouring through the open door. Ambra was first, running towards them, followed by Alfie and finally Aleanor. Ambra ran right to her mother, shy in the presence of her eldest brother whom she had only seen a handful of times since her birth and didn't really know, but Alfie knew him. He ran straight for Atlas and rammed into his legs.

"Atlas!" he shouted. "Look at me! I am big, too!"

Atlas crouched down beside his little brother, pulling the boy into his embrace. "King Alfie," he said, affection in his tone. "I expected to see you outside with your horse guard. Do you still have one?"

Alfie allowed Atlas to hug him for about two seconds. After that, he was finished with the greeting and grabbed Atlas' hand.

"I have a great guard," he said, tugging. "Come and see them!"

Atlas laughed softly as his brother yanked on him, but Amabella put a hand out to stop Alfie from pulling his brother's arm from the socket.

"In a moment, Alfie," she said. "Atlas has only just arrived. Let us go into the solar and speak to him for a few moments. Would you not like to speak with your brother?"

Alfie was still yanking, only this time it was towards the open solar door. "Come inside," he commanded. "Do you want to play with my sticks? I am building a castle."

Atlas was still grinning as he allowed himself to be pulled into the chamber with his mother and sisters in tow. Amabella was holding Ambra as Aleanor tucked in behind her, shy from a brother she had hardly seen over the years. Alfie pulled Atlas over to his pile of sticks and forced him to sit.

Amabella simply shook her head.

"Alfie, your brother may not wish to play with your sticks," she said. "Did you even ask him?"

Alfie looked at Atlas as if the thought hadn't occurred to him. "You *do* want to play, don't you?"

Atlas lowered himself onto the floor. "Of course I do," he said, picking up several sticks. "I do not have much of a chance to build at Castle Questing. I am always working."

Amabella sat down in the chair nearest her boys, propping Ambra on her lap. "You look fine, Atlas," she said. "They do not work you too hard there, do they?"

Atlas shook his head. "Nay," he said, focusing on putting a new floor on Alfie's castle. "I am quite content there. My master, Tobias, says I will be a great knight someday. I will be a tribute to the Abril dynasty."

He was speaking of Amabella's family, not the House of de Sauque, in yet another display of his animosity towards his father. Even as a young boy, Atlas treated his father like a stranger, but Roget was to blame for that. He'd never shown much interest in his eldest son.

There was history there, and none of it good.

"You are already a fine tribute to your family," she said quietly. "We are all very proud of you."

Atlas carefully laid out small pieces of wood before looking at his mother. "I will bring back the honor that Roget destroyed," he said. "I have been in the solar below with Berwick and Markus and Shand. I know what Shand has done, Ama. He is as greedy and underhanded as Roget ever was and I have made the decision to send him away from Trastamara."

Amabella stared at him. "Away? To where?"

"I do not care where he goes, as long as he leaves. I do not want to see him ever again. I have Berwick's full support in this matter."

She looked at him in shock. "Shand is going… forever?"

"Forever."

It was too much for Amabella.

Words she never thought she would hear.

Tears sprang to her eyes and she looked away, struggling to compose herself. Atlas saw this and he quickly stood up, taking Ambra from his mother and handing her over to Savia, who patted Atlas fondly on the cheek. A few whispered words from Atlas to the old nurse had the old woman taking all three children away. As they disappeared, perhaps in search of yellow eggs, Atlas sat down next to his mother and took her hands in his.

He studied the woman for a moment, the mother he loved with all his heart but had never been able to help. As a young boy, that had devastated him, and as a young man, the ache was even deeper. Deeper because he understood the helplessness of his position.

But he was no longer helpless.

"Ama," he whispered. "You needn't worry anymore. I am in command now and I promise you will have a good life. I will make sure that you do. I know what Roget did to you. You and I have had conversations about it and I've heard what others have said. I am telling you that you will no longer have to bear that shame. I will take care of you from now on."

Amabella looked at her big, brave son, trying so hard to be a man in a world of older, more seasoned men. He'd grown up so much since she'd last seen him, that was true, but in her eyes, he was still her little boy. She still wanted to protect him from what he would be facing, but she knew that she had to back away and let him take the lead. He was a man now and he'd been well-trained. Moreover, he had the entire House of de Wolfe behind him.

He would succeed.

She had to believe that.

"I know you will," she said softly, touching his face. "You will do a very good job of it."

He smiled timidly but he ended up averting his gaze, having a difficult time looking at her.

"One of the first things I intend to do is go to Mordrington and evict Fenella," he said quietly. "She will be the first shame you no longer have to bear."

Amabella could see how difficult it had been for him to speak those words, a family shame that was not a secret. Truth be told, she'd stopped caring long ago. She couldn't stand for Roget to touch her and was relieved when he would run off to Fenella. It had been a small price to pay to keep her husband off of her, but she didn't need to tell Atlas that. He saw it for what it was – a family shame. He didn't know that his mother had actually grown comfortable with the arrangement.

She squeezed his hand.

"Fenella has two sons," she said quietly. "I told you of them. They are not very old; mayhap the same ages as Alfie and Ambra."

Atlas stiffened. "I do not care," he said. "They are bastards, mistakes that should have never been born. They are not my brothers, nor will I ever call them that. Fenella can go back wherever she came from and take those two aberrations with her."

"She is from Clan Hume. You do not want to offend the clan, so be fair when you deal with her."

Atlas looked at her, then. His brow furrowed. "Fair?" he

repeated. "Was Roget fair with you when he took that… that *whore* to his bed?"

Amabella shushed him. "You will not speak so in my presence," she scolded softly. "You cannot change the past. All you can do is change the future, and you are already determined to do so. I do not want the name of that woman or her poison entering our world, Atlas. Get rid of her, but be fair about it, and we will speak no more of her. Ever."

Atlas calmed down a little, knowing his mother was correct. "Agreed," he said. "But once she is gone, I will station fifty men at Mordrington and send an army of servants to clean it out and scour every piece of it. Then, you may go there whenever you like, secure in the knowledge that the home has no trace of her in it."

Amabella smiled at him. "You are very thoughtful and I love you for it," she said. "It was such a lovely house, though I've not seen it in years."

"It will be lovely again," Atlas said firmly. "All of this will be lovely for you again, Ama. It is what you deserve."

Amabella kissed him on the cheek, her courageous and protective son. It did her heart good.

"You are already a fine lord," she said. "But there is one more thing you must attend to."

"What is that?"

"Your father's burial. Shand was going to send to St. John's for the priest. Mayhap you should do that now."

Atlas nodded, but it was clear that he was not enthusiastic. "If it was up to me, I'd throw his body in the river and let the fish consume him," he grumbled. But when he saw his mother's expression, he lifted a hand to her. "I know; that was cruel, but it is how I feel. Short of feeding the fish, what do you want done with him?"

"He can be buried at St. John's with your grandfather and

grandmother."

Atlas scowled. "You would put him next to people I respect and admire?"

Amabella lifted a dark eyebrow. "As I told Shand, put him next to my father, a man he was happy to see die. Let him spend eternity explaining his actions to him."

Atlas rather liked that idea. "I will," he said. Then, he released her hands and stood up. "Now, if you do not require me, I should get about my duties and my first duty is to send Shand on his way. I want that man out of Trastamara this very moment."

Amabella stood up, studying her son's serious face. "Be fair," she said softly. "How you deal with men, even men who have wronged you, will define your command."

Atlas snorted. "That is the same thing Berwick said."

"He is correct."

Atlas nodded as he headed for the door. "I will be fair because it is required of me," he said, reaching for the door. "But I would truly like to kick that man right in the arse for all he's done."

Amabella fought off a grin. "You can still do it," she said. "Just make sure no one sees you."

Chuckling, Atlas quit the chamber and quietly shut the door, leaving Amabella to ponder the man her son had become. Up until just a short while ago, she was looking at a future of fear and uncertainty. Now, all she could feel was hope.

Hope and joy.

Everything was going to be all right.

CHAPTER SEVEN

T HEY WERE ALL lined up with their stick horses and leaf banners.

King Alfie was delivering commands.

Markus stood at the gate leading into the kitchen yard, grinning at the sight. While his father was over near the gatehouse speaking with Anson and Damien, Markus was wandering the grounds, looking for any sign of insurrection. He saw Hermes and Shand over near the stables, and young Kieran was with them, which gave him confidence that Shand was being contained for the moment.

Markus could wander, unhindered.

He'd heard a child shouting when he'd neared the kitchen yard, peeking inside the gate to find Alfie and his guard. They weren't hard to miss. The children had crowns of vines on their heads. In one case, one of the boys was wearing an old bucket with part of it pulled away so he could see, and they all had weapons or shields they'd fashioned out of scraps they'd come across.

The horse guard in all its regalia.

As Markus watched, Alfie drilled his guard – first they went one way in a line and then they'd turn about and go the other way, all in a line. One of the boys tripped, and the two children following him fell over him. It ended up a pile of children in the dirt as Alfie stood over them, hands clasped behind his back, and told them to be more careful. He had a big stick in his hand that he waved around, but he made no attempt to strike anyone.

And then there was the goose.

As the children marched in a line, a fat, white goose followed. When the children moved faster, the goose moved faster. When the children turned around and headed towards the goose, the bird would honk and rush out of the way only to continue honking at the children as it once again attached to the rear of their guard.

The best part came when Alfie would yell at the goose and shake his stick at it, only to have the goose chase Alfie. Poor King Alfie ended up running a lap around the kitchen yard with the nasty goose chasing him. He would finally take a stand and shake his stick at the goose again, who would waddle away and pretend it had business elsewhere.

It was some of the best entertainment Markus had seen in a long while.

He stood there and laughed as Alfie and the goose fought for control of the horse guard. The lap around the yard happened twice and at the end of the second go-around, Alfie caught sight of Markus standing in the open kitchen gate. He came to a halt.

"Sir Knight!" he yelled. "You will join my horse guard!"

Grinning, Markus entered the yard, heading towards Alfie and the gang of children who had come to a halt as the massive knight approached. They cowered somewhat, unused to seeing strange knights.

But Alfie was brave. He pointed to the children behind him.

"You will have a place of honor in my horse guard," Alfie said. "You will be my champion."

Markus' eyes twinkled at him. "You are a king," he said. "Don't you already have a champion?"

Alfie looked at a servant boy, perhaps eight or nine years of age, wearing the old bucket on his head. "Just Aldwin," he said. "You will fight him and the winner will be my champion."

Markus looked at Aldwin, whose eyes widened to enormous proportions. The terror in the child's face was evident at the prospect of a fight against a real knight and Markus fought off a smile.

"Sir Aldwin," he said formally, dipping his head to the boy. "I surrender to you. You may continue to be King Alfie's champion, for I am certain that you are far greater than I."

The declaration did nothing to allay the terror on Aldwin's face. "But I dunna even have a real sword!" he cried.

Markus put his hand over his mouth so the children wouldn't see him grin. "You will need one as King Alfie's champion," he said. "Mayhap I will see about having one made for you. But there should be more than one knight. A king needs many knights."

Aldwin looked at two other boys near his age, skinny and blond. "Bartram and Manley are knights," he said, pointing to the pair. "We have taken an oath."

"Is that so?" Markus said. "What oath is this?"

"All hail King Alfie the Bold. We say those words and we are knights."

Markus nodded; an oath was an oath, even among servant children, no matter what the words were.

"Alfie the Bold, indeed," he said. "Make sure you serve him well."

The three boys nodded eagerly, looking over the enormous knight and a little more comfortable with him now that they had engaged in conversation. They began to study him, looking at the massive broadsword strapped to his leg, the assortment of daggers on his waist, the mail coat he wore that went to his knees, and the leather boots that covered up his feet and calves.

It was fascinating.

"The sword," Aldwin said, pointing. "It has a dog's head."

Markus looked at the sword that was longer than some of the children were tall. He put his gloved hand on the hilt.

"Not a dog," he said. "A wolf's head. My family name is de Wolfe."

The boys were brave enough to come a little closer. Even Alfie came closer, all of them looking at the exquisite wolf's head with the ruby eyes. Then, he looked at Markus' tunic and pointed.

"The wolf head is on your tunic," he said. "Is it everywhere, then?"

Markus nodded. "Everywhere," he said. "I even have it on my body, a mark of the House of de Wolfe."

That brought great interest from Alfie and his knights. "What kind of mark?" Alfie asked. "Is it burned on you?"

Markus shook his head. "It is drawn on," he said. "In ancient times past, it was called a *stigmata*. It is a mark, a picture of something, that is made with something sharp upon the skin. Then, an ink is put in the little wounds that make the mark permanent. When I take off my mail, I will show you. It is the de Wolfe's head, the mark of the grandsons of William de Wolfe of Castle Questing."

Alfie was fascinated by the suggestion of a permanent mark upon the skin, but something else in Markus' conversation caught his attention. "Castle Questing," he said. "That is where Atlas lives."

Markus nodded. "He serves at Castle Questing, the heart of the de Wolfe empire," he said. "But there are other castles, too. Berwick is one and that is my father's castle. It is by the sea."

Alfie's eyes lit up. "I want to go there," he said. "I want to take my horse guard and go to the castle by the sea. Is that where you live?"

Markus nodded. "I do," he said. "I live there with my mother and father and brothers and sisters. But I am not going to be there much longer."

Alfie looked at him with concern. "But why?"

"Because I am going to London to protect King Edward."

That brought expressions of awe from the children. Even the little girls, who were wrapped up in vines and dried flower garlands, seemed impressed. But the goose suddenly appeared and tried to nip Alfie, who howled and lifted his stick to the goose. It was a standoff because the goose wouldn't run away until Alfie told his horse guard to go vanquish the evil dragon.

But it was really a goose.

The horse guard proceeded cautiously, and for good reason.

"*Ow!*"

Aldwin was on the receiving end of a goosey pinch as Markus stood there and snorted. He was, however, wise enough to back away because even he didn't want to tangle with the big goose. He had a feeling slaying it in front of the children might not be well-met. He watched four boys try to fend off the aggressive fowl, turning his head away so they wouldn't see him laugh. As he did, he caught sight of his brother, Cassius, over at the yard gate.

"Cass," he called, waving an arm. "Come over here."

Cassius de Wolfe was eighteen months younger than Markus. He had his mother's blue eyes, quite the handsome lad, but he had curly hair when no one else in the family did. Everyone else had straight hair, or hair with a slight wave to it, but Cassius' hair was silky and kinky, in ringlets that a woman would envy. He came over to his brother, eyeing the gaggle of children and the naughty goose.

"What are you doing?" he asked his brother.

A smile played on Markus' lips. "Watching a mighty battle," he said. "St. George fought the dragon. King Alfie fights the goose."

Cassius had no idea what he was talking about. "*King* Alfie?"

Markus nodded, waving the children over when the goose seemed to tire of the fight and waddle off.

"Meet King Alfie and his horse guard," he said to his brother. "King Alfie is the younger brother of the new Lord of Trastamara."

Cassius lifted a dark eyebrow. "And just what is Alfie king of?"

"King of the kitchen yard, of course."

Cassius nodded in understanding. "Charming," he said drolly. "It is a pleasure to meet you, King Alfie."

Alfie inspected Cassius with the same naked curiosity he had inspected Markus. "What's your name?"

"Cassius de Wolfe, my lord."

Alfie looked between Markus and Cassius. "You are brothers?"

"Indeed, we are," Cassius said.

"I have a brother."

"I know."

"Do you want to be in my horse guard?"

Cassius lifted his eyebrows as he looked at Markus. "Do I?"

"Of course you do," Markus said. "It is a great honor."

Cassius merely shrugged. "I am sure it is," he said. "But mayhap later. I hate to take you away from this royal duty, but Papa is looking for you. He says you are to go immediately to the lord's solar inside the keep."

Markus frowned. "I just saw the man at the gatehouse."

Cassius nodded. "I know, but Atlas has emerged from the keep and Papa took it as a sign, evidently," he said. "He is heading for the keep. Then, Hermes took Shand by the arm and they, too, are heading to the keep. What's going on?"

Markus was acutely aware that Alfie was watching them. "Did you not hear anything at all?"

"About what?"

Markus turned away so that Alfie couldn't hear him. "Atlas is sending Shand away," he muttered. "The lad doesn't want Bexwell here and I don't blame him. He's been positioning to take over Trastamara."

Cassius frowned. "Who told you that?"

"He asked Lady de Sauque to marry him so he could act as Atlas' regent."

Cassius wasn't stupid. He could put the pieces of the puzzle together, too. "I see," he said. "So it is as we suspected. The man's ambition is showing."

"It certainly is."

"Then you had better get into the solar if that is what they are about to do. They may need your strength to physically remove Bexwell if he does not move under his own free will."

Markus suspected as much, though he hoped that was not to be the case. "And you," he said. "You are fully armed, so come with me. It may take both of us if Bexwell does not give up without a fight."

Cassius was up for the challenge. Leaving Alfie and his horse guard in the kitchen yard, Markus and Cassius headed for the keep. They made an imposing pair as they crossed the bailey, drawing looks from some of the Trastamara soldiers. They'd already seen the Earl of Berwick heading for the keep along with Shand, who was their commander. But word had spread among the men that Atlas de Sauque had also arrived, and he was now their liege.

It was an unsettling time for the men of Trastamara.

But Markus and Cassius ignored the looks of curiosity and

concern. They had a job to do and they were running by the time they hit the stairs to the keep, rushing up the steps and into the cool, dark entry. The door to the solar was partially open and they slowed their pace as Markus opened the door, admitting Cassius first before following.

They walked into a standoff.

Shand was over against the wall, eyeing Atlas with a baleful expression. Patrick was standing near the door, as was Hermes, and Patrick held up a hand to Markus and Cassius, indicating to them to be still and silent.

The knights immediately complied.

Over against the wall, Shand glanced at the two latest arrivals to the solar.

"So you send for de Wolfe's sons because you think I will not obey your command?" he said, his attention back on Atlas. "Why did you not simply speak with me about this, Atlas? Why do you need to send me away? You need me, much as your father needed me. I know Trastamara better than you could ever hope to. I will be invaluable to you, as the new lord."

He sounded as if he were pleading, but Atlas stood his ground. "Shand, I will explain my position to you so there is no question as to why I have ordered you away," he said. "My father was poison. He infected everything at Trastamara that he touched. He only married my mother to gain her family fortress and when my grandfather died, he seized everything and treated my mother no better than a servant. She was a prisoner here and you know this. Worse still, my father's poison touched you, Shand. You have been enforcing my father's immoral and apathetic commands since the beginning and I do not want you here. You are as shallow as he ever was, but I am learning something about you. You have ambition. You gave that away when you asked for my mother's hand."

Shand's eyes flickered, but only for a moment. He was adept

at concealing his surprise that Atlas had been told of his offer to Lady de Sauque when the truth was that he shouldn't have been surprised at all.

He should have expected it.

"It was what your father wanted," he said evenly. "You have only seen seventeen years. He knew that you needed a seasoned man to help you govern and as your mother's husband, I would have more freedom to do that."

Atlas could read him beneath the surface. He could see the man who wanted everything he had.

"You would also have the power of Trastamara in your hands and I do not intend to fight you for my inheritance," he said. "Regardless of if it was my father's wish for you to marry my mother, it is not *my* wish. Better to send you away than have a dagger shoved into my back at some point. I will send you with enough money to take you wherever you wish to go, but you *will* go."

Shand was staring Atlas down as if his glare could cause the young man to change his mind.

"This is not fair," he finally hissed. "I have given ten years of my life to Trastamara and this is how you repay me?"

Atlas, surprisingly, remained calm, impressive for so young a man. He could have easily become emotional and angry, but the words from his master, Tobias, had taken root.

Emotion will get you killed, lad.

It was a lesson Atlas had taken to heart, or at least tried to.

"You have been paid many times over, I am sure," he said. "You have had fine weapons, a roof over your head, food to eat, and I would suspect a good horse. Did you purchase any of these things yourself?"

The tic in Shand's jaw began to grow worse. "Your father wanted me to have the best equipment money could buy," he said. "I am his captain. My weapons, my dress, directly reflect upon him."

"Then he bought it for you."

Shand hesitated before spitting out the words. "As my liege, that was his obligation."

Atlas studied the man. He took a good, hard look at him before taking a step in his direction. "Show me your sword."

Shand had the scabbard of his broadsword strapped to his waist and thigh. He unsheathed the weapon but as he did so, both Markus and Cassius unsheathed theirs. They moved towards Shand, the message obvious.

Move against Atlas and you will die.

Shand saw the knights advancing on him and he slowed his movements. His focus was fixed on Markus.

"He asked to see my sword," he said, almost belligerently. "I must be permitted to unsheathe it."

Markus didn't say a word, but he came to stand next to Atlas. Cassius stood on the other side, his sword in a position that could easily slice into Shand should he bring up his hand.

Frustrated, and clearly fighting a losing battle, Shand finished unsheathing his sword carefully and gripped it so the hilt was in Atlas' direction. The young man took the sword from him, inspecting it.

"This is very fine," he said. "Where did you get it?"

"From a sword maker in Madrid."

"Spanish?"

"They make some of the finest weapons."

"And my father purchased this for you?"

Shand sighed heavily. "He commissioned it."

"Give me a straight answer. Did he pay for this?"

"He did."

"Then I shall keep it."

Atlas handed it over to Markus, who took it without hesitation and then extended it to Hermes, who came forward to collect it. Shand watched his beautiful Spanish sword slip from his grasp, unable to do anything about it.

Atlas, however, had no qualms about what he had just done. At least, not on the outside. With Markus and Cassius standing on either side of him, he was very brave. He proceeded to frisk Shand for anything else of value that his father might have purchased for him, coming across two very fine daggers. He handed those over to Markus as well, but he left Shand his coin purse, belt, and shoes. Then, he stood back.

"You are to proceed to your chamber and collect your possessions," he said. "You will only collect what you brought with you to Trastamara ten years ago and no more. You will leave your Trastamara tunics behind as well as anything else that identifies Trastamara – mail, helm, protection. Leave it. Then, you will come to the stables. I will meet you there with money for your journey."

There was nothing Shand could say at that point. He was outnumbered and without a weapon, so any show of rebellion or anger would not be well met. He simply couldn't believe that ten years of his life had come to this moment, wasted as if it had been dust upon the wind. He could see those years blowing away before his very eyes, vanishing into memory, and it cut him to the bone.

Everything he had worked for was gone.

Taken from him by the son of the man he'd been so loyal to.

God, but hatred was blooming in his heart. Hatred and vengeance. It simply wasn't fair, any of it, but if he fought back now, they would kill him. Perhaps that's what they wanted to do. Maybe they were hoping he would resist.

But he wasn't going to. At least, not now.

But the time would come.

With a heavy sigh, Shand pushed past Markus and headed towards the chamber door.

"Go with him," Markus muttered to Cassius. "Hermes, you also."

Hermes handed over the confiscated weapons to Patrick as he followed Cassius and Shand out of the chamber. When they were gone, it was only Patrick, Markus, and Atlas left in the room. Atlas turned to Patrick.

"Was I fair enough, my lord?" he asked.

In that moment, his youth became evident. So did his nervousness in a situation he'd faced bravely. Covering those nerves had been impressive, but in that question, he sounded like a boy looking for approval.

Patrick nodded.

"Indeed, you were," he said. "I thought you handled the situation well."

Atlas seemed relieved by that, but he didn't seem entirely comfortable with the situation as a whole. He turned away, wandering over to the windows that overlooked the bailey.

"I intend to take his warhorse, too," he said. "I am sure my father purchased the animal for him as well, wanting his captain to have a fine steed. I will give him another horse to ride."

"I approve of your decision."

Atlas was silent a moment. "Thank you," he said. "But I have a feeling that he will not leave easily. Trastamara was his home for ten years. Looking into his eyes, I can see how badly he wants it. It is as if he feels… he feels that he is deserving of it. That it belongs to him. He resents me greatly."

Patrick came away from the wall, heading in Atlas' direction. "Then he is delusional," he said. "Any knight worth his oath would never look at his liege's property as his own. But I would not worry about him if I were you."

"Are you certain?"

"I am. We will escort him far away so he cannot trouble you."

Atlas nodded, but he still didn't seem very relieved. "Thank you, my lord."

Patrick's gaze lingered on him for a moment, hearing his doubt. He turned to Markus.

"Send word to Questing and the other de Wolfe properties that if Bexwell shows up looking for a position, they are to turn the man away," he said. "We do not need that man's venom infecting our ranks. They will not know what has transpired here at Trastamara and will view him as an ally. We cannot take that chance."

Markus nodded. "I'll do it right away," he said. "Anything else?"

"Have four of our soldiers escort him away from Trastamara," he said. "Whatever direction he chooses to go is fine, but tell the men to make sure he is far away. At least a two days' ride away."

"It shall be done."

Before Markus could leave, Atlas stopped him.

"Can you please ask my mother where my father kept his coinage?" he said. "I have promised Shand money and I do not know where my father kept it."

Markus frowned. "That is a question you should ask her."

Atlas nodded, but there was uncertainty to his movements. "I will admit my encounter with Shand has me questioning… things. I do not wish to explain myself to my mother right now, not until I get a few things straight in my own mind."

"Like what?"

"That I did not let my anger make my decisions for me. I tried not to, you know."

Markus gave him a reassuring smile. "You did fine."

Atlas needed the reassurance. He'd just dismissed a man with maturity beyond his years, which had left him questioning himself.

He very much wanted to do the right thing.

Quitting the chamber, Markus left his father to counsel the young lord who was trying very hard to make just and lordly decisions.

CHAPTER EIGHT

MBRA AND ALEANOR were painting.

At least, Aleanor was painting. Ambra was doing… something. She said they were flowers and trees, but they didn't look much like flowers and trees. They looked like squiggly shapes with colors. There were little brown splotches that were supposed to be people and other round things with stick legs that were horses. Ambra was happily painting an entire village of splotch people.

For all of Aleanor's nervousness and odd propensities, she was surprisingly patient with her younger sister. She made the paints herself out of onion skins and dandelion roots, any number of colored berries, or even fresh, green grass. She and her sister would paint on scraps that would come from a variety of sources – pieces of ruined clothing, or sometimes even tree bark.

Amabella watched her daughters work on their paintings intermittently as she stood by the window overlooking the bailey. Since her conversation with Atlas, she'd been unable to return to the sewing she'd been doing, unable to focus on anything other than reliving the discussion with her son.

She worried about him, a young man now with great responsibilities thrust upon him. That, more than anything, pressed upon her. Finally, her restlessness soon got the better of her and she left her daughters to their painting and headed from the chamber.

It had been quite a day. So much had happened that Amabella needed a few moments alone to process it. The past two days had been life-changing, twenty years into a marriage that had been hell on earth. She didn't know what the future held for her and her family now, but with Atlas now the Lord of Trastamara, she knew one thing –

They were all free.

As the afternoon passed and the news of Atlas and the removal of Shand began to sink in, Amabella broke down in tears more than once. It came in waves. Her moments of tears were brief, but they were tears of joy and relief. Tears that God had been merciful in a way she could have never imagined.

It was more than she could have ever hoped for.

Leaving Aleanor and Ambra painting the splotch people in her solar under Savia's watchful eyes, she was just coming down the stairs with the intention of heading to the kitchens to check on the evening meal when she heard a door open. Shand suddenly appeared, followed by two knights she didn't recognize, both of them heavily-armed and both of them bearing de Wolfe tunics.

Amabella froze on the stairs, carefully watching what was happening on the entry level. She could hear voices in her husband's solar, recognizing one of them to be Atlas. It occurred to her that she had just witnessed Atlas sending Shand away, under an armed escort no less, and it was difficult to contain her disbelief. She'd just witnessed something she never thought she would see and given her conversation with Shand earlier that day, things had happened quickly, indeed. She'd gone from terrified of being forced into a marriage to relief beyond measure.

Quietly, she made her way down the remainder of the stairs. The solar door was cracked open and she could still hear voices, but her attention was on the wide-open entry door. She could see into the bailey beyond and she watched as Shand marched across the dusty bailey with his de Wolfe escort.

Evidently, they were heading for the outbuildings that sheltered some of the soldiers. It was also where Shand was housed, near the gatehouse. As she stood in the doorway and watched, she heard a voice behind her.

"Lady de Sauque?"

Startled, she turned to see Markus standing behind her and her momentary fright turned to relief. She put her hand on her chest to ease her racing heart.

"Sweet Mary, you surprised me," she said, smiling. "You are as quiet as a mouse when you move."

Markus returned her smile. "It is all of that intense training I have gone through," he said. "I have learned to sneak up on unsuspecting women."

There was humor in his reply, something that was quite endearing. "Then you learned your lesson well, for I never heard you."

His eyes twinkled. "That is good, for I have worked hard on it," he said. "In fact, I was just coming to see you. I have a question that mayhap only you can answer, but I see that you are going about your duties. Is this an inconvenient time?"

Amabella shook her head. "Not at all. I was simply going to the kitchen to see to tonight's meal." Quickly, her smile faded. "That is not entirely true. I was standing here because I saw Shand crossing the bailey with an escort. Is… is he leaving?"

Markus looked over her head, towards the gatehouse where the knights' quarters were located. "He is."

"For good?"

"For good."

Amabella drew in a long, pensive breath as she let that sink in. But in that same breath, she also found herself looking at Markus. Their first meeting a short while ago had been brief and intense, and she thought back to her initial impression of him – handsome and young.

But he'd made her feel worthy.

In just the brief few moments they'd spoken, he'd made her feel safe and comforted. As the sunlight streamed in from the bailey and hit him like a beacon, she found herself taking a second look at him.

As a man.

Amabella was coming to think her eyesight must have failed her the first time around because she didn't remember his eyes being so pale and lovely. The virtuous young knight made her feel strangely alive. Giddy, even. She hadn't felt that way in over twenty years, so it came as something of a surprise.

Markus de Wolfe arrived and, suddenly, everything seemed brighter. The future itself looked brighter.

Amabella couldn't have been more grateful.

"That is something I never expected to happen," she said belatedly. "To think that he is finally leaving is difficult to believe. And my son? How did Atlas handle the situation?"

"With great maturity," Markus said. "In fact, my father is in the solar with him right now. They are discussing the details of Shand's situation, but Atlas specifically asked me to inquire about his father's coinage because he must give some to Shand as a parting gift. He thought you might know where it was hidden."

Amabella cocked her head thoughtfully. "I think so," she said. "If it is not in his solar somewhere, which I doubt, it would be in his bedchamber, which is on the top floor of the keep. But a word, Sir Knight… Shand might know where it is, too. He and

Roget were very close. If he is leaving, you will want to ensure he is not taking my husband's money with him."

It was a good point. "I will make sure he is searched before he departs," Markus said. "He has two seasoned knights guarding him and they will not let him get away with anything. Meanwhile, may I ask you to come with me to search his bedchamber? Atlas wants control of the coinage, for obvious reasons."

Amabella immediately moved to grant his request. "Of course I shall help," she said, heading back towards the stairs. "Although Roget never confided in such things to me, I am going on assumptions. My father had a hiding place for his money in his chamber, which became Roget's chamber, so I am assuming Roget used the same spot."

Markus followed her up the stairs, her swaying backside nearly eye-level with him because of the angle of the stairs. He found himself staring at her gently swaying hips as he followed her up to the floor above.

There wasn't one part of the woman that wasn't lush, as he'd noticed the first time, but being in such close proximity to her buttocks was making him feel a little flushed. A little… hot. He was so hypnotized that he failed to notice a young girl rushing from the small solar by the time they hit the landing.

"Ama!" the girl cried. "Ama, I want to find Alfie!"

She crashed right into Amabella and the woman paused to pick the child up. "Are you finished painting, then?" she asked.

The child nodded firmly. "I want to play with Alfie now."

Markus could tell that this was one of Lady de Sauque's children because she favored her mother greatly with hair the exact same color, only on the child, it flowed freely. It was long and curly, a magnificent mane of red hair, and her eyes were as green as emeralds. She was an astonishingly beautiful child.

"I saw Alfie with his horse guard in the kitchen yard not

long ago," Markus said helpfully.

Amabella turned to look at him, smiling. "That is his favorite place to play," she said. "This is his sister, Ambra. She is my youngest."

Markus smiled faintly at the little girl. "My lady," he greeted formally.

Ambra turned her big, green eyes on him. She looked him over before grinning shyly, sticking her finger in her mouth. It was apparent that it was all the conversation she was capable of at the moment and Amabella smiled apologetically as she set Ambra to her feet.

"She is not much for conversation unless you are discussing food," she said. "Then, she will not stay silent."

Markus chuckled. "Food, is it?" he said. "I've heard that about men, but never women. What kind of food do you like best?"

Ambra still had her finger in her mouth, chewing on it as she clung to her mother's skirt. "I don't know," she said. "I like a lot."

Amabella bent over, looking her daughter in the face. "What about the yellow eggs?"

Ambra nodded eagerly. "I like yellow eggs!"

Markus grinned. "Yellow eggs? What are those?"

Amabella glanced up at him. "Stuffed eggs," she said. "The cook makes them with raisins and saffron. Ambra loves them."

Markus was still focused on the child. "They sound delicious," he said. "Will you share some with me?"

Ambra giggled, pressing her face into her mother's skirts. "Nay!"

Markus feigned great shock. "You won't?" he said. "I am terribly hurt."

He made weeping sounds, enough to force Ambra out of her mother's skirts. She stared at him for a moment, momentarily mystified at his weeping, before emitting peals of naughty laughter.

"I will give you none!" she said.

Markus covered his face with his hand, pretending to weep loudly, before suddenly stopping and peering at her through spread fingers just to make sure Ambra was watching. She was smiling broadly at him, quite entertained that he should be so crushed. When she saw that he was looking at her, she laughed again.

"You get *none!*"

That triggered the crying again, which thoroughly delighted her. But Markus couldn't keep a straight face for long and ended up grinning at her through his splayed fingers.

"I understand," he said. "No eggs for me. I will not ask again."

Ambra giggled, enamored with the big knight, but the subject of eggs and food was quickly forgotten as she tugged on her mother's skirt again.

"Ama, please," she said. "I want to find Alfie!"

Amabella put up her hand to silence her begging child before calling out to her older daughter. "Ally?" she said. "Please come to me."

It took a moment, but Aleanor eventually appeared in the doorway, eyeing Markus with her usual inherent fear before responding to her mother.

"Aye, Ama?"

Amabella held out Ambra's hand. "Please take your sister to play with Alfie and remain with them," she said. "I do not mind Alfie being out of my sight, but not Ambra."

Aleanor didn't want to go outside. She didn't want to go out of the chamber, but she knew that Ambra wouldn't be peacefully corralled. She'd given up on the painting and was now looking for new entertainment.

With a reluctant sigh, she nodded.

"Very well," she said, coming out of the chamber and taking her little sister by the hand. "Let us find Alfie."

Ambra went happily, nearly yanking her sister down the stairs. When they disappeared from view, Amabella looked at Markus apologetically.

"I am sorry for the interruption," she said.

Markus waved her off. "Not at all," he said. "She is delightful. Cruel, but delightful."

Amabella laughed softly. "She can be a handful," she admitted. Then, she motioned for him to follow her. "Come, we shall continue to Roget's chamber."

She was heading up the stairs once more, leaving Markus to watch her backside again, only it was worse the second time around. Something about the woman was appealing to him no matter how much he tried to ignore it. She was older than he was, a widow with four children, but that didn't seem to register with him. She was shapely and beautiful, and he liked that. In desperation, he tried to distract himself by saying the first thing that came to mind.

"What do your children call you?" he asked. "It is not Mama."

"Nay," she said as she neared the top of the stairs. "It is *Ama*. It means 'mother' in Spanish."

Markus understood. "My father told me that your family was from Aragon."

They reached the third floor. "That is true," she said. "I am the first in my family to be born in England. My father was born in Aragon, but my mother was born in Algiers. Have you heard of it?"

Markus nodded. "It is across the sea from Spain," he said. "Beyond Ibiza, I think. I seem to remember my grandfather telling me that, once."

"It is a faraway place," she said as they reached a chamber door, one of two on this dim and musty-smelling level. "My mother's family came to Aragon from Algiers and that is how my father met her. Her family was exiled royalty, so I'm told. The House of Hemada."

Now, the conversation about Lady de Sauque was starting to come back to Markus. Damien had mentioned she had the look of the Berbers, but Markus didn't see that at all. She looked English to him except for her eyes – there was some unearthly quality about the color that he'd never seen in England. The English he knew didn't have eyes that bewitch like that. There was, indeed, something different about her, but it wasn't strange or alien.

It was wildly attractive.

"Then you and I have something in common," he said as she opened the door to a vast, messy chamber. "My mother's father is a Norse king. Magnus the Law-Mender, they call him. He gave me my name, in fact. *Markus* – he said the strongest, greatest man he'd ever known was named Markus. He wanted to honor him."

She paused before continuing into the chamber, looking at him with some warmth and curiosity. "You are the grandson of a king?"

"I am."

A smile flickered on her lips. "I would believe that," she said. "You are tall and powerful and handsome. Of course you are the grandson of a king. You have greatness about you."

Markus was usually the arrogant one, but Lady de Sauque's praise had him close to blushing, something he was quite unaccustomed to.

"That is kind of you to say so," he said. "Magnus is a very great man and I do my best to honor him. He is also pushy, intrusive, and arrogant at times. But… he is my grandfather and

I adore the man."

She laughed softly. "It is a good thing that you do," she said. "I am surprised he did not name you after himself."

"He saved that for my third brother. He named me and the next eldest brother after his friends."

"That is sweet," she said. "My name has a story, too. I was named for the woman my father wanted to marry but was denied. How my mother allowed him to name me Amabella Najima, I will never know."

She giggled as she said it, causing Markus to grin. "Najima?" he repeated. "I have never heard that name."

"It means 'star' in the language of the Arabs."

"It is a beautiful name. It suits you." When he realized he'd just given the woman a compliment, he was mortified. Even though she had complimented him, he wasn't comfortable flattering her. He didn't want to sound inappropriate, given the circumstances of their association. After that, he was quick to change the subject. "This is where your husband slept?"

He took a step into the chamber, leaving Amabella at the door. If she was offended by his compliment, she didn't let on.

She followed him into the chamber.

"This was Roget's domain," she said. Then, she pointed to the hearth. "There is a stone in the bottom of the hearth that is loose. Pull it free and there is a hidden hole beneath it. That was where my father hid his wealth."

Markus headed straight to the hearth, dark and cold and full of ashes. Going down to one knee, he swept away the soot with his hand, clearing the black stones beneath. One stone was larger than the others, right in the middle of the hearth, and he pushed on it, seeing that it was, indeed, loose. Using the fire poker, he managed to pry it up and set it aside as Amabella peered over his shoulder.

"Can you see anything?" she asked.

Markus couldn't. "It is too dark," he said. "May I reach inside?"

"Please."

He reached down with his left hand, not his sword hand, in case there was a trap, but there was no trap to be found. He put his hand on a leather sack, pulling it out. He handed it over to Amabella before reaching in again and pulling forth yet another sack.

It ended up that there were four sacks total, all of them heavy leather and tightly bound, but they were clearly full of coins. He carried two sacks and Amabella carried two sacks, making their way over to the messy bed.

Amabella straightened out the coverlet first before setting her sacks down upon it. Without a word, she unfastened the leather ties. Markus saw what she was doing and he, too, unfastened the leather ties. Soon, the contents of all four sacks were spilled out onto the coverlet.

It was a pile of coins, of great wealth. Three of the sacks had been silver marks, but the fourth was gold. Lots and lots of gold. Awed, Amabella picked up one of the silver coins and held it up to the weak light coming in through the window.

"This is Spanish money," she murmured.

Markus came up behind her, trying to see what she saw. "I have not seen that type of coinage before," he said. "How do you know it's Spanish?"

She held it up to him, pointing to one side of it. "Do you see this shield?" she said, watching him nod. "It is the shield of King Alphonse of Navarre, the four lions. I know this because my father showed me these very same coins and explained it to me."

Markus could see the four lions within the three-point shield. "So, Roget never spent these," he muttered. "Interesting."

Amabella turned to look at him. "My thoughts, as well," she said. "There have to be hundreds of them, don't you think?"

Markus was about to agree until he realized how close he was to her. The mere thought seemed to suck all of the thoughts right out of his head. This elegant, lush, mature woman had all of his senses engaged as no one ever had. He found himself looking at her, at the delicate lines of her face, and into those eyes that were so mesmerizing. She was a woman; so many females he knew were only girls. Young and silly and giddy, with slender bodies and immature minds, but Amabella... she seemed beyond that to him.

She was what every woman should be but seldom was.

It was an effort to turn away from her.

"At the very least, hundreds," he said, pretending to focus on the coins. "And look at the gold coins; there have to be at least fifty of those alone. You expressed concern that Shand may have taken some of it. Do you believe it is all accounted for?"

Amabella shook her head. "There is no way of knowing," she said. "I do know that Roget paid him steadily because I overheard him once say that he paid Shand two pounds a month."

Markus pondered that. "How long has he served him?"

"A little over ten years."

Markus did the mathematics in his head. He'd always been extremely good at doing sums in his head, calculating the largest numbers with great accuracy. In fact, his father entrusted all of Berwick's finances to Markus because of the gift.

The man had a keen and analytical mind.

"That is a great deal of money over the course of ten years," he said. "If those figures hold, then Shand should have around two hundred and forty pounds. Even if he only spent a small amount of that over the years, it would make him an extremely wealthy knight."

Amabella looked to the coins spread out all over the bed. "More than what is here?"

Markus looked at the money. "Nay," he said. "Those gold coins alone are worth twenty pounds each. I would say there is at least a thousand pounds in gold coins, but the silver – that is quite a bit as well. Hundreds of pounds at the very least."

Amabella looked at it all, picking up another silver coin and seeing the head of King Henry on it. The coins had been minted in the last century, mixed in with the Spanish coinage.

"Well," she said after a moment. "It is comforting to know that the money is still here. At least we will not starve. But if Roget paid so much money to Shand that the man has well over two hundred pounds, I do not know why Atlas needs to send him on his way with more money."

Markus nodded. "Agreed," he said. "But Atlas does not know that. He was going on the assumption that Shand would need the money to find his next position."

"Then we shall tell him that is not the case."

Amabella immediately went to the bed and began loading the coins back into the heavy leather sacks. Markus helped her and, soon, they had them all secured and back into the hole beneath the hearth.

"Atlas is probably still in the solar with my father," Markus said. "If he is not, then I shall find him for you. You should not wander around the castle until this business with Shand is finished. It would be safer if you did not, at least until things are settled."

She looked at him as they headed for the chamber door. "If you believe that is best," she said. "But I must still go to the kitchens to see to the evening meal. May I?"

"Aren't there others who can see to the task?"

She shook her head. "Nay," she said. "That is my duty, especially since we have special guests. I want to ensure your meal is to your liking."

Markus opened the door for her. "Except your daughter has denied me yellow eggs," he said. "If I cannot have yellow eggs, I shall protest greatly."

Amabella appreciated his humor, lightening the mood a little. She laughed softly. "I shall give you some when she is not looking."

"I see. Slide them to me under the table?"

"Exactly. And do not let her see that you have them."

"Will she fight me for them?"

"Probably."

They grinned at each other as they headed to the stairwell, a moment of levity and warmth in a day that had seen little of either. But this moment, just the two of them, was rather special.

At least, Markus thought so.

Following Amabella down the stairs didn't have nearly the same view as following her up them but, at that point, it didn't matter.

Any view of Lady de Sauque was fine with him.

He was coming to look forward to the next one.

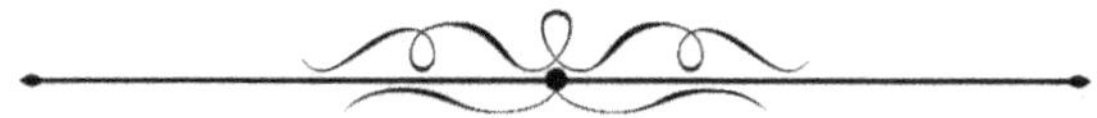

SHAND BEXWELL LEFT with only the money he had on him, money he'd kept stored in his small chamber, hidden in the wall behind a loose stone. Markus wasn't sure how much there was, but it was a great deal, enough for two leather sacks to weigh down his saddlebags.

Markus stood with Patrick, Atlas, Hermes, and Cassius in

the late afternoon, watching Shand depart Trastamara on a sturdy, young horse. It wasn't the great silver beast that Roget had purchased for him a few years ago, but the horse would get him where he needed to go. Shand was accompanied by four heavily-armed de Wolfe soldiers who were told to escort him at least two days away from Trastamara before letting him go on alone.

Shand departed without any fanfare and without a fight, which had been surprising to all concerned considering the man had just been banished from his home of the past ten years, a home he'd tried hard to hold on to until Lady de Sauque sent her missive to Berwick. Perhaps he realized that he'd held on so tightly, everything he'd wanted for himself simply slipped through his fingers. He'd taken a gamble and he'd lost, and with the odds stacked against him, he did the only thing he could do.

He departed.

Even so, it was clear that the Trastamara soldiers were confused by it, so much so that Patrick had them all rounded up so that Atlas could immediately address them. As the young lord had expressed, he wanted to be open and honest with his men in the hopes of earning their trust.

It had to start somewhere.

As Patrick and Markus and the rest of the de Wolfe knights stood by, Atlas explained the situation to the Trastamara soldiers without going so far as to point out Shand's ambition or actions. In fact, he didn't incriminate Shand at all, but simply explained that Shand's service had been flawless for Roget, but now that Roget was dead, Shand would be moving on to serve a new lord.

He left it at that.

Truth be told, none of the soldiers seemed too upset about it. A few grumbled, but most didn't seem to care, much to the relief of the de Wolfe knights. There was no great rebellion on the horizon. They seemed to accept young Atlas as the new lord without hesitation and, given that he was Roget's son, he was the legitimate heir.

No one questioned that.

Regardless, Patrick gave quiet orders to his own soldiers to watch the Trastamara men for any hint of unrest. The evening meal was swiftly approaching as the sun began to set and the western sky turned shades of gold and orange, and Patrick suggested to Atlas that they have plentiful ale that night so the men would know what a generous new lord they had.

Atlas heartily agreed.

Two senior de Sauque soldiers were put in charge of organizing the additional ale as Atlas, Hermes, Kieran, and Damien remained in the bailey, talking to the men and becoming familiar with the usual routine at this time of night. It was all part of Atlas becoming familiar with his unexpected command, and he asked a good many questions as the de Wolfe knights followed him around to be of any assistance.

As the servants were preparing the great hall for the coming feast, Markus found his father and brother inside, getting an early taste of the ale that was being rolled out from the storage vaults beneath the keep. The hall itself was of an older style, with a steeply pitched roof and a fire pit in the center of the hall. Smoke drifted up to the roof, finding its way out among the many vents. Markus sat heavily across from his father, pouring himself a cup of ale from the wooden pitcher.

"This day has gone better than I'd hoped," Patrick said. "I truly did not know what we would experience today with Bexwell. I will give the man credit for knowing when he is defeated. He left without a fight."

Markus gulped down half of the cup of the cheap ale with chaff in it. "Maybe so," he said. "How is Atlas doing after the confrontation?"

"He seems better," Patrick said. "Once he got over the shock of making a difficult command decision, he seems much better. The last I saw, he was in the stables, looking over the horse that used to belong to Shand. Quite an animal."

Markus nodded, thinking on the entire event with Shand's dismissal. "The man did not seem particularly upset to lose it," he said "In fact, it seemed to me that he gave in fairly quickly once he realized there was nothing more he could do. It was futile to resist. But it was almost… oh, I don't know. *Too* easy, I suppose."

Patrick peered at him curiously. "*Too* easy?" he repeated. "He gave us an argument once he realized we'd discovered him. He tried to make it seem as if his actions were all for Atlas' benefit."

Markus nodded, grabbing at a hot loaf of bread that a servant set down near him. "I know," he said. "But the man did not immediately notify anyone of de Sauque's death because he didn't want anyone to know. He wanted to put his own scheme in place before he made the notifications, but he was unable to do so once Lady de Sauque sent her missive to Berwick. She thwarted his plans and a man like that does not give up so easily."

"What are you saying?"

Markus shrugged. "I am saying that Atlas should be on his guard for some time to come," he said. "You mentioned you were going to leave Damien with him. Do you still intend to?"

Patrick nodded. "Aye," he said. "In fact, I am wondering if it wouldn't be a good idea to remove Lady de Sauque from Trastamara completely, at least for the time being. Move her to Berwick or even Questing or Northwood until the situation here settles a bit. She has three children that should be kept protected until we know for certain that Bexwell isn't going to come back and harass them."

Markus shoved bread into his mouth. "Have you not seen King Alfie and his horse guard?" he said. "They would make excellent protectors if they were old enough. Cass met them. Tell him, Cass."

Cassius, well into his second cup of ale, merely shrugged his shoulder. "He's a child with children following him around."

"He's a brave little lad who demanded I fight one of his knights," Markus insisted. "I thought the child was going to faint from sheer fight. There is something about Alfie that reminds me of my younger years. Papa, do you remember when Poppy gave me my first sword? How old was I?"

He was referring to Patrick's father, William. All of the grandchildren had called him Poppy and they still spoke of him in the present tense at times. William de Wolfe had lived such a long and noble life that even now, four years after his death, no one could quite bring themselves to talk about him as if he were gone. To them, he wasn't.

Patrick nodded his head.

"I do," he said. "He had it made for you when you were born and he tried to give it to you when you first started walking, but Matha would not let him. It came to the point where he would have to hide it from her, but she was clever and would find it. He'd get it back from her only to hide it again, but she always found it. Once, Poppy couldn't find that sword for six damned months. He was furious."

Matha was what the grandchildren called William's wife, Jordan. She was the strong and beautiful matriarch of the de Wolfe clan, deeply loved by all. Markus and Cassius started to laugh at the memory of their wily grandfather and their cunning grandmother, battling it out over a small, dull sword.

"He had swords made for every grandson he had," Markus said. "It was a rite of passage with Poppy. We all had to be properly armed even as infants."

Patrick smiled at the memory of his father, so incredibly proud of every grandson he had, and there were dozens. Forty-nine, to be exact, adopted and natural, and every single one of them had a sword from their Poppy.

But it had been the same thing every time – William would have a sword commissioned, in secret or so he thought, and his wife would somehow track the sword down and take it away. William would find it and the game would go back and forth. Jordan, the grandmother of over seventy grandchildren, had never approved of the very young children with the dull swords William would give them.

It had been a running family joke for years.

"Aye, it was a rite of passage," Patrick said after a moment, his smile fading as he thought on the father he loved so much. "He was the greatest knight of his generation. It was only right that his grandsons reflect that greatness and the weaponry was part of it."

Markus and Cassius watched Patrick sink into the familiar depression that occurred when discussing his beloved father. Markus even reached out, grasping Patrick by the hand and giving him a squeeze.

"He *was* the greatest," he said softly, with affection. "And his sons are the greatest knights of their generation. We all miss Poppy, Papa. You are not alone and you know that."

Patrick nodded, but he couldn't help the melancholy. "I know," he said. "Men die all of the time. Fathers die all of the time. Even so, I was not ready for mine to die. I am sure that sounds strange for me to say this, but I can still hear him saying 'Atty'. Sometimes I think I hear it just behind me and when I turn around, no one is there."

Markus knew that his grandfather's death had hit his father particularly hard because they were very close. It was rare for

Patrick to express his grief, but this moment had come about so organically that Markus simply held his father's hand and let the man speak.

"I think he *is* still here," he said after a moment. "Whenever I go to Castle Questing, I swear I have seen him. Not really seen him, as if he were a ghost, but I have seen flashes of what I thought was him. As if he'd just gone around a corner and I caught a glimpse. I think as long as Matha lives, Poppy will not leave Questing. I truly believe that."

Patrick nodded, using his free hand to take a big swallow of his ale. "I think you're right," he said. "What Poppy and Matha had went beyond earthly confines. Their love is legendary. But… I still miss him deeply."

"I know, Papa."

"And Uncle Paris. God, we lost him barely four months after Papa passed. That was a difficult year."

"It was."

Patrick tended to be emotional these days and the moment turned heady as thoughts of William de Wolfe and his best friend for over seventy years, Paris de Norville, were spoken of. Knights who were legendary along the border, in life and in death. Patrick knew that better than most. Finally, he drew in a deep breath and squared his shoulders.

"Enough of sorrowful memories," he said, trying to sound as if he were focusing on business again. "We were speaking on the status of Trastamara, so let us continue. With Bexwell gone, I see no reason for me to remain here any longer, so I shall return home on the morrow. I will take Hermes and Anson with me, and leave Cass and Damien and Kieran. I think it will be good experience for Kieran to remain and, being closer in age to Atlas, he may be of more comfort to the new lord."

Markus and Cassius went along with their father as the man dodged the emotions of his father's passing. That was usual.

Soon enough, they were back on the subject at hand.

"What of Lady de Sauque?" Markus asked. "Are you going to insist she move to Berwick or Questing?"

He tried not to sound hopeful as he said it, but thoughts of Lady de Sauque settling in at Berwick were not unpleasant. In fact, he realized that he would like that very much. But his father merely shrugged.

"Mayhap," he said. "I will speak with her and express my concerns. I will not force the woman, but it may be in her best interests to go where she and her children will be safe. Away from Trastamara and soldiers who were once loyal to her husband and to Bexwell. Atlas will have enough on his mind without worrying over his mother and siblings, too."

"Here is your chance," Cassius said, picking up the wooden pitcher of ale to refill his cup. "Here she comes."

Patrick and Markus turned to see the servant's entrance opening. Lady de Sauque was at the head of a contingent of servants, all of them carrying great trays of food. In fact, Lady de Sauque was carrying one herself and before Markus could think, he was on his feet, heading in her direction.

"My lady, that looks too heavy for you," he said, reaching out to take a large wooden tray that carried several bowls. "Permit me to help you."

Amabella looked at him in surprise even as he took the tray from her. "It is not terribly heavy," she insisted weakly. He was just standing there with the tray, so she gestured to the table. "Please put it in front of your father. I thank you for your assistance."

Markus did as she instructed, setting the tray down. Amabella removed the bowls of butter and stewed fruit, and two more big loaves of bread. She smiled her thanks at Markus as she collected the tray, rushing back to the kitchen as he watched curiously.

"Why is the woman serving?" he wondered aloud. Then, he looked around the hall, only seeing three servants. They were spread out, putting bread on the tables. "It just occurred to me that I have not seen many servants here. Have you?"

He looked at his father and Patrick shrugged. "I have not been paying particular attention, but it does seem to be rather devoid of servants," he said. "This is a large hall. There should be several."

Markus nodded as he looked around. "Yet, I only see three. Odd."

He sat back down, producing a knife and pulling apart more bread, which they then began to butter. Amabella appeared again shortly thereafter, carrying the tray, which was now laden with more food. She set it down at the end of their table and began distributing more bowls with butter and fruit.

Markus watched with increasing curiosity.

"Lady de Sauque," he said. "Is it usual for you to personally serve the tables of your hall?"

She looked at him, bowl of butter in-hand. "Aye," she said, but she seemed somewhat uneasy. "I have a few kitchen servants and a nurse for the children, but there are no maids or servants for the hall. Roget did not believe in them."

"What do you mean he did not believe in them?"

She sighed faintly as he forced her into a distasteful confession. "I am the Lady of the House," she said frankly. "He believed I should serve him and everyone else here."

Markus had never heard of such a thing. He opened his mouth to say so, but Patrick kicked him under the table. When he winced and looked at his father, Patrick shook his head faintly.

"Thank you for your kind attention, Lady de Sauque," he said politely. "We are greatly honored to be served by the Lady of the House."

Amabella forced a smile and collected her tray, rushing back through the servant's entrance. When she was gone, Markus bent over to rub his shin where his father had kicked him.

"Why did you do that?" he demanded unhappily.

Patrick cocked an eyebrow at him. "Because you were embarrassing the woman," he said. "You must know when not to press, Markus. Can you not see it is a humiliating situation for her?"

Markus had and now he was coming to feel badly about pressing her. "The more I find out about how Roget de Sauque treated his wife and family, the less I like the man," he grumbled. "The woman shouldn't be serving the entire Trastamara army."

Patrick shook his head. "All the more reason to take her and her children to Berwick where they can enjoy peace and safety among people who will be kind to them," he said. "Your mother will talk to her and explain to her how the Lady of the House should be treated. Let your mother straighten out Lady de Sauque. She should be no man's servant."

Markus completely agreed. "Then speak to the woman and convince her to come back to Berwick. I will personally escort her."

"I will."

Men began to trickle into the great hall now that the sun had set. What few servants there were had begun lighting the big iron sconces along the walls, torches soaked in fat that burned black, sooty smoke into the air. Trastamara soldiers were entering, finding a place at one of the three big feasting tables, pouring themselves cups of the cloudy ale. The low hum of conversation began to fill the stale air of the hall as Amabella began to bring out steaming trenchers.

Patrick was the first man served, followed by Markus and

Cassius. The big, stale bread disk was filled with fish, which was surprising. Usually, men on a grand scale were served beef or mutton, so fish was not the usual feasting fare. The trencher also contained boiled onions and peas, and Markus noticed that his trencher in particular had yellow, stuffed eggs.

"There," Amabella said. "I brought you some yellow eggs."

He grinned at her. "Does Lady Ambra know?"

Amabella's eyes twinkled at him. "She is in the kitchen with me," she said. "It was she who told me to give you some. I told you she likes her food, and believe it or not, the fish is something she created with the cook. Our cook was my father's cook many years ago, from Spain, and she is very good. She and Ambra create dishes together. Try it; it is delicious."

Markus looked at the white fish, covered in a clear sauce with bits of spice and onion. He didn't even hesitate; he stabbed his knife into it and put a rather big bite in his mouth. After chewing only a couple of times, he looked at her in surprise.

"It *is* good," he said. "Lady Ambra *made* this dish?"

Amabella smiled proudly. "She simply tells the cook what flavors she likes," she said. "She doesn't actually cook it herself, but she is very good with flavors. My daughter has a discerning palate."

By this time, Patrick and Cassius were carving into the fish, agreeing that it was quite tasty. Seeing that her guests were pleased, Amabella turned for the kitchen, leaving Markus to watch her from the corners of his eyes.

He found he couldn't take his eyes off her.

"Who is this Lady Ambra?" Cassius asked, interrupting Markus' thoughts. "Is she married?"

Markus snorted. "She is a child of five years," he said. "She is too young for you."

Cassius shoved more fish into his mouth. "It does not matter," he said. "If she can create dishes like this, I will have Papa negotiate a betrothal this very night. I will wait for her to become of age."

Patrick shook his head at his gluttonous son as he thought that culinary talent was a good enough reason to marry. Truth be told, however, the child had a great talent if what her mother said was true. He was deep into his fish when a small girl came bouncing into the hall, climbing up on the bench next to Markus. When he saw her coming, he tried to cover his food.

"If you have come for your eggs, you cannot have them," he told her. "These are mine. Your mother said so."

Ambra grinned brightly, a mouth full of little baby teeth. "I've already had many," she told him. "More than you. *Many* more than you."

He frowned, exaggerated. "I am going to eat mine right now so you cannot have them," he said, popping one into his mouth and realizing it was delicious. He looked over at Cassius. "This is Lady Ambra, Cass. Still want that betrothal?"

Cassius looked at the little girl, his mouth full of fish. She was an adorable little thing with big, green eyes. "Tell me something, my lady," he said to her. "Did you really make this dish?"

Ambra looked at the fish on Cassius' trencher then looked to the remains of the fish on Markus' trencher. Reaching out, she snatched a piece of Markus' fish and shoved it into her mouth.

"I told the cook how it should taste," she said, chewing with her mouth open as tiny pieces of white fish flew onto the table. "There is onion and honey and vinegar. It tastes sweet, but it also tastes sour, like it has been pickled."

"Do you know what pickled is?"

She nodded firmly. "I do," she insisted. "I like pickled carrots and pickled cucumber and pickled beets. Cook makes them for me and they make my mouth go like this."

She suddenly puckered up her lips and squeezed her eyes shut, a true reaction to sour pickling. It was amusing. But she also spoke with a knowledge and diction beyond her years, which was surprising. Lady Ambra was an unusual child, indeed, and Cassius fought off a grin at the food flying from her lips when she spoke.

"My compliments," he said. "Are you married yet?"

Ambra laughed out loud and food went flying. "Nay!"

"Are you certain?"

"Aye!"

"I think I will marry you myself if you can create food like this."

She giggled, pointing her finger at him. "You're too old."

"I am now, but not in twelve years. I will be just right."

Ambra shook her head, the red curls whipping around. Pieces of fish from her lips were sticking to them. "You're silly!"

She was ridiculously adorable. By this time, Markus, Patrick, and Cassius were laughing at her and she giggled with them, not realizing they were laughing *at* her. She took another handful of fish from Markus' trencher and as she pushed that into her mouth, Amabella emerged from the servant's door, carrying more food. One look at her daughter eating off of Markus' trencher and her eyes widened in horror.

"Ambra," she hissed, quickly setting down the trenchers in her hand so she could grab her daughter. "You do not eat off a guest's meal. That is the lord's food."

Ambra looked at her mother as if she had no idea what the woman was talking about, but clearly, her mother was appalled and that upset her. It didn't occur to her that all of the food in the hall, regardless of whose trencher it was on, didn't belonged to her. She didn't often eat in the hall because Roget didn't like his children around when he was eating, so the consequences of that were poor table manners.

Her lower lip began to tremble when she realized she was being scolded. She turned big, watery eyes to Markus.

"Can I have your fish?" she said, wiping the tears pooling in her eyes.

Markus shoved the trencher in front of her. "Eat, sweetheart. You can have all of it."

She was trying very hard not to cry as she looked at her mother, who was looking at Markus apologetically.

"My lord," she said quietly. "You did not have to…"

Markus cut her off gently. "She can have it," he said. "You can bring me more."

Amabella smiled at him gratefully as she turned for the kitchen once more. Markus found himself watching the little girl as she took handfuls of the fish, which was cooled by now, and shoveled it into her mouth. The tears seemed to be forgotten and, at one point, she held out a sticky piece for him, like an offering. He grinned as he took it, putting it in his mouth, much to her delight.

Being the eldest of six siblings, Markus was comfortable around younger children because he happened to have two younger sisters of his own. For all of his size and strength, he was quite gentle when it came to the female sex because he enjoyed them. He thought women and girls, as a whole, were charming and intelligent. Ambra was no exception.

He was coming to like her.

As he took bits of fish from her sticky fingers, some commotion at the hall entry caught his attention and he looked over to see Damien, Anson, Hermes, and Kieran entering the hall. Atlas and Alfie were leading the pack. Atlas had hold of his little brother as they headed straight for the table with Markus and Patrick and Cassius.

"Sir Knight!"

Alfie was halfway across the hall when he caught sight of

Markus, shouting to the man. Yanking free of his brother, he began to run. There was a table between them, but that didn't matter to Alfie. He climbed up on the table and nearly kicked Patrick's trencher in his haste to get to Markus. In fact, Markus ended up standing up, picking the child off the table, and then setting him down next to his sister.

All the while, Alfie had eyes only for Markus.

"Did you make the sword for my knights?" Alfie asked eagerly. "For Aldwin, I mean. He needs a sword."

Markus caught his father's curious expression. "Papa, this is King Alfie," he said. "Alfie, this is the Earl of Berwick, my father. Greet him properly."

Alfie had to lean forward to get a good look at Patrick. "Do you have many knights, my lord?" he asked.

A grin flickered on Patrick's lips. "I do," he said. "I hear you have some also."

Alfie nodded, climbing onto the table again so he could talk to Patrick without Markus and his sister between them.

"I have three," he said excitedly. "Sir Knight was going to give them real swords so that they could protect me."

It was clear that Alfie only addressed Markus as "Sir Knight". To him, Markus was *the* knight. When Patrick looked at Markus regarding the sword declaration, the man merely shrugged.

"They were using sticks as weapons," he said. "I told them I would see if I could find someone to make them swords."

Patrick nodded in understanding. "Just like Poppy, I see."

Markus grinned. "Except Matha isn't here to take them away."

"Nay, but Lady de Sauque is," Patrick said. "If you are serious, you should ask her permission."

"My lord!" Alfie demanded because Markus and Patrick were talking between them. When Patrick looked at him, he scooted closer to him along the tabletop. "My lord, someday I will be a great knight, too, like Sir Knight. He *is* a great knight, isn't he?"

Patrick's eyes glimmered with mirth at the enthusiastic young boy. "He is the greatest knight you will ever see," he said. "So is his brother, Cassius. They are so fearsome that the Scots runaway at the mere sight of them."

Alfie looked at Cassius, who wasn't quite finished with his meal. "Have you fought many Scots?"

Cassius was still chewing his bread. "I have."

"Did they beg for mercy? Did you cut their heads off and watch their blood spill out?"

Cassius looked at him in surprise before breaking down into laughter. "I think I like you, King Alfie," he said. "You have an impressive bloodlust."

By this time, Atlas and the others had settled in, all of them taking a seat on the benches, reaching for ale and bread. All except Atlas; he reached for Alfie, pulling his little brother off the table.

"Sit here with me," he said. "You are not to sit on the table like a little animal. Do you see any of these men sitting on the table?"

Alfie looked at the table, seemingly embarrassed by behavior he didn't even know was questionable. The men were eating, not paying much attention to him, but his gaze moved between Markus and Cassius. Big, powerful knights he was enamored with. Suddenly, he scrambled up onto the tabletop again.

"I want to sit with Sir Knight," he said.

Atlas made a swipe for him, but he was already to the other side of the table, pushing himself in between Ambra and Markus. Ambra didn't take kindly to be separated from Markus and angrily, she hit Alfie on the side of the head with her open, sticky palm. Unhappy with the fish sauce on his head, Alfie gave

Ambra a big shove and over she went, falling onto the floor.

Screams erupted.

As Atlas leapt up to intervene between his battling siblings, Amabella came bolting out of the kitchens. She had trenchers in her hands but when she saw her daughter on the ground with Alfie standing over her, she quickly set the trenchers down and went straight to her misbehaving children.

"I permit you to eat with our guests and this is how you behave?" she said, incredulous, as she picked Ambra off the ground. "Shame on both of you for your terrible manners. You have made me ashamed of you."

She had Alfie in one hand and Ambra in the other now, and Ambra began to cry. Unsympathetic, Amabella hauled her children off as Atlas stood there, looking after them with great concern.

"It was Alfie's fault," he called after his mother. "Ama, did you hear me?"

Amabella was already out of the hall, through the servant's door. Sheepishly, Atlas turned to the men at the table.

"I am sorry," he said, slowly reclaiming his seat. "My father never allowed them into the hall, so I do not think they know how to behave."

No one seemed particularly disturbed by it and Patrick waved him off. "I have had several young children myself," he said. "Six, in fact, with four boys born fairly close together. There was a time when my hall was a chaotic circus, so you needn't apologize for your siblings. They will learn."

Atlas nodded, still embarrassed, suddenly realizing that his mother had left two full trenchers at the end of the table. He quickly retrieved them, giving one to Damien and the other to Anson. As he sent a servant for more food, Markus stood up.

"Has anyone seen to our sleeping accommodations this night?" he asked the table.

The knights looked at each other, eventually shaking their heads, and Markus put up a hand. "I will," he said. "Finish your food. I shall return."

"Where are you going?" Patrick asked.

Markus pointed towards the servant's entrance. "To find Lady de Sauque and ask her where she intends to house us," he said. "I also want to make sure she does not punish her children too severely. They caused no trouble."

Markus had always been the peacemaker in the family, so his inclination towards Lady de Sauque and her children was not unusual. Patrick waved him off and Markus headed for the servant's door, following Amabella's path from the hall.

But it was an excuse, all of it.

Markus simply wanted to see Amabella again because he clearly had some manner of odd infatuation with her. This proud, beautiful woman with a husband who treated her so poorly. The fact that Roget had expected her to serve an entire hall of men spoke of incredible disrespect, and yet she projected a quiet dignity. No matter how poorly Roget had treated her, it seemed to Markus as if the man hadn't been able to break her. At least, not on the surface.

He was starting to see that more clearly now.

It intrigued him more than he could control.

The kitchens were open for the most part and the servant's entrance had taken him out into the kitchen yard. Knowing Amabella would have taken the children into the keep, he headed for the big, stone bastion, silhouetted against the starry sky. He could see a light emitting from the windows on the second level, so he entered the dimly lit foyer, with only a single torch to light the fairly large space.

And he could hear crying.

Taking the torch, he went into the larger solar on this level and found several tapers, lighting a fat one that was wedged into an iron candle holder. He replaced the torch in its iron sconce before heading up the stairs to the next level with his single taper.

He could hear Ambra's angry and hysterical voice.

The level with Amabella's solar on it had two more chambers, smaller ones, and the door to one of them was open. That was where the commotion was coming from. Markus stuck his head into the doorway in time to see Amabella pulling a sleeping shift over Ambra's head.

"I don't want to go to bed!" Ambra wailed. "Ama, I want to go back to the hall! My fish!"

"You may not go back to the hall," Amabella said steadily. "Not tonight. It is time for sleep. Alfie, you will get into bed and stay there. I do not want to see your face until morning."

Alfie was standing next to the bed, frowning and unhappy, until he caught sight of Markus in the doorway. Then, he bolted.

"Sir Knight!"

He ran to Markus, grabbing the man by the leg as if his savior from motherly punishment had finally arrived. Markus reached down to disengage the boy from his limb.

"Your mother gave you a command," he said. "All good kings must obey their mothers. Get into bed."

Alfie's face fell. "But... but you *came.*"

Markus took the boy by the arm and led him back over to the bed. "Aye, I came," he said. "But I came to speak to your mother. Meanwhile, I expect you to be a good king and do as she says."

Alfie did, but it was begrudgingly. He climbed onto the bed, looking at Markus most longingly.

"But will you be here on the morrow when I wake up?" he asked.

Markus nodded. "I will."

"You are not leaving?"

"Not tomorrow."

That seemed to give Alfie the push he needed to close his eyes. Amabella lifted Ambra into the bed, pulling the coverlet over her two youngest children.

"Now," she said. "No more fighting, no more talking. I want you both to go to sleep right away so that you can see Sir Markus in the morning."

Alfie was already trying to go to sleep, but Ambra was still sniffling, hiccupping on occasion, as she rubbed her red eyes. She looked up at Markus with such sadness that he had to refrain from comforting the girl.

"Did you like my fish?" she sniffled.

He smiled faintly. "It was delicious."

"And my yellow eggs?"

"They were also delicious."

"I-I will eat them all so you cannot have any more."

He was about to reply to the contrary when he realized that wasn't what she wanted. She had said the same thing to him earlier when he pretended to weep. Suspecting that was what she wanted from him, he put his hand over his face and made a crying sound.

That brought instant sunshine. Ambra's frown turned to a smile in an instant and she laughed.

"No more for you!" she said.

That brought an exaggerated and pathetic howl from Markus, much to the delight of both Ambra and Alfie, who opened his eyes to watch Markus weep. They lay there and laughed at his antics until he removed his hand from his face and pointed to them both.

"Your mother said for you to go to sleep," he said. "Obey her."

The children were still grinning, but they nodded. Alfie

closed his eyes tightly again. Ambra, however, kept hers open, smiling adoringly at her newfound friend. Suspecting they wouldn't go to sleep until he left, Markus departed the chamber with Amabella right behind him.

"Quiet, now," she whispered as she stood at the door. "May the saints and angels watch over you while you sleep, my little ones."

With that, she carefully shut the door, turning to Markus with an appreciative smile.

"Thank you," she said sincerely. "When Ambra weeps like that, sometimes it can take an hour to calm her. You did it quite swiftly."

Markus shrugged. "I have two younger sisters of my own," he said. "I know how little girls can be."

"You are very good with children. Are you not married? You have none of your own?"

He shook his head. "I am not married, and I have no children of my own," he said. "But I hope to be, and have, someday."

Amabella laughed softly. "I am quite shocked that some maiden has not snared you for her own," she said. "When she does, she will be quite fortunate to have you as the father of her children. It seems you have many talents, not only limited to warfare."

There she was, praising him again. He felt as if he very much wanted to accept her praise because it was coming from someone he was coming to both respect and admire, but he was positive there was nothing personal about her praise. She was simply being kind.

It wasn't as if she were interested in him.

She couldn't be.

... couldn't she?

He cleared his throat softly.

"I suppose I am a man of many facets," he said. "As for marriage, I've simply not yet had the time. Moreover, I am due to assume an appointed position with King Edward soon and marriage does not fit into that plan, at least not now."

She grew serious. "Oh?" she said. "You will be leaving Berwick?"

He nodded. "I have been appointed as Edward's Lord Protector," he said. "It is a prestigious position as the king's personal guard, which means I will spend all of my time with him. If he is in London, I will be in London. If he goes to battle, I go to battle. His life shall become my life."

Amabella was properly awed. "What a proud thing," she said. "Your father must be delighted."

"He is."

"And your mother?"

He fought off a smile. "She is happy for me, but she does not want me to leave her," he said. Then, he shook his head. "I am her oldest child. I have seen thirty years, but still, she does not want me to leave her bosom."

Amabella giggled. "I understand completely," she said. "I did not want Atlas to leave me, either, but when I see him now, I know it was the right thing for him. He has returned to Trastamara as a strong, educated young man. Your mother, too, will understand that going to serve the king will be the right thing for you."

"I suppose. But she is currently in the denial stage."

Amabella understood a mother's pain at being separated from a child, something Markus didn't seem to appreciate.

"All will work out as it should, I am sure," she said. "Now, did you require something more from me? You did not have to trouble yourself by leaving your meal to seek me out. I planned on returning to the hall as soon as I put Alfie and Ambra to bed."

Markus shook his head. "I did not require anything," he said, realizing she was asking him to explain his appearance. He didn't want to tell her the truth, that he simply wanted to see to her. "I came to tell you that… that my father will be returning to Berwick upon the morrow, but he will be leaving men behind to assist Atlas during this transitional time. He will also be leaving most of the soldiers he brought with him, but he wanted to speak to you about the possibility of you returning to Berwick for a time. He thought it might be better for you and your younger children to be at Berwick where it is safe while Atlas settles Trastamara."

She looked at him curiously. "Is it so unsafe here that we should leave?"

"Probably not, but my father is concerned about Shand. He wants to make sure that the man does not try to return."

"Does your father think he might?"

"Not really," Markus said. "But Shand is an ambitious man and up until today, this was his home, something he was intent on keeping. My father simply doesn't want you to be part of any trouble he might try to bring if he's vengeful enough."

Her eyes widened. "God's Bones," she murmured. "I hope he does not try."

"As do I," Markus said. "If you do not want to go to Berwick, you do not have to. However, you should give it some thought. For the safety of King Alfie and the Lady of the Fish."

Amabella was back to grinning as he mentioned her children. He had quite a way about him, a subtle humor that was endearing. "You enjoyed her food and that is all she cares about," she said. "She will speak of nothing else for months to come."

He was smiling because she was, feeling a warmth in his chest when he looked at her that he couldn't begin to describe. It was something heated and liquid, making his palms sweat like a giddy squire.

"She has every reason to be proud," he said. "It is quite an interesting talent she has. An interesting lass with an interesting name. In fact, I have never heard that name before. Is it a family name?"

Amabella shook her head. "Ambra is not her given name," she said. "Her given name is Anne Mary Barbara Rose Amalie Abril de Sauque. My husband named her after his mother and grandmothers, and also an aunt. Ambra is simply the first letter of each of those names."

Markus thought that was fascinating. "How clever," he said. "Who came up with that?"

"I did. I was not going to call a tiny babe Anne Mary Barbara Rose Amalie. The name was bigger than she was."

He snorted. "Very wise, Lady de Sauque."

Her smile faded, her emerald eyes riveted to him. "I would be pleased if you would call me Amabella," she said. "I… I realize we have only just come to know one another, but you and your family have done so much for us that I feel as if there is no need for formalities. We are utterly in your debt. You and your father have saved us, in every way a family can be saved. You have given us hope for the future where before, there had been none at all. Hope that Atlas can restore the good name of Trastamara Castle and undo the damage done by his father."

Markus could feel her sincerity. She was vulnerable and open in that moment, and he appreciated that. "I am honored to call you Amabella," he said quietly. "You may call me Markus. Or, Sir Knight, as Alfie seems to think is my name."

Amabella chuckled. "He is enamored with you."

"The feeling is mutual."

Amabella was still smiling and Markus could feel a pull between them, like an invisible embrace that threatened to pull them together. It was something he'd never before experienced, a feeling that had only become stronger by the hour. It was strange, and unexpected, perhaps even uncomfortable at times, but he couldn't deny how marvelous it made him feel.

Surely it was only an infatuation.

It couldn't be anything else.

"Well," Amabella finally said, breaking into his thoughts. "I should return to the hall. There are always a thousand tasks to complete on nights like this."

Markus nodded as they turned towards the stairs. "Aye, you should get back," he said. "But not to serve. You will sit with my father and brother and me. You will enjoy a meal with us as we discuss the future of Trastamara. Then, tomorrow, I will send to Berwick for more servants. You cannot do with only a handful of servants in a place like this and you should not be working like a common wench. You are the Lady of the House and should be treated like one."

She paused at the top of the stairs, looking at him. "You are not returning to Berwick with your father tomorrow?"

His gaze lingered on her in the dim light. "Nay," he said after a moment. "I am one of the ones remaining here to help settle Trastamara."

It wasn't exactly the truth, but by the time Markus got down to the hall and told his father that he intended to remain behind, it would be.

As long as Amabella remained at Trastamara, he wasn't going anywhere.

CHAPTER NINE

Mordrington Manor

I T HAD TAKEN him five days.

Five days to return to what he knew best – the Trastamara properties.

Shand had ridden with his de Wolfe escorts south to Alnwick, where they had left him in an inn for a night he spent drinking and eating and fornicating with one of the serving wenches. He'd had a night of it, getting drunk and enjoying himself for the most part. But when he departed the next morning in a heavy mist, he could see the de Wolfe escort watching him from the north side of the city.

They had been waiting to see where he would go.

Therefore, he had to outsmart them. They were only soldiers, anyway, so in a battle of wits, Shand knew he had the advantage. He'd gone south, out of their line of sight, until he came to a road that went east.

He took it.

It was the beginning of doubling back and heading north again. Only this time, he'd taken an inland road and not one that ran parallel to the coastline. It had taken him three days to return to the border, whereupon he crossed the River Tweed in

Coldstream and not terribly far from Castle Questing, and headed into Scotland, to the area he was familiar with.

He had a destination in mind.

Roget had been either heading to, or coming from, Mordrington Manor where he kept his long-time mistress at the time of his demise. Shand didn't know if Fenella Foulden Hume knew of Roget's death, but if she didn't, he intended to tell her. He also intended to seek shelter at Mordrington for as long as he could remain.

Shand didn't know what Atlas' plans were for Mordrington, but he could guess. Atlas had been unabashed in his scorn for his father's mistress, so he suspected that Atlas intended to banish the woman from the property.

Until that time, however, Shand needed a place to stay. To think. To plan.

Vengeance.

At the time of his removal from Trastamara, he'd presented the very model of a submissive and obedient knight. He'd let Atlas humiliate him and order him away, because the truth was that he'd had little choice in the matter. With Berwick and his hulking knights present, any show of resistance would have been painfully met. He knew that.

Shand may have lost the battle, but he'd not lost the war.

In fact, he intended to win it.

With his knowledge of the intimate workings of Trastamara Castle, he had a lot to offer the reivers and hostile clans of the borders. Roget had his share of enemies, and Shand knew that he could very well sell his services to the highest bidder. Knowing that Fenella Foulden Hume was Scottish, he was going to use her clan connections to get what he wanted. There were rich outlaws and clan chiefs willing to pay for what he knew, and he had no qualms selling it.

He'd been loyal to the House of de Sauque for ten long

years and he had nothing to show for it. Therefore, his loyalty to them was at an end. He'd been treated poorly and cast aside, and he wasn't going to let that humiliation stand.

He was going to regain what had been so wrongfully taken from him.

Lady de Sauque and Trastamara Castle.

The ride to Mordrington was wrought with peril, however. Roget had paid the price for that. With that in mind, Shand used his knowledge of the area and kept to the trees and meadows, staying off the road, avoiding heavily forested areas where outlaws were known to congregate.

Traveling that way had taken him extra time, but towards the end of his fifth day since leaving Trastamara, the big walls of Mordrington finally came into view. He was very nearly to his destination.

But what he saw did not surprise him.

There were Scots, everywhere.

The manse itself had big, lovely walls to protect it and it was quite a fine home, but the drawbridge was wide open and men were milling in and out of it, men dressed in long tunics of traditional Scot's dress. There were no guards, no one up on the battlements to suggest there were any security measures in place, and nothing to suggest it was a Trastamara garrison.

The manse was simply open and there were dozens of Scots infesting it.

Knowing that Fenella was Scots, somewhere in the back of his mind, Shand could recall that she had a brother as well. He remembered Roget mentioning a Baldwin Foulden in passing, who was a warrior with Clan Hume. But given what he was seeing, it was clear that the Scots had all but moved into Mordrington. Had Clan Hume taken over? Had Roget known about it?

It was all a bit of a mystery.

Given that Shand was evidently heading into a nest of the enemy, he dropped his weapons and money back along the road, hiding them all beneath a rock bridge over a bubbling brook to ensure that he could not be robbed of his possessions. His life was another matter. He could only hope he didn't fall to the same fate Roget had.

Carefully, he approached Mordrington astride his hairy, mediocre mount, his arms raised to show that he had no weapons on him. The men in the front of the manse were digging a hole of some kind, passing a jug of drink between them, and when they saw Shand approach with his hands up, they immediately came to a halt. They pointed at him, looking at each other curiously, before heading towards him with their shovels wielded like clubs.

Shand slid off his horse, hands held high.

"My name is Shand Bexwell," he said. "I have come seeking Lady Fenella."

The men paused momentarily, looking at each other with confusion, before suddenly rushing him.

"Kill me and you will not know how I can make you rich!" he shouted quickly. "I have come to make Lady Fenella rich!"

All but two of the men slowed down as his words registered, but those two who didn't slow down ended up throwing Shand to the ground. He landed heavily on his back as one man jumped on his chest, holding the shaft of his shovel across Shand's neck.

"Who are ye, Shand Bexwell?" he demanded, sweat and spittle flicking onto Shand's face and neck. "Where did ye come from?"

Shand had the wind knocked out of him by being thrown onto his back and he coughed a couple of times before speaking.

"Roget de Sauque is dead," he said, avoiding the questions.

"Did you know that?"

That seemed to bring some pause from the men. Someone reached down to yank the burly Scotsman off Shand while still another man hauled Shand to his feet. He continued to cough, rubbing his ribs where they'd hit the ground.

"We know he's dead," one man said. "What do ye want here, *Sassenach*?"

Shand faced the man because he seemed to speak succinctly. He didn't sound like a crazed animal, like some of the others did.

"I have come to speak with Lady Fenella," he said evenly. "I have a business proposition for her. Will you please announce me?"

The Scots weren't sure what to think. They eyed him and each other until the same man who had pounced on him took another swipe at him. He grabbed Shand by the arm and spun him around, grabbing at his waist, his tunic, looking for his purse or weapons or anything else of value.

Shand let them poke.

Finally, the Scotsman realized that there wasn't anything on Shand other than tunics, a mail coat, a belt, shoes, and little else. Nothing of value. With that awareness, he released him.

"What business proposition do ye have for her?" the rational Scotsman asked. "How did ye know tae come here?"

Shand debated about how much to tell him. He was still facing away from the group and he slowly turned around, thinking to perhaps tell them the truth. At least, as much as he dared. They were starting to attract a crowd because more dirty Scots were spilling from the manse, heading in their direction.

Shand put down the hands he'd been holding aloft.

"I told you that my name was Shand Bexwell," he said. "I served Roget de Sauque until his death. Then, his son, the new Lord of Trastamara, exiled me from my home of ten years. I was dismissed as if I was the filth of the earth and not a loyal warrior. If you want money, and if you want to overrun Trastamara Castle and regain her Scottish lands, then I can help you. I have come to present my services to Lady Fenella because I have valuable information on how this can be accomplished. *Now* will you tell her I have arrived?"

As he'd hoped, his explanation brought a positive reaction from the men. Not strangely, they seemed very interested.

"Is it vengeance ye seek, then?" someone asked.

Shand lifted his eyebrows as if it were a ridiculous question. "Clearly."

"And ye need us?"

"I need men willing to fight for great reward."

The sane Scotsman reached out and grabbed him by the arm. "Then come inside," he said. "I think Fenella will want tae hear this. But God help ye, *Sassenach*, if ye're lying."

"I would not have come all the way here just to lie to you."

The man's gaze lingered on him. "For yer sake, I hope not."

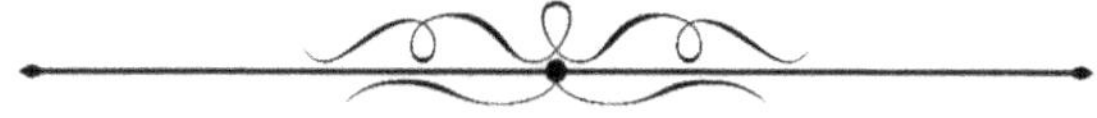

"Aye... I know the name. I know who ye are."

Fenella seemed wary. Confused, even. She kept looking at the sane Scotsman who had dragged Shand into the manse, puzzled by what was going on. He'd told her, briefly, why the Sassenach had come, but she needed more of an explanation. She finally returned her focus to Shand, waiting for him to fully explain his presence.

A most baffling presence.

Shand didn't explain himself immediately. He was still looking at his surroundings. He remembered, years ago, coming to Mordrington before Fenella had taken up residence. It had been a favored home of the Lords of Trastamara with a beautiful garden, a small lake, and a hall that was draped with tapestries and fine furniture. It had been a lovely place and most definitely a woman's place. Shand seemed to remember hearing that Lady de Sauque's mother had been quite fond of it.

But now, it was a shadow of its former self.

The hall smelled like a barnyard. It was devoid of any furnishings and what furniture there was seemed to be broken or half-repaired, certainly not the fine pieces he remembered.

The small number of Scots outside the manse had belied the reality of dozens inside, living in a central courtyard like a great communal encampment. In all, it was a horrific sight, a once fine mansion now destroyed by animals disguised as men.

But Shand kept his focus on Fenella, who had become round and slovenly over the years. He remembered seeing her once, a long time ago, and she had been a lovely, full woman with beautiful hair. Now, she simply looked… old.

Shand found it difficult to believe that Roget kept this piece of baggage on the side when he had a wife as beautiful as Amabella.

Strange, indeed.

"We actually met several years ago, my lady," Shand said, ignoring the Scots who were eyeing him like hungry hunters. "I was with a group of soldiers Roget had brought to Mordrington and we were not formally introduced, so I am not surprised that you do not know me on sight. But I am indeed Shand Bexwell and I was Roget's commander. I have come for a purpose."

Fenella nodded. "That's what my brother has told me, briefly," she said, indicating the sane Scotsman standing next to her. "This is my brother, Win. He told me what ye said when ye arrived. A proposal?"

Shand glanced at the brother before replying. "It seems to

me you know of Roget's passing."

"I know."

"May I offer my… sympathies."

She nodded, but she averted her gaze. There was something there, like guilt or shock or… something. It was difficult to tell. When she finally fixed on him again, her gaze was uncertain. "Ye've not come tae remove me?"

Shand shook his head. "As I told your brother, I have come with a business proposition and it has nothing to do with removing you from Mordrington," he said. "In fact, if you help me, you can keep it for good."

"What do ye want?"

"An introduction to your clan, or at least access to your warriors."

"Ye want men tae attack Trastamara?"

"If they help me, I will tell them how to defeat Trastamara. I know the place quite well."

Fenella looked at him for a moment before sitting down in one of the only chairs left in the hall. Her expression was still full of doubt.

"I dunna understand," she said. "Ye served Roget for years. He spoke of ye, so I know it is true. And now ye want tae ruin his castle?"

Shand cocked an eyebrow. "It is not his castle any longer," he said. "It belongs to his son, a whelp who has been away for years. He has come back to assume his father's command and he is weak. So very weak. It will be a simple thing to overrun Trastamara and gain her wealth – and there is a good deal of wealth to be had."

Fenella pondered that. "But why should ye want tae do that?"

Shand sighed sharply. "As I told your brother, I have been dismissed," he said. "I was humiliated and wrongly sent away.

Instead of respecting my position with Roget and my years of loyalty to the man, I was treated like dirt. That bastard of an heir had no right to do what he did."

"What did he do?"

"He took my command."

"But he is Roget's heir."

Shand was becoming annoyed with the woman. "So he is," he said. "That does not mean he is fit for command, nor does he even deserve it. And what about your sons? You have two with Roget. Do you think these lads will be provided for by Atlas de Sauque? Of course not. They will be shunned and ignored. They will have no part of their father's legacy. Don't you want them to have their due? What is fair to them? Help me and your sons shall have what they deserve."

Fenella regarded him for a moment. "Then this is about vengeance," she said. "Ye want tae punish Roget's heir for treating ye poorly."

Shand's expression tightened. "He may have been Roget's heir, but he did not serve his father as I did. I should be the one in command of Trastamara, not him."

Fenella still wasn't sure about anything. She could see a man before her, a man bent on revenge for an offense against him. Real or imagined was up for debate. She sensed great arrogance from him, and ambition, because he lusted after something he felt was his due.

Fenella had been around enough ambitious men to know one when she saw him. It was a mood, a feeling, or perhaps even the way the man carried himself. Looking at Shand Bexwell, a name she'd heard many times over the years, she could see that he was determined to harm what Roget held dear.

Not that it mattered to Fenella.

In truth, Shand was correct. Her sons would receive nothing from their father's estate and that was something Roget himself had made clear over the years. He considered her sons mistakes and little more. As long as Roget provided a roof over their head and put food in their bellies, Fenella didn't complain. It was as good as she could hope for. But now…

Now, she saw a chance for her children where there hadn't been one before.

Perhaps in death, Roget was about to provide for his bastards in a way he wouldn't in life.

Fenella had never been particularly ambitious. She'd stopped loving Roget years ago and he'd become a habit more than anything, her keeper, her tormentor, and little else. She'd become so very complacent in life, simply living day to day without any excitement or hope. Roget's death at the hands of her brother had not upset her in the least, but she had worried for the future a little, knowing that, at some point, Roget's army would come to remove her. It would be a battle, too, because her brother's men would put up strong resistance.

But none of that had happened yet.

It was possible it wouldn't happen if what Shand was offering was true.

"Very well, Shand Bexwell," she said after a moment. "I'm willing tae listen tae what ye have tae say. I'm sure my brother will, too. And we keep Mordrington."

Shand nodded with satisfaction, realizing he had her interest. "You shall, indeed," he said. "But I keep Trastamara."

"Then what did ye have in mind?"

"Feed me and I shall tell you."

The long, exhausting day turned into a long night.

CHAPTER TEN

Trastamara Castle

"Part of being lord of the castle is understanding the various ways a castle can make money for you," Markus said. "I know you have been taught this, Atlas, and it is especially important. Look at Berwick; we have massive herds of sheep that we sell for both meat and wool, and we also have a small fishing fleet to sell fish to the fishmongers in town. From what I can see from the records your father kept, he hasn't done much other than sheep to create a source of money for the castle. Increasing your money-making potential is something you should look in to. It is important to increase your wealth."

They were in Roget's former solar on the sunset of a cool and calm day, a solar that now belonged to Atlas. In the week since his arrival at Trastamara, Atlas had been forced to grow up very quickly. Not only had he buried his father, but now he was under the tutelage of Markus and Cassius and Damien, who were trying their best to drive their lessons home. The young man had learned a great deal during his years at Castle Questing, but he hadn't learned everything he needed to know about managing a castle.

Now, the lessons were coming fast and furious.

Atlas had no problem grasping the military aspects of Trastamara. He'd been an excellent student when it came to military training. However, he'd never been a very good student with his sums or writing, but he had a sharp mind. He could speak three languages and he was a surprisingly excellent musician with a lute. Therefore, he could be taught, and that's what Markus had been trying hard to do today.

The young man had to grow up quickly.

Atlas sighed heavily. "But why?" he asked. "We have two big sheep herds and my father seemed to make a good deal of money from the sale of the sheep and lambs. I don't understand why I have to make all of the money in the world now."

Markus could see that he was becoming frustrated with his lessons and Markus glanced over at Cassius, who was sitting at the big, cluttered table. They had been working in tandem today, beating the lessons into Atlas' skull. But Cassius, too, could sense the irritation and he shook his head in resignation.

Dealing with the new young lord hadn't been an easy time of it.

"You do not have to make all of the money in the world," Markus said after a moment. "But you must ensure that Trastamara has enough wealth to sustain her for generations to come. That is what your grandfather did and why you have so much coinage at your disposal. But if you do not add to that, you are going to run through it at some point. Then what will your children have?"

Atlas' eyes widened. "I am having children already?"

Markus cocked an eyebrow. "If you want heirs, you must. Not tomorrow, but someday."

Atlas sighed with relief. "I thought you were trying to marry me off already."

"Not yet."

"That is good. But just so you know, I will choose my own

bride."

"Anyone in particular?"

"That is for me to know."

Markus fought off a grin as Cassius tossed a stale crust of bread across the table, hitting Atlas in the shoulder. It was a playful gesture, one meant to ease the tension.

"Do you have one in mind already?" Cassius demanded. "Tell us now."

Atlas brushed the crumbs off his shoulder and looked away. "If I do, that is my affair," he said. "But we were not speaking of brides. We were speaking of sheep. And money."

Cassius and Markus exchanged amused glances, unable to let his comment slide so easily. They'd both come to like Atlas a great deal, a young man who truly wanted to be a good liege now that he'd inherited an empire. His heart was in the right place. Being that Markus and Cassius had younger brothers, they were well equipped to deal with him.

"We are not ready to speak of sheep and money yet," Markus said. "Personally, I want to explore this future Lady de Sauque. Who is this young lady you have your eyes on?"

Atlas shook his head. "I will not tell you."

"So there *is* one."

"Possibly."

"Then tell me about her."

"I will *not*."

"Why? Is it a terrible secret?"

Atlas shrugged. "It is not terrible. I simply do not want to discuss it."

Markus headed over to the hearth, with the low flame snapping softly, and sat on a big chair that was cushioned with leather pillows. As he sat back, he stroked his chin thoughtfully.

"I know for a fact that you have been at Castle Questing for the past six years," he said. "I do not believe you have traveled any further than Kelso, or mayhap even to Carlisle if Tobias had a mind to. You also spent time at Roxburgh Castle with him."

Atlas looked at him. "What does that have to do with anything?"

Markus looked at Cassius. "How many young ladies do we know at de Wolfe properties?"

Cassius scratched his head. "We have many girl cousins who would be eligible," he said. "There is Uncle Scott's daughter, Sorcha. She's very pretty."

Markus nodded his head. "True. And Uncle Troy's daughter, Elspeth."

"She's a beauty."

"There is also our younger sister, Kristiana."

They both suddenly looked at Atlas, glaring at the mere thought that his secret love might be their baby sister. Atlas' eyes widened as he found himself being stared down by two very big, very protective older brothers. He put up his hands.

"I've no inclination towards Lady Kristiana, I swear it," he said. "It is not her!"

Markus and Cassius were pleased to hear the panic in his voice. It was immensely satisfying.

"Well and good that it is not," Markus said, backing down. "When Thora married, we put her husband through hell. The poor man. I'm surprised Callum ever spoke to us again after what we did to him."

Cassius nodded in agreement. "He's a strong man," he said. "He's a de Reyne, and they are mighty."

"He fought back a little."

"He did."

They snickered like naughty boys, leaving Atlas to look at the pair impatiently. "We were speaking of *sheep* and *money*," he stressed again. "I don't want to speak of women!"

Markus held up a hand to him in a silencing gesture. "We

are not finished yet," he said. "We will run through all of the eligible young women we know until you tell us. Now, who else is there? Uncle Blayth's daughter, Isabella."

Cassius nodded firmly. "A beautiful lass," he said. "Aunt Evelyn's daughters Adele and Aline."

Markus frowned. "Pretty, but they have the de Norville look. And attitude. Atlas, you do not want to get mixed up with the de Norvilles. They are mad."

He was jesting and Cassius snorted wickedly. Finally, Atlas rolled his eyes. "Enough," he said. "If I tell you, will you leave me alone?"

Markus and Cassius nodded. "Of course," Markus said. "Who is the young lady who has caught your eye?"

Atlas looked at him reluctantly. "You must promise you will not say anything to your Uncle Scott," he said. "I do not want Warenton to know. Promise me or I will not say another word."

Intrigued, Markus nodded. "You have my vow."

"And mine," Cassius said. "Is it Sorcha, then?"

Atlas shook his head. "Nay," he said. "When I get older, I hope to ask for Lady Caria's hand."

Markus' good humor vanished. So did Cassius'. They looked at each other, shocked by what they were hearing but, in the same breath, perhaps it wasn't that shocking, after all.

Caria de Wolfe.

They had completely neglected to mention the adopted daughter of William and Jordan, having come to them as a newborn. William and Jordan's children were all grown and married at the time little Caria came into their lives, and they'd both doted on her as if she were their very own flesh and blood. Caria had grown up protected, coddled, and loved.

But she wasn't who she seemed.

Very few people in the family knew of Caria's origins, but Markus and Cassius did because their father had told them in the strictest confidence. All of the children of William and Jordan knew, and a few de Norville and Hage senior family members, but it was a closely guarded family secret.

Caria was actually a full-blooded Welsh princess.

Born Tacey de Shera ferch Dafydd, one of the very last of her kind, she had come to William and Jordan through Penelope de Wolfe de Shera, their youngest daughter, who had married a hereditary Welsh king, Bhrodi de Shera. Caria was Bhrodi's niece and had come to William and Jordan for protection against the English crown, who would have liked nothing better than to have her as a hostage, or worse. Caria did not know her origins and the de Wolfe family intended to keep it that way. She was a precious commodity to be protected.

And that meant she was out of Atlas' reach.

"You have excellent taste," Markus said after a moment. "But I do not think Uncle Scott will permit Caria to be married any time soon. I also think he has hopes for a prestigious marriage for her. No offense, Atlas, but I believe my uncle wants an earl or a duke for Caria. I'm afraid she may be out of your reach."

Atlas' jaw ticked stubbornly. "Then he is in for a disappointment," he said. "She loves me."

Markus' eyebrows flew up. "She *what*?"

Atlas was defiant. "She loves me and I love her, and we want to marry someday," he said. "She has seen eighteen years, I have seen seventeen years, so we know that we must wait, but we *will* marry. Mayhap in five years or so. I can provide well for her, Markus, I swear it. You are teaching me right now to provide well for her and I promise I will learn."

Markus stared at him with his mouth hanging open before looking to Cassius, who was equally shocked. The brothers gazed at one another, the reality of the situation with Caria passing in silent words between them. They both knew what

Atlas didn't.

Markus finally closed his mouth.

"I take it that my uncle does not suspect your feelings for Caria," he said.

Atlas shook his head. "He does not." He looked between Markus and Cassius, seeing their shock. "We have loved each other since we first met. There has never been anyone else for me. Why is that so wrong?"

Markus shook his head, unwilling to elaborate on anything with regards to Caria. "It is not wrong to love," he said. "But Caria… I do not think that she is meant for you."

Atlas lifted his chin. "We shall see."

Markus wasn't going to argue with him and neither was Cassius. What had started out as good-natured teasing had turned into something else. Something a bit sad, to be truthful. Atlas had no idea the woman he loved was as rare as a unicorn – a Welsh princess of pure blood.

In fact, it was a little tragic.

Markus changed the subject.

"Mayhap," he said. "Meanwhile, let us return to the subject at hand – sheep and money. There's something else to consider – orchards. Trastamara used to have a great one, hence the name of The Orchard crossing, but your father let those trees go to waste. Berwick has a small orchard that isn't half the size of what Trastamara's used to be and we make a good deal of money from our fruit. I would suggest you revitalize those pear and apple trees because you are literally sitting on a fortune."

Atlas opened his mouth to reply when the door to the solar suddenly creaked, as if someone were leaning against it. All conversation ceased as they looked to the door, listening to it creak and pop. Atlas was the closest. Lifting a finger to his lips to beg for silence, he quietly made his way to the door, put his hand on the latch, and yanked it open.

Several little bodies fell forth.

Alfie was on the top of the pile, quickly scrambling to his feet. Beneath him, his "knights" were all struggling to stand up. Two out of the three had small wooden swords in their hands, a definite improvement from the sticks they used to wield. They had Markus to thank for that, who had found the castle's wheelwright and had the man make small, dull swords from scraps of wood.

But that meant they were properly armed.

And determined.

"We've come to take over the solar and claim it for me!" Alfie declared. "My knights have come to fight you!"

Atlas started to laugh but Aldwin used the flat side of his sword to smack him right across the groin. As Atlas doubled over, startled and in pain, Aldwin and Alfie and another boy named Manley charged into the solar, prepared to fight.

Markus and Cassius rose from their seats.

"Surely there must be a peaceful solution to this," Markus said steadily. "We do not need to fight to the death."

Alfie had bloodlust in his eyes. He pointed at Markus. "You have made us weapons and now we shall use them against you!" he said imperiously. "Give us this chamber. My horse guard needs a place all their own!"

Markus looked at Cassius for his reaction, only to see that the man was trying very hard not to burst into laughter. Seeing his brother's struggles only made Markus want to laugh, too. It was a naughty, bold child who would try to usurp his brother's private chamber.

But it was typical Alfie.

"Your horse guard can have a place of their own, but not this chamber," Markus said. "Go now in peace and I will forget that you barged into a private meeting. Test my patience and I will take your weapons by force."

Rather than intimidate Alfie, Markus' words were a challenge. Markus and Alfie had become very good friends over the past week, spending a good deal of time together as Markus helped train Alfie's horse guard. Not only did they have suitable dull weapons now, but they even had two real helms, both of them having belonged to Roget. In fact, Alfie had one of those helms on his head at this very moment, which made him feel particularly powerful.

"Atlas has this whole castle," Alfie said. "I have nothing. I deserve a chamber of my own, too."

By this time, the sting of being slapped in the groin with a sword had worn off and Atlas came up behind Alfie, grabbing his brother by the neck.

"You little devil," he scolded. "I am going to tell Mother what you have done and…"

"What has he done, Atlas?"

Amabella was now standing in the doorway, a basket of freshly dried clothing in her arms. She had just come in from the kitchen yard and heard the argument. For a moment, no one said a word, and certainly not Markus and Cassius, because they didn't want to get involved in what had simply been a family dust-up. But Atlas still had Alfie by the neck; his grip tightened and he thrust the child at his mother.

"Take this demon-child away from here," he said. "He charged in here and demanded we turn over the solar to him or he would fight us. He needs a swift beating."

Amabella's gaze immediately turned to her youngest son, who was trying to pry his brother's fingers off his neck.

"Did you do this?" she asked with underlying hazard in her tone.

Alfie was unrepentant. "Atlas has everything and I have nothing," he said. "I want a chamber for my horse guard. I am the king!"

Atlas let go of his brother and gave him a kick to the buttocks. "You are *not* the king," he said. "Get out of here."

Alfie didn't take to be kicked kindly. He rubbed his bum before rushing his brother, little fists balled, and Atlas was forced to push him away by his head. Alfie landed on his buttocks, but he didn't stay there for long. He came up swinging.

"Enough," Amabella snapped softly, reaching out to grab Alfie by the arm before he could make contact with his brother. She yanked the boy from the chamber. "You will behave yourself, Alphonse. One more offense against your brother and you will no longer be able to play with your horse guard. I will send them all away."

That was a serious threat for the king. Alfie looked at his mother, trying very hard not to weep now that he realized that he was thwarted.

"But I need them," he sniffled.

"Then you will behave yourself," Amabella said sternly. "Now, take your knights and go back to the kitchen yard. Do as I say."

Alfie turned to his knights, standing fearfully near the door, and motioned to them. With hung heads, the children followed their king from the chamber, ashamed of their failed coup.

Amabella stood in the doorway, arms folded across her chest, her disapproval evident at the would-be raiders. When Alfie and his cohorts trickled through the entry and out into the bailey, she turned to the men in the chamber.

"My apologies," she said. "I hope they did not disturb you overly."

Atlas was standing the closest to his mother and answered her. "We can withstand his invasion attempts," he said. "But he is very bold, Mama. He is going to get into trouble when he gets older."

"He will be fostering by then," Markus said, his gaze on Amabella. "He is young, still, but in another couple of years, he will go off to foster and they will temper that boldness. Let him be young while he still can. He has a fearlessness that few dare."

Atlas shook his head at his brash, fearless brother, while Amabella smiled.

"I hope that always holds true," she said. "And thank you for being so understanding of him."

Markus simply nodded his head while Amabella collected her basket again and headed about her business. But even after she left the chamber, Markus' thoughts were on her.

And that was the end of his attempts to school Atlas for the afternoon.

These days, Markus could think of little else *but* Amabella. The past week at Trastamara had been mostly spent with Atlas, especially since his father departed. Patrick seemingly had no issue leaving Markus behind for a time to help Atlas acclimate, so Markus had taken command for the most part, helping Atlas most of the time and Alfie some of the time. He genuinely liked the de Sauque lads.

The lasses were another issue altogether.

Aleanor still turned pale with fright when she saw him, but she was getting better about it. Ambra was nearly as bad as Alfie with her demands for his time, but he didn't really mind. When she wasn't with her nurse, she was with her mother, and sometimes she would slip her little hand into his big one as he went about his duties, following him.

That meant her mother sometimes followed, too.

Even if he was simply around Amabella, he was content. She was very polite with him, warm most of the time, but she had yet to cross that line that she would consider showing romantic interest in him. In fact, she treated him pleasantly and respectfully, as one would the son of her liege. But after a week of being pleasantly, politely, and respectfully treated, he was becoming dissatisfied with it.

It wasn't as if he weren't the most handsome, capable knight on the border.

But Amabella wasn't falling at his feet for some reason.

He was thinking that he wanted to change that.

As Cassius took over the discussion on expanding Trastamara's agricultural empire with a revitalized orchard near The Orchard crossing, Markus stood by the lancet window overlooking the bailey. He saw Alfie and his horse guard as they retreated to the kitchen yard and he stood there long enough to see Amabella leave the keep and head towards the great hall.

Tonight, the feast in the hall was going to be the start of something different.

He hadn't remained at Trastamara out of the goodness of his heart. In the beginning, it had been out of his seeming infatuation with Amabella, but he remained because the infatuation had turned into something else. He wasn't sure what.

But he was going to summon the courage to find out.

TRASTAMARA HAD SETTLED into a routine with shocking speed now that Roget was gone.

As the Lord of Trastamara, Roget had treated the evening feast like court and only his favored were allowed to attend. The great hall was fairly large, enough to accommodate at least two hundred men, but Roget had only allowed a select number of favorite soldiers in, mostly men who had come into service after he'd inherited his properties from Amabella's father. He considered those men loyal to him and the men who once served Alonzo Hemada Abril to be questionable.

As Markus had discovered, there has been a definite hierarchy when it came to the soldiers at Trastamara. Atlas, however, felt everyone should be treated equally and even though the hall wasn't big enough for all of his soldiers, they were all invited on a first-come, first-served basis.

Men who had served Atlas' grandfather now found themselves with a seat at the lord's table once again while the smaller force of Roget's men were split. Some were inside, some were outside, eating their meals around a big bonfire that burned near the kitchen yard.

But all of them were unhappy with the new lord's rules.

Markus had seen within the first two days that the Trastamara soldiers were starting to split into two factions – those who had served Alonzo and those who had been brought in by Roget. It was concerning, something he expressed to Cassius and Damien and the other de Wolfe men, but it wasn't something he expressed to Atlas. He didn't want to create a situation in the young man's mind until they could see if it righted itself.

But a week later, supper on this cold, clear evening was shaping up to exhibit the same division of men – Alonzo's against Roget's. As Markus approached the hall with Cassius, he could see the same Roget loyalists around their bonfire in the bailey, separating themselves from the rest of the men in the hall.

It had become a familiar sight.

"What do you intend to do about the army separating itself like that," Cassius said, gesturing to the men around the bonfire. "We've been watching this for the better part of a week. An army in factions is ripe for defeat."

Markus knew that. "As you know, I have refrained from

saying anything to Atlas because I had hoped the situation would resolve itself," he said. "I am still hoping it will ease, with time, especially once they see what a fine lord Atlas will be."

"Do you think we should send word to Papa?"

Markus shrugged. "If it is still like this next week, mayhap," he said. "Meanwhile, it bears watching. We must think of things to draw the men together, like drills or exercises. We cannot let them separate like the chaff from the wheat."

"I think the time has come to tell Atlas what is happening. It is his right, after all."

Markus reluctantly agreed. At that point, they entered the hall, which was half-full with soldiers. Damien and Kieran were already at one of the tables along with Alfie and Atlas. As Markus and Cassius drew near, they could see that Aleanor and Ambra were there, also, but they were at the head of the table, with Ambra seated upon her sister's lap.

Markus made his way down to the end of the table.

"Good eve to you, my ladies," he greeted the sisters as he sat on the very end of the big table. "It is agreeable to see you here tonight."

Ambra had a big hunk of bread and butter in her hand. She was chewing happily, with butter smeared on her cheek.

"Mama said we could eat with everyone," she said. "Cook is making chicken with cinnamon and onions in sauce. It is a stew. You will like it!"

Markus smiled at the young lady with the culinary inclination. "I will?" he said. "Is that one of your dishes?"

Ambra nodded firmly. "I was in the kitchen and I tasted it," she said. "It is very good. And she is making rice with raisins."

Markus nodded as he reached out to pour himself a cup of wine from the pitcher on the table. The entire week had been an adventure in culinary dishes, things he'd never had before in combination, all of them a creation of Ambra's imagination.

There had been mutton and eggs with honey and pepper, more stewed mutton with clove and vinegar, and other dishes he couldn't even recall because every night was something different.

Everything revolved around mutton or fowl or fish, because those were the most readily available, and Ambra liked her cinnamon and cloves and onions and honey, so there was a good deal of that as well, but Markus never thought he'd eat food concocted by a five year old and like it.

But he had.

"I am certain it will be delicious," he said. "You will make some man a fine wife someday and feed him until he is so fat, he will not be able to get through the door."

He grinned as he said it and Ambra crowed at his humor. "I don't want a husband!"

"Why not?" Markus asked. "Remember that my brother, Cassius, has expressed an interest in marrying you."

Ambra looked across the table at Cassius, smearing more butter on her cheek when she took a bite of her bread.

"He is too old," she said flatly, which was what she said the first time the subject had come up. "But he can marry Aleanor. She needs a husband."

Aleanor, who had thus far remained invisible at the table, suddenly appeared stricken with fear to hear her name mentioned. Her eyes darted to Cassius, sitting across the table.

"I… I do not need husband," she said quickly. "I am not old enough. Mama said I do not need to marry until I am ready, and I am not ready."

That was the most Markus had ever heard come out of her mouth at one time and she had only uttered the words because she was so terrified. He put up a soothing hand.

"Truthfully, Cassius is not ready, either," he said. "Not to worry, my lady. We are not trying to foist my brother upon you."

Cassius, who had been speaking with young Kieran, heard his name. He turned his attention to Markus, frowning.

"Who is foisting whom?" he said. "You are the one who should marry, not me. You are the heir and you need to make a gaggle of little heirs."

Markus opened his mouth to reply but he caught movement out of the corners of his eyes, turning to see that they were being joined by Amabella. She only had one trencher in her hand this time and she put it in front of Markus as several servants spilled through the servant's entrance bearing more food and drink.

But Markus had eyes only for Amabella.

"I see that you have only brought one meal with you," he said. "And now, you shall sit and enjoy the feast while the servants do the rest. I did not send all the way to Berwick for servants only to have you continue doing their job."

Amabella smiled at him, some uncertainty in her expression. "And I told you that you did not have to do that," she said. "I was not troubled by helping in the kitchens."

"And I told you that *I* was troubled that you did," Markus said, moving down the bench so she could sit. "You are the Lady of Trastamara and you should not be serving your guests or the army. You should be charming us with your wit and graciousness."

He wasn't cruel about it, but he was firm. The warm glimmer in his eyes told Amabella that he truly wasn't irritated with her. In truth, he had that warm glimmer in his eyes when he looked at her most of the time, an expression of approval and friendship, something she was coming to long for every time she saw him. It had been years since she'd last seen a gleam like that in a man's eyes where it pertained to her and she wasn't even entirely sure Roget ever had that gleam.

But Markus did.

Sweet, beautiful, strong, and brilliant Markus.

The past week for Amabella had been one of bliss. Her days with Roget seemed like another lifetime ago even though it had only been a few days. Eight to be exact. But those eight days had changed her life in ways she couldn't have possibly imagined, and Markus de Wolfe had been at the head of it.

He'd been her knight in shining armor.

It wasn't that he spent an over amount of time with her, because he hadn't. His time had been spent with Atlas, and rightfully so. Once the Earl of Berwick departed, Markus took command and he'd done a great deal with Atlas, and Trastamara in general, in that short amount of time.

The servants had been part of those efforts.

He didn't like that Roget had treated Amabella like a servant, so two days after his father left, Markus sent word to Berwick for servants – kitchen servants and maids, mostly. In response, his mother, Lady Berwick, had sent ten kitchen servants and kitchen helpers, plus four maids, all of them reporting directly to Lady de Sauque.

Now, Amabella had a veritable army of servants under her command and she was still trying to become accustomed to it. She was so used to doing for herself that to have others doing for her had been a drastic change. Markus, for his part, saw her as a woman to be treated with respect and he was doing everything possible to set that example.

Amabella couldn't help but adore the man for it.

Aye, she adored him. She adored him as someone who had come to her rescue and the rescue of her family. She adored him as one does when something is brilliant and unobtainable, a beacon of hope and strength that is the standard for others to follow. That was how she viewed Markus. She was so very grateful to the man.

And so very unworthy of him.

She knew that. She'd always known that. He was handsome and charming, and she had watched him with her younger children to see how sweet he was with them. He was the father her children should have, not the distant bastard who had fathered them. Ambra and Alfie adored him and even Aleanor was coming out of her shell. At least she was in the hall for the feast, which was something she never did. But she was here now.

Amabella couldn't have been more grateful.

It was amazing how life opened up without Roget to stifle them.

All of them.

"I promise that I am not serving the army," she said after a moment's reflection. "But I would still like to oversee the meal. It is still my table and my reputation is at stake."

Markus nodded with some reluctance. "Very well," he said. "If you must. But let the servants do the heavy work. That is not for your delicate hands."

Amabella flushed, looking at her hands. She turned them over, inspecting them. Once, they had been soft and white, but working in the kitchens without benefit of servants had seen them turn red and chapped. She even had calluses on her palms. Tucking her hands away so Markus couldn't see them, she forced a smile.

"I swear that I am not working any longer," she said. "You have been very kind to do everything you have done for us. I am sorry that we have been such trouble. It seems that when you came here, there was much to fix."

Markus took a long drink of his wine. "It was hardly a bother," he said. "Atlas is coming along nicely in his indoctrination, by the way. Today, we discussed reviving the orchards down by the river. Your father planted those, did he not?"

Amabella shook her head. "Actually, my grandfather plant-ed those trees many years ago," she said. "It was quite a thriving orchard until I married Roget, but he did not see the value of it. I fear it has been sorely neglected."

"It has," he said. "But those trees still bear fruit, I would think."

"They do," she said. "But we do not harvest them. Peasants come from the villages and take what they can."

"That is going to change," Markus said. "Atlas sees the value in revitalizing those trees and making money from the produce."

Amabella reached for a cup of wine but Markus was faster and handed it to her. "Thank you," she said as she collected her cup. "And I am glad you spoke to Atlas about the orchard. It used to be a very important part of Trastamara. I can remember riding my pony in the orchard as a child when the trees were starting to flower. The smell of the blossoms is one of my best memories."

"Mayhap it shall be again."

She smiled at him, sipping at her cup. The conversation lagged, but it wasn't unpleasant. Amabella couldn't help but notice that Markus didn't touch his meal until she was served and until his brother was served. Then, he delved into the chicken stew with gusto, but the wait had been polite manners on his part. It had been a long time since she had seen a man with such manners.

She'd almost forgotten they existed.

As soon as he started, however, Ambra climbed off her sister's lap and made her way to Markus without hesitation or reservation. She pushed herself right onto his lap as he was sopping up the stew with bread and began picking pieces of chicken off his trencher and shoving them into her mouth.

"Ambra," Amabella scolded softly, reaching out to pull her

daughter from the man's lap. "Come and sit with me, *querida*. You can have some of my food."

But Markus put out a hand to stop her. "Not to worry," he said. "I've become accustomed to sharing my meal with Lady Ambra. She is welcome to what I have."

Amabella sighed reluctantly as the little girl settled on his lap again and literally took food out of his hand to put in her mouth. Markus simply picked up another piece and ate it. No fuss, no scolding. He let Ambra do as she pleased.

All the while, Amabella found herself watching the interaction, watching her daughter do something that she normally wouldn't ever do with her father. She was comfortable with Markus, so much so that she was planted on his lap as if she'd been doing it her entire life. What she saw was a child starved for fatherly attention, which Markus had provided in the short time that he'd been there.

God, it warmed her heart to see it.

She wondered if Markus would ever know what these few short days had meant to them.

To her.

The meal progressed uneventfully and, across the table, even Atlas and Alfie were getting along. Cassius was sitting between them, so Amabella suspected he might have been the reason, but she ate her meal in silence, watching Alfie try to convince Cassius to join his horse guard. Cassius had a good manner with children, much as his brother did, but he was more apt to show less patience with a demanding little boy.

When Alfie tried to steal bread off his trencher, Cassius retaliated by taking the child's entire trencher and pouring it onto his. That left Alfie with no food, a soggy trencher, and a frown as the table roared with laughter. But Cassius was only jesting with him; he returned what he took and then some, but after that, Alfie was no longer willing to steal bread from the man.

In truth, it had been a wonderful meal. Her children were enjoying the company of the de Wolfe knights and even Aleanor had a conversation with Markus about the food she was eating. He asked her what she liked to eat best and they actually had a conversation about it. Amabella couldn't have been more astounded.

It seemed that all of her children were willing to listen to Markus.

She found herself wishing he would never leave. A foolish thought, but one she couldn't seem to shake.

A secret wish and nothing more.

Sweets and nuts were brought out at the end of the meal, something that all four children pounced on. Especially Aleanor; she loved her honey puffs and sweets, so when the servants brought out fried dough balls filled with figs and basted with honey, she began shoving them into her mouth at an alarming rate.

"Allie," Amabella said. "Slow down, *querida*. You are going to make yourself ill."

Aleanor looked startled that her mother had noticed her greedy eating. She had one in her hand, halfway to her mouth, but it was frozen there as she debated what to do. Her mouth was too full to speak. Before she could make a decision, or even swallow, Alfie plucked the dough ball from her fingers and devoured it.

Aleanor was crushed.

"Alfie," Markus said. "A good king does not steal from his subjects. Mayhap you should have asked your sister if you could have her sweet before taking it."

Alfie considered that, realizing he hadn't done something very kingly in that gesture. "But she already has many of them in her mouth," he pointed out. "I have not had so many."

As Markus glanced at Amabella to see what her reaction was, he caught a glimpse of the hall entry. Four soldiers had just entered and it took him a moment to realize they were the soldiers who had been sent to escort Shand when he departed Trastamara.

Instantly, he was on his feet.

Cassius, noting his brother's posturing, stood up as well. "What is amiss?" he asked.

Markus nodded his head in the direction of the hall entry. "Look," he said quietly. "Those men were Bexwell's escort. They have returned."

He was on the move, followed closely by Cassius. When Damien saw the returned escort, he, too, stood up, followed by Kieran and finally Atlas. The five of them made their way over to the escort that was just starting to scope out the chamber for those in command. When they saw Markus approaching, they made their way towards him.

"My lord," the soldier in the lead spoke. He was a man who had been with Berwick for many years, with red hair and a grizzled appearance. "Has the earl gone home?"

Markus nodded. "Shortly after you left," he said. "Well? Is Bexwell away?"

The soldier sighed heavily, wiping a gloved hand over his dirty face. "We are not certain, my lord."

"What do you mean?"

"May we speak in private?"

Markus didn't like the man's tone or his question. It suggested something ominous.

He lifted a dark eyebrow.

"I think we'd better."

CHAPTER ELEVEN

A MABELLA WATCHED MARKUS lead his knights, Atlas, and a few soldiers from the hall.

"Curious," she muttered. "I wonder where they are going?"

The only person in earshot was Aleanor, who had stuffed herself silly on the fig pastries and was wallowing in gluttonous misery.

"Who, Mama?" she asked.

Amabella's gaze lingered on the hall entry, peering through the smoke and the heat of the hall, before turning away. "Your brother and Viscount Ravensdowne," she said. "They have all departed."

Aleanor was uninterested. She yawned. "I would like to leave, too," she said. "Mama, may we?"

Amabella looked around the table. There was really no reason to remain now that all of the men had left. Alfie was yawning and Ambra was seated on her mother's lap, rubbing her eyes. Amabella finally stood up.

"Come along, then," she said, cradling Ambra in her arms. "To bed, everyone."

Alfie was too tired to argue and Aleanor simply followed in silent obedience. They made their way out of the hall and out into the crisp night, heading towards the keep. By the time Amabella hit the stairs leading up into the structure, Ambra was already fast asleep.

The three maids that had been sent from Berwick were in charge of the keep and having the extra help to manage it had changed the keep dramatically. Usually, it was only Amabella and Savia tending to the keep – cleaning and sweeping, tending the children, making sure the chambers had enough peat for the fire.

With the additions of the maids, however, the chambers were spotless. The women had scrubbed the entire building from top to bottom and fresh rushes were in every chamber, bed linens had been washed, mattresses re-stuffed, hearths lit, and any number of details that needed to be done and seldom were. Therefore, Amabella entered the keep that smelled like fresh rushes and was blissfully warm because the hearth in the entry, which was almost never lit, had been cleaned out and stoked.

For the first time in years, it felt like a home.

As soon as Amabella came through the entry door, Savia was waiting to take the younger children and Amabella handed them over. Savia would not eat in the hall, given that she was a servant and servants did not sup with their lords. But she diligently waited for her charges to return, and Amabella watched the old nurse take the two younger children up the stairs.

"Mama?"

Amabella turned to Aleanor, standing next to her. She smiled, reaching out to smooth errant hair from her daughter's face.

"What is it, *querida*?"

Aleanor went to her mother, putting her arms around her waist and holding her tightly. It seemed to Amabella as if

Aleanor needed to be held, so she put her arms around her and kissed her head.

"What's wrong, Allie?" she asked softly.

Aleanor sighed heavily. "I don't know," she said. "I feel… I feel as if everything is so different now that Father is gone. Don't you feel that way?"

Amabella had been thinking the exact same thing in the hall. "I do," she said. "Things *are* different. Atlas is going to make a magnificent lord. Lord Ravensdowne and his knights are going to see to it. Life will be better for us, I promise."

Aleanor lifted her head, looking at her mother. "Must I marry soon?"

Amabella grinned at the unexpected question. "Why do you ask?"

"Because Ambra said so," she said, somewhat annoyed. "She told Lord Ravensdowne that I need a husband. I don't have to marry soon, do I?"

Amabella laughed softly and turned her daughter for the keep entry. She put her arm around the girl's shoulders.

"Walk with me," she said. "Let us speak of your future while Savia puts your brother and sister to bed. It is a lovely night to walk and talk. I do not think we have done much of that."

That was true because Aleanor didn't like to leave her chamber, or the keep for that matter. She had been a sickly child, and immature in her behavior, but she was growing up now. Things like marriage would be on her mind. Amabella led her daughter back out into the crisp night, with a million stars overhead, spread across the black sky.

"Don't you want to marry, Allie?" Amabella asked softly as they headed to the southeasterly part of the bailey. "You should not let it frighten or intimidate you. Marriage is nothing to fear."

Aleanor pondered that statement in direct contrast from

what she had witnessed with her own parents. "Are you glad you got married?"

That was a question with many answers. Amabella gave her daughter a gentle hug. "I am very glad I had you and Atlas and Alfie and Ambra."

Aleanor looked up at her. "But Father was not kind to you."

Amabella didn't reply for a moment. There was some embarrassment in her own daughter commenting on the issue of her marriage to Roget, but it wasn't as if it had been a secret. Aleanor was a bright girl and she'd seen how Roget had treated her mother. His inherent apathy was how he'd treated his entire family.

"Not all men are like your father," she finally said. "There are men who are very kind to their wives and children."

"Will you marry a man who is kind to us?"

It was a heartbreaking question, one that brought a lump to Amabella's throat. She could hear how starved her daughter was for a father-figure to be kind to her, just like the rest of her children were. Even though Atlas pretended otherwise, she suspected he longed for such a thing, too. He was a sensitive young man.

She felt like a failure.

"I think *you* should marry a man who is kind to you," she said. "I have been married; I do not need to marry again. But you will, someday, and we will make sure he is very kind and handsome. Ambra, too. We will select a kind and handsome husband for her, as well."

Aleanor was still looking at her mother, still lingering on the subject of a kind husband. "Will you not be lonely when we marry and leave you?"

Amabella smiled. "Of course I will," she said. "But you will bring your grandchildren to me and then I shall not be lonely."

The very idea of grandchildren made Aleanor blush. "I am

not certain I want babies."

"Why not?"

"Because they will be like Alfie and Ambra, and they will run around and scream."

Amabella laughed softly. "I assure you that they will be a joy," she said. "It is different when it is your own children."

"Mama, why do you not want to marry a kind man now that Father is gone?"

They were back on that subject again and Amabella thought she'd better give her daughter a reasonable answer or it might keep coming up. It wasn't that she didn't want to marry someone kind; she did. But the shining example held up to her of male perfection since Roget's demise was Markus and she wasn't sure she'd ever find a man as handsome and flawless as he was. Now that she'd seen what a man could be, she wasn't sure that she could accept anything less.

Markus de Wolfe *was* perfection.

"I am old, Allie," she finally said. "I was married to your father for twenty years."

"How old were you when you married him?"

"I had seen twenty years."

"But that does not make you too old, Mama."

Amabella shrugged. "It makes me old enough," she said. "I have had my time to be married and I am content to be a widow, watching watch my children grow and thrive. And I will be here to help Atlas manage Trastamara. I shall be quite busy with that."

"Too busy for a husband?"

"*Too* busy," she said, giving her daughter a squeeze to essentially signal the end of that subject. "You needn't worry about me, *querida*. Please. I will be fine."

Aleanor got the hint. They were over by the southeast tower now, casting shadows in the bright moonlight. The southeast tower housed men, mostly, but the lower floor was also the armory. They could hear voices of men inside the tower as they continued walking, men inside the tower, laughing and probably drinking. They sounded quite happy.

Since Roget's death, everyone at Trastamara seemed… happier. Certainly, Amabella and her children were. The night seemed deeper, the stars brighter.

Everything seemed brighter.

Amabella was feeling content and grateful to be walking with her daughter and having a meaningful conversation, right on the cusp of Aleanor's womanhood. Amabella was glad that Roget wouldn't be around to influence his eldest daughter's marriage. God only knew what kind of a husband he would select for her. As they reached the end of the tower and Amabella turned them around to head back for the keep, they heard a voice behind them.

"Lady de Sauque."

Amabella came to a pause. Three men were coming out of the shadows of the wall, heading in her direction. A quick assessment of the men beneath the silver moonlight told Amabella that these men were part of the crew Roget had brought in when he'd taken command. She knew at least one of them because he was missing an eye. These men weren't loyal to her. Only to her husband.

They were also rough, crude, and selfish. She'd always stayed far away from the army and particularly far away from Roget's men, but tonight, that seemed to have changed. Her heart began to race, just a little. Something told her there might be trouble.

She didn't want her daughter involved.

"Allie," she whispered. "Run away. Find Lord Ravensdowne or one of the other knights and send them to me."

Aleanor looked like a frightened rabbit. Her eyes were big

and she was beginning to cower from the unfamiliar men.

"But… Mama…"

"Go. *Hurry!*"

Amabella gave her daughter a shove towards the keep and Aleanor nearly stumbled. But she started to run, as fast as her shaking legs would carry her, because her mother told her that she should. Somewhere, she had to find that courage buried deep inside. She didn't even really know if she had it, but she tried.

Fear, at this moment, dictated courage.

As her daughter bolted off, Amabella faced the soldiers.

"What can I do for you, good men?" she asked steadily.

The three of them came to within a few feet of her. "Do you even know who I am, Lady de Sauque?"

It was the one-eyed soldier speaking. Amabella looked at him. "I do not know your name," she said. "My husband would not let me speak with his men and he did not tell me your names, so I only know that I have seen you."

The man's gaze lingered on her for a moment. "I'm Mickleton," he said. "Where's Shand?"

Amabella shook her head. "I do not know," she said honestly. "I was not part of the decision to send him away. You have been at Trastamara long enough to know that I have no control over anything. That still holds true."

The soldiers looked at each other, looks of disgust and frustration on their features. "Berwick," Mickleton grumbled. "He did this."

"If you are truly concerned, then you need to speak with Viscount Ravensdowne and not me," Amabella said. "If that will be all, I must return inside."

"That is *not* all," Mickleton said, considerably more unfriendly than he had been before. "No offense intended against your son, Lady de Sauque, but Shand Bexwell is a fine commander. He has been our commander for ten years and we don't want another one."

Amabella was trying to move away from them, very discreetly, one tiny step at a time. "As you well know, I have nothing to do with that," she said. "I did not make the decision to send Shand away, but I will tell you this – Atlas is Roget's heir. He is your commander now. If you do not wish to serve him, then you can leave. Nothing is holding you here."

Mickleton frowned. "Is that what Shand was told?" he said. "That he could serve the boy or leave? There's something to be said for loyalty, Lady de Sauque. You live in your keep with your fine food and warmth and money, and you never have to worry about your future. Well, I've put in too much of my time here at Trastamara and I want something for it. I'll not leave until I get it."

They took a step in her direction and Amabella took an obvious step back. "Your argument is not with me," she said, her heart beginning to pound faster. "Speak to Ravensdowne of your issues."

Mickleton came to a halt when he realized she was moving away from him. But the message in his eye was obvious; it was about to become a hunt, with the hunter chasing down the prey. He wanted something and he was going to get it. Lady de Sauque, alone, would be the perfect bargaining chip. There had been trouble brewing for days now, ever since Shand was sent away, so the moment was ripe.

There might not ever be another chance like this.

"I am speaking to you," he said after a moment. "You are the lady they are listening to now. I have seen how Ravensdowne listens to you when you speak. Roget's heir listens to you also. You will give them our message."

Amabella continued to back away. "What message is that?"

Mickleton suddenly sprinted at her, grabbing her by the

arm before she could get away. She yelped as his fingers dug into her.

"You tell Ravensdowne and your lad that there are many of us who don't like how things have changed," he growled, his foul breath in her face. "We are the men who were loyal to Roget and we deserve consideration."

Amabella was trying desperately to pull her arm from his grip. "What consideration?" she demanded. "Be plain."

He yanked on her to stop her from trying to escape. "We want the hall returned to us," he snarled. "We won't eat in the bailey, with no roof, like animals. We…"

He was cut off by movement coming from the keep. Men were spilling out, rushing in his direction, and he could see the flash of weapons in the moonlight. Realizing the knights were coming for him, he tried to pull Amabella with him so he could retreat into the tower and use her as a hostage, but Amabella had seen the knights, too.

Help was on the way.

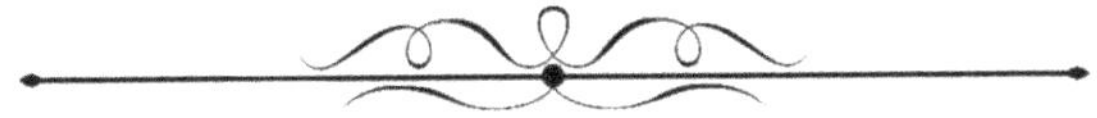

"WHAT HAPPENED TO Bexwell?"

Markus asked the question as soon as they were behind the closed doors of the solar. Having brought Bexwell's escort to the keep for some privacy, he faced the scruffy, redheaded soldier while Atlas, Cassius, Damien, and Kieran stood around, listening carefully.

The red-haired soldier sighed heavily.

"We escorted him as far south as Alnwick," he said. "We all spent the night at a tavern in town but before dawn, the four of us went to the northern end of town to ensure Bexwell didn't try to come north again. We waited much of the day and didn't see him, so I sent one of my men to the livery to see if the man had departed and the livery keep told the story of Bexwell riding north and spying us before turning south. If you know that area, my lord, you know it is relatively flat. There is a moor to the west. The livery keep said he saw Bexwell head west through the moor."

Markus cocked an eyebrow. "Did you follow his trail?"

The old soldier nodded wearily. "We did, to the next town on the westerly road."

"And?"

"And there is a small village at the crossroads of the wester-ly road and a road heading north, near Cartingdon," he said. "The villagers know strangers and they told us that they saw Bexwell head north along that road. We followed fresh horse tracks until the rains came and washed them away. After that, we could do no more. We hurried back to tell you that the man headed north again. You've not seen him?"

Markus grunted unhappily. He dragged a hand over his face in frustration, turning to see how Cassius and Damien were dealing with the news. Cassius sighed sharply and shook his head while Damien stepped forward, focusing on the soldier he'd served with for twenty years.

Damien knew the man and knew that he was no fool. If Bexwell got away, then it was because Bexwell was clever about it, which seemed to follow Shand Bexwell's pattern.

The man was sly and subversive.

"We've not seen Bexwell, but that does not mean he is not around," Damien said. "How far did you follow his trail?"

The soldier considered the question. "Halfway to the village of Wooler," he said. "It was a long ride, but the rains came and washed away the fresh horse trail we'd been following. After that, we had no choice but to hurry back here."

"But where could he possibly go?" Markus wanted to know. "He knows that he is not welcome at any Trastamara property."

"Does he?" Damien said, looking at him. "Have you sent word to Mordrington? What about the other properties? There are a few, aren't there?"

Markus conceded the point. "There are," he said. "I did not send word to them, never dreaming that Bexwell might actually try to go to one. He'd be foolish to try. But our allies have received word about it. I made sure to tell them of the situation should Bexwell show up on their doorstep."

"He knows this entire area very well," Atlas said. "He must; he served my father for ten years. He knows where he can go and hide."

Markus scratched his head. "But why? Why would he return to a Trastamara property? To try and turn what few soldiers are manning the outposts against the new lord?"

Damien, older and wiser, and having seen much of the evil men could inflict upon each other, simply shook his head.

"Who is to say?" he said as Atlas scratched his head worriedly. "One thing is for certain – he can only be up to no good if he has returned to these lands, so we must be vigilant. We must be very cautious of young Atlas because if Bexwell manages to remove him, he could possibly try to decimate the entire family and try to take control of Trastamara."

That was what Markus was thinking, only he didn't want to frighten Atlas. The young man had enough to deal with, and adjust to, without a rogue knight out to kill him.

"Then we should send word to all Trastamara properties about this," Markus said, looking at Atlas. "Would you not agree?"

Atlas was trying very hard not to look unnerved about the situation. "I do," he said. "I…"

He was cut off when there was a great pounding on the

solar door, a frantic beating until Kieran opened the panel to reveal Aleanor standing there, her pale face flushed. She stumbled into the chamber, wringing her hands.

"My mother," she gasped. "There are men – out in the bailey – they will hurt her!"

Immediately, everyone was rushing towards the door, towards Aleanor, who shrank away as men rushed in her direction. Cassius happened to be the closest to her and he reached out, gently grasping her by the arm.

"Where, sweetheart?" he demanded softly, swiftly. "Where are they?"

Aleanor looked at him, wide-eyed and terrified. "That way," she said, pointing with her free arm. "The tower near the smithy stalls."

Markus was already out the door, drawing his weapon. "The southeast tower," he said. "*Move.*"

Markus de Wolfe's commands were not meant to be disobeyed. The knights unsheathed weapons, charging out into the night. Markus was in the lead with Cassius right behind him. He was able to see enough beneath the silver moon to see Amabella hit a soldier holding her arm and then run away in his direction. He could also see a group of soldiers behind her, gathered by the tower.

Rage surged.

He didn't know why she was on this side of the bailey, alone. There would be time for questions later. All that mattered was that he punished the men who assaulted her.

Kill them.

Markus paused long enough to ask Amabella if she was well and when she nodded her head quickly, he charged after the other knights, now beginning to engage the soldiers who first tried to run, but then decided to turn and fight.

But it turned out to be more of a fight than Markus had

expected.

After slaying a soldier with a missing eye and wounding two others, more soldiers spilled out of the tower, armed. Because it was dark, they really couldn't see what was going on other than men fighting and killing in silver moonlight. That made it confusing, and chaotic, and Markus and the knights had to shout to the men pouring from the tower to drop their weapons so they wouldn't kill each other.

But that didn't work very well.

It took Markus and the others a short time to realize that the men holed up in the southeast tower were those loyal to Roget. They didn't *want* to stop fighting. When they saw their colleagues down, they went after Markus with a vengeance, and Atlas was forced to run for reinforcements from the de Wolfe troops.

Reinforcements weren't long in coming and the sheer number overwhelmed those from the tower. In short order, the situation was under control, but Markus had his men enter the tower to clean it out, once and for all, of any remaining soldiers who happened to be loyal to Roget.

The time had come to merge the army or purge it.

Some men didn't seem to want to fight and surrendered immediately, but there were those who were quite vocal about the situation and the way they'd been treated. Between the de Wolfe troops and the four knights and Atlas, they managed to sequester those who surrendered easily and those who seemed to want to fight until the death.

When all was said and done, there were four wounded, two dead including Mickleton, and about forty men who had been separated into two groups. The dissident group was herded to the gatehouse while the group that surrendered was kept outside of the tower where Atlas had a few words to say to them.

Atlas gave them the opportunity to leave in peace with the others who were being thrown out or remaining at Trastamara under supervision. All of them chose to remain with supervision, which meant they would probably be reduced to serving the quartermasters or even in the kitchens, but it was better than being thrown out into the cold, cruel world.

Their loyalty to the Roget faction only went so far.

When the men were finally allowed to return to the southeast tower under guard, Markus turned to Atlas.

"You did well," he told the young man. "I will admit that I suspected something like this might happen. There are men who are still quite loyal to your father, so this was not unexpected."

Atlas watched as the men were directed back to the tower for the night, with Cassius and Damien and Kieran shouting at them and shoving them when they did not move fast enough.

"I am not entirely sure I want to keep them on," he said. "Men are hard to change sometimes. I remember hearing Tobias say that. I wonder if those men are capable of giving me their loyalty at all. I will not be like my father."

Markus shook his head, but his expression was one of pride. Atlas wasn't his son or brother or even a relative, but he found pride in the young man and how well he'd handled the situation.

"Nay, you are not like your father," he said quietly. "Thank God for that. But you did the benevolent thing by giving those men a chance to change their loyalties. That was quite lordly of you."

Atlas looked at him, a smile flickering across his lips at the compliment. "I hope they will take the chance."

"You have done all you can do."

"I have been thinking about something else, Markus."

"What is that?"

Atlas turned in the direction of the keep and Markus followed. "Mordrington," he said. "As you are aware, my father took it from my mother and kept his mistress there. I want it back and I want her out of it, and anyone else who is living there. They, too, are loyal to my father. I must purge them and let my mother have the manse returned to her."

"That is a good decision."

"But there is something more."

"What is it?"

Atlas cocked his head. "If those at Mordrington are loyal to my father, and Shand is loyal to my father, do you think he might go to Mordrington?"

"I suppose anything is possible."

"It seems to me that he might," Atlas said. "You mentioned other Trastamara properties and there are a few, but I do not know if he would go to them. Mordrington is the biggest and he would know that everyone there is loyal to Roget."

Markus was listening. "How many men did your father keep stationed there?"

"I do not know."

As they both pondered what the possibility could be, Markus scratched his head. "I saw the deeds in your solar when we were discussing your holdings and making them profitable," he said. "Mordrington was one, Kirkbank Tower another. I think our next order of business should be to make the rounds to these properties and determine how many men your father kept stationed at each one. We must ensure they are loyal to you."

"Agreed. I'll find the maps and deeds so we know as much as we can before we proceed."

It seemed like a good enough plan, something that needed to be done sooner rather than later given the near-revolt they'd just had. They were nearing the keep and Markus looked up, seeing the warm light emitting from the windows against the starry sky. Taking the stairs up into the softly glowing innards, Atlas headed straight to the solar, but Markus stopped him.

"You should see to your mother, Atlas," he said quietly. "She and your sister should have been your first thought when you came through the door. They have had quite a fright tonight."

Atlas paused at his table, looking at Markus with some chagrin. "I was going to look at the map that shows Kirkbank and Mordrington," he said. "I will see to them in a moment. I promise that I shan't be long."

But Markus shook his head slowly, pointing a big, gloved finger towards the stairwell. "Your maps can wait," he said. "Go see to the women. They should be your priority."

Atlas sighed heavily but he didn't argue. He knew that Markus was right. Sheepishly, he headed up the stairs with Markus behind him.

The doors on this level were all closed and, as Atlas discovered when he tried to open one, they were bolted from the inside. He knocked softly on his mother's solar door.

"Mother?" he said. "It is me. You need not be afraid anymore."

They could hear the bolt being thrown and the door slowly creaked open. Amabella stood there, her eyes riveted to Atlas.

"Are you well?" she asked. "You were not hurt in the fight, were you?"

Atlas shook his head. "I am well," he said, glancing at Markus. "We are all well. I wanted to make sure you were well also."

"You were his first thought, Lady de Sauque," Markus said as if praising the lad.

That only made Atlas feel more guilty. "Are you unharmed, Mother?"

Amabella nodded. "I am," she said, her gaze moving between Atlas and Markus. "But those men… they probably would have tried to harm me had you not come when you did. They said that they were loyal to Roget and they blamed me for Shand leaving."

This time, it was Markus who answered. "We know," he said. "As I was telling your son, I suspected it was only a matter of time before the men loyal to Roget made a move. I am just sorry they made their move on you."

Amabella nodded wearily, opening the door wider and moving aside so that Atlas and Markus could enter the warm, fragrant solar. As they entered, they could see Aleanor curled up in a ball on one of the big, cushioned chairs. She appeared quite unsettled, still.

"You were quite brave tonight, my lady," Markus said to her. "You quite possibly saved your mother and are to be commended."

Aleanor wasn't used to praise of any kind coming from a man, but having spent this past week coming to know Markus just a little, she was more receptive to speaking to him. His words had some effect on her and she lifted her head, perhaps just a little less fearful.

"I… I ran as fast as I could," she said.

Markus smiled faintly. "And you did a fine job."

Amabella picked up on Markus' kindness, turning to look at her daughter. "I have always told her that she is very courageous," she said. "Tonight, she had the opportunity to prove it."

That seemed to bring Aleanor out of her balled-up state, just a little. She sat up straight and unwounded her legs, comforted in the words of praise. Something terrifying had happened, that was true, but she'd survived it. Perhaps she was a wee bit stronger for it. Amabella smiled encouragingly at her daughter before returning her attention to Markus and Atlas.

"Thank you both for coming to my aid," she said. "May… may I speak with you privately, please? Outside on the landing, if you will."

Atlas backed out of the chamber, followed by Markus. Amabella was the last one out, shutting the door softly behind her so her daughter would not hear.

"Atlas," she said quietly. "I believe your father had documentation about all of the soldiers he kept here at Trastamara so that he could pay them regularly. You may want to go look for that, as it might help you determine just how many men he has and who might be loyal to him. There have always been two factions at Trastamara – one loyal to your grandfather, one loyal to Roget. What happened tonight has happened before, but not in many years."

Atlas nodded quickly. "I will see if I can find the documents."

"They should be kept with the financial documents of the castle. Can you remember seeing them at all?"

Atlas looked at Markus, who shook his head. "We've not come across them yet, but I will go now and see what I can find."

As he began to descend the stairs, Markus moved to follow, but Amabella put a hand on his arm to stop him. When he looked at her, questioningly, she put her finger to her lips in a silencing gesture. Markus understood and he kept still. When Amabella was certain Atlas was out of earshot, she turned to Markus.

"What are you going to do about this?" she whispered. "Those men do not want my son in command of Trastamara. They mentioned Shand."

"What did they say?"

"They told me that Shand was a fine commander and they did not want another one."

Markus mulled that over before leaning against the wall behind him. His movements were slow with thought.

"As I said before, this rebellion was not unexpected," he said. "But you should know that after Bexwell was exiled from Trastamara, his escort lost sight of him. They followed his path north again, but they do not know where he went."

Amabella's features tightened with concern at the news. That wasn't something she had wanted to hear. After a moment, she lowered her gaze, her distress more evident by the moment.

"I did not think he would go so easily," she muttered. "He went from trying to keep Roget's death a secret to being ousted from the very castle he wanted so badly to keep for himself. Somehow, I knew he would not surrender so easily."

Markus could see her fear, her apprehension. "We will formulate a plan this very night to keep him away from Trastamara and away from you," he said. "If Bexwell thinks he can outsmart me, he is sorely mistaken."

Amabella looked at him, then. "This has nothing to do with me," she said. "I am not worried about me. I am worried about my son who has just assumed command of an important outpost. He is only seventeen years of age, Markus. Atlas is the one we should all worry over."

Markus' eyes glimmered at her. "I wondered if you remembered."

"Remembered what?"

"My name."

She eyed him with confusion. "Of course I know your name," she said. "You gave me permission to use it. Did I do wrongly just now?"

His lips twitched with a smile. "You did not," he said. "But I have been here over a week and you have not called me by my name, not once. I thought you had forgotten."

He was looking at her with that familiar warmth again, a pleasant and endearing warmth that she was coming to expect from him. Somehow, the focus of the conversation was shifting away from her concern for Atlas and to the fact that she had not yet called Markus by his name. It didn't seem to be an appropriate shift in conversation, but in the same breath, she didn't seem to care.

When Markus smiled at her, nothing else seemed to matter.

"I have not forgotten," she said quietly. "But in my defense, you have continued to address me formally, also."

He grinned. "In front of my men, I will show you all due respect," he said. "But in private, as we are now, I will freely call you Amabella."

Amabella smiled because he was. "Sometimes it is such a long name," she said. "My father called me 'Ama' because he said it was too exhausting to speak my entire name."

"Then your father was a lazy man."

She broke down into laughter and he followed suit. "He was a practical man," she said, her smile fading. "There was practicality in everything he did. That is why he agreed to a marriage contract with Roget, in fact. He saw practicality in it."

"How did he know Roget?" Markus asked. "De Sauque is not a name I've ever heard here in the north, at least as a family name."

"Roget was my father's knight," she said. "He came to serve my father when I was away to foster. When I returned, Roget had already been at Trastamara a couple of years. He was a decent knight, but once I returned from fostering, it seemed as if Roget drew quite close to my father. He became indispensable. When Roget asked for my hand, my father was quite happy to give his consent."

Markus looked at her curiously. "And your father never had any doubts in how Roget showed respect to you?"

She smiled, but it was an ironic one. "Roget was a perfect gentleman while we were courting," she said. "He was attentive and kind. He continued to be that way until my father passed away. Then… then, it was as if everything changed overnight. He became distant, cool, apathetic, and immoral. It was as if he had simply been playing a role until my father died and once the man was gone, Roget no longer had any reason to pretend."

"Pretend what?"

"That he was a decent man. He wasn't, you know. He was a beast."

Markus took a good, long look at her. It seemed that all he ever did was look at her, but now… now, he was seeing something deeper than just the cursory impression he'd first had of the woman.

A lush, beautiful woman.

She was still lush and beautiful. There was no doubt about that. She was the kind of woman who made him feel glad that he was a man because something about her seduced him without even trying. A look, a smile, and he was putty in her hands. After having come to know her over the past week, he could also see that she was wise and compassionate and incredibly tolerant of the tribulations she'd been dealt in life. And her children… she was fiercely protective of her brood, something that reminded Markus of his own mother.

But that was where the comparison ended.

He didn't want to bed his own mother, but he certainly wouldn't mind bedding Amabella.

Aye, he could admit it to himself.

He didn't care that she was older than he was. In fact, that was one of the things that made her so attractive. She'd had four children and she'd been married for twenty years, and as far as he was concerned, that made her more alluring and sensual than any woman he'd ever met. There was something very attractive about an experienced woman. It was true that he appreciated her good qualities, but he wasn't ashamed to admit that the more he looked at the swell of her full bosom and the nip of her slender waist, the more he wanted to put his hands on her.

"Not all men are beasts, Amabella," he said softly. "I hope… I hope that one day, you will allow a man to show you that."

She looked at him. "Me?" she said. Then, she shook her head. "It is funny you should mention that because just this evening, Aleanor was asking me if I would marry again."

"Would you?"

She chuckled. "I will tell you what I have told her," she said. "My time for marriage is over. I am content in my widowhood and watching my children grow. Truly, I am not troubled by it."

Markus was still leaning against the wall, still watching her, and trying desperately not to give away what he thought about her.

"Then you are depriving some man of an excellent wife," he said. "You have beauty and wisdom. I cannot tell you what valuable commodities those are. I realize your marriage to Roget was unpleasant at best, but that does not mean all marriages are unpleasant. You should give yourself the opportunity to discover that for yourself."

She looked at him as if he had lost his mind. "I am not a valuable commodity," she said. "I cannot bring anything to a marriage – no property, no wealth. All of that belongs to Atlas now. I have nothing to offer."

"You have a great deal to offer."

"To whom? A man so rich and titled that he does not care that he is getting a woman with nothing to offer?"

Markus shrugged. "For argument's sake, let us say that I was a prospective husband," he said. "I would take wisdom and beauty over money and property. I don't need a woman's money or property. I much prefer a woman who is a companion and a friend and a lover over a cold contract marriage."

She smiled as she listened to him speak. "Then you are a rarity," she said. "And you can command the finest wife in all of England, Markus. You have breeding, training and titles. You are your father's heir, are you not?"

"I am."

"Then you shall be an earl someday. And why is it you are not married yet? At your age, you should be."

He eyed her. "How old do you think I am?"

She looked him up and down. "I would say you've seen no more than thirty-two summers."

"I have seen thirty."

"Then you are in the prime of your life."

"So are you."

She shook her head. "I am past my prime."

"You cannot possibly be."

"I am older than you."

"It would be rude of me to ask how much older, wouldn't it?"

She laughed softly. "It would, but I do not mind telling you," she said. "I do not guard my age like some women do. I married Roget when I had seen twenty years. I was married to him for twenty years."

He shook his head. "You look ten years younger than that," he said. "You are ageless."

Her smile turned genuine. "That is very kind of you to say so," she said. "It has been a long time since I have heard such sweet lies."

As she chuckled, he shook his head. "That was not a lie, I assure you," he said. "I do not lie, not even for flattery. It was the truth, upon my oath."

Her smile faded. "I did not mean to offend you, truly," she

said. "'Tis simply that it has been a long time since someone has been so kind to me. I have almost forgotten what it feels like."

"If you allow, it will not be the last time I flatter you."

She wasn't catching on to what was a potentially flirtatious tone. "But you do not need to," she said. "I can live contently for the rest of my life on what you have said to me. I will treasure it, and you, always."

"Do you mean that?"

"Of course I do."

He pushed himself off the wall, standing tall and strong before her. "Good," he said. Then, he reached out to take her hand, bringing it to his lips for an unexpected and tender kiss. "Because I intend to hold you to that. I intend to flatter you a great deal and, in time, mayhap more. You are not too old, Amabella Hemada Abril de Sauque. I think you are perfect. Now, I am going to help Atlas figure out what we need to do about Shand's mysterious whereabouts and the faction loyal to Roget. I would suggest you and your daughter retire for the night. It has been an eventful evening."

With that, he kissed her hand again, let it drop, and headed down the stairs.

Amabella stood there for the longest time, virtually in a state of shock. She wasn't sure she'd heard right. In fact, she wasn't entirely convinced that she hadn't gone stark raving mad in the last few seconds. Surely she must have because a man like Markus de Wolfe did not speak of things like flattery and perfection to a woman like her.

She was old.

He was young and handsome and titled, and completely out of her grasp.

... wasn't he?

Heart pounding in her ears, Amabella tried to walk back to her solar but she couldn't seem to walk in a straight line. She ended up opening the door and leaning against the door jamb, gazing off into space, thinking on Markus' words.

I think you are perfect.

Maybe she was, maybe she wasn't. But she knew one thing – he most definitely was.

CHAPTER TWELVE

I T WAS THE folly of youth.

The next morning following the small revolt of Roget's loyal soldiers, Atlas was on the road for Mordrington.

Alone.

But he'd planned it this way.

He'd spent a good portion of the night in conference with Markus, Damien, Cassius, and Kieran about the Trastamara properties. In addition to Mordrington and Kirkbank, there was another smaller manse closer to Berwick called Lamberton that was evidently lived in by an old man and his wife who were somehow related to Roget because their family name was de Sauque.

But Atlas didn't have any idea who they were, and he didn't care. He would deal with them later. At the moment, he was focused on Mordrington because he knew his father's other family lived there.

Perhaps that was what had him so worked up.

He remembered when his mother told him about the births of his father's two bastard sons, how jealous and inadequate he'd felt. He'd never admitted those feelings to anyone and, in truth, it was difficult for him to admit them to himself, but he'd been very jealous his father had other sons.

Brothers.

Brothers who took attention away from him, vying for the attention of a father who hardly gave anything to his legitimate children. They might even try to lay claim to anything Roget had, but now that Atlas was the Lord of Trastamara, that wasn't going to happen. His jealousy had turned into rage; rage that his father had thought so little of his legitimate family that he should go and have a second one. He'd heard the knights of Castle Questing speaking of his father once and they used words like *careless... foolish... filth.*

Those words had stuck in Atlas' head.

The knights of Castle Questing, and his master in particular, had never treated Atlas any differently just because of his father. They'd always treated Atlas like any other pledge, but Atlas suspected that, at times, they'd treated him with some sympathy because of who his father was.

But Roget de Sauque's legacy wasn't going to be his son's.

Atlas would see to that.

Last night's lengthy discussion with Markus had spurred his determination to finally do something about his father's indiscretions. He'd hardly slept, tossing and turning, his mind whirling with the situation in general. It was clear that he was threatened; his father's legacy seemed to breed resentment towards him, not loyalty. Shand's removal had only aggravated it. Therefore, he had to clean out any remaining loyalists and he intended to start with Mordrington.

He was alone on the road, at the dawn of a cloudy day, heading towards the manse. That was his folly; he'd come by himself because he felt he needed to. Up until now, Markus had been by his side for every major issue, every problem, every victory. Atlas knew it was necessary and he appreciated that the House of de Wolfe was determined to help him in his new lordship, but that was the problem – Atlas felt as if they were doing too much. He was afraid of becoming dependent upon their strength and advice.

He wanted to do something by himself this time.

And that was Mordrington.

For all he knew, it was simply his father's whore, her two sons, and just a few men. That was the assumption from the documents they'd examined last night. Strangely, there weren't many records in his father's solar of Mordrington other than an old list of inventory – sheep, foodstuffs, things like that. Markus thought it was rather odd, and suspicious, but Atlas, in his impetuous youthfulness, was convinced that meant there wasn't much going on there. He thought he knew everything about it.

Unfortunately, he was wrong.

He began to realize that as he came within sight of the manse, her gray walls emerging from the misty morning, a fine piece of country living that Atlas remembered being quite bucolic in his youth. He remembered visiting with his mother and father as a small child, when Aleanor had been an infant. But, as he neared the manse, he began to smell something. Pigs, animals, filth… *something.*

It was a horrific smell.

He realized the morning breeze was coming from the east, blowing westerly, and it was blowing the smell from Mordrington right into him.

Then, he saw it.

Men in *leine* tunics, the kind that the Scots wore. They were emerging from the lowered drawbridge, carrying what looked like a body between them. As Atlas slowed his horse to watch, they threw the body right into the moat and it was sucked down into the putrid mud.

Shocked, Atlas threw himself off his horse and quickly pulled the animal into the trees. It was a cloudy morning, a fine fog hanging just above the treetops, and he was able to pull back into the shadows of the darkened forest that embraced the south side of the road. In stealth, he made his way along the road, just inside the trees, keeping his eyes on Mordrington.

Atlas may have been impulsive and young, but he wasn't stupid. He could immediately see that something out of the ordinary was going on at the once-lovely manse. For one thing, the smell permeated everything. The moat had a least one body in it and from the stench that covered the land, he suspected there was more than one.

And there was the matter of Scots, everywhere.

Settling down on his haunches where he could watch the front of the place, Atlas watched the activity that seemed to be fairly busy so early in the morning. The drawbridge remained open, as if there were no concern for safety. Mordrington had an enclosed courtyard with battlements that encircled the manse and he could see men on the battlements who weren't soldiers. If he could guess, he would say that they were not his father's men. In fact, it appeared as if the Scots had taken over the place.

Clan Hume.

His mother told him that Fenella had come from Clan Hume and it occurred to Atlas that Clan Hume must have taken over Mordrington. Had his father known? Or had he even encouraged it? The Scots had tried to raze Trastamara many times since Atlas' grandfather had built it, so was it possible that his father had given Mordrington to the Scots to keep them away from Trastamara? If that was the case, then Atlas would need help getting them out.

Perhaps coming here alone hadn't been the smartest idea.

He was beginning to rethink his impetuous action.

Suddenly, a hand clamped over his mouth. Terrified, Atlas grabbed at the dagger he kept on his belt, but a massive hand stilled it. He was trapped by an unearthly strength and when he strained to get a look at his accoster, Markus' face came into view.

"If you scream, you will be very sorry," Markus growled in his ear. "Shut your lips, you foolish whelp. I should beat you senseless for sneaking off as you have. When I remove my hand, you will be silent. Do you understand?"

Atlas nodded fearfully. The hand was removed and Atlas sucked in a ragged breath, lightheaded with relief to see that a Scot hadn't gotten hold of him. From the furious expression on Markus' face, however, a Scot might have been preferable.

"Markus, *look*," he whispered, jabbing a finger in the direction of the manse. "There are Scots everywhere. They've taken Mordrington!"

Markus' enraged gaze lingered on Atlas a moment before turning his attention to the wide-open manse. There were a couple of men on the drawbridge but those were the only men he saw at all. For the most part, the place seemed quiet. After a moment, he nodded his head.

"I saw them as I came up through the trees behind you," he hissed. "Atlas, I cannot tell you how foolish this was. Thank God Kieran was on the wall and saw you leave before sunrise. If you do not come back with me this very moment, I will bodily remove you and throw you in the vault when we reach Trastamara. Is this in any way unclear?"

Atlas was torn between blind obedience of Markus' directive and the fact that there were Scots all over his family's property.

"But… but the Scots have Mordrington," he whispered urgently. "We must do something!"

Markus sighed heavily. "We will," he said. "But not with just the two of us. We have no way of knowing just how many there are. It would be suicide to charge in there now and try to evict your father's mistress. Clearly, she has permitted some of her clan to occupy the manse along with her. We must return to Trastamara for the army."

Atlas knew that. He was embarrassed because he was so upset by what he saw that he wasn't thinking entirely clearly.

"You are right, of course," he said. "I suppose I'm too angry. I just want them out."

Markus put an enormous hand on his head. "I know," he said, his anger cooling. "And we will get them out. But with more than just you and me. I am a great knight, but even I do not think I can clear out an entire manse full of Scots."

"Do you think there are many?"

Markus' gaze moved over the manse in the distance. "Probably," he said. "The only safe thing to do is return for the army and then we can…"

He suddenly trailed off, his eyes narrowing as something at Mordrington caught his attention. Atlas had been looking at Markus but when he saw the man's jaw tighten, he quickly turned back to the manse to see what had the man so riled.

It didn't take long for him to see it. Coming across the drawbridge and speaking to the two men who were pissing over the side was the very man they'd been looking for.

The devil had revealed himself.

"Shand," Atlas hissed, his eyes wide with surprise. "It's *Shand!*"

Markus could only nod. Shand Bexwell was at Mordrington and so were several Scots. The mystery of Shand's whereabouts was solved, but that only threw more confusion into the mix. There were no English soldiers to be seen, Roget's soldiers, but there were plenty of Scots.

What in the hell is going on?

Markus tugged on Atlas' sleeve.

"Come," he said in a tone that left no room for disobedience. "We must get out of here now."

This time, Atlas didn't argue. He followed Markus back to the trees where the man's big-boned warhorse was tethered. They led the animals out of the trees, towards the south and away from the manse before mounting. Once on horseback, Markus and Atlas tore off through the forest, heading for the road that would lead them back to Trastamara in a hurry.

A strange situation just took on a rather sinister turn.

CHAPTER THIRTEEN

Mordrington Manor

"WE DINNA SEE them, but someone was definitely there," a burly Scot spoke to Shand and Win. "There was movement in the trees but they were gone before we could catch up tae them. Their horses were swift."

Shand was listening with concern. The men had gone on a routine patrol, prowling around the lands surrounding Mordrington just after dawn, and noticed recent signs of men moving in the trees south of the manse. Footprints in the mud, disturbed bushes, and there were also signs of at least one horse, probably two.

Mordrington was being watched.

"Which direction did they go?" Shand asked.

"South," the Scotsman said. "Straight down the road to-wards Cocklaw and Kirkbank and Trastamara."

Shand turned to Win. "Spies from Trastamara," he said with certainty. "I told you that boy wanted to clean out Mordrington. He must have sent men to do it and when they saw the Scots, they turned around. Now the de Wolfe knights are going to know that there are Scots here. This takes away any element of surprise we had."

Win wasn't entirely upset like Shand was, mostly because he was a man who could never admit someone might have the upper hand on him. That was his nature. Take no responsibility, admit no failings.

Like now.

As he saw it, this was to their advantage.

Since Shand had come to Mordrington yesterday with his proposal for laying siege to Trastamara, a great deal had been discussed through the night. Win knew of Shand Bexwell, or at least he'd heard the name, but he was coming to see an intelligent man who believed he was very much due Trastamara in spite of the fact that Roget's heir had taken control. It wasn't that the man coveted the property or was greedy about it. He simply believed it should belong to him, pure and simple.

But Win liked his message – remove all traces of the House of de Sauque and the properties would belong to them – Trastamara to Bexwell and Mordrington to the Scots. As a man who happily took what did not belong to him, Win couldn't have agreed more. Mordrington would make a hell of a base for his band of reivers and Bexwell would let him operate as he saw fit.

He wasn't going to lose this opportunity.

"Ye worry too much," he said after a moment. "I've spent a day and a night listening tae ye tell me everything I wanted tae know about Trastamara Castle and her weaknesses, so we simply move forward earlier than we'd planned."

Shand frowned. "Move earlier?" he said. "Don't you understand? Trastamara is probably mustering the army as we speak."

Win looked at him, smiling. He had a handsome smile, but there was so much evil in his blood that it negated any semblance of attractiveness or honor. A smile on his face was simply a wicked gesture, his black eyes reflected his black soul.

"I hope they are," he said. "I hope they plan on marching right up tae the door of Mordrington. But we willna be here, lad."

"What do you mean?"

Win was quite pleased with himself, for he saw a great advantage in Trastamara taking the army to Mordrington.

"Just what I said," he said. "We'll be gone. As they're marching tae Mordrington, we'll be using the trees tae shield us as we move tae Trastamara. While they're here tae attack us, we'll be climbing over their walls and killing the men they left behind. When they return tae Trastamara, it'll be ours. *Now* do ye understand?"

Shand looked at him in shock. "Are you serious?"

"Of course. Just show us the weak places on the wall and we'll make short work of them."

Shand was somewhat embarrassed that this reiver had thought of this plan of attack and he hadn't. But, then again, reivers were sly and underhanded, so it wasn't surprising. In truth, it was rather brilliant. While Trastamara's army was removed from the castle, the reivers would strike.

After a moment, Shand nodded.

"Then we go," he said. "Muster your men and I will show you where to place your ladders. But be prepared for a fight because if de Wolfe left his men behind, the de Wolfe soldiers will not give up without trying to kill you first."

Win waved him off. "I've fought my share of de Wolfe men over the years," he said. "Berwick, Questing, Wark, and as far west as Wolfe's Lair. I know them and they know me. It may take some time, but we'll triumph in the end. With yer help, we will."

Shand wasn't as confident as Win, but he didn't argue with the man. He simply nodded, thinking on what lay ahead. Finally, his chance to regain Trastamara, as it should have been his when Roget was killed. It was never meant for that little whelp of a son. He wasn't man enough to handle such an outpost.

Shand also knew that this would lead to trouble with de Wolfe and de Norville, and the other allies along the border. With the House of de Sauque, and Abril, no longer in control of their hereditary home, the allies would have questions. His possession of Trastamara wasn't legitimate.

But he couldn't worry about that now.

First, he had a castle to gain.

"I'll help," he said. "But I suggest you get your men moving. If I know de Wolfe, they will muster the army as soon as they receive the word that Mordrington is overrun with Scots."

"We can be ready in an hour or two," Win said. "My men travel fast and light. We can move quickly."

Shand nodded, but his thoughts were lingering on something else, something he'd been thinking of since he'd left Trastamara the first time.

Lady de Sauque.

"One more thing," Shand said. "Roget's wife… you will spare her and your men will not touch her. She belongs to me."

Win gave him a knowing smirk. "Is that so? Have yer eye on her, do ye?"

"She was the heiress of Trastamara when Roget married her. I need her to hold the castle."

Win didn't give up his teasing so easily. "Are ye sure it's not more?" he said. "When Roget was bedding my sister, ye were bedding his wife?"

Shand shook his head. "Nay," he said. "But, God willing, that will change."

Win snorted, but he was already moving. The time for jesting was over. They had preparations to make and little time to do them. In short time, the reivers of Mordrington Manse were preparing for what could possibly be their biggest prize yet, that great and glorious castle that protected The Orchard crossing bridge.

Trastamara.

CHAPTER FOURTEEN

"AND THEN WE hurried back," Markus said. "Now, you know what we know. Mordrington is overrun with Scots and Shand is with them."

He had just finished speaking to a room full of stunned men – Cassius, Damien, Kieran, Atlas, and a couple of senior de Wolfe sergeants, including the red-haired soldier who had been at the head of Shand's escort. They were all looking back at him in various stages of disbelief. All except Atlas; he stood there, head hung, struggling not to be overwhelmed by everything.

More than anything, there was a sense of shock in the air. But it was more than shock; there seemed to be a sense of realization as well. Realization in the fact that Shand's determination to return to Trastamara was as great, or greater than, they could have imagined. The man had denied his ambition at first, and he had made it seem as if he genuinely had Atlas' best interests at heart, but the truth was that he wanted Trastamara, so much so that he had returned for it.

"But the Scots," Damien said. "I simply do not understand. Is Shand allied with them? Has he been allied with them since the beginning?"

"It is possible that Roget's death was not an accident," Markus said. "I seemed to recall speculation of that, considering we still would not know of Roget's death had Lady de Sauque not sent her missive to Berwick. It is possible that Shand has been at the head of this all along. Mayhap Shand allied himself with the Scots do to away with Roget in exchange for Mordrington."

Damien sighed heavily. "Anything is possible," he said. "but one thing is for certain; we must ride to Mordrington and clean it out. And we cannot leave Bexwell alive when this is over."

It was a brutal statement, but a necessary one. No one in the chamber disagreed. But Markus imperceptibly nodded his head in Atlas' direction and Damien took the hint. They were not in command here; a young lord was. All of this was his decision. Therefore, Damien turned to Atlas.

"Of course, my lord, we will do whatever you wish," he said. "This is your command. We are your servants."

Atlas, who had thus far been standing near the cluttered table lost to his thoughts, lifted his gaze to look at the men in the chamber. Powerful, seasoned men at his disposal. He knew they meant well, and would do as he said, but the truth was that he felt like a fool. So much of this situation, as he saw it, was his fault.

"I underestimated how much Shand wanted Trastamara," he said. "I was trying to do what I felt best, by being benevolent and lordly, when I should have thought like a ruthless lord. Shand wants what I have. I should not have treated him so kindly."

Markus felt somewhat responsible for that. He had applauded the lad for being gracious to his enemy. Now that was coming back to bite them both.

"You behaved appropriately," he said. "It is Shand who has shown dishonor, not you. Do not question your actions, Atlas.

They were indeed lordly."

"Listen to him, my lord," Damien said. "The way you deal with men defines you. You dealt with Bexwell in a fair manner. Now, you will simply have to deal with him in a way his behavior dictates. He has shown how ruthless he can be and now you must do the same. He has returned to take Trastamara from you. Will you let him?"

Atlas looked between Damien and Markus. "Nay," he said flatly. "Trastamara is mine and I intend to keep it. He has no right to it, no matter what he thinks. I will fight him to the death if I have to."

He sounded very grown up in that statement. Atlas had been trying so hard to grow up in the past week, and the knights had been trying so hard to help him, that it was good to hear the strength in his voice. He meant what he said.

Now, they needed to help him achieve it.

"What are your orders, my lord?" Markus asked. "Tell us and we shall carry them out."

The grown-up young man was trying not to look uncertain again. There was a battle to plan, something he'd never done before, but he'd certainly been around enough of them. He knew what to do, at least in theory. He drew in a deep breath, summoning his courage.

"We should prepare the men to ride to battle," he said. "But not all of them. Markus, how many men do we have right now?"

Markus thought quickly. "To the best of my knowledge, my father took one hundred men back with him to Berwick," he said. "That leaves us with four hundred de Wolfe men and about one hundred and fifty Trastamara soldiers."

"Then assimilate the Trastamara soldiers into your army," Atlas said. "I want them to march with us to Mordrington. Leave as many de Wolfe men behind as you see fit."

Markus shrugged. "Since we do not know how many Scots are at Mordrington, I would feel comfortable taking four hundred men in total," he said. "That leaves the smaller group to man the battlements until we return."

"Can you make it so?"

"Aye, my lord."

Atlas then turned his attention to Damien. "Can you make sure all of the men are properly armed?" he said. "We will also need to muster the quartermasters. I will leave that up to you."

Damien nodded shortly, motioning to Kieran, who was already moving to quit the solar. Lastly, Atlas turned to Cassius.

"I would like you to ride at the head of the army with me and Damien, as I will rely on you to supervise the battle." As Cassius nodded, Atlas' focus returned to Markus. "I would feel better knowing you are here protecting my mother and brother and sisters. You are the fiercest knight in all northern England and I believe my mother deserves that protection. Will you remain behind with the smaller force and protect Trastamara?"

Markus' lips twitched with a smile. "As you wish, my lord."

"Are you disappointed that I've not asked you to ride to battle?"

"You've asked me to perform a much more important task."

Atlas seemed relieved that Markus was not upset that he would not be facing a battle. Truly, he felt much more at ease knowing Markus would be with his mother and siblings. He simply didn't want to leave them without the best protection he could provide, and that was Markus. With that, he nodded shortly, confident he was making the right decisions.

"Then let us go about our duties," he said. "Markus, will you cull the army now? I want to go with you and see how you do it."

Markus nodded and, with that, they were all moving with a purpose.

To save a young lord from a vicious and determined opponent.

ORGANIZING THE MEN who would go with the army and the men who would stay behind didn't take an over amount of time. Markus was done with it in an hour and after that, he had little to do.

But he knew where he was going next.

The kitchen yard.

As he'd gone about his duties, he happened to see Alfie in the kitchen yard with his horse guard, so when he'd finished with Atlas, he'd made his way to the yard to check upon the king. He hadn't seen Alfie since last night and he missed the little lad. Seeing him had become one of the highlights of his day.

Therefore, Markus entered the kitchen yard, smiling when he saw Alfie and his eight-man guard over near the small pond they kept to provide the fish that Ambra liked to sauce. The children had their bucket helms and stick swords, but once they caught sight of Markus, they ran in his direction.

"Sir Knight!" Alfie shouted, trying to keep the oversized helm on his head. "The army is going out! Can we go with them?"

Markus glanced over his shoulder at the gate he'd just come through. Beyond in the bailey, the army was gathering and the children had undoubtedly noticed. Reaching out, he righted Alfie's tipping helm.

"Not this time," he said. "You and your horse guard still have much practice before you can go into battle."

Alfie appeared momentarily unhappy but that quickly changed with the next request. "Can we have more helms?" he asked. "Aldwin and I are wearing the ones you gave us, but Bartram and Manley need one. They cannot be knights without them."

Markus grinned at the child. "I'll see if I can find you two more."

Alfie pointed out into the yard. "There is the armory," he said. "There are many in the armory."

"But those are for real soldiers, going into battle."

"I *am* a real soldier. I am a king!"

Markus wasn't entirely sure that Alfie didn't really believe that he wasn't the king of the kitchen yard, so he didn't argue with him. As far as Trastamara was concerned, Alfie really *was* a king in his own world.

It was good to dream.

"Indeed, you are," he said after a moment. "But this king does not go into battle, nor does his guard. In fact… in fact, I have a very special assignment for you that is just as important."

Nine pairs of eyes lit up at him. "What is it?" Alfie asked anxiously.

Markus swept a hand around the kitchen yard. "This is your domain," he said. "As you have seen, the army is indeed mustering for battle. But you must protect this kitchen yard. It has the postern gate in it, which is very important. If the enemy was to get in through that gate, they could destroy Trastamara. It will be your duty to protect it and ensure it is always locked."

The children turned to look at the postern gate, which was of an odd design. It wasn't tall enough for a man to stand up and walk through, but rather had been specially designed so that it was wide enough to pull a hand cart through, but men had to bend over to enter. Therefore, if the gate was ever breached, men could bash the lowered heads of the enemy coming through. Coming in hunched over, it would be difficult to meet castle defenders head-on.

The children took off at a run towards the gate with Markus walking behind them at a leisurely pace. By the time he reached them, they were squealing excitedly, jumping up and down and grabbing hold of the very heavy iron gate. It was locked and bolted into the surrounding stone, making it impossible for any attackers to pull it loose, but the horse guard tried to climb up it and Markus ended up ducking beneath the low entry to pluck children off the grate and set them on their feet.

"This is not something to treat lightly," he told them, bent over to nearly half his considerable size as he stood next to the gate. "This is where battles are lost and won. You must always watch this gate as part of your duties in the kitchen yard. Do you swear to do this?"

The children all nodded solemnly, and Markus came out of the doorway, standing up straight. Alfie and the others followed him.

"If we are to watch the gate, then we must have real weapons," Alfie said. "Wooden swords will not fight off enemies."

Markus saw it as a ploy by a clever child to get real weapons and he fought off a grin. "For now, wooden swords will have to suffice," he said. "But anything else in the kitchen yard can be a weapon. Look around you. A fire poker, an iron spit, a firebrand like the ones the smithies use to smooth the hides. You can use anything at all in a fight."

The children were looking around the yard at the everyday implements that could be considered a weapon. The yard was vast and there were two massive cooking fires over near the kitchen. One fire had iron pots situated over it with everything from hot water to broth to some kind of stew bubbling over it, while the second fire had tools for the various trades – fire-brands and fire pokers, and other things that were variously used.

Alfie pointed to the second fire.

"Can we burn men with those things?" he asked.

Markus nodded. "Absolutely," he said. "But you more than likely cannot kill a man with them, so you must try to disable him so that he cannot hurt you. Burn his hands, his eyes, the parts of his body he will need to fight with. If you cannot kill a man, then you must disable him."

Alfie considered that seriously. Then, he looked at his wooden sword, lifting it up. "How can I disable him with this?"

Markus held up his hands as if wielding an imaginary club. "Instead of trying to stab him, use it like a club and strike him."

That wasn't the answer Alfie wanted. He very badly wanted to stab a man, especially in battle. Eyeing Markus doubtfully, he turned his wooden sword around so that he was holding on to the dull blade and exposing the surprisingly heavy hilt, and whacked Manley on the shoulder with it. The child howled as Markus reached out and plucked the sword from Alfie's grasp.

"I said an enemy," he said sternly. "Not one of your horse guard."

Alfie was grabbing for the sword as Markus held it over his head. "But I wanted to see if it would work!"

Markus lifted a disapproving eyebrow before handing it back to the lad, who embraced it greedily. "I told you it would work," he said. "Do not do it again. A good king does not abuse his men."

Alfie knew what he meant but he essentially ignored him. "We will watch the gate," he said. "No one will come in."

"You have to let the farmers in," Markus reminded him. "There are people who come to do business with the cook. You must let them in."

"I will."

Alfie was on a mission to protect the postern gate at all

costs, so he gathered his guard and made them all line up against the iron grate to "protect" it. It was a line of children, as determined and brave as they could be. Chuckling at the antics, Markus turned away with the intention of heading back out to the bailey when he caught sight of Amabella and Ambra entering the kitchen yard.

His heart skipped a beat.

Pretending the sight of Amabella wasn't making him feel the least bit giddy, he smiled politely as the woman and her youngest daughter approached. Ambra pulled away from her mother and ran over to the horse guard. Markus opened his mouth to greet Amabella, but one look at the expression on her face as she drew near and the greeting died in his throat.

The woman's brow was furrowed with worry.

"I heard what you did this morning," she said. "You saved my son from doing something very foolish. I am so angry with him for going to Mordrington that it is all I can do to keep from beating him senseless. What on earth possessed him to go there, alone?"

Now, Markus understood her fury. "Did he tell you?" he asked quietly.

Amabella nodded. "He did," she said. "He told me that you prevented him from getting himself killed. He also said that Shand is at Mordrington. Is there truth in this?"

Markus nodded faintly. "There is."

Amabella's unhappy expression morphed into something strained and apprehensive. As Markus watched, it looked as if she were blinking back tears.

"Then he did not go away like Atlas told him to," she said tightly. "My God… he really came back."

Markus nodded. He didn't know what to say to her. The heavyset nurse came wandering into the kitchen yard, heading for the children, and that gave Markus the opportunity he needed to pull Amabella away so that he could speak with her. Clearly, she was distraught, so with the children being minded, he grasped Amabella by the elbow.

"Come with me," he said softly. "Let us go somewhere to speak about this in private."

Amabella simply nodded, allowing Markus to take her out of the kitchen yard. She kept her head down, not uttering a word, as he took her over to the keep. As they passed through the bailey, Markus could see Atlas with Damien inspecting the troops, as Damien pointed out things to watch for on each man.

It was a swift education on command for Atlas, but he seemed up to the task. Kieran was with the quartermaster and Cassius was in the armory tower. Markus could see his brother ensuring that the men were properly equipped. As they neared the keep, Amabella came to a pause and looked in Atlas' direction.

"Look at my son," she said quietly. "He is just a boy. Markus, he should not be riding to battle. He is a squire. He will not be a full-fledged knight for another four years. He has no business going to battle against the Scots."

Markus didn't say anything. He encouraged her to move, escorting her up the stairs into the keep, but he didn't take her into the lord's solar. He took her upstairs to her small solar, thinking she would be calmer and more comfortable if they spoke there.

Entering the warm chamber, cluttered with sewing for Aleanor and poppets for Ambra, Markus directed Amabella into the nearest chair.

"Sit down," he said. Then, he looked around. "Where is Aleanor?"

Amabella sighed heavily as she sat down. "She is in her chamber, sewing."

"Doesn't she usually do that in here?"

Amabella glanced at him. "Shall I tell you a secret?"

"Please."

"Swear you will not repeat it."

"I swear."

"Her chamber window overlooks the corner of the bailey with the armory. Your brother is there, is he not?"

Markus nodded. "He is."

"I think Allie wants to watch him."

Markus stared at her a moment before breaking down into soft laughter. "If I could tell him, he would be most flattered," he said. "But she is a bit young for him. Besides, he wants to marry Ambra because she has a talent for food."

His laughter had Amabella smiling, however wearily. "Then he will be in for a long wait," she said. "But your brother is the first man Allie has ever shown interest in. I am encouraged that she will not grow up a spinster or a recluse."

Markus shut the door to the solar before making his way over to a chair near the hearth. "Your two younger children are quite amiable and friendly," he said. "Has Aleanor been abused or hurt that she should be so fearful of people?"

Amabella shook her head. "Nay," she said. "That is simply her nature. She was a sickly child and she has always had an unnatural fear of people she does not know, especially men. But you have been kind to her, so very kind, and that has helped her a great deal."

"I'm glad," Markus said, his eyes glimmering warmly at her. "Now, you wished to speak on your son."

Amabella's smile faded. "Aye," she said. "Markus, he is too young to be riding to battle. I do not understand why you are allowing it."

Markus leaned forward, his elbows resting on his knees. "I am not allowing anything," she said. "Trastamara belongs to Atlas. This is his command. If he wants to ride to battle, I cannot stop him."

Amabella's features tightened. "But he is only a boy. He's still learning what it means to be a man."

"Children have fought wars throughout history," Markus said. "Do not diminish him simply because you believe he is young. I can tell you that Atlas is quite skilled thanks to his training at Castle Questing. He is not inexperienced by any means. He has been to battle."

"Aye, but as a squire," Amabella insisted. "Never as a warrior."

"He has been taught to fight," Markus said quietly. "You must let your son grow up. He wants to be a good lord, a good warrior, and he needs your support and your encouragement. You will cause him to doubt himself if you demand he not fight and that will only harm him in the end. I am sure that is not what you wish to do."

Amabella could see his point, though it didn't make her feel any better. "Of course not," she said. "But… but he is only a boy."

"He is a man," Markus countered with quiet firmness. "You must start treating him like one. He wants to do well for you and for his siblings. The best thing you can do is show him complete and utter faith, no matter how fearful you are for him. Trust him, Ama; you must do that if he is going to succeed as the Lord of Trastamara."

He used her nickname, something he'd not done before. It caused Amabella to look at him, feeling her heart pound and her palms sweat at the familiarity he was taking with her. Ever since had kissed her hand, she felt there was something more between them. Now, he was calling her by a pet name.

Her heart beat just a little faster.

"You are correct, of course," she said after a moment. "I just do not want to see him hurt. He has a great future ahead of him."

"He does," Markus agreed. "And the first step towards that future is exactly what he wants to do – cleaning out Mordrington and making sure all Trastamara properties are safe and well-manned. Atlas has a great empire here and he knows it. He will make a fine ally for the House of de Wolfe."

Amabella was proud of her son; that was clear. But as a mother, she worried. She would always worry. But she also knew that at some point, she would only be hurting him by trying to protect him. Markus was correct. Atlas was a man and she needed to treat him like one. But all she could see when she looked at him was that little child with the dark hair that flopped down over his eyes.

Those days were gone.

"Thanks to you," she said, gratitude in her tone. "Everything Atlas has become is because of you and your men, and the knights at Castle Questing. I did not see how his master, Tobias, trained him, but I have seen how you have tried to mold him and give him advice. You have been a wonderful teacher, Markus. Your heart is full of kindness and generosity. Atlas is very fortunate to have you."

Markus smiled faintly. "He is a good student," he said. "He has had to do a good deal of growing up in the past week, but he is learning. I believe he will do very well. I hope that you will continue to keep me informed of his progress even after I leave."

Amabella knew, in theory, that Markus would not remain at Trastamara forever, but to hear him speak of it made it a reality. She began to feel a longing for the man she couldn't begin to describe and he wasn't even gone yet. All she knew was that, somehow, it saddened her.

Hurt her.

"Are you leaving soon, then?" she asked.

Markus sat back in the chair. "More than likely," he said. "I was never meant to remain here for any length of time. In fact, I plan to assume my position as Lord Protector next month."

"Will you go to London?"

Markus shook his head. "Edward is making a push into Scotland and he will be here in the north, soon, if he isn't already," he said. "He is due at Berwick soon and I will assume my position then."

Amabella thought on that for a moment. "Edward is invading Scotland?"

Markus chuckled softly. "There are a few things Edward wishes to do with Scotland."

"That means it will be difficult on the borders," she said. "Trastamara sits on Scottish lands, yet we are loyal to the English. This could go badly for us if Edward is intent on war."

It was an astute observation. Markus couldn't, in good conscience, deny such a thing because it was the truth.

"I will not let anything happen to Trastamara," he said. "I will put the de Wolfe troops here to protect you, so do not worry about that. You will always have the protection of de Wolfe. And me."

There was something in his tone that suggested there was more to that statement than met the eye and Amabella's heart began to race again. The last time they'd spoken, he'd kissed her hand and told her that she was perfect. Was it only flattery? Or was it something more? Markus didn't seem like the type to deliver idle flattery. He seemed more sincere, deeper than most men, and he was certainly more compassionate than most. As she'd told him, he had a great heart.

But he'd also made it clear that he was leaving with Edward, to become the king's protector. Surely a man like that couldn't be thinking about courting a woman, or even marrying a woman. Certainly not with a woman who was older than he was.

… could he?

"You have been a very good friend to Trastamara," she said, looking into his eyes and unable to pull away. "I do not know how we can ever repay you, but I promise that we shall be good allies forevermore."

Markus smiled faintly. "That is exactly how you can repay us," he said. "By being good allies and neighbors. And I hope that…"

He suddenly stopped himself, giving her an embarrassed little smile and averting his gaze. He was sitting there, looking at his hands, and Amabella watched him closely. For the first time since she'd known him, he seemed uncertain, which was completely unlike him. Usually, Markus was the paragon of confidence and strength.

But in his vulnerability, she found courage. He'd indicated that he wanted to flatter her and he'd even said that, someday, it might be more. What *more* was on her mind. Perhaps it was foolish and futile and all of those things, but she had to know.

She had to ask.

"Markus," she said after a moment. "May I ask you a question?"

He nodded, glancing up at her. "Of course."

She took a deep breath. It was now or never. "What did you mean when you said that you intended to flatter me a great deal and, in time, mayhap more?" she asked. "I have been trying to figure out what you meant and forgive me for being dull, but it seems to me… that is to say, if I was a woman to be courted, you might be hinting towards such a thing. Could you possibly put my mind at ease about what you meant?"

His gaze lingered on her for a moment before he suddenly stood up. He took a deep breath as he did it, making it sound long and laborious, as if she'd just asked him an insurmountable question. He took a few steps towards the hearth and ended up leaning against the mantle above it. All the while, he was looking into the flame as he considered his answer.

"It was clumsy of me, wasn't it?" he said softly. "I do not think I made myself very clear."

Amabella shook her head. "You were not clear at all. But your kiss to my hand... that was very sweet. I've not been flattered like that in twenty years."

He smiled, but it was a weak one. He continued to stare into the fire as it softly snapped. "I do not know how to answer you," he said. "I suppose I never should have said those things, but I could not help myself. Ama, I have known many women in my life. I have had more than my share of female admirers."

Amabella laughed softly. "You do not need to tell me the obvious," she said. "I knew that the first day I saw you. How many fathers have come beating down your door with offers of marital contracts?"

His smiled turned embarrassed. "A few."

Her laughter grew. "I would say it was probably more than a few," she said. "And you've not accepted any of them?"

He looked at her, then, shaking his head. "Nay."

"Why not?"

He shrugged. "Because they were for marriage to a girl," he said. "I am not interested in young women who have yet to grow up. I have never been interested in someone like that."

"What have you been interested in?"

His gaze was intense. "May... may I make a confession?"

"Please."

He sighed heavily, turning back to the flame, the mantle, looking at anything but her. "The first day I saw you, I remember thinking what a spectacular example of womanhood you were," he said. "Roget de Sauque had a goddess for a wife and what did he do? He spit on that fortune. He shite upon it. He did everything he could to diminish the fact that he was married to a lush, compassionate woman of unearthly beauty. He was the most fortunate man in the world and he didn't care."

Amabella was stunned by his words. She opened her mouth to reply but had no idea what to say. At least, for a moment. She had to let those words sink in, like salve for her soul.

"Oh… Markus," she breathed. "That is the kindest thing anyone has ever said to me."

He looked at her, then. "I know," he said. "That's the problem. I know how badly de Sauque treated you. Atlas knows. Every allied knight serving in de Wolfe properties probably knows. Atlas hates his father so much that he will only address him as Roget because he, too, knows how badly the man treated you. And that makes me so angry at Roget that if he wasn't already dead, I would probably kill him. I would have given anything to be in Roget's place when he married you, but I would have done it because of the magnificent woman you are, not because I would inherit a property. I would care not for Trastamara and her wealth. It's you… *you* are the true prize, Amabella. It's a pity Roget never realized that."

Amabella was staring at him, wide-eyed. As Markus watched, her eyes filled with a lake of tears that suddenly spilled down her cheeks. Swiftly, he went to her, standing in front of her as she sat upon the chair.

"I am sorry," he said quickly. "I did not mean to hurt or offend you. If I did, please forgive me. I did not mean to."

Amabella blinked and tears splattered, but she reached up to take his hand and squeeze it. Markus took a knee in front of her, holding her hand in his two enormous mitts. It was a moment before she could compose herself enough to speak.

"You are the kindest, most compassionate man I have ever met," she whispered tightly. "You will never know what your words have meant to me. It is difficult to speak of it. I… I am not sure how to…"

He cut her off gently. "You do not have to speak of it."

But she shook her head, strongly. "I must," she said. "I want you to understand why your kindness has meant so much to us. To me. I have spent the past twenty years being treated as a possession, an afterthought, a breeder of heirs. That is all Roget ever saw me as and that is something I have never confessed to anyone. Up until a week ago, I was resigned to the fact that it was all my life would ever be, but so much has changed since then. You have changed our world more than you can ever know. *My* world. And I shall be forever grateful."

Markus smiled faintly before bringing her hand to his lips, kissing it gently. "I am supposed to assume a new position next month, a very important one," he said. "It will bring me wealth and prestige, and it is something that will make my father very proud, but now… now I am not entirely sure I want to accept it."

She looked at him, startled, as she wiped her cheeks with her free hand. "Why not?" she said. "Markus, you must. You have done great things here at Trastamara, but this is not your destiny."

"Why not?" he said, overlapping her last word. When he realized he'd been forceful, he took a deep breath to steady himself. "What I mean to say is what if a man's destiny isn't what he'd planned? Sometimes destinies are expected. Some- times they just… happen."

She wasn't quite following him. "Trastamara was never your destiny. It belongs to Atlas."

"That is true. But you do not."

"What do you mean?"

"What if *you* are my destiny?"

Amabella blinked in surprise. Then, her eyes widened.

"What… what do you mean?"

He shook his head. Then, he snorted like a man who was about to lose his mind. "I am not entirely sure," he said. "But I do not think I want to leave this place or you. You consume me, Ama. I do not even know how it happened. But the moment I saw you, I knew you were something unique. I have never had a woman catch my eye as you have. I feel… I feel as if we are destined to know one another. Mayhap even belong to one another."

Her wide eyes grew wider. "You… Markus, you cannot mean that," she said. "I am older than you are. Much older."

"You are ten years older than I am. That is not terribly old."

She sat back in her chair, staring at him in disbelief. "I have had four children," she said. "I have been married. I told you that I have had my time. But you… you have not had your time. You must find a young and lovely woman who can give you a dozen children, fine tributes to the de Wolfe name."

"I do not want a young and lovely woman to give me a dozen children," he said. "Amabella… you are ageless in my eyes. Do you not understand? You are wise and mature and reasonable. You are everything a man could want."

Amabella could hardly believe what she was hearing. When he'd told her that he wanted to flatter her, she could have never imagined this was what he'd meant. But he seemed unsure, even as he said it, torn between whatever he was feeling for her and the destiny as Edward's Lord Protector that await him.

He was torn as she was torn.

She was older than he was. Ten years older, as he'd pointed out. But it didn't matter to him in the least. Was it possible that it mattered to her? Perhaps it did in the sense that he was in his prime, a young and powerful knight who deserved a young, beautiful, and virginal wife.

Not an older woman with four children who had already

been married.

But the truth was that she probably fell in love with him the very first day she met him. He'd been so very gentle with her, and kind, and he treated her in a way she hadn't been treated in years. Add his male beauty and powerful form, and there was nothing about that man that was imperfect.

Did she want him?

There was no doubt in her mind. This beautiful, impetuous boy had her attention.

He had her everything.

Gently, she disengaged her hand from his, and both of her hands came up to cup his face. For a moment, she simply looked at him, those gorgeous blue eyes, the nearly-black hair, the straight nose and square jaw. My God, he was spectacular.

It had been such a long time since she'd longed for a man's touch that when the feeling crept over her, it was difficult to resist. In fact, she didn't even try. She knew what it felt like to have a man make love to her, from long ago when Roget had actually been gentle with her. She remembered the excitement, the pleasure, something she never thought she'd ever experience again.

But here it was, in front of her.

Before Amabella realized it, her arms were around Markus' neck as her lips slanted over his.

The magic began.

Markus responded instantly to her, engaging in a heated kiss as tongues plunged deep. He was so surprised, and so overcome, that he ended up pulling her out of the chair and into his arms. He tried to stand up with her but in his haste, he ended up tripping, backing into a wall with his big arms around her as if to never let her go. Amabella had her arms around his neck, his head, trapping him against her, and when she suckled on his tongue, Markus nearly went out of his mind. With a growl, he picked her up and set her on the table of her solar.

Amabella was no shrinking maiden. She was a woman, with woman's needs that had been pent up for years. They were needs she had resigned herself to never being fulfilled again until Markus came into her life.

Until he kissed her hand.

Now, she was on fire.

Amabella took on the aggressor role. She wrapped her legs around his waist, skirts and all, holding him tightly as they furiously kissed one another. Markus's hands were beginning to roam, gaining confidence, as he went from holding her tightly to stroking her back and arms. When she didn't stop him, he grew bolder and moved to her buttocks, squeezing them and pulling her body up against his. Her legs were parted and his body was wedged in between them even though they were fully clothed. Markus sincerely wished, at that moment, that they were not.

He'd never been more consumed by a woman in his life.

Markus' mouth went to her neck, gently suckling her tender skin, and a hand began to gently pull back the neckline of her garment. It wasn't too tight, and he was able to pull it off her right shoulder, baring her skin, as his lips suckled her delicious flesh. He could hear her grunting with pleasure, her hands on his head, her face in his hair. He made no move to touch her breasts, but he continued to slowly and steadily pull her bodice off her shoulder, exposing the swell of her right breast.

Still, she didn't stop him.

Markus grew bolder.

He hadn't been with a woman in over a year. He simply hadn't had the time. Now, he had the woman of his dreams in his hands and he was consumed with her. If she wasn't going to stop him, he was going to keep going, and the bodice was pulled further down. When the fabric resisted, he snaked his hands in behind her and untied the laces that were secured on the side of the garment.

It loosened the dress considerably.

Markus' mouth was on her cleavage now, that delightful cleavage he had noticed the first day he ever saw her. That lush, beautiful body was in his hands and he feasted. Half of her bodice was pulled down her chest and he continued to pull, kissing the flesh as it became exposed, until he finally uncovered her right breast.

Amabella cried out softly as his mouth clamped over a tender nipple. She began to pull at his tunic, trying to undress him, and Markus went right along with her. He wanted her as badly as she wanted him, not stopping to think about the consequences of his actions. He didn't care. All he knew was that he wanted her so badly that he couldn't stop himself from pulling her bodice down around her waist to expose her full, luscious breasts.

His clothing was coming off in pieces until he was finally nude from the waist up. Mouth on her succulent breasts, he flipped up her skirts without any resistance whatsoever. In fact, she was working on his scabbard and his breeches, and he had her skirts up about the time she pulled loose his ties. His broadsword cluttered to the floor and his breeches slipped down to his mid-thigh.

He was between her legs, their bodies naked from the waist down, and his big arousal pushed at her. Markus was a big man and his male member was proportionate, and Amabella's eager hands moved to his thick erection as she guided him into her. He was a hunter seeking his target, and when he felt her slick, wet heat, he thrust firmly into her.

Amabella bit off her cries of pleasure, sinking her teeth into his left bicep. It only served to inflame him. She was exquisitely tight and hot, and he thrust again, feeling her legs wrap around him and draw him in deeper. His arms went around her, holding her tightly against him as he began to move.

Markus' mouth was on hers, kissing her deeply, as he made love to her on the well-made oak table of her solar. It was everything he knew it would be. He felt things for Amabella that he had never felt in his life, for anyone, feelings of attraction that he couldn't control. It was more than the act of sex itself. It was a demonstration of emotions that had completely conquered him.

Amabella was nearly incoherent in her passion, feeling every move with the greatest of pleasure. He was so big, and thrusting himself so deeply, that the pleasure-pain of it was quickly driving her towards release. She'd never made love like this in her life; nothing had even come close. Markus was a spectacular form of a man that she had never seen equaled. Perhaps she was older than him, but it didn't matter any longer. This moment between them was right and she knew it.

She never wanted it to end.

She wanted all of him.

Markus' thrust grew harder, firmer, and he ground his pelvis against her every time he plunged deep. He suckled her nipples as he thrust, listening to her gasp with pleasure. It was moving and beautiful and powerful, and after one particularly deep thrust, he felt her release around him and pants of ecstasy escaped her lips. Still, he continued to make love to her, feeling another climax a few moments later. Their lovemaking was reaching frenzied proportions and he could no longer stop his own release.

Markus tried to pull out of her, but her legs were wrapped around him. He ended up spilling himself into her sweet body, feeling every last twitch and spasm with more pleasure than he'd ever known to exist. But he still kept moving, feeling what he'd put into her, having absolutely no regrets. Normally, he was much more careful about where he put his seed, but with Amabella… it seemed like the most natural thing in the world.

That's how he knew that his feelings for her were real.

With his body still joined to hers, Markus finally opened his eyes to look down at her. Her bodice was down around her waist and her skirts were hiked up over her pelvis, her legs open wide to receive him. The sheer sight of it was enough to cause him to heat up again. Gently, he bent over, kissing her shoulder, the tops of her breasts, before gently taking a nipple in his mouth again and suckling tenderly.

In his arms, he could feel Amabella shudder. She had her arms around his neck, but when he started suckling her again, she put one hand down to where their bodies joined, gently fondling his testicles. Her warm, gentle fingers were wildly arousing and Markus could feel himself growing hard again. The woman's touch set him on fire. His mouth captured hers again and she responded readily until a faint cry filled the air.

"Ama! Eggggggggggs!"

Mouth still fused to hers, Markus' eyes flew open and he found himself staring into her deep emerald green eyes.

"Ambra," she breathed against his mouth. "She has awakened from her nap and she is hungry."

Markus withdrew from her in a flash, pulling her off the table as he pulled his breeches up. As Amabella tossed down her skirts and yanked up her bodice, Markus grabbed his tunics and began pulling them over his head in no particular order. The padded tunic close to his body ended up backwards on him, but he didn't stop to fix it. All that mattered was that he dress, no matter how sloppy that dress turned out to be.

Next to him, Amabella managed to very quickly fasten her garment and she helped him straighten out his tunics. The belt with his broadsword had fallen to the ground and he swiftly picked it up as she rushed over to a chair that was near the windows overlooking the bailey. There was some sewing there that she'd left, little breeches for Alfie, and she quickly picked them up just as Markus finished buckling his scabbard onto his waist. He looked as if he'd dressed in complete darkness and Amabella struggled not to laugh. He bared his teeth at her menacingly, but it was in good humor.

The door to the solar rattled. Markus managed to lean casually back against the wall next to the hearth, quite a distance from Amabella, as the door flew back on its hinges and Ambra charged in with Savia on her heels. The little girl headed straight for her mother.

"Ama," she said, climbing onto her mother's lap. "I want yellow eggs."

Amabella set her sewing aside, cradling her sleepy daughter, who was rubbing her eyes. "I do not know if there are any left, but we can see," she said. "Can you greet Sir Markus?"

Ambra stopped rubbing her eyes and looked at Markus, just now noticing him over by the hearth. She grinned brightly and pointed an imperious finger at him.

"No eggs for you!"

Markus knew what was expected of him. He put a hand over his face and made sniffling noises, much to Ambra's wicked delight. Markus chuckled at the devious little girl as he lowered his hand and turned for the open door.

"If you will excuse me, Lady de Sauque, I will go along my way," he said. "If you have any further questions about Atlas and the situation we are facing, do not hesitate to ask. I am at your service."

Amabella watched him cross the floor, with his tunics askew and his belt twisted, and his hair mussed from where she ran her hands through it. She noticed these things, but she wondered if anyone else would.

Not that she cared.

The price was well worth it.

"Thank you, my lord," she said. "You have been most… gracious in your explanation."

Markus merely smiled, quitting the chamber without another word.

Even as Ambra yanked her mother off the chair with her demands to go to the kitchen, Amabella's thoughts were still on Markus, still on his miraculous touch. It had been an awakening for her, an awakening that showed her what she was truly capable of in the arms of a man. More than that, it showed her what she was truly capable of with Markus.

When he touched her, the sparks flew.

Roget had been inadequate and demanding in bed. He'd taught her what he liked, but as the years went on, she could never bring herself to do it, knowing she was sharing him with another woman. But with Markus, that reserve was gone. She was willing to explore everything with him and then some, and if their encounter was a foretaste of what the future held for them, she felt as if this went beyond an awakening.

A rebirth.

Come what may, Markus de Wolfe had done that for her, in more ways than she could imagine.

CHAPTER FIFTEEN

THE ARMY FROM Trastamara moved out before dawn the next day.

The trek to Mordrington was a short one, all things considered, and Cassius and Atlas rode at the head of the army while Damien was positioned at the back of the column, watching their rear. With one provisions wagon and four hundred heavily-armed soldiers, they moved with surprising speed on a morning that had dawned misty at first, but had soon cleared.

It had rained the night before, leaving the roads a bit muddy, but nothing that was impassable or particularly difficult. The pace was quicker than normal because Cassius and Damien knew that any patrols from Mordrington would pick up the approach of an army and it was quite possible that they would run headlong into a shield wall of Scots before they could even get to the manse. Therefore, they wanted to give the Scots less time to prepare for their arrival.

The men were moving swiftly.

The knights were in full battle gear, while Atlas' mode of dress was a little different. He was taller than his father, but not quite as heavy, so he was able to wear almost all of Roget's mail and protection, including a beautiful broadsword that had once belonged to Amabella's father. It was Spanish, from the great metalworkers of Aragon, much as Shand's broadsword had been. But Shand's broadsword was back at Trastamara, probably never to be used again, at least not by Atlas. He couldn't bring himself to touch the thing. But he carried his grandfather's sword quite proudly.

He was also wearing the old Trastamara colors of red and white, old tunics that had been stored when Roget had become the Lord of Trastamara and had commissioned tunics of red and blue, representing the House of de Sauque. But Atlas refused to wear them or show tribute to his father in any way. He and several old soldiers who had served under Alonzo Abril had hunted down the old tunics, and now many of the old guard were wearing their tunics proudly once again.

So was Atlas.

In fact, he rode at the head of the column as puffed up as a peacock, this young lord who now commanded his hereditary army. Cassius and Damien kept passing amused glances because Atlas was singularly focused on the road ahead as if nothing else in the world existed. Cassius had to remind him, twice, to keep his attention on the land surrounding the road so he wouldn't be surprised by any marauders brave enough to take on an army. Sheepishly, Atlas did.

Nearly an hour into their march, Atlas had the army slow because they were approaching Mordrington. They could smell it, even at this distance, but they hadn't met any resistance so far, which they took as a hopeful sign that the Scots weren't alerted to their presence. Cassius asked for permission to disperse the army around Mordrington and Atlas agreed, so Cassius split the army into two factions. A smaller group split off, with Damien at the helm, and headed into the trees to flank Mordrington on three sides while Cassius and Atlas took the bulk of the army to the front of the manse.

Having never seen the manse, Cassius wasn't quite sure what to expect, but once it came into view, he could see that it wasn't a very big structure. Surely no more the fifty Scots could be inside because it simply didn't have the size that a castle would. As they approached, they could see that the drawbridge was down, but there didn't seem to be anyone moving about, not like Atlas and Markus had seen the day before.

In fact, it appeared strangely deserted. Within full view of the manse, Cassius called a halt to the army, who began spreading out to form the front line. Cassius, next to Atlas, scratched his head.

"It does not look as if anyone is there," he said, confused. "And you are sure you saw men here?"

Atlas nodded firmly. "Most definitely," he said. "There were Scots and they threw a dead body into the moat. Shand came out to speak with them."

Cassius thought on that. Then, he emitted a low whistle between his teeth, summoning a couple of men. He gave them orders to send scouts out into the surrounding countryside to make sure there wasn't a Scots army lying in wait for them, waiting to pounce and box them in between an attacking army and the castle walls. As four men mounted steeds and charged off, Cassius returned his attention to the manse.

"The army will remain here and position archers," he said. "You and I will approach. Bring your shield."

Atlas nodded, sliding off his horse and collecting the shield that was strapped to the saddle. Unlike most shields, which bore an animal like a bear or a boar or a falcon, or even a symbol of war, the old Trastamara shield bore the Archangel Michael. It was the simple design of an angel with big wings and a sword in the right hand. It had been the symbol of the House of Abril in battle for a century until Roget de Sauque used it, but the shield Atlas had in his hand had belonged to his grandfather. Other than the armor, which he wore only because it fit, he didn't intend to carry on anything his father brought to Trastamara.

The House of Abril would shine again.

Beside him, Cassius carried his de Wolfe shield, with the recognizable wolf's head. It was the same design that he had tattooed on his left shoulder, a symbol of the grandsons of William de Wolfe. Like Markus and the rest of the extended male cousins, he wore the *stigmata* proudly.

Shields in-hand, the two of them cautiously made their way to the lowered drawbridge. There was a sense of concern since the place appeared deserted. It didn't seem natural. The drawbridge was open and they could see into what appeared to be a courtyard with a roof overhead, or even a hall of sorts. It was difficult to tell. The shadowed light of whatever was beyond told them there was something overhead and they could both clearly see that there was someone standing in the hall, waiting for them.

Cassius and Atlas came to within ten feet of the drawbridge before Cassius called a halt. Shield lifted, he called to the figure inside.

"Show yourself," he boomed. "I bring four hundred men, so any resistance will be strongly met."

The figure moved immediately, coming out of the shadows towards him. As it came through the doorway, Cassius and Atlas could immediately see that it was a well-dressed woman with two small boys, one in each hand. The three of them emerged from the manse without hesitation, coming out onto the drawbridge.

Atlas knew immediately who they were.

"The whore," he hissed. "That is my father's whore."

Cassius didn't take his eyes off her, but he could hear the loathing in Atlas' tone. The woman was not unattractive, with red hair and a rather round body, and both boys were dark-haired, like Atlas was. In fact, they looked a little like Atlas, but Cassius didn't comment. He could already sense how tense Atlas was at the sight of them.

"Stop," he commanded the woman. "Who are you?"

The woman looked between the two men. "My name is Fenella Foulden Hume," she said. "These are my sons, Edmund and Emrys. Why do ye bring yer army here? Who are ye?"

Cassius regarded the woman for a moment. "You were standing inside, waiting for us with the drawbridge open. Surely you know."

"I saw ye coming from the battlements. I wanted tae show ye we posed no threat."

Cassius considered that, glancing at Atlas to see the young man's reaction. There was none. He returned his focus to the woman.

"Where are the Scots who fill this place?" he asked.

"Gone."

"Gone *where*?"

"I dunna know," she said. "And ye have not identified yourself."

"I am Atlas de Sauque," Atlas said, suddenly moving in her direction. "You are my father's whore, but now that he is dead, Mordrington belongs to me. You will pack your bags and your bastards and get out today. If you are still here when the sun sets, I will have the army remove you."

Fenella's eyes widened as she stared at him. "Atlas," she breathed. "Is… is it true?"

"Of course it is. I would not lie."

She looked him up and down, almost proudly. "I can see that it is because ye have the look of yer father about ye," she said. "He spoke of ye often and fondly and said that ye…"

Atlas cut her off rudely. "Shut your lips," he said. "I do not want to hear your voice. I do not care about you or what my father told you about me. All I care about is that you pack your things and leave."

Fenella acted as if she didn't hear him. She bent over, speaking to the boys beside her. "Look," she said, pointing at Atlas. "That is yer brother. Ye must greet him properly."

Atlas moved closer to her. "Lady, are you deaf?" he said. "I told you to pack your bags and get out. If you do not, I will turn this army loose on you."

Fenella looked at him, finally forced to address his demand. "I have nowhere tae go."

"That is not my concern," he said. "I want you out, and out you shall go. And where is Shand Bexwell? Why was he here yesterday?"

Fenella cocked her head. "I dunna know what ye mean."

Atlas marched up to her, posturing angrily over her. "Aye, you do," he said through clenched teeth. "Stop playing stupid. I know he was here yesterday and I want to know why. And where are all of the Scots that were here yesterday? I want answers and you'd better give them to me, or I will separate you from your sons and you will never see them again. Do you understand me?"

That seemed to strike some fear into Fenella. She clutched the older boy but before she could grab the younger one, he pulled away from her and would have run off had Atlas not grabbed him. The child screamed, Fenella screamed, and Cassius came forward to take the screaming child from Atlas.

It happened that fast.

"My bairn!" Fenella cried. "Dunna hurt him! He's only a babe!"

"I have no intention of hurting him," Atlas said. "But you *will* get out. Once you pack your bags and leave, I will give you back the lad. Refuse me and I will take him back with me to Trastamara."

Fenella began to panic. "How can ye do this?" she wept. "He is yer brother!"

"He is *not* my brother," Atlas roared. "He is my father's bastard. He has nothing to do with me and I care less for him even than I care for you, so do as you are told, woman. My patience grows thin."

Fenella had gone from being fairly excited to finally meet Roget's son, thinking that somehow, someway, he would have a heart for her plight and the plight of his half-brothers, to being terrified and furious. She had been told by Shand that Atlas wanted her out of Mordrington, but she didn't really believe it until now. It was clear that Atlas had no use for her. There was no warmth in his eyes, no consideration.

No mercy.

This was not how she had planned this day.

She knew Trastamara was coming. Win and Shand had told her of their plans because they wanted her to try and keep the Trastamara army at Mordrington as long as she could so that they would have ample time to breach the walls of Trastamara Castle.

Of course, Fenella was willing. She had heard the talk from her brother and his men, and Shand, when they spoke of how they would divide up the de Sauque properties once Trastamara surrendered to the *reiver* army. Win even spoke of calling upon the other reivers in the area, *Na Bràithrean,* and creating a large outlaw army to capture Trastamara, but that idea was discarded because Win knew he'd have to share Mordrington with them. If his brethren reivers helped capture a castle, they would want a part of the spoils.

And Win didn't want to share.

Therefore, he took his men and, along with Shand, made his way south to Trastamara before dawn, knowing full well that the Trastamara army would more than likely be mobilizing on them. It was really a lucky guess based on the fact that there were spies watching Mordrington the day before, but it was more like an educated guess. If Atlas de Sauque really wanted to throw Fenella from Mordrington, then it stood to reason that once the Scots were spotted, Trastamara would move quickly.

And they had.

Clearly, the spies had been from Trastamara because Atlas knew of Shand and he knew of the Scots. But the situation had spiraled out of control once Atlas took charge of Emrys, who was screaming in the grip of an enormous English knight. Fenella was willing to do what she could for her brother, and for her future at Mordrington, but that was until the *Sassenach* caught hold of Emrys.

Then, she wasn't so willing to go along any longer.

"Ye want tae know about Shand and the Scots?" she finally hissed. "Give me back my lad or I'll tell ye nothing!"

At that point, Cassius came forward, still gripping the weeping child. "Then you do know about them."

"I'll tell ye nothing!"

"If you want your son returned, you most certainly will."

She took a step back, whispering something to the other boy, who ran inside the manse and disappeared. That forced Cassius to emit a piercing whistle between his teeth as two soldiers rode forward. As the men drew near, he lifted the child to them, but Fenella started to scream.

"Nay!" she cried. "Give him back tae me!"

Cassius still had hold of the child, now lifted up in his big hands. "Answer our questions and he will be returned to you."

She shook her head, her frizzy hair whipping back and forth. Cassius promptly handed the boy over to one of the soldiers, who took off in the direction of the army with a screaming child in his arms. Cassius motioned to Atlas, who began to follow Cassius back the way they had come.

Fenella could see that they weren't going to give her back her child until she told them what they wanted to know. She was normally a calm woman, but not when it came to her children. Living with animals as she did, she had seen men kill one another for little to no provocation and she'd always managed to keep her children away from it.

But not now.

Convinced the army from Trastamara was going to kill her younger son, she began to scream.

"Ask me!" she cried, following them as they walked away. "Ask me what ye will, but give me back my bairn!"

Cassius came to a halt and Atlas right after him. They both turned to look at her.

"Where is Shand?" Cassius asked.

Fenella was shaken, wiping the tears from her eyes. "Please," she whispered desperately. "My bairn…"

"I will not ask again. Where is Shand?"

She swallowed hard. "He's not here," she said. "Ye can search the place if ye like, but he's not here. No one is."

"Then there were Scots here."

She nodded unsteadily. "My brother and his men."

"From Clan Hume?"

She shrugged. "We are part of Clan Hume," she said. "But my brother… his men come from other clans, too. Men seeking money."

It took Cassius a moment to realize what she meant. "Reivers."

Fenella nodded. "They… they do as they please."

"Is Shand part of them?"

She shook her head. "He only came here two days ago," she said. "He said… he wanted their help tae lay siege tae Trastamara. He wants the place."

"We know he wants it," Cassius said. "Where did he go?

Where did they all go?"

"South."

"South *where*?"

"Along the road ye came on. The one that leads tae The Orchard crossing."

"We did not see them and we were on the road since we left Trastamara."

"They stayed tae the trees, out of sight."

An ominous feeling swept Cassius and, suddenly, he was standing in front of her, his expression tight. All of her clues were leading to one destination.

"Is *that* where they are?" he demanded. "Trastamara?"

Fearfully, she nodded. "They knew ye would come here," she said. "They knew there were spies here yesterday and they knew the spies came from Trastamara. They figured ye would come tae rid Mordrington of Scots and I see they werena wrong – ye *did* come. They went south this morning as ye came north."

Cassius' eyes widened for a split second as he realized Trastamara was being targeted and her army was gone. He and Markus and all of the knights had badly misplayed this situation. They'd done exactly what the Scots at Mordrington, and Shand, had wanted them to do.

They'd left Trastamara with hardly enough men to defend her.

Suddenly, Cassius turned on his heel and began to bellow.

"Give the woman her son!" he boomed. "We return home *now*!"

CHAPTER SIXTEEN

A T DAWN, MARKUS had been on the battlements of Trastamara, watching his brother lead the four-hundred-man army out of the gatehouse and to the road heading north. He and Kieran had watched the men march out, followed by the wagon, a relatively small army as far as de Wolfe armies went. Markus had seen thousands of men march out at one time from Berwick or Castle Questing, two of the larger outposts in the de Wolfe empire.

It wasn't like the army wasn't going to face a major battle that would determine the course of a family but, in a sense, it was a serious enough battle. They were going to purge the Scots, and Shand Bexwell, from Mordrington Manse and Damien had specific orders to kill Bexwell on sight. Atlas didn't know about that particular order because the young man had enough on his mind. That order was between Markus, Cassius, and Damien.

It would be carried out, no matter what.

Markus had watched the army move north along the road until they disappeared from view on a surprisingly bright morning after the mist had lifted. He had followed the wall walk around until he ended up above the kitchen yard. Even at the early hour, he could see Alfie prowling around below with his wooden sword and Roget's old helm. A couple of the horse guard were out with him, drilling, and Markus watched them for a few minutes, smiling at the sight.

There was something settling about watching children play. It brought back memories of a more peaceful time in his life, a time when he didn't have a care in the world. Watching children play without any thought to war or intrigue told Markus that there was indeed peace in the world, still. Sometimes he wondered. Being a de Wolfe, he'd been raised in a military household and that was all he knew. That was his world.

But there was part of him that longed for the peace that Alfie knew.

He envied the child his sense of tranquility.

Ever since his encounter with Amabella the day before, Markus had his own sense of tranquility he'd never had before. He couldn't even begin to describe it – it was like a piece of him he never knew to be missing was suddenly found. He felt whole, complete, and happy beyond measure. He'd seen men fall in love before and he had his own parents and grandparents as an example of that, but he never truly believed it would happen to him. It simply wasn't something he thought about or longed for.

But now… now, he understood what the fuss was about. As he watched Alfie play with his friends, he understood the joy in the simple things, in the things that all the money or glory in the world couldn't bring him. A new world was presented to him and he wanted every single part of it. But if he took it, he knew the title of Lord Protector would have to be sacrificed. He couldn't spend days and months and years with Edward, as the man's premier warrior and protector, because that meant he would have to sacrifice his own happiness.

He would have to sacrifice Amabella.

That very thought had been heavy on his mind since yesterday. It wasn't that he was torn, because he really wasn't. It was more that he was concerned how his father was going to react.

Patrick had wanted this so very badly for him.

Patrick himself had been offered the position many years ago but had ultimately relinquished it in favor of marrying Markus' mother. In that respect, Markus was certain his father would understand. He might not be happy about it, but he would understand.

But then came the subject of Amabella herself.

She was older than Markus was. She was a woman who had been married twenty years and had four children of her own. As Amabella herself pointed out, she didn't come with any great dowry or titles. She essentially had nothing of value to offer. In a world where marriages were based on such things, it made her a dismal prospect, but not to Markus. He already had a title and wealth, and upon his father's death, he would become an earl.

Amabella would make a magnificent countess.

He smiled at the thought, of how proud he would be to have such a beautiful, wise wife. The fact that she was older only made her more beautiful to him and when he touched her… no maiden could have responded the way she had. Even the thought of her flesh against his set him on fire. She was perfect in every way, as he saw it. But he could only hope his father saw it that way, too. He had to admit that he was concerned.

Leaving Alfie to practice with half his guard during this early hour, he came off the wall and went to check in with Kieran, who was at the gatehouse. They had about fifty men on the walls and the rest were going about various duties inside the bailey. With the bulk of the army away, they were on heightened alert.

Posts were set and men were vigilant, enough so that Markus felt comfortable going inside to check on the women.

He was certain they were tucked away in Amabella's solar, which is where they should be, but when he entered the keep and made his way to the solar, he could see that it was empty.

A fire burned in the hearth, making the chamber cozy, and two of the Berwick maids were sweeping and cleaning. They acknowledged Markus with a curtsy.

"Where is Lady de Sauque?" he asked.

One maid, an older woman in charge of the maid brigade, pointed a finger to the floor above.

"She must still be in her chamber, m'lord," she said. "The nurse took the wee ones to the hall, but I've not seen the lady."

"What about her older daughter?"

"I've not seen that one, either, m'lord."

Markus turned for the stairs, his destination being the floor above. Normally, a visiting knight wouldn't think to wander unrestrained around a family's keep but, in this case, he had no such qualms. He would be respectful of their privacy, but he wanted to make sure both Amabella and Aleanor were well this morning.

He could tell himself all he wanted that this was part of his duty, as the knight in command of Trastamara, but deep down, it was more than that where Amabella was concerned. He'd spent an entire night away from her and very much wanted to see her lovely face this morning. He wanted to know how she felt after their encounter yesterday because they hadn't discussed it. There hadn't been the opportunity.

Truth be told, he was a wee bit nervous. That big heart he had, a true de Wolfe heart, was a fragile thing when exposed as it was now.

Coming to the top of the stairwell on the top floor of Trastamara, he knew there were two chambers on this level – one was Roget's cluttered, dusty mess of a chamber, but there was a second one that he assumed was Amabella's. He'd never actually been on this floor with the exception of the one time he'd come with Amabella in search of Trastamara's riches. Going to the second door, he knocked softly.

"My lady?" he called softly.

The door opened almost instantly. Amabella stood there, a smile on her lips, and Markus knew instantly that she was feeling the same delirium that he was. He could see it in her eyes. The same joy, the same happiness. The same realization that yesterday had not been an impulsive mistake.

It had been real.

There was no doubt in his mind.

"Good morn to you, Markus," she said. "I saw the army depart this morning. You did not go with them?"

Markus shook his head. "Atlas asked that I remain in command at Trastamara to protect you until the army returns," he said. "Naturally, I did not argue with him."

He said it with a twinkle in his eyes and Amabella's smile broadened. "I am glad you did not," she said. "He came to see me before he left, you know."

"He did?"

She nodded. "I did what you said – I did not undermine his confidence," she said. "I have not said a word to him about not wanting him to ride to battle."

"Then you did well," Markus said. "Did you see him ride out?"

She nodded, her smile fading. "He was wearing mail and protection. Where did he get it? I did not know that he had any of his own."

Markus leaned against the door jamb. "Most of it was his father's," he said. "Did you see the tunic he wore?"

She shook her head. "I could not see very well in the darkness before dawn."

Markus lifted an eyebrow. "He would not wear Roget's," he

said quietly. "I was unaware that Roget commissioned new tunics when he became the Lord of Trastamara. We dug around in the old armory until we came across several that had been worn by your father's soldiers. They identified the Abril tunics. The old Trastamara soldiers were happy to wear the old red and white tunics again and that was what Atlas wore as well."

Amabella sighed and put her hand over her heart. "How touching," she said. "My father was so proud of Atlas. He was still a very small child when my father died, but my father never had any sons and he doted on Atlas. I wish… I wish my father had seen him grow up. He would have been so proud of him."

Markus could see how much Atlas' gesture meant to her. "Indeed, I'm sure he would have been," he said. "He's a good lad, Ama. He will make a fine lord."

Her smile returned. "I know," she said, her eyes alight with hope and joy. "As I said yesterday, we owe you and your men much thanks. You have all taken a great deal of care with him. But this battle coming up… I have a question I am afraid to ask."

"Why?"

"Because it sounds as if I am worrying again."

He grinned. "You are his mother," he said. "You are the only one allowed to worry. What is your question?"

She took a deep breath. "The knights… they will watch out for him in battle, won't they? Knowing he is not a full-fledged knight?"

He pushed himself off the door jamb. Reaching out, he put a big hand on her arm, gently. "They are all watching him very closely," he said. "Cassius will not leave his side, and my brother is a knight of astounding talent. Trust me when I say that Atlas will be well protected."

She smiled gratefully. "Thank you," she said sincerely. "I will not worry any longer."

"Aye, you will."

"You're correct. I will."

They shared a gentle laugh together, but the air between them was electric. There was so much that Markus wanted to say to her, but he wasn't sure how to. He looked into her chamber, over her head, as if searching for something.

"Where is Aleanor?" he asked.

"In her chamber on the floor below," Amabella said. "Though I will say that when the army left this morning, she watched with me from the windows in my solar. I watched my son ride away from the walls and she watched Cassius."

Markus chuckled. "I am afraid she is going to have to give up her dreams of Cass," he said. "He has no interest in a wife right now."

"She is still too young. But she will not be in a few years."

"Then, in a few years, if Cass has not yet married, you should approach my father about it."

Amabella chuckled. "I will if she ever gets over her abject terror of men in general," she said. "Hopefully, it is something she will outgrow with age."

"Time will tell."

The conversation died, but it wasn't unpleasant. Markus simply stood there, a faint smile on his lips while Amabella looked up at him, waiting for him to say something. What happened yesterday was hanging over them like a cloud, obvious, but neither of them was willing to point it out. The more the moments dragged on, the more weighty the cloud became.

"You mentioned that Aleanor will have to give up her dreams of Cass," she finally said. "Tell me, Markus, must I also give up my dreams of you?"

His gaze lingered on her for a moment before slowly shaking his head. "Nay," he murmured. "I am yours, Ama. If you want me."

Amabella's heart swelled with joy. "More than anything in the world," she whispered. "My age does not bother you?"

"I told you that you are ageless to me."

"But I am more than likely past childbearing years."

"I hope to discover that you are wrong."

Her breath caught in her throat, hardly believing what she was hearing. Indeed, it was like a dream. In fact, she wasn't entirely sure everything that happened yesterday wasn't a dream when she woke up this morning. It had all seemed so surreal. But looking into Markus' eyes, she could see that it was no dream.

It was very, very real.

"Oh… Markus," she breathed. "I do not know what to say."

He took a step into the chamber, standing so close to her that he could feel the heat from her body. It was arousing, titillating, so much so that his palms began to sweat. His heart was thumping against his ribs. Everything about the woman seemed to stir every corner of him until he could hardly think of anything else.

"Tell me that you'll love me the rest of your life," he whispered. "Because I will love you for the rest of mine."

She nodded, unable to articulate the joy in her heart, and she threw her arms around his neck just as he pulled her into a crushing embrace. His mouth descended on hers with powerful passion and in that brief and magnificent moment, he claimed her.

She was his.

But Amabella was quite willing. She wanted to be claimed, to be dominated. Her arms tightened around his neck and she was aware of being picked up and carried towards her bed. Markus had enough presence of mind to kick the door shut and throw the bolt.

As he had done yesterday in her private solar, his lips ravaged her, his tongue gentle, firm but experienced. His strength was too much for Amabella to match so she surrendered to him easily, responding to his fierce kisses. When his mouth left her lips and he nibbled hungrily down her neck, it was all she could do to catch her breath.

The man sucked every last bit of air out of her.

Markus didn't stop with fiery kisses. He wanted more. Something about her heated flesh in his arms turned him into a madman. He pulled the top of her shift out of the way to reveal a delicate white shoulder and Amabella could hear him growl as his mouth suckled her flesh, feeling the heat from his lips like a fire brand.

Markus pulled harder on the surcoat she was wearing and ended up tearing it. The coat came apart in his hands and he threw it to the floor. She was clad now in only her shift and he slowed his frenzied pace, taking a moment to feel her flesh underneath the thin material. He rubbed her breasts, her belly, her hips. It was slow, gentle, and erotic. He gazed into her eyes as his hands cupped those lush buttocks, pulling her against his arousal. It was clear what he wanted.

She wanted it, too.

Markus was in full protection, but it began to come off in a steady rhythm. Amabella wasn't very proficient at helping him, but she tried. He was doing more work than she was, his mouth rarely leaving hers as he worked, and when he was down to his heavy breeches, he paused long enough to rip off his tunic and throw her onto the bed.

He was on her in an instant.

Mouths locked in a passionate embrace, Markus lay her back on the neatly made bed, one hand behind her head and the other moving down her slender torso. Her breasts were full and luscious in his hand and he was suddenly angry at the shift that was still between them. He pulled it off, indelicately, leaving her completely nude. He gazed at her a moment in the weak light of the chamber, his breath catching in his throat.

He'd never seen anything so beautiful.

"God, you're magnificent," he muttered.

Amabella gazed up at him, completely comfortable in her nudity. She lifted a leg, rubbing his thigh with her foot as he stood over her, his gorgeous nude form drawing her hungry eyes. But something caught her focus, a mark on his enormous bicep.

"That mark on your arm," she said softly. "What is that?"

Markus glanced at the de Wolfe standard on his arm. "This is the mark of the grandsons of William de Wolfe," he said huskily. "We all receive this stigmata when we come of age. It is a birthright that we wear with pride."

She lifted her hand to touch it, but unable to reach him, she simple fondled his fingers. "It is unique and powerful," she whispered. "Like you, my beautiful lad. Don't make me wait for you any longer. Come to me."

Her words inflamed him. Quickly, his breeches came off and he smothered her with his massive form.

Instinct took hold. Markus kissed her so passionately that Amabella couldn't breathe with the force of his lust. His big hands moved the length of her body, gentle yet powerful. When he closed over a bare breast, she encouraged him. When his hot mouth finally descended on a tender nipple, she held his head fast against her. Her body was quivering with excitement as his lips moved over every inch of her sweet, round breasts.

When he wedged his big body between her legs, she welcomed him. Her legs parted easily, inviting him into intimate places. Markus accepted the invitation and plunged into her, feeling her body arch against him as the first waves of pleasure rolled through her.

Gathering her against him, he began his measured thrusts into her sweet body, overwhelmed by the smell and feel of her. She was slick and hot and tight. Never in his life had he experienced anything so arousing, nor had he ever expected to, but the woman in his arms was just this side of heaven. He savored every thrust, every withdrawal, feeling her body draw him in deeper and deeper.

He was trapped.

Markus' mouth moved to hers again, kissing her deeply. Amabella's hands were on his buttocks, her nails leaving crescent-shaped marks in his flesh. In the throes of her passion, she drew blood, causing Markus to spill himself sooner than he had hoped. The pleasure-pain had been too much for him to take and he spent himself with the greatest of ecstasy. Even after he savored his release, he continued to kiss her, unable to let her go. He couldn't stop himself from making love to her once more before both of them fell into an exhausted sleep, content in each other's arms.

When next Markus realized, alarms were going up all over the fortress.

IT WAS MORNING and the army from Trastamara had ridden out a couple of hours earlier. It was a bright day, with the sun shining and the birds singing, and would have been a pleasant day had there not been a hint of tension laying over the castle. With the army gone to a skirmish, the inhabitants of Trastamara were understandably a little edgy.

But not Alfie. He was down in the kitchen yard with his horse guard, drilling them, forcing them to march one way and then the other. He was preparing them to guard the postern gate and he wanted them to be ready. When he felt they were ready, or at least all moving in the right direction, he marched them over to the bolted gate so they could assume their posts.

It was cold in the passage underneath the wall and some of the horse guard weren't properly dressed against it. Manley's lips were turning blue as he shivered, but Alfie was unsympathetic. He demanded they form a line in front of the gate and stay there. The guard managed to maintain their position for a while until boredom overtook them. They were starting to beg for water, or bread, when Alfie caught sight of something on the other side of the gate.

He pushed Manley and Bartram out of the way as he peered at the movement.

"There are *men* out there," he finally said, astounded.

The entire horse guard turned around, startled. Trastamara sat on flat ground with a slight slope that led down towards the orchards and the River Tweed, but there was a clear field of vision fifty feet all the way around the property. Beyond that were heavy trees and it was in those trees that Alfie saw the movement.

Suddenly, men in long tunics bearing short swords and ropes were skulking towards the walls. Some of them even had crude ladders between them.

Alfie's eyes widened.

"Go get the branding irons," he hissed to his guard.

Aldwin, Manley, and Bartram ran to get them while the rest of the guard backed away from the gate fearfully. But Alfie stood there, watching with some fascination, as men rushed up to the gate. Faces he didn't recognize peered through the iron grate at him.

"Laddie," one of the men said. "Will ye let us in? We need protection."

Alfie frowned. "From what?" he asked. "You have swords. You can protect yourselves."

There were several men crowding up against the grate, making Alfie nervous enough that he backed away. Someone stuck an arm out, grabbing for him, and he backed away further.

"Go away!" he shouted. "Go away or I'll tell Sir Knight!"

"Help us, laddie," the man said again. "Will ye not help protect us?"

Alfie shook his head. "You have swords," he said. "If you needed to be protected, you would not have swords. Who are you? Why are you here?"

More hands were reaching out, trying to grab at him, but by this time, Manley and Aldwin had returned with red-hot fire brands. Alfie took one from Manley and wielded it menacingly at the men on the other side of the grate.

"Go away!" he said again. "Go away or I'll fight you!"

The men at the grate were no longer so pleasant.

"Open the gate, ye little whelp," one man said, taking a swipe at Alfie. "Open it now!"

His hand was reaching out and, frightened, Alfie lashed out with the fire brand, jabbing the man in the hand with it. It seared into his flesh and he screamed, which terrified the entire horse guard. The children screamed, the man screamed, and Alfie was spurred into action. He began jabbing anything that moved with his fire brand, making contact on several occasions as the men on the other side of the grate pulled back, fearful of being burned. They also tried to grab at it to take it away from him.

But Alfie could see there was a serious problem. He knew these men shouldn't be here and he knew, instinctively, that they were bad. He barked at his horse guard, telling them to get more fire pokers, while he sent one of the little girls running for his friend, Sir Knight.

His greatest hero had to know there was trouble at the postern gate. Little did Alfie know that, at the moment, there was trouble all around Trastamara.

The attack had begun.

The alarms began to sound.

CHAPTER SEVENTEEN

T HE WALLS OF Trastamara weren't as easy to breach as Shand had made it sound.

Win and his fellow Scots figured that out within the first hour. They'd been unsuccessful at trying to convince the child in the kitchen yard to open the postern gate. In fact, the little bastard had taken fire pokers and burned their hands when they tried to grab him.

Shand had seen the child. He knew him on sight. He named the child as Alphonse, son of Roget, but he'd stayed out of sight, not wanting the child to see him. Since Shand had been exiled from Trastamara, he didn't want the lad telling people that he'd seen his father's knight in the mix of Scots who were now encircling the castle with ropes fastened to grappling hooks and ladders built from wood from the nearby forest. Shand wanted to make sure he remained out of sight until absolutely necessary.

The truth was that Shand hadn't been entirely truthful about the difficulty in breaching the castle, mostly because he didn't want the Scots to refuse his proposal. Now that they were here, they could see that the big, gray walls were smooth, so it was difficult to get any kind of a foothold on them. Not only that, but they were built out at the bottom, which made them very difficult to scale.

Difficult, yes, but not impossible.

It was more difficult for the ladders because they couldn't get a good bracing against the wall. There were several ladders, built that morning by hungry Scots, and they'd tried to put them up for a solid hour before they gave up and concentrated on the grappling hooks. Then someone got the idea to use the ropes from the grappling hooks to tie on to the ladders so they could stabilize them. A man could climb the ladder with the rope from the grappling hook secured at the top, providing no one from the castle loosened the rope or the hook, and then use the rope to climb all the way to the battlements.

Every wall had soldiers on it and they'd brought one hundred and seven men with them. They had no way of knowing how many men were still in Trastamara and there weren't a great number of them on the battlements, which was encouraging.

But then, the arrows started.

Flying from the bailey and raining down on the Scots, the first barrage of arrows managed to strike several of the men, who went down screaming. But Win and his men bellowed at them, demanding they rip out the arrows and continue trying to mount the walls. The Scots were, if nothing else, tenacious, and no man would give in to pain at this early point in the battle.

The reivers were a tough bunch. They were also driven by greed and Trastamara promised to be a fine prize. On the western wall, some men managed to get onto the battlements, but the biggest knight they'd ever seen was waiting for them, tossing them right back over the wall as if they weighed no more than children.

Word spread quickly.

Shand watched as Markus de Wolfe threw men to their deaths, with two men landing right on their heads. The rest of them, and there were six who had managed to make it on the wall, landed heavily and wounded some part of their body. One man broke a bone that poked through his skin.

But that didn't discourage the reivers.

More men made attempts to mount the walls and someone managed to get onto the wall near the gatehouse, which brought some serious fighting and the death of two more Scots. Still, Shand didn't engage. He stayed out of it, watching from a distance as Win Foulden's men worked hard for little reward.

With all of that going on, Win joined Shand at one point and he did not look pleased.

"It seems tae me that this wasna as easy as ye led us tae believe," he said, sweaty and grimy from having tried to scale the gatehouse. He jabbed a finger in the direction of the castle. "They have a knight on the walls throwing my men tae their deaths."

Shand nodded. "I know," he said. "That is Markus de Wolfe of Berwick."

Win cocked his head. "Berwick?" he repeated. "De Wolfe? The Earl of Berwick is a de Wolfe."

Shand nodded. "And that knight on the wall is his son and heir," he said. "The man is a monster. As long as we can only get a few men to the walls at a time, he will continue to defeat us."

Win was becoming frustrated. "Then ye led us here tae a futile action?"

Shand looked at him. "I would not do that," he said. "I thought your men would be able to scale the walls easier than they have, but it is not futile."

Win pointed to the gray walls in exasperation. "It seems that way tae me."

But Shand shook his head. "Come with me."

Win followed him over to the area of the wall where the postern gate was. There was a big tower on one corner, used for storage, but there were soldiers on it, preparing to fight off Scots who were still trying to mount the walls. On the corner, near the tower, were two arched drainage openings, grated with iron like the postern gate. Shand pointed to them.

"See those?" he said. "They are protected, but the iron grates do not go terribly deep and it is not anchored in any rock. If you put men to digging on those, we can dig a deep enough hole to get underneath the grate and into the drainage culvert. There is another grate on the other end, with the kitchen yard beyond, but if your men can dig underneath both of those grates, we can gain access."

Win peered at the grates. They were mostly buried in muck and mud, and all of the foul things that drained out of the kitchen yard, but there was enough of a space to make them passable should they be able to dig down and get underneath them. Shaking his head in disgust, he eyed Shand.

"This damnable castle had better be worth it," he grumbled.

Shand looked at him. "Is Mordrington worth it?" he fired back. "And think of all of the lovely revenue you can collect when we control The Orchard crossing."

The potential for controlling that bridge alone made this all worth it, but Win wasn't going to admit it. Gathering some of his men, he pointed to the mud and explained what needed to be done.

Disgusted, but determined, the Scots got busy.

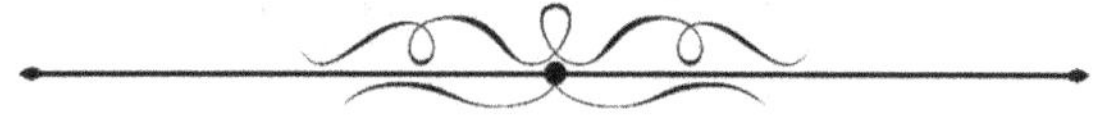

"AMA! I MUST fight!"

Amabella was holding on to Alfie as tightly as she could. He was a little boy, that was true, but he had a surprising amount of strength. Locked up in her chamber at the very top of the keep, Amabella was sequestered with Aleanor, Ambra, Alfie, Savia, the three maids from Berwick, and Alfie's entire horse guard.

When the battle had started, Markus had made sure they were all in one room, locked up in the highest chamber of the keep, and armed with daggers, clubs, and fire pokers. Whatever he could find, he gave them. They were under instructions to not open the door for anyone but him or one of the other de Wolfe knights.

But Alfie had other ideas.

After the initial alarm had sounded and Markus had dressed in a hurry, he found Alfie and his horse guard using red-hot fire pokers to ward off the Scots who were trying to coax them into opening the postern gate. He'd grabbed Alfie and calmly commanded the rest of the children to follow him, and they made their way into the keep. The children had been fighting admirably but the fact remained that they were children, and vulnerable, so Markus had corralled all of them into Amabella's chamber so he could focus on the battle.

But that was exactly where Alfie wanted to be.

"Ama!" he cried, trying to pry her arms from around his waist. "I am the king! I must fight for my people!"

Amabella hung on for dear life. "Alfie, please," she said. "Listen to me; you know you cannot fight. You are simply making this worse. You must behave yourself and sit with your guard, do you hear? Markus will send for you if he needs you."

Using that logic, Amabella was able to calm her son down, just a little. Alfie was still frowning, but at least he wasn't kicking any longer.

"Will he?" he asked his mother dubiously.

She nodded seriously. "Of course he will," she said, loosening her grip. "He put us in this chamber for a reason and if you leave, you will put everyone here in danger because an open door is a door that the enemy can get through. You do not want to do that, do you?"

Alfie didn't. He looked at her, unhappy, but even at his young age, he understood. "But what should I do?"

Relieved that Alfie was no longer going to charge the door and put them all in jeopardy, Amabella loosened her grip on him and put him on his feet. Alfie was so much like Atlas; young, but wanting so much to grow up and be a man. She had two very brave boys on her hands and she knew that, so she knew better than to try and take that fighting spirit away. Markus had told her not to diminish a young man's will to fight simply because he was a child.

That meant Alfie, too.

She pointed to the door.

"You must protect all of us," she said. "Take your guard and stand in front of the door. If men come, you must fight them off and protect the women. Will you do that?"

Alfie nodded solemnly, mostly because it sounded like a very serious task. He was the king, after all, with a well-trained guard. He was more than willing to protect his mother in this battle situation. Even if he couldn't go help Sir Knight, he could at least defend his mother and sisters.

"I will," he said, motioning to his guard. "We can fight off anyone who comes."

Amabella stood up from her chair, distracted by the sounds from the bailey outside her window. "Good lad," she said. "Form a line; that's right. And stay there to make sure no one comes in."

Alfie and his guard did. The children, including the "knights", were frightened and even a little unsteady about the situation, but Alfie assured them they were doing important work. The whole thing had disoriented and terrified them, but not enough to make them cower. Perhaps it should have, but they were strong.

Thanks to Alfie.

As Alfie and his guard took their positions, Amabella found herself wandering over to the window, looking out to watch the Scots down below and the soldiers on the wall. It was rather terrifying and when Aleanor wandered over to her, she deliberately turned her back on the window to partially block it from her daughter's view. Aleanor was nervous enough without seeing men with weapons down below, trying to breach the castle.

"Ama," Aleanor said, hugging her mother tightly. "When will this be over with?"

Amabella wrapped her arms around her daughter. "Soon," she said, though she wasn't sure she believed it. "Sir Markus will make short work of these Scots. Have no fear."

But Aleanor wasn't easily quelled. She looked up at her mother, her pale face strained. "But what if he doesn't?" she said. "What if they enter the keep? What then? They will try and kill us!"

Amabella shushed her daughter softly. "Not so loud," she said. "Do not frighten your sister and brother with such talk."

"But what if…?"

Amabella shook her gently. "If the Scots get into the keep, then we must pull Alfie and his guard away from the door," she said. "You can hide under the bed or in the wardrobe. In fact, I want you to be responsible for Ambra. Take her with you and hide. Will you do that?"

Aleanor nodded warily, fearful of having such responsibility, but in the same breath, it made her feel… grown up. Her mother was trusting her with something important and that hadn't really happened before.

"I will," she said. "But what of you?"

Amabella sighed heavily. She turned her head slightly to catch a glimpse of the battle going on outside. She didn't want to think of the possibility that the Scots would make it into the keep. That would mean Markus was…

Nay.

She couldn't think such thoughts. She *wouldn't.* God didn't bring Markus de Wolfe into her life only to cruelly snatch him away. Markus was alive and he was going to stay alive. God had overlooked her all her life and she refused to believe that He was about to play yet another wicked joke on her by taking away a man who had literally changed her life.

All would be well.

But even so… she prayed fiercely.

God, help us!

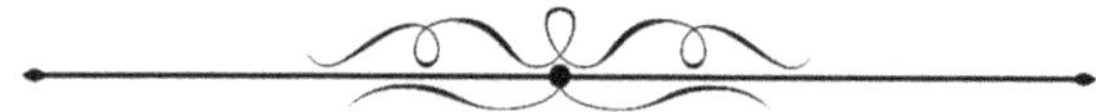

AS FAR AS battles went, it wasn't a particularly brutal one. He'd been in worse.

But this one had consequences.

There were about one hundred Scots from what he could tell trying to scale the walls of Trastamara any way they could – ladders and ropes, mostly, although some were trying to scale the gatehouse without benefit of either of those things only to be kicked off or thrown off by Kieran.

While Kieran held the gatehouse and the nearby walls with about fifty soldiers, Markus took the rest of the walls and spread out about seventy soldiers on the two of them. The Scots were few, but they were everywhere, like vermin, so the soldiers on the walls were there to cut the ropes or kick back the ladders.

And on it went into the afternoon.

The remaining soldiers from Trastamara were positioned in the bailey, both watching for any errant Scots who might actually make it over the wall and also lobbing arrows at the attackers. It was firing blind for the most part, but they'd managed to take a few Scots down.

Markus hadn't worked up much of a sweat. In fact, he'd rather enjoyed tossing Scots off the walls or kicking them in their faces when they got to the top of the ladders and close enough to his big feet. He knew that, eventually, they'd get tired and skulk off, more than likely around dusk, so it was simply a matter of keeping them from doing any real damage and, so far, they hadn't.

But that opinion faded when he saw Shand.

The man wasn't difficult to miss. He was the only one in the group not wearing a long *leine* tunic, but rather a mail coat and padded tunic that Atlas hadn't stripped from him. He was lingering back in the tree line, trying to stay out of sight, but Markus had excellent eyesight. He could see him clearly. The fact that Shand was here unnerved him because the man knew Trastamara better than anyone, Atlas included. He knew her strengths and knew her weaknesses.

That began to concern Markus.

Therefore, he put several of the soldiers in the bailey on patrol in the bailey itself. He had them prowl every inch of the yard, the stables, and kitchen yard.

And that's when they found something.

Markus came running as the soldiers in the kitchen yard sounded the alarm. There were two big drainage swales that went from the kitchen yard, through the wall, and dumped out on the other side. They discovered that Scots were digging under the iron grates, trying to use the swales as a way to breach the castle, so Markus put the men on gathering all of the hot water and stew bubbling over one of the big kitchen fires. The hot water alone was perhaps fifty gallons and they took it up to the wall and positioned it right over the diggers.

Down it went.

Men screamed as they were scalded by the hot water. The stew went down in chunks, clinging to skin and burning. It was enough to chase the Scots away from the digging, but Markus knew they'd be back. Shand was clearly exploiting that weakness in the wall, so Markus put the soldiers on stuffing as much debris as they could into the drainage swale, hoping to clog it up so the Scots couldn't get through. As Markus put some of the men to boiling more water, shouts could be heard from the top of the wall.

Markus raced up the stairs to the wall walk in time to see a small army approaching from the north. It didn't take him long to figure out who it was because he could see the red tunics, even from a distance.

A smile spread across his lips.

The Trastamara army was returning.

Now, things were going to get interesting.

CHAPTER EIGHTEEN

A TLAS WAS SO panicked, and so angry, when he saw the swarm of reivers surrounding Trastamara that he spurred his horse forward at a rapid gallop, which caused Cassius to do the same to prevent the young man from getting himself killed. That left Damien to command the army and he gave the attack command.

Pick your targets!

The Scots, seeing the approach of an army four times their size, were forced to turn away from the walls and face the incoming troops. Most of them were concentrated over by the gatehouse, with a secondary concentration near the drainage swales, and even though they carried weapons, they were without any shields they might carry because of the ladders, hooks, ropes, and digging implements they had been carrying. But the incoming Trastamara army changed that very quickly as men began running for the shields they'd dumped in the tree line.

Unfortunately for them, that made them an immediate target because the Trastamara army arrived and put themselves between the Scots running for the shields and those who were still at the wall. An army split is a weakened army.

The initial clash was loud and violent.

Only half of the Trastamara army was on horseback, so those were the ones to arrive first, including Atlas and Cassius. Broadswords were produced and the Scottish short swords were no match against a great sword. Blood was spilled and men fell to the ground, overwhelmed by the fearsome war machine known as the English knight.

Cassius was dynamic in battle, a tribute to his de Wolfe blood, and he quickly cut down three Scots who had been caught between the wall and their shields. Atlas, who had never faced a battle on horseback, still knew how to wield a sword properly and he did very well when faced with a Scot with a pike who nearly took his head off. Atlas lashed out with his grandfather's sword, cutting the man down, looking both startled and sickened that he'd just eviscerated a man. He glanced up, saw Cassius' encouraging smile, and that bolstered his courage.

But he was looking for one man in particular.

Atlas had come into this battle looking for Shand. He knew the man was here, somewhere, and he was fed by the rage and embarrassed that Shand should betray his mercy as he did. As he was searching the group of Scots, looking for any sign of Shand, Damien roared up on his charger with the bulk of the infantry.

Cass!" Damien shouted. "I'm going to move the foot soldiers in next to the walls to drive the Scots back!"

Cassius was trying to control his snapping warhorse. "We've got trouble near the drainage holes on the north side," he said. "I haven't been to the gatehouse yet, but the men at the drainage holes need to be dispersed."

Damien waved him off. "You see to it," he said. "I'll move the foot soldiers into position and then head to the gatehouse. Atlas, you come with me!"

Atlas didn't really want to. He wanted to search for Shand, but he also didn't want to disobey Damien. This was his first real battle as a warrior and he didn't want to fail. Damien and Cassius took off to their assigned tasks and as Atlas turned his horse to follow Damien, he caught sight of the man he'd been looking for.

Shand.

Bexwell stood just inside the tree line about twenty feet to Atlas' left, watching the battle, watching the knights. As Atlas looked at the man, he felt uncontrollable fury bubble up in his chest. He couldn't even begin to describe it. All he knew was that he felt anger as he'd never felt before and he dismounted his horse, taking his grandfather's broadsword with him as he ducked into the trees. Since Shand was watching the battle, Atlas intended to come up behind him and catch him unawares.

The hunter had sighted his prey.

With stealth, Atlas made his way through the trees, watching Shand from behind. Someone began to shout because the English infantry was shoving men away from the wall and killing those who were still climbing on it. The tides of war were turning against the Scots and the fighting was beginning to turn vicious. Some men were even beginning to retreat from the English soldiers who were better armed and better prepared.

Atlas dared to take his eyes off Shand for a brief moment to see that the English troops that seemed to be fighting the most fiercely were wearing the red and white Abril tunics. It did his heart good to see that. Finally, the pride of Abril was returning to Trastamara after the slander of de Sauque. Atlas decided at that moment that from this day forward, he would no longer bear the name de Sauque. He would follow his honorable Spanish ancestors, men so great that they had led the Kingdom of Sobrarbe, the great kingdom that existed before Aragon ever came into being.

Atlas would be known as an Abril forever more.

He was going to erase the name of de Sauque from Trastamara, forevermore.

But he couldn't focus on that now. It was a powerful thought but quickly pushed aside. Up ahead, he could see Shand with his back to him. He couldn't believe the man hadn't seen him coming. He had been so vigilant about everything else, but his failure to see Atlas sneaking up on him would be his undoing.

Atlas was going to kill him.

But all that changed when Atlas was nearly upon him and he happened to step on a stick, which snapped under his weight. It was enough of a noise to cause Shand to spin around, sword leveled, and catch Atlas with the sharp edge right across the chest. It was a deep, nasty slice, and a heavy blow, and Atlas stumbled back, falling onto his arse as he did so. As he fell, he looked Shand in the face only to see that there was a smile on the man's lips.

Perhaps he hadn't surprised Shand at all.

It seemed to him that Shand had known he was coming all along.

After that, the fight was on.

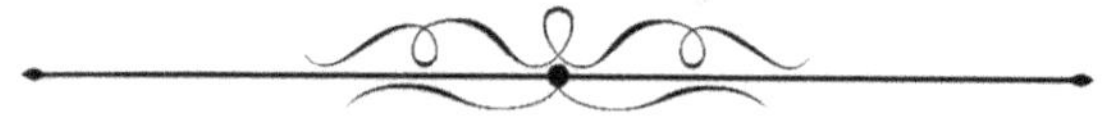

STANDING ON THE battlements, Markus watched as the Trastamara army, with mostly de Wolfe men, went after the reivers with a vengeance.

Cassius and Damien were making short work of those trying to trench the drainage swale and those trying to scale the walls. At that point, Markus felt rather useless simply watching, but he couldn't chance opening the gatehouse until the battle was under control, and it wasn't yet. There were pockets of heavy fighting going on and until those had been quelled, he would wait to open the gate.

But that was until he saw Atlas.

He saw the young lord ride up at the head of the army, straight into the gang of Scots trying to mount the walls, but Cassius had caught up to him very quickly and it had been mostly Cassius fighting off a group of Scots who decided to move against both him and Atlas. Atlas, however, did his best and it wasn't bad for a lad who had never faced battle on horseback.

Most de Wolfe squires were relegated to following their knight into battle, but mostly waiting from the edges of the battle itself in case their knight needed assistance. It was rare when they were called upon to fight, though some did simply for the experience. Markus wasn't sure how much battle Atlas had actually fought personally, but he did very well against men more experienced than he was.

Markus was feeling some confidence in Atlas' ability until Cassius and Damien took off, leaving Atlas behind. As Markus watched, the young lord started to follow Damien but swiftly came to a halt and slid off his horse. Markus had no idea why until he happened to spy Shand standing at the edge of the trees.

Atlas was going for Shand.

Markus' confidence dissolved in an instant.

He knew that Atlas was going to try to kill Shand, but Bexwell was a seasoned knight. He wasn't going to let the young man get the upper hand on him. Not only that, but Atlas had what Shand wanted. Shand was apt to kill Atlas out of pure hatred.

What Atlas was doing was a very bad idea.

Fighting down panic, Markus began to run towards the tower with the drainage holes because that's where he'd seen Cassius heading. He looked over the side of the battlements but couldn't see his brother and when he did, Cassius was in a fight of his own and Markus didn't want to distract him.

Markus began to run the other direction, looking for Damien or any of the senior de Wolfe sergeants, anyone who could go and head off Atlas or at least help him. But the battles below were intense, and Markus wasn't apt to distract anyone in a fight for their lives.

He had to think fast.

Shand was right at the edge of the trees and Markus could see Atlas getting closer. Since he couldn't get anyone down below to help Atlas, he would have to do it himself. It wasn't as if he could jump off the wall, and all of the grappling hooks and ropes he could see had been tossed off, now cluttering the ground below the wall.

Damnation!

Something caught his eyes in the bailey and he turned to see a group of soldiers with bows and arrows, preparing to launch them over the wall at the next command. Markus frantically motioned them up to the wall and they came running, flying up the stairs that led to the wall walk.

Markus snatched the bow from the first man he came to, turning to focus on Shand and preparing to launch an arrow right into the man's chest. But just as he lifted the bow and got the arrow into position, Atlas came up behind Shand and Markus saw clearly when Shand abruptly turned and cut Atlas right across the chest with the sharp edge of his sword.

After that, both men disappeared into the forest.

"So you thought you'd catch me from behind, did you?" Shand said, stalking Atlas as the young man tried to scramble to his feet. "I was your father's knight for many years. I have eyes in the back of my head, Atlas, or at the very least, I am aware of my surroundings. I saw you dismount your horse and slip into the trees. I knew you were coming for me."

Atlas was in a great deal of pain, bleeding all over the place because Shand's cut had sliced him deep. Pieces of mail and tunic were embedded in the gash, which ran across his chest, from one side to the other. But his fear of Shand overruled the pain and he finally managed to get to his feet, wielding his grandfather's broadsword in front of him.

"You bastard," Atlas hissed. "Trastamara is mine. It is mine by rights and heredity. You have no right to it, no matter how much you want it. I showed you mercy when I sent you away. Know that I will not make the same mistake twice."

Shand smiled thinly. "I realize you showed mercy," he said. "That is why I did not kill you just now. But my mercy is only extended once. The next time I slash this sword at you, it will be to cut your head off."

Atlas believed him. Truth be told, he was increasingly unnerved and trying desperately not to show it. He knew that Shand was an experienced knight who had fought in many battles and, strangely enough, in the times that Atlas had contact with his father over the years when Shand was present, the man barely said two words to him. He'd always seemed silent and obedient.

But it had been an act.

Atlas could see now that beneath that obedient surface was

a man of great determination and ambition, which included Trastamara. Atlas had tried to use the element of surprise to kill Shand, but he had failed.

If he wanted to keep Trastamara, he was going to have to fight for it.

"You can try," he said, backing off and circling around as Shand tracked him. "But I do not understand why you feel you have any right to my hereditary home. Don't you have your own home to return to?"

Shand's humorless smile never left his face. "Do you want to know how I became a knight?" he said. "My father was a wool merchant in Norfolk and a wealthy one. I have five older brothers and having no use for me, he essentially sold me as an apprentice to a French knight who was passing through Norfolk on his way north. This French knight taught me well, but his lessons were brutal. When I became of age and he beat me one too many times, I killed him. Everyone thought it was an accident, but it was not. In answer to your question, I do not have a home to go to. Trastamara is the only home I have ever known."

Atlas probably should have felt sorry for Shand, but he couldn't bring himself to. "Even men who have difficult paths in life do not resort to ruthless ambition to steal another's inheritance," he said. "My father thought you were a fine knight and so did the de Wolfe knights. You could have easily found a position somewhere else with your skill."

Shand's smile faded. "You are not hearing me," he said quietly. "Trastamara is the only home I have ever known. I know it better than you do and I have served it with more dedication than you could ever show. I deserve to be here."

"It belongs to me."

"It will not after I am finished with you."

"But you cannot simply take it. My allies will not allow it."

"I will deal with that when the time comes."

With that, he lunged at Atlas, who managed to get his sword up. It was a heavy blow and although Atlas had been training with a sword for several years, he wasn't at Shand's level and he knew it. The best he could hope for was dodging the man and trying to wear him out.

But it wasn't going to be easy.

Shand was fast and he was accurate. After two fairly forceful barrages at Atlas, he managed to clip the young man on the arm. It didn't draw blood, thankfully, but it smarted, and Atlas managed to dodge behind a tree with the next onslaught from Shand. The forest was acting as a shield for him and he used the trees to his advantage, at least as much as he could, until Shand began to anticipate his movements and cut him off the next time he tried to dodge behind a tree.

Unfortunately for Atlas, the only one being worn down was him. He simply wasn't Shand's caliber, at least not yet, but he was giving him an admirable fight. Whether or not he could actually kill the man remained to be seen, but he wasn't backing down.

He would fight to the bitter end.

Which might be sooner than he hoped.

Atlas thought to get out from behind the trees because, at this point, they were creating a problem because Shand was using them, too. Frightened and bleeding heavily from his chest gash, Atlas made a dash to leave the dense collection of trees but was summarily stopped when Shand unsheathed a dagger and hurled it at Atlas, catching the young man behind his right knee.

Atlas went down.

The big dagger had him impaled enough so that he couldn't bend his knee at all, nor could he stand up, and he could see Shand bearing down on him. In excruciating pain, he tried to remove the dagger, but he couldn't get a good grip on it and crawl away from Shand at the same time.

It was then that Atlas began to think his life might be over. He didn't feel any real panic for himself, only a great concern that his mother and siblings would be left to the mercy of Shand Bexwell. That was his only thought as he struggled to crawl away, pausing long enough to lift his sword and protect himself from the down parry that was inevitably coming in his direction.

But then, something unexpected happened.

A shadow fell across Atlas and, suddenly, a massive body stood between him and Shand. Shielding his eyes from the sun, Atlas craned his head back to see that Markus was standing between him and certain death.

Help had arrived.

"Since you seem to like to fight with astonishing dishonor, mayhap you would like to use your dirty tactics on me."

Markus was facing Shand. In full armor, with the de Wolfe tunic front and center, he made perhaps one of the most formidable sights ever to behold on the field of battle. In his left hand, he held the wolf-head sword, the one his father had given him when he'd received his spurs. It was bigger, heavier, and sharper than most swords.

He raised it.

"What?" Markus said. "No swift response? Since when do you keep silent, Bexwell?"

Shand backed up; he had to because he was within range of that enormous sword. "This is not your fight, de Wolfe," he said. "If Atlas is going to be a man, then you need to let him face his own battles."

Markus wasn't swayed. "I would let him face a battle against a worthy opponent, but that is not you," he said. "You are the slime in a pig's sty, the scum on a pond's surface, and the vomit in the sewer. You are all those things and more, wholly unworthy of Atlas and utterly unworthy of me. I fight men, not dogs, but I will make an exception in your case."

Shand's jaw ticked at the barrage of insults lobbed at him. "The only reason you have what you have is because you rely on your family name," he said. "You have achieved nothing on your own, so do not be so quick to call me unworthy."

Markus cocked an eyebrow. "Has the king offered you a position as his Lord Protector?"

Shand's brow furrowed. "He has not."

"I didn't think so," Markus said, deliberately insulting the man's achievements, or lack thereof. "But I, in fact, am worthy enough for such an offer. Now, let's get on with this. I have more important things that require my attention."

He flinched and the fight was on. Shand went to raise his sword, but he wasn't fast enough. He was right-handed, and Markus left-handed, and he brought his sword up as if preparing for a strike from a right-handed man. Because he didn't have his sword in the right place, Markus managed to spin that enormous blade up and over, coming down on the top of Shand's right shoulder.

It was a move that nearly cut Shand's shoulder clean from his body. In an instant, his collarbone was broken, tendons severed, and his sword hand completely useless. It was a devastating and brutal blow. As Shand began to howl, Markus switched hands with his sword, wielded it like a club, and swung it with both hands at Shand's neck.

The man's head went rolling into the foliage.

In a few short seconds, the fight was over.

Markus hadn't even raised a sweat. He took a couple of steps towards Shand's body, now collapsed upon the bed of the forest. He observed his handiwork before turning to Atlas, who was sitting up, hand on his wounded knee, and looking at Markus with eyes the size of saucers.

Markus could see the young man's shock.

"I am sorry I had to intervene," he said. "But I could not let him get the best of you. You have a great future ahead of you, Atlas. Let no man as lowly as Shand Bexwell take it from you."

Atlas, still stunned, nodded. Then, he vomited all over himself in a spectacular display of nerves. Markus chuckled sympathetically.

"Is that the first time you've seen a man's head cut off?" he asked.

Atlas shook his head. Then, he nodded, greatly embarrassed. "Like that, it is," he admitted. "He… he said he was going to do that to me."

Markus sheathed his sword. "Not as long as the House of de Wolfe is around," he said, moving over to the lad. "Roll onto your side. Let me see that knee."

Atlas did, stiffly, and Markus knelt down, taking hold of his knee to steady it and yanking the dagger from it in one swift motion. Atlas grunted but he didn't cry out. Markus knew how painful it must have been, but the lad had shown courage.

Great courage.

Reaching down, he pulled Atlas to his feet, very gently. "Can you walk?"

Atlas was shaken, and in great pain, but he was alive. "Aye," he said. "I can walk. But I'll do it alone, Markus. Those men out there… I am in command of them. I'll not let them see me leaning on you. I think I've leaned on you enough."

Markus smiled at the brave young lord, letting him go when

he was certain he had his balance.

"It has been my honor to have you lean on me, my lord," he said. "I will always be here if you need me."

Atlas smiled weakly. He genuinely liked Markus, more than he could verbalize, a true and noble man to look up to. Hand to the gash on his chest, he limped from the trees and out into the clearing where the Trastamara army was finishing up the Scots. Those who hadn't run away, or hadn't been killed, had been gathered up in a small group over by the gatehouse.

The battle, for the most part, was over.

The land surrounding Trastamara was torn up and many of the trees had been cut to make the ladders, so there was a sense of devastation. Bodies of the dead littered the ground, all Scots, and Atlas limped by the arrow-ridden body of Win Foulden, having no idea that the leader of this band of reivers had been killed. All he knew was that the fight was over, Shand was dead, and Trastamara's mighty walls were still standing.

That was all he cared about.

Markus walked beside Atlas, proud that the young lord was determined that his men see him bloodied but not beaten. It would have been very easy to have allowed Markus to carry him into the castle, but he wasn't going to let that happen.

He was going to walk.

As they neared the gatehouse, which was now open, Cassius came running in their direction.

"Christ," he hissed when he saw Atlas. "What in the hell…?"

"Atlas and Shand had a battle of their own back in the trees," Markus said. "Shand's headless body is back there, in the foliage. When you are cleaning up the field of battle, make sure to collect his body and burn it with the rest of the rubbish."

Cassius looked at his brother. "Who killed him?"

Markus threw a thumb in Atlas' direction. "The young lord

knows how to fight," he said. "Make sure his men know that."

Cassius looked at Atlas, a smile of approval on his face. "Well done, my lord," he said. Before Atlas could reply, however, he returned his attention to his brother. "Markus, an army has been sighted on The Orchard crossing. They will be here within the hour."

Markus' brow furrowed. "What army?"

"They are flying Berwick and royal standards."

Markus' eyes widened. "Edward?"

Cassius nodded. "He has finally arrived," he said. "Papa must be escorting him here because he knows you are still at Trastamara."

That made sense, but Markus found himself looking at the keep, knowing Amabella was there. That was his only thought at the moment. Edward had finally come for him, but he didn't want to go. He wanted to remain with the little girl who sauced fish, the little boy with his horse guard, the nervous young woman who had eyes for Cassius, and the young lord who was trying so hard to do his family justice.

But most of all, he wanted to remain with a woman he knew he couldn't live without.

"Then send riders out to meet them if you haven't already," he said without enthusiasm. "I will meet them in the bailey."

"I've got men mounted already," Cassius said. He could sense something in his brother's dour mood that had him puzzled. "Aren't you happy about this? Your moment of glory has finally arrived."

Markus was still looking at the keep. "Cass," he said slowly. "I think my moment of glory has already come. And Edward did not bring it."

With that, he walked away with the limping, wounded Atlas, heading towards the keep. Cassius watched him go, having no idea what he meant. He didn't even have a clue.

But he soon would.

CHAPTER NINETEEN

"**H**E SHALL RECOVER," Markus said quietly, trying to pull Amabella out of the chamber because Atlas was passed out, asleep, on his bed. "You have tended him quite well, my lady. Leave him to sleep now. He needs it."

Amabella was still standing over her son. He was snoring softly, boiled linen bandages wound over his chest and around his right knee. She'd cleaned the wounds, doused them with wine, and wrapped them up tightly to heal, but still, she felt as if she hadn't done enough. She still wasn't over the shock of seeing her bloodied, beaten son and hearing the story behind it.

"He looks like my little boy upon those linens," she whispered. "He *is* my little boy. Markus, when I think of what would have happened to him had you not intervened…"

She trailed off, tears filling her eyes, and Markus finally went to her, took her by the hand, and pulled her to the door. There, he wrapped her up in his big embrace, holding her tightly as she struggled not to weep openly.

"He shall recover," he whispered into the top of her head. "Shand is no longer a threat and Atlas shall go on to rule Trastamara with honor. You said he has a great future ahead of him; I can assure you that he does. And so do we."

Amabella held him fiercely, her head against his chest. "I would wish so with all my heart," she said softly, finally releasing him long enough to look into his eyes. "But… how? We have only just… how can we make plans for the future?"

Markus pulled her out of the chamber, closing the door softly. It was Roget's former chamber, and Alonzo Abril's former chamber, now belonging to Atlas. They stood in the landing as he put his big hands on her arms, forcing her to look at him.

"That is what I need to speak with you about," he said. "Before I brought Atlas into the keep, I was informed that an army is approaching from the south."

She looked concerned. "An army? Whose army?"

"It is my father and King Edward," he said calmly. "In fact, they should be here any moment and I must go down to the bailey to greet them, but before I do, I must ask you something."

Amabella was looking at him with fear in her eyes. Nay, more than fear… it was disappointment of the greatest magnitude. Disappointment that these few days of joy and pleasure were ending, or at the very least, changing.

He could see her entire body tensing up.

"You said that Edward was coming north," she said. "He is here to take you into Scotland with him."

He looked at her pointedly. "Did you hear me? I have a question to ask you."

"Of course you may ask."

"Will you be my wife?"

Amabella's eyes widened. "You… you wish to *marry* me?"

"If you will consent."

As he watched, her eyes filled with tears. "Markus, I would love nothing better in this world," she said. "You honor me greatly. But I cannot leave my children and they would not be able to come with us into Scotland."

He smiled gently. "Silly wench," he said softly. "I will not go with Edward. The title of Viscount Ravensdowne comes with the Cheswick Castle. It sits right on the coast, watching the sea, between Berwick and Bamburgh. It's the oldest castle in the north and has fended off many a Northman raid. I would take you and the children there. We would be very happy there, I promise, and Atlas can make his life here as the Lord of Trastamara. He can have his own family here, someday."

As she realized what he was saying, she gripped him by the arms. "Then you do not intend to go with Edward?"

He shook his head. "Nay," he said. "The title Lord Protector… it is only a title, after all. It is not my destiny. Being the husband of Lady de Wolfe is and I can think of no finer calling."

Amabella studied him to see if she saw any hint of regret in his features, any suggestion that this decision had him torn. But she saw nothing. He seemed confident and determined. Reaching up, she cupped his face between her two soft hands.

"Are you certain?" she asked quietly.

"Never more certain of anything in my life," he said. "If you will have me, of course."

"If you will have *me*."

He grinned. "I knew the first day I saw you that I would have you," he said. "I just had to convince you that I was not too young for you. You seem to have a problem with a younger man."

She broke down into giggles. "Never," she said, reaching up to kiss his cheek softly. "You are my angel, Markus."

"Then tell me that you'll love me the rest of your life," he whispered. "Because I will love you for the rest of mine."

She smiled sweetly at him as she heard the words he'd uttered before. "I will love you for the rest of my life and beyond," she murmured.

He kissed her deeply, then, pulling her against him and feeling that familiar fire fill his veins. But there wasn't any time to do what his natural instincts dictated. His father and the king were approaching and he had to deal with them first. He had to let them both in on a life-changing decision and hope they took it well.

Kissing Amabella's hand, he left her with her injured son and headed down to the bailey.

IT SEEMED THAT they had ridden into a war zone.

Patrick and Edward, King of England, exchanged concerned glances as they approached Trastamara Castle. There had clearly been a battle here that had only recently ended because there were bodies and debris scattered everywhere. The castle, however, didn't seem damaged.

Still, the army was cautious. The king's men, fully armed, spread out to protect the monarch and the Earl of Berwick as they closed the gap to the gatehouse. Patrick had several of his own knights, including Hermes, Titus de Wolfe, and Anson. They charged on ahead into the bailey as Edward and Patrick followed.

The bulk of the king's army remained outside the walls, in a protective group in front of the open gatehouse so that no one could enter now that the king was inside. But it was clear that whatever happened here had only happened outside because the bailey was business as usual. The first thing Edward and Patrick saw was Markus and Cassius, approaching them from the keep.

Patrick called a halt to their group. As he and the king dismounted, Patrick and Cassius closed the gap between them.

"Welcome to Trastamara, your grace," Markus said to Edward. "You arrived on a most… interesting day."

Edward faced perhaps the finest knight England had seen since William de Wolfe and further back still, the likes of William Marshal and Christopher de Lohr. At sixty years of age, Edward had seen more than his share of good knights, death, doom, battle, and politics. He was still tall at his age, still vital, but that head of fair hair had turned white over the years. He eyed the biggest, strongest de Wolfe knight.

"I would believe that," he said, turning to peer through the open gatehouse. "What happened?"

Markus followed the king's focus. "A good deal, actually, but I believe it is under control," he said. "Did my father tell of the death of the Roget de Sauque, Lord of Trastamara? That is why I am here."

Edward nodded, fixing on him once more. "He told me," he said. "He also told me that the new Lord of Trastamara is a seventeen-year-old squire who used to serve the House of de Wolfe."

"That is correct, your grace," Markus said. "But what you see now has nothing to do with the youth of the new lord. It is the result of greed. When Roget died, his captain tried to commandeer Trastamara. What you see is the result of the captain making a final push to wrest Trastamara from Atlas de Sauque, the rightful heir."

"I take it that he did not succeed?"

"He did not, your grace."

"Who is this captain?"

"His name is Shand Bexwell, your grace."

"Where is he?"

"Dead."

That was enough for Edward. Squabbles between lesser barons didn't concern him much, but Patrick had something to say about it. Considering he was here when the entire situation started, he was somewhat astonished to see the results of Bexwell's return.

"Shand came back?" he asked his son, surprised. "We saw dead Scots outside the walls. Did he bring them?"

Markus nodded. "He did," he said. "They belong to the brother of Roget's mistress. It's a long and complicated story. Let us retreat into the hall and I will explain everything over some food and drink."

Patrick started to move, but Edward shook his head. "I cannot," he said. "Markus, I am only here to collect you. We have a date with your Uncle Scott for this evening and I do not want to delay. I have waited a long time to have a de Wolfe at my side, so this is a momentous occasion for me. It is time."

He was smiling wearily and Markus knew he could not delay the inevitable. He'd hoped to tell Edward of his decision over a pitcher of wine, to fully explain his reasons, but it looked as if that was not to be. They were expecting him to depart with the king, and Markus could see his father smiling proudly at him. He had known this moment was going to be difficult, but the more he looked at his father's smiling face, the more difficult it became.

But not difficult when he thought on *why* he'd made this decision.

Amabella.

"My lord, I cannot go," he said, looking Edward in the eyes. "Though I am greatly honored by the appointment, I am afraid that I must decline. Every man has that moment in his life when he sees something greater than himself. I have had that moment, here at Trastamara. With the sincerest apologies to you, it is my intention to remain in the north, marry the woman of my choosing, and serve my father."

Edward looked at him in surprise while Patrick looked at him in utter shock. "Marry?" Patrick repeated. "Since when? Have you been back to Bamburgh and Emmalina de Vesci?"

Markus grinned and shook his head. "Nay, Papa," he said. "I do not need Emmalina when I have Amabella. It is my intention to marry her."

Patrick blinked. That wasn't the answer he had been expecting. "Amabella?" he said after a moment. "De Sauque's widow?"

Markus nodded. "She is to be my wife," he said. "She has consented. I cannot serve two masters and no offense intended, your grace, but I do not love you like I love her. She is also prettier than you are. I choose her."

Edward didn't quite know what to say. He didn't appear angry, but he did appear frustrated. He looked at Patrick.

"Again?" he said. "This is happening again? Something tells me that de Wolfe knights are not meant to personally serve me."

"That is not true," Markus said. Then, he looked to Cassius, standing next to him with a stunned expression on his face. "Cassius would make an excellent Lord Protector. He is one of the finest knights I have ever served with. Please consider my brother in my place, your grace. He is a de Wolfe, after all. He will serve you well."

All eyes turned to Cassius. At least, all eyes except Patrick's. He was still looking at Markus, still shocked by what he'd heard. As Edward moved to speak to an astonished Cassius, Patrick grabbed Markus by the arm and pulled him away.

"Markus," he hissed. "What is this about? Have you gone mad?"

Markus smiled at his father. "I have," he said. "Mad in love. And I have never been happier."

Patrick was growing increasingly agitated. "But de Sauque's

widow? Lad, she is a woman with four children already."

"I know."

"She is a good deal older than you are."

"She is ten years older than I am."

Patrick's eyes widened. "Markus, when I told you that I wanted you to marry, I did not mean an old woman with children," he said. "There is an entire country full of young, lovely maidens who would be thrilled to be your wife."

Markus' smile faded. "Amabella is not an old woman," he said. "You will never call her that again, Papa. I mean that. She is not some silly halfwit girl. She is a wise, reasonable, and beautiful woman in ways I never knew existed. She is exactly what I want in a wife."

Patrick sighed sharply. "How would you even know? You have not entertained enough young women to know what you want."

"Did you know what you wanted when you met Mama?"

That caused Patrick to falter. "You know that is different," he said. "The circumstances of meeting your mother were different."

Markus wouldn't be put off. He knew exactly how his parents had met and the chaos that had ensued. "You married her against the will of the church and against the will of Poppy," he said quietly. "Did your father give you the same lecture you are giving me?"

That shut Patrick up. He had, indeed, married his wife against the wishes and advice of his father, and there had been a major argument because of it. In fact, he could remember that argument as if it happened yesterday and all of the things he wanted to tell Markus were the same things his father had said to him.

When he realized that, he began to feel sick to his stomach.

"Poppy accused me of being illogical about your mother,"

he finally said. "That is the same thing I was going to say to you. But I know from experience that love knows no logic. Do you love her, lad?"

Markus nodded. "I do," he said. "I do not know how it happened, but it has. I cannot and will not leave her, not even for Edward."

Patrick sighed again, only this time, it was from resignation. He understood completely and there was nothing more he could say.

"Very well," he said. "I did say that I wanted you married and you are complying. I suppose I should be grateful."

Markus' smile was back, and he put his big arm around his father's shoulders. "Aye, you should be," he said. "And you should be grateful that it is for love. You have met Lady de Sauque, so you know she is a beautiful woman."

Patrick grunted. "A beautiful woman that Roget abused," he said. "Lad, you're not marrying her because you feel… pity for her, are you?"

Markus shook his head. "I am marrying her because she is the most remarkable woman I have ever met," he said. "She is kind and sweet and mature… she is a woman, not a girl. And I very much want a woman."

Patrick looked at him. "And the children? You will be assuming her family."

Markus laughed softly. "And you will finally have grandchildren," he said. "That should make Mama happy. And I already love them as if they were my own. They are bright, sweet, and intelligent. I cannot describe it better than that, Papa. This was meant to be."

Patrick could see the joy on Markus' face and, in that moment, he was no longer resistant. He could see that Markus meant every word and it did his heart good to see his eldest so happy about such simple pleasures. Markus had never been the simple type, so to see the transformation was quite astonishing. He patted his son on the cheek before turning his attention over to Cassius in conversation with Edward. Cassius was nodding firmly before Edward finally waved him away and the man headed off in search of his horse and possessions.

Patrick shook his head ironically.

"It looks as if at least one of my sons shall assume the Lord Protector position," he said. "I must go speak to Cass. And then we shall take your lady and her children, and return to Berwick for a marriage. Your mother will want to plan the feast."

Markus was greatly relieved. He had hoped this moment wouldn't create problems between him and his father, and he was overjoyed to realize that his father was in agreement. It could have so easily gone badly.

But it didn't.

Markus stood there, watching his father intercept Cassius and hug the man, so very proud of him and his new appointment. It made Markus smile, knowing that Cassius would make an excellent Lord Protector. But his joy encompassed more than that; it was in knowing that Cassius had a future, that his father was at peace with his eldest son's decision, and in the knowledge that every day for the rest of his life, he would wake up next to Amabella, knowing the life he chose for himself was the best life possible.

No glory upon the fields of battle, or on the fields of Scotland, could come close.

As he stood there, something caught his attention out of the corners of his eyes and he turned to see Amabella standing on the steps of the keep, with Alfie and Ambra running down to the bailey. Alfie was followed by his eight-man horse guard, who had been bottled up in the keep until this moment, and he watched as Alfie ran all the way across the bailey to Edward, who was wearing expensive regalia as befitting a king.

He saw, clearly, when Alfie pointed out his horse guard to the monarch.

King Alfie.

With a grin, Markus made his way over to Edward and King Alfie before Edward realized there was another usurper in Scotland. Alfie probably had no idea who the well-dressed man was but considering he was infatuated with knights, he had targeted the strange man with the beautiful dress. That was typical Alfie.

And he loved the lad for it.

Markus spent several minutes explaining to Edward that Alfie was not a threat, and Alfie eventually retreated to the safety of the kitchen yard that he had helped protect. Markus would remember this moment years later when Alfie found himself in the personal guard of Edward II, a protector of monarchs and a great knight in his own right, thanks to his father, Markus.

A great destiny, indeed.

It seemed that they were all destined to have one.

EPILOGUE

January, Year of Our Lord 1302
Cheswick Castle

IT WAS VERY late on an icy January night as the fire snapped softly in the hearth. It had been blazing the entire day in the lord's solar of Cheswick, so much so that the stones had warmed and, even now, gave off radiant heat into the dark of night.

And it was a crowded room.

Markus was on his feet, unable to sit. Over to his left, his father was sitting on a chair near the hearth with Ambra snoring softly against him. His brothers, Titus and Magnus, were both there along with his Uncle Scott, the Earl of Warenton.

Scott had brought his wife, his two eldest daughters, and all of his younger children and they had come two weeks ago. But it hadn't been a social call. It had been to bring Lady Jordan to Cheswick because a great-grandchild was due any day and Markus had asked for her help.

The old woman had been more than happy to come.

But there was also another man present, a larger-than-life presence.

Magnus the Law-Mender was sitting next to Patrick on the most comfortable chair in the entire castle. He'd purposely tested them all out before he selected that particular chair. After a long journey across the North Sea, he'd come about a month ago with three longships and about sixty men, all of them now holed up in Cheswick, awaiting the birth of the Law-Mender's first great-grandchild.

In so many ways, this was a very important birth.

Markus was so worried for his wife that he could hardly stand it. Her pregnancy had been easy enough, but her belly had been absolutely enormous, which frightened him to death. How in the world was she going to birth that giant offspring he'd planted within her? She'd merely laughed at him and assured him that it could be done. That was why he'd sent for both his mother and grandmother. Between them, they'd birthed sixteen children. They knew how these things worked.

He didn't.

God, please let Ama come through unscathed!

"How much longer?"

Markus heard the words, looking down to see Alfie standing next to him. He forced a smile at the child. "Not much longer, I would hope," he said. "Shouldn't you be asleep like your sister?"

Alfie looked over at Ambra, sleeping with her mouth open and drooling on Patrick's chest. "Nay," he said. "I want to wait with you."

"Very well," Markus said. "We shall wait together."

He faced the window overlooking the sea, watching the waves down below. It was a clear night, with a full moon in the sky, making it absolutely beautiful. It gave him some peace. But Alfie couldn't see the ocean, or the sky, and he grew bored quickly and wandered over to Magnus, who smiled at his adopted grandson.

Magnus, who had a rather fearsome look about him with his long, graying hair and weathered face, genuinely liked Alfie. In fact, he was enamored with a lad who had his own horse guard, even at Cheswick, and demanded weapons. He wanted to take the boy back with him to his homeland, but both Patrick and Markus had discouraged him. The lad needed an English education, they had said, not one from the Northmen who hated the English.

Magnus was still trying to figure out how to smuggle the boy onto the longship when he left.

Markus could hear Alfie trying to negotiate with Magnus, striking up a conversation that had to do with the fact that Alfie needed more than seven horse guards, which was all he could scare up at Cheswick. His original horse guard remained back at Trastamara. Alfie was trying to recruit Magnus, which Markus thought was humorous. He listened to the boy bargain, and Magnus' polite denials, but he wouldn't give up.

Fidgety, Markus came by the window and went to sit next to his uncle.

Scott de Wolfe, Earl of Warenton, was a powerful man in command of a massive empire. He also had ten children, so he understood Markus' nervousness well. As Markus sat down beside him, Scott put a comforting hand on the man's shoulder.

"I know from experience how unsettling this is," he said. "But your wife has the best of care. Sometimes babies just take a while to come. My youngest took almost two days. That was two days of no sleep for me, so I understand your worry completely."

Markus looked at his uncle. "Ama's pains started last night," he said. "It has almost been a full day and a full night."

"As I said, sometimes these things just take time."

Markus nodded. Then, he leaned forward, elbows on his knees, and put his face in his hands. "She told me that she thought she was past childbearing years," he muttered wearily. "I wouldn't believe her. When she became with child, we were both so thrilled, but now… mayhap I should have listened to her."

Scott gave him an ironic smile. "There is nothing to worry over," he assured him. "My wife has had six children. Women are much smarter and stronger than we are, even when they're small. If my daughters were men, they would make magnificent knights."

Markus took his hand away from his face and looked at him. "That reminds me," he said. "I must speak to you about Caria."

"What about her?"

"Has she expressed any interest in being married? To anyone?"

Scott frowned at the change in subject. "Nay," he said. "Why would you ask that? She cannot marry *just* anyone. You know that."

Markus nodded. "I do," he said. "But I am asking for a reason."

"What reason?"

Markus sat up and leaned closer to the man, lowering his voice. "On behalf of my son, Atlas, I would like to discuss a marriage between him and Caria," he said. "Uncle Scott, I know Caria isn't meant for just anyone, but Atlas isn't just anyone. He is of Abril stock, from the royal house of Aragon, and he loves Caria. He would make her a fine husband and she would remain close to Questing. Moreover, a marriage between Trastamara and de Wolfe would forever link the houses. It is the perfect solution, really."

Scott looked at him as if he'd suddenly developed a searing madness. "Are you serious?"

Markus nodded, holding up a hand for the man to keep his

voice down. "Atlas told me about his love for her right after Roget died," he said. "He knew he was too young to marry, but he came of age last year. He has been asking me ever since to speak with you and I haven't done it. You know that he and Caria meet secretly, don't you?"

Scott's mouth dropped open in outrage. "What are you talking about?"

"When she makes her weekly visits to Coldstream with Matha? Atlas is always there waiting for her."

Scott was genuinely astonished. "My mother knows about this?"

"Knows about it and encourages it," Markus said. "She is Caria's rightful guardian, you know. She approves. But she hasn't brought it up to you because that is my duty. I just haven't found the time or the courage, to be truthful. But right now… we are waiting for a new de Wolfe to enter the world. It seems like the right time to speak of a new life for two people we love."

When he put it that way, Scott couldn't get too angry. He shook his head with exasperation.

"So this… *this* love affair has been going on behind my back?" he asked.

Markus shrugged. "Matha knew," he said. "Aunt Avrielle probably knew, too. Women know these things. As you said, they are stronger and smarter than we are."

Scott looked at him, trying to appear stern, but he ended up breaking down in a grin. "I have just been made a fool of by my own words," he said. "Well played, Markus."

Markus smiled in return, hoping that this would be the breakthrough that Atlas had been hoping for with Caria. Perhaps it wasn't the right time but, somehow, it had felt right in the moment. He'd explained it well enough.

Reaching out, he squeezed his uncle's hand.

"You know I adore you," he said. "So does Atlas. He has always had the greatest respect for you and you know what a fine man he is."

Scott nodded. "He is very fine," he said. "There is no question about it. How is he faring, by the way? I've not seen him in several months, but Trastamara seems to be peaceful. I've not heard anything to the contrary."

The subject changed again, slightly, now veering back onto Atlas and the status of his Trastamara lordship.

"He is doing quite well," Markus said. "After that nasty business with Bexwell and Mordrington, Papa left Damien at Trastamara to help Atlas and it has worked out splendidly. The big orchard by The Orchard crossing is operating again and Mordrington Manse, the property that was part of the issues back then, is peaceful once more. Atlas wants to give it to Caria as a wedding present."

Scott rolled his eyes. "Are we back on that again?"

"I thought you should know."

Scott snorted. "So now, I know," he said. "But the place is much coveted by the reivers. Are you sure they will not come back for it at some point?"

Markus shook his head. "Nay," he said. "Fenella and her bastards returned home, to Clan Hume, and her outlaw brother was killed at the siege of Trastamara. Papa has his own men staffing the place, so the Scots haven't tried to reclaim it. They won't, or they risk Berwick's wrath. It would make a lovely honeymoon cottage."

Scott hissed in exasperation. "Oh, do shut up about that."

Markus laughed softly. "Very well," he said. "No more talk about it. I promise I will…"

He was abruptly cut off when Aleanor suddenly burst into the solar. Her eyes were wide, her face flushed, and when her gaze fell on Patrick, she bolted for him.

"Ama had *two!*" she blurted. "Two babies!"

"What?" Markus bolted to his feet, suddenly feeling light-headed. "Two of them?"

Scott was up beside him, holding on to the man so he wouldn't topple. The entire room began to laugh.

"Two children," Scott said. "Congratulations, Markus!"

Patrick, with Ambra sleeping on his big shoulder, made his way over to Markus and hugged the man, but Markus was still focused on Aleanor.

"Is your mother well?" he demanded. "Are the children well? What are they?"

"Male."

They all looked over to the doorway to see Jordan de Wolfe standing there. The woman looked weary, but her cheeks were rosy with joy. Even at her advanced age, she looked positively ageless, even more so now that she'd helped deliver her great-grandchildren. It was the circle of life that just kept going. When she saw Markus, she stepped into the chamber.

"Two boys, Markus," she said in her soft Scottish accent. "Yer wife had a time trying tae bring them into this world, but they are here and they are healthy. Ye have two beautiful sons."

Markus stared at her a moment before collapsing back onto his chair. As Patrick and Scott kissed their mother, and Scott congratulated Patrick on becoming a grandfather, Jordan went to her overwhelmed grandson.

"Ama is doing very well," she assured him softly. "She is weary, but that is understandable. Come and see her. She has asked for ye."

Markus looked up at his grandmother. The rock of the entire de Wolfe pack, a woman whose love and advice he valued more than any other with the exception of his own wife. She meant so much to so many people. Reaching out, he took her two small, warm hands in his. He was fighting off tears.

"Two sons," he whispered. "I… I can hardly believe it. And they are well?"

"Screaming like banshees."

"And Ama is well?"

Jordan kissed him on the forehead. "She's fine, lad," she said. "Please believe me."

Markus nodded, blinking back the tears. "I do, I swear," he said. "I just… this is such a big moment. I find myself wishing Poppy was here to share it with us."

Jordan smiled. "He is," she said. "Can ye not feel him all around ye? He's here, Markus. Have no doubt of that. Now, come along. Come see the newest members of yer family."

Markus nodded, taking a deep breath before standing up again. He didn't want to chance toppling over because he was still feeling a bit woozy. He hadn't taken two steps when Magnus, holding on to Alfie's hand, spoke up.

"'Tis a good thing you had two," he said sternly. "I reserve the right to name one of your sons, as I named you."

They all looked over at the big Northman. "I knew that was why you came," Markus said, his eyes twinkling with humor. "Of course, it was to see your daughter and your grandchildren, but your first great-grandchild is something to be proud of. I suspected you would demand to name it if it was male."

Magnus made his way over to his grandson, looking up at him because he was so tall. There was adoration and amusement in his expression.

"I named you after the greatest warrior I ever knew," he said. "His name was Markus Haakonsson and there was no man finer or braver in all the land. But for your firstborn son, I have chosen the name Magnar. That was the name of my mother's father and I loved him dearly. He was wise beyond measure, generous to a fault, and one of the fiercest men I have ever known. It is a great honor for your first born to carry the name of Magnar."

Markus grinned at him. Truly, he knew the man would demand naming rights, so he had forewarned Amabella. That meant they were both prepared for this moment.

No one wanted to disappoint a Norse king.

"Aye, it is," he agreed. "Let me go see to my sons now. I shall whisper their names in their ear and Magnar will know that his great-grandfather has named him. But his middle name shall be Patrick, after the greatest man I know. I must honor my father, too. Magnar Patrick de Wolfe."

They all turned to look at Patrick, who was overwhelmed with gratitude by the naming. He thought for certain that his wife's father would have taken over that particular aspect of their lives like he had with their other children. But Magnus didn't have complete control; Markus still managed to honor his father. Patrick and Markus shared a special moment, just between father and son, before Markus quit the chamber and headed to the keep to see his wife and new children.

He could still hardly believe it.

When he arrived in the lavish and warm chamber, it was to his own mother's smiling face. Brighton de Wolfe hugged her enormous son, pulling the physic and her daughters from the chamber so that he could be alone with his new family. When the door was shut and the room was still, Markus crept up on the bed to find Amabella lying there, nursing the dark-haired infants, one on each breast.

Markus couldn't help it; the tears came.

"Oh… Ama," he murmured. "Look at them. They are magnificent."

Amabella smiled up at her emotional husband. "Sit next to us," she said softly. "Allow me to introduce you to your sons, *querida*. We hoped for one and were blessed with two."

Markus sat on the edge of the bed, looking down at the contented infants. He reached out a timid hand, gently touching the one nearest him.

"They are beautiful," he said. Then, his gaze moved to her. "As are you. At this very moment, you are the most beautiful creature I've ever seen."

Reaching out, he took her hand, kissing it reverently. Amabella touched his face, watching him as he kissed her palm.

"Are you well?" she asked. "You look a bit pale."

He laughed softly. "I am fine," he said. "Now that I know you are well, I am perfectly fine. But I will admit I was nervous."

Amabella laughed softly, looking down at the infants tugging on her breasts. "Truth be told, I was a little, too," she said. "These two were happy and content in my belly. It took a while to coax them out."

"That is what my mother said."

Amabella snorted. "She has had twins twice," she said. "I have no idea how she managed such a thing. Once is enough for me."

"My mother is a strong woman."

"She is," Amabella agreed. "But you and I did not expect two sons and we only selected one name."

Markus grinned. "Not to worry," he said. "Magnus has taken care of that, as I told you he would. He insists that the first born be called Magnar and I have agreed. It would make an old man happy."

"Magnar," Amabella repeated, rolling it over her tongue. "I like that. Magnar and his brother, Mateo, after my own grandfather."

"As the great-grandsons of a Norse king, England's greatest knight, and Aragon royalty, they will be the finest knights the world has yet to see," Markus said. Then, he bent down so that he was peering at the infants. "It is an awesome legacy you bear, Magnar Patrick and Mateo Alonzo. Through you, great men will live on."

Amabella watched him as he spoke to the babies, reaching out to hold Markus' hand tightly. "They are the sons of Markus de Wolfe," she said. "Through them, *you* shall live on, too. There is no question that their legacies shall be the greatest England has yet to see."

Markus leaned over her, kissing her sweetly, tenderly, as the infants nursed. To see the results of their powerful love was enough to bring tears to his eyes again. He'd only heard of such contentment, told by men he had, at times, considered fools. Surely no man could be content with a woman to love and children at his feet. Men needed glory and warfare, properties and wealth in order to be truly happy.

At least, that's what he'd thought, once.

But Markus had come to realize that true contentment did indeed come from things that all of the money in the world couldn't buy. Through the children now dozing off against his wife's bare breasts, Markus knew that he'd found the greatest contentment of all.

The power of love.

The man with the heart as big as a wolf had found his noblest destiny.

◌ THE END ◌

Children of Markus and Amabella
Atlas (formerly de Sauque, now Abril)
Aleanor (de Sauque – de Wolfe)
Alphonse (de Sauque – de Wolfe)
Ambra (de Sauque – de Wolfe)
Magnar & Mateo
Gaetan
Thor
Angelia

ABOUT KATHRYN LE VEQUE

Medieval Just Got Real.

KATHRYN LE VEQUE is a USA TODAY Bestselling author, an Amazon All-Star author, and a #1 bestselling, award-winning, multi-published author in Medieval Historical Romance and Historical Fiction. She has been featured in the NEW YORK TIMES and on USA TODAY's HEA blog. In March 2015, Kathryn was the featured cover story for the March issue of InD'Tale Magazine, the premier Indie author magazine. She was also a quadruple nominee (a record!) for the prestigious RONE awards for 2015.

Kathryn's Medieval Romance novels have been called 'detailed', 'highly romantic', and 'character-rich'. She crafts great adventures of love, battles, passion, and romance in the High Middle Ages. More than that, she writes for both women AND men – an unusual crossover for a romance author – and Kathryn has many male readers who enjoy her stories because of the male perspective, the action, and the adventure.

On October 29, 2015, Amazon launched Kathryn's Kindle Worlds Fan Fiction site WORLD OF DE WOLFE PACK. Please visit Kindle Worlds for Kathryn Le Veque's World of de Wolfe Pack and find many action-packed adventures written by some of the top authors in their genre using Kathryn's characters from the de Wolfe Pack series. As Kindle World's FIRST Historical Romance fan fiction world, Kathryn Le Veque's World of de Wolfe Pack will contain all of the great story-telling you have come to expect.

Kathryn loves to hear from her readers. Please find Kathryn on Facebook at Kathryn Le Veque, Author, or join her on Twitter @kathrynleveque, and don't forget to visit her website and sign up for her blog at www.kathrynleveque.com.

Please follow Kathryn on Bookbub for the latest releases and sales: bookbub.com/authors/kathryn-le-veque.